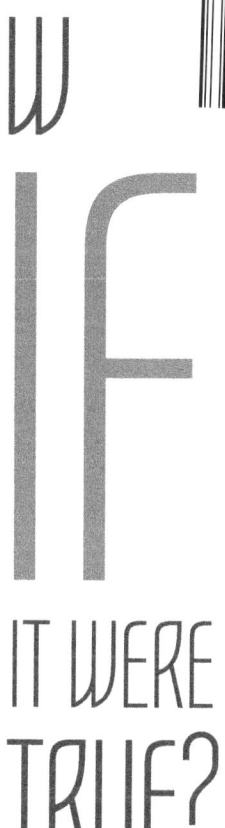

W

IF

IT WERE
TRUE?

WHAT
IF
IT WERE
TRUE?

EILEEN WESEL

atmosphere press

DEDICATION

To Mrs. Jacobs
Wherever You Are

Your Words Were Never
Forgotten!

EVERYTHING HAPPENS FOR A REASON! EVERYTHING

please...

DON'T KILL
THE MESSENGER

1

∞

Going to devote as long as it takes to finish a bucket list item—learn who I am and why I am here on planet Earth. A huge undertaking, I know.

Here's your invitation to acquire what I'm about to research. The construct of this work will be threefold: write personally to you throughout, interject conspiracy theories and possible scenarios, and coincide my findings with an epic sci-fi tale.

Two problems have always stopped me from writing: how to separate from my world as I know it, and, I need total quiet. I will be a recluse. So, how do I tell my family I'm isolating myself for however long this will be?

I am retired now and I have a hubby who would fully support this effort, but I love my large family. For the first time in my life I can choose to have them around or not. To write, I must sacrifice my time with them. Not easy.

Something happened to me when I was in junior high. A teacher named Mrs. Jacobs took me aside and asked if I wrote the essay that I had handed in. I was taken aback by the question, as who would help me with anything? I told her yes, and she said, "You should consider writing as a career." I felt pride, probably for the first time in my life. I'll never forget her and her kind words.

Once, I attended a writing seminar. I had been writing a little and wanted the work critiqued. I was directed to read the material out loud. The feeling of putting myself out there was surreal, but the class and the teacher said they liked it.

The teacher asked if I knew where the book was going. I said, "No, not yet." She told me to give it a beginning and an end in my head and then write it, but did I? No. (More on her comment later). I didn't have the discipline. So, I allowed life and insecurity to postpone my writing for twenty-two years.

This is day two. The great-grandkids have left. I'm thinking about writing, so...why am I not preparing?

I did get a push to consider writing again. My girlfriend sent me a Christmas present, which I opened early. It was a book titled, *You've Got a Book in You*. I haven't read it yet; it's sitting right next to me, but I'm already inspired to try this writing thing.

Day three, out comes my red folder titled "Novel." Its label is faded and my notes are mostly handwritten. Yikes. I'm looking for any dates and found three: 1987, 1993, and 2014. There are about thirty pages in all, mostly my handwritten attempts. I apparently typed some pages I didn't date— perhaps 2014?

Damn it, I'm distracted again. Now I know for sure that was the reason I haven't done this. I am a very focused person. I need total quiet.

Two days have gone by. Geez. How serious am I? I did start to read, okay browse, through the book from my friend. Really good tips, some I think should come naturally to a writer and others very helpful!

Now it's day four. I have thought seriously about disciplining myself. Was I inspired by the book? I bought a new computer, hired someone to help me transfer stuff into it, bought a new cool laptop pillow with a light attached and am in my bed with the laptop at eye level. I texted my daughter and my granddaughter not to call. Hubby is using the headphones, so I don't hear the TV. I'm looking at my folder with trepidation, wait, anxiety? Oh, they're the same thing. Duh. Is this what new writers feel? I don't know.

Wait, got to get a cup of coffee. Be right back. Procrastination?

Back and focused. It's 12:53 pm, Thursday, December 20, 2018. Hmmm...I was born on a Thursday...

The handwritten work needs to be put into this Word program. That's a task! My thought is, will I be changing the story as I go along? I'm going to keep it as it is and review it later. Yes, that's my goal. Here goes...

2

Dr. Kaplan walked into his reception area Friday morning and exchanged a cordial greeting with Teresa, his assistant. When he entered his office, he noticed a large manila envelope on the desk. The instructions on the package said REVIEW IMMEDIATELY. No postage, no forwarding address.

He pressed the intercom and was a little surprised at the seductive voice that answered. It was his new assistant, Linda. Just hired, he's had little time to adjust to her being in the office. He asked what she knew about the envelope. "A courier came to the office earlier this morning, Doctor, and said it was confidential."

He thanked Linda, then began studying the envelope. The seal was tightly taped, but with a scissor he was able to pry the package open. A letter, a check, and a thick maroon pamphlet fell out onto the desk. He picked up the check first and found it only revealed one name: T-HE-RE. Odd, he thought. The amount on the check was $4,000. A retainer? Dr. Kaplan put the check down and picked up the pamphlet. He found this item odd also; it looked like an extensive dossier dating back to 1996. Usually, patient referrals come with a case file.

The enclosed memo was on a formal letterhead of the same name, but again, no other information was forthcoming.

The message stated a psychologist, Dr. Richard A. Stone, had highly recommended him for this case study and that privacy was crucial.

The requirements specified he consult immediately with a woman named Dawn Coleman. He was informed Ms. Coleman knew they were to meet as often as possible. A phone number for Ms. Coleman was handwritten, but legible.

Further, it was understood he would use his discretion when interviewing any relatives or friends, and have the sessions transcribed and forwarded to the email address provided.

The letter ended with, "If you were to accept these terms, payments will be arriving weekly via a courier in the amount of $4,000."

Dr. Kaplan walked around to his chair and sat down. His first thought was of his patients. *What would taking on a case like this do to my schedule?* Another real concern was the speed at which he was to psychoanalyze this person. *Will this method interfere with my modus operandi?*

Then he realized it was going to take him all weekend to review the dossier if Ms. Coleman was immediately scheduled. Unfortunately, that meant he couldn't attend his sister's cocktail party. She held one every year to gather with her brother and friends. Her goal, if it were known, was that one of her friends and her brother might hook up.

He muttered out loud to himself, "She's not going to be happy if I don't attend!"

After weighing the pros and cons, he acknowledged it was too lucrative an offer to turn down. He also realized this could be the case to advance his career.

If one was to describe Dr. Kaplan's looks, the comment most heard would be, "He's got it all: tall, slender, gorgeous wavy blonde hair, sexy emerald eyes, and what a body." This is usually followed up with, "He's also genuinely a nice person."

Dr. Kaplan had a reputation for not following the standard Psychiatric Assessment format. He didn't initially ask his patients questions like, "Why do you think you are here?" or, "Does anyone in your family have a psychiatric history?"

He's had some real breakthroughs with his method of treatment. Perhaps his colleagues are finally taking notice. Furthermore, being offered this opportunity by a prominent psychologist, he thought *Well, doesn't that beat all!*

He reached for his intercom. "Linda, could you come in here a moment?"

"Yes, Doctor," Linda replied.

Walking slowly, Linda entered the office. She was beautiful, no doubt. She stood around five feet four inches tall, with brown, silky hair flowing freely to her waist. Her figure was picture-perfect and one couldn't ignore that she was well endowed. Her eyes were wide and a deep crimson, of which some would swear were really a fiery red.

Without looking up, Dr. Kaplan inquired, "Linda, how many cases do I have scheduled for the rest of this week?" She replied, "Nine, Doctor."

"I see. I'm going to need more time on this new case I've been offered. Can you see if Dr. Stein can handle some of my most recent cases? I'll still see Mr. Brown and my long-term patients." Thinking to himself *Especially Mr. Brown, I've got to find out why he thinks he's an alien!*

Softly Linda informed him, "I've already put a call into his office." He looked over at her, and wondered how she knew exactly what he needed.

"Wow, thanks Linda, that's great," he responded. They exchanged a smile and Linda walked out of his office.

Dr. Kaplan never went to his sister's party, and, as he suspected, she was quite upset about it. He spent the whole weekend in his home, on his bed, reading the three hundred nineteen-page dossier on Dawn Coleman.

∞

Whew. I did it! First few paragraphs done. But...so much for not changing a word!

∞

3

∞

I love the quiet. My hubby Dave just left for an appointment and I'm totally alone. Oh, if I could just have more of this... Did I mention it's raining?

∞

Dawn looked up at the impressive professional building with its brassy gold lettering that read Capital 248 Professional Centre, Nostrand Avenue, Brooklyn, NY. She walked through the heavy glass doors and over to the elevators. The elevator door opened, and a quick review of the directory indicated David S. Kaplan, PhD was on the sixth floor.

Dawn stepped into the office and was amazed to find the room empty of clientele. She walked over to the reception area where a very pretty young lady was busy working. The woman looked up and said, "Hello, you must be Dawn Coleman. I'm Teresa Del. Dr. Kaplan is expecting you. Please, come with me." Dawn smiled, nodded her head, and followed behind Teresa.

The room Dawn entered was breathtakingly beautiful with rounded walls, offering her an immediate sense of enclosure. The drapery and furniture were white. Both the pillows and drapery were accented with a coordinating design of an ancient symbol. She recognized it immediately. Strange, yet so comforting.

Dr. Kaplan was talking with Linda when he noticed Teresa and his new client enter the room. He stood up from his desk and walked over to greet her. She held out her hand and looked up at him with a smile.

The moment he took her hand, a small jolt shot through their arms. Both reacted the same way by immediately stepping backward and looking up at each other. For one split second there was an affinity, a bonding that confirmed they knew each other very well...somehow.

Embarrassed, Dawn looked down at her hand and chuckled. "Oh wow, so sorry. I'm so..."

When Dawn looked up at Dr. Kaplan again, he started intently staring into her eyes, but she was used to that. After all, they were the color sapphire. He finally caught himself and chuckled, "Oh no, I'm sorry. I guess the rug has static. Wow. Never had that happen before. Ah...oh, I'm Dr. Kaplan, but...you know that already."

Linda witnessed the exchange but didn't acknowledge it. Teresa chuckled. Dr. Kaplan gave Teresa an embarrassed look and excused her with a nod of his head, while Linda approached Dawn. Their eyes met. Immediately Dawn sensed an uneasiness and looked away, but Linda's gaze was penetrating. She asked Dawn if she would like coffee or perhaps a cup of herbal tea.

"No, thank you," she replied.

Dr. Kaplan said, "Dawn; can I call you Dawn?"

"Of course. Yes."

Slapping his hands together he said, "Okay, won't you sit down?" Dawn noticed the patient lounger was situated near the window. She walked over to it and sat down. She felt comfort in feeling the heat from the sun warming that area of the room. This position was directly across from Dr. Kaplan's desk.

Dr. Kaplan and Linda were standing near the desk when he said, "Dawn, this is Linda Chalmers, my assistant. If you cannot reach me, she'll track me down. Linda, can you get me one of our cards?" Linda, still gazing at Dawn, smiled and walked out of the room.

"Now, just so you know, Dawn, whatever we discuss here is private, so rest assured you can be comfortable with me."

"Well, that's going to be the problem, Dr. Kaplan, being comfortable I mean. I know I'm here for you to evaluate what's happening with me, but I've got an innate sense that you'll need to report that information." Dawn looked down at the floor then up to the doctor's face. "I have an ability that's causing too much attention, I'd better tell you now. I can telecommunicate. Well, that's what I call it. It actually involves some other gifts...I say gifts..."

Dr. Kaplan's mouth opened, but before he could speak, Dawn continued, "Don't be alarmed, I know a little of what's going on. But I will be forthcoming, as I need to get insight, which I'm hoping you'll provide. I also sense there is a need to keep this arrangement quiet, but that's fine with me. I have been given this opportunity to see you by one person, yet I'm beginning to wonder his motives."

Dawn noticed Linda enter the room and walk towards her, so she instinctively stopped speaking. Linda handed her a business card, which gave Dawn a reason not to look up, as she was very well aware of Linda's gaze. Dawn kept her eyes glued to the card, until Linda turned and walked out of the room.

Dr. Kaplan sat down at his desk and opened the dossier, but he really didn't know where to start. Does he tell her he has one on her? He thought *What if she gets inquisitive? I don't know if I can expose what's in this file. This isn't going to be an easy beginning. It's at best a conundrum!*

As if reading his mind, Dawn said, "Dr. Kaplan, I see you're a little uncomfortable. I understand. I get that a lot. Let's just start talking about you." Dawn turned her attention to his wall display. "Your degrees on this wall: a Masters in Holistic Health Care, a PhD in Clinical Behavior, a Doctor of Psychology." She turned her head back and faced him. "You seem pretty young to have accomplished these credentials. I'd say you're around thirty-five, am I right?"

"Yes, wow. Right on. So...I'm not too young."

Dawn smiled, "Please, don't think I was questioning your accomplishments, I'm just impressed at your tenacity. I'm also a little surprised your address is not on Park Avenue in Manhattan." Dr. Kaplan was so taken aback he couldn't find the words to respond. Dawn just giggled. Then they both laughed. He knew what she was doing, but he hadn't experienced a patient try that tactic on him. Yet, it worked: both felt a little more relaxed.

"Yes, Dawn, I have parents who wouldn't hear of anything but the best for their boy. I am a product of their upbringing for sure. But, if truth be known, Manhattan's not for me."

Dawn's eyes were browsing across the room. A picture behind Dr. Kaplan's desk caught her attention.

Dr. Kaplan continued, "You might ask, why have you settled in Brooklyn? That's simple, I'm drawn here." He let that sink in. He looked for an expression; did he get it? Dawn made no comment, as she was engrossed in the painting.

So much for lightening the mood, he thought.

"No, really, I was born here. My parents are here. I've thought of moving a few times but Brooklyn feels right. Have you ever felt like that about a place?"

Dawn turned to Dr. Kaplan, "Oh yes, too often I'm afraid. I always have the feeling Earth isn't truly my home." While he pondered the remark, Dawn took a few seconds to stare at him. He started to speak but she interrupted him. "So, your parents live here and I see you're not married." At that point, she turned her attention back to the painting.

Dr. Kaplan looked incredulously at Dawn then down at his hands. "Ah...yes." Then he held up his left hand and said, "And no, I'm not. Hey, you'd make a good detective!"

It was the doctor's turn to take advantage of Dawn's preoccupation with the painting. He stopped talking and gazed at his new patient. He liked the fact they were of the same age. Her hair was platinum and shoulder length, but pulled back off her face in a pony tail. Her figure was just what he liked in a woman, perhaps a size ten. She was wearing a light pink shirt with jeans. Her long legs...*Wait, I shouldn't be studying her this way,* he thought. With that he turned around and looked up at the picture.

"Interesting, isn't it?" No reply. "Dawn?"

"Hmm?" She turned her gaze toward him.

He asked, "What does it say to you?"

"I know that place, although I've never been there... physically."

"Really?"

"Yes, it's the Abu Sir, at the Abu Ghurab site in Egypt." She was studying the picture. "You probably know...some-how...that my views are pretty far out there. I've often wondered if this site was used as a portal."

"Do you? Me too," he exclaimed, before realizing he just told her of his belief in time travel! "I've never been to Egypt, but my fascination started when I was a kid, and to this day I can't get enough. I love the history, the myths. Trying to separate in my head what's fact from conspiracy is a pastime of mine. So, we both believe they could be portals. So, I guess I'm out there too, huh?"

Dawn smiled then changed the subject. "I noticed the furniture and draperies in your waiting room. How exclusive. Did you have them custom made?"

"Uh huh, I saw this design…"

"Yes, I know it," Dawn exclaimed. "It's an ancient Tibetan Drusta script meaning…" and they both said in unison, "Everything happens for a reason." They looked at each other and laughed.

Then, they both became quiet for a moment, reflecting on what that symbol meant to them. Dawn spoke first, "Like I said, my abilities are attracting unwanted attention. But why do I feel something more is going on? I just want answers."

4

∞

Halfway through my handwritten notes! Not bad for day five. I did tell a few people not to mention what I'm attempting in case I find I don't have the discipline. I am apprehensive. But right now, it's quiet. Might as well keep plugging away.

∞

When Dr. Kaplan began to explain his psychiatric approach, Dawn positioned herself on the lounger and started staring up at the ceiling.

"Dawn, I have a non-clinical approach in the way I conduct my sessions. It's my practice to have patients begin by discussing past events. The sequential order of occurrence brings clarification to both the patient and me. Even if your family or friends come here on your behalf, they must begin with what they know of your younger life first. Okay?"

"Yes, that's fine."

"Oh, and I take notes and use a recorder. Does that bother you?"

"No, go ahead," she said, then positioned herself on the

lounger with her head on a small pillow.

"Are you comfortable, Dawn?"

"Yes. I'm fine."

Dr. Kaplan got up from his desk and walked over to a chair next to the lounger. He placed the chair to the right and behind Dawn. He pressed a button on the recorder, nestled near the lounger on a small table, then stated:

"Dawn Coleman: Session 1, September 12, 2018"

Dr. Kaplan started the session in his usual way; asking a few preliminary questions like how far back in her memory could she go, who did she feel influenced her at a very young age, inquiries along those lines. Then he guided Dawn to recall any specific memory that affected her when she was a child. His technique was calming, his voice soft, comforting.

"Well, that would be the bus accident. I remember I must have been around seven. All of us were bussed, due to living so far from our school. I was sitting in my usual seat, in the middle of the bus, on the right. I liked that seat, as I enjoyed being near the window, especially when the sun came through.

"We were going over a small bridge and I felt the bus starting to sway from side to side. Then it started swirling around in circles. It was happening so fast. The bus hit something, and I was forced forward and my head hit the seat in front of me and pushed me back again. I felt like I was turning upside down and then another jolt, this time much harder. This must have been when the bus hit the water.

"Everything felt like it was happening in slow motion after that. I felt wet and very cold. I remember hearing kids screaming for their mothers, some cried for help. I don't remember crying.

"For a moment, I realized I couldn't breathe. Then I felt myself sliding down to the floor. My eyes sensed the light quickly turning a shade of gray. I wondered if I was drowning.

"The crying noises stopped. Everything slowed down even more.

"Suddenly there was a flash of white blinding light. I felt a pressure as if I were being enveloped in a large warm enclosure. I closed my eyes as the light was too bright. This pressure swept me upward and was forcing me to the top of the water. My head pushed through and I gasped for air. I opened my eyes and saw the river bank nearby. I swam over and when my body felt the stones, I knew I was safe. At that moment I passed out.

"When I woke, I heard beeping noises. There was a band around my forehead and it was too tight. I was lifting my arm to loosen the band when I saw something stuck into my arm. I screamed. That's when my mother and sister ran over to me. They were both talking at once, but managed to tell me I was in a hospital. My mother put her hand over the intravenous hose to prevent me from tearing it out. At that point my mother told Carole, that's my sister, to be quiet and she tried to explain what was happening. I really wasn't listening, I was just so happy to see them. Then, I noticed tears on my mother's cheeks, so that's when I started paying attention to what she was saying.

"Apparently, my bus got into an accident. Mother kept saying how grateful she was she gave me those swimming lessons and swears that's what saved my life. She didn't tell me till we got home that I was the only one to survive. Carole kept hugging me. I guess you could say we were close, even though she was almost thirteen. She always had a way of comforting me, still does as a matter of fact.

"So that was my first episode, and little did I know, there were more experiences to come."

∞

Getting serious. I made a date to attend a writing group at a nearby library next week. What does one bring on their first day? Notes? Part of their work? Nothing? I will say it took a lot of thought as to whether I wanted to go to this or not. My age kept tugging at me, seventy-one.

5

Damn it, doorbell. Well, it is Christmastime and packages are due. Oh, it's our friend, Art. Told him I'm writing and asked if he wanted to play pinochle later. He said, "Let me ask Norma." That's always his answer. Sweet.

It felt good to say I was writing. Still feeling disciplined. Dave's not back yet and Snooky (our 17-year-old shih tzu) is sleeping...

Three hours have passed. I'm tired now. Did a lot of research today and my brain is fried.

∞

Dr. Kaplan said, "That was quite an experience for you, Dawn. You were so young. Do you remember anything else around that time of your life that might coincide with this incident? You know, anything that you felt was out of the norm...or any uneasy feelings?"

Dawn answered, "Just that I felt...different, more anxious. I started watching a lot of TV, yet not my usual programs. The news channel became my favorite show, but this I could tell was upsetting my mother.

"In school I got into trouble asking teachers too many questions. They didn't like being challenged, but I was so inquisitive. A few trips to the principal's office taught me to seeks answers elsewhere. One teacher who I really liked, Ms. Lyons, started avoiding me whenever possible. I must have frustrated her to the point of anger."

Dr. Kaplan watched as Dawn's expression told him she was reliving in her mind the lonely time she had experienced. "I really had no one to talk to. My sister Carole was concerned. Even as a young child, I could tell she was at a loss as to how to help me."

Dr. Kaplan's silent alarm vibrated. *An hour, already?* he thought.

"Dawn, let's stop here. We covered a lot today. That makes me think you're at ease with my method of working with you."

"Yes, I am, Dr. Kaplan. I'm very relaxed talking with you."

He stood up and went over to his intercom, pressed a button and said, "Teresa, please schedule Dawn to come back in..." He looked over at Dawn and continued "In two days, what's that? Friday? Dawn nodded her head yes.

Teresa replied, "Yes, Doctor."

Dr. Kaplan and Dawn started walking over to the door when they both stopped and stared at each other. He motioned to take her hand when he realized that might be a bad move. Flustered he said, "Uh...till then, Dawn." Dawn grinned at his hesitation, nodded, and slowly left the room.

Dawn walked around the curved wall and into the reception lobby. She was surprised to find Linda there. "Here's your next appointment date, Ms. Coleman." Dawn had no choice but to look at Linda. They stared at each other. Dawn immediately felt the hair on the back of her neck rise. She took the card and said a hurried thank you.

She looked for Teresa but didn't see her. When she opened the door to leave, she nearly bumped into her. "Oh, there you are. I was hoping for a chance to say goodbye."

Teresa was flustered but replied, "Well, isn't that nice. Goodbye, Ms. Coleman." Dawn wasn't sure why, but she purposely meant for Linda to witness this exchange. Once outside the front entrance she scheduled an Uber.

As was his custom, Dr. Kaplan reflected after every patient session. He sat back into the white leather office chair, placed his feet on the desk and arms behind his head, and began the ritual of staring at the ceiling.

Although Dr. Kaplan always compared the original case file (or a dossier in this instance) with his handwritten session notes, this time, the information in the dossier didn't add up to what his assessment of the client indicated.

The Dawn he met today didn't fit the portrayal of the woman described in the dossier. She showed no signs of psychosis, nor was she aggressive. She didn't pull any parlor tricks or try to telecommunicate. Was she being evasive? He didn't think so. After meeting Dawn, his initial thoughts of her perhaps being a phony psychic or soothsayer didn't ring true. She seemed to understand that she needed help. He was thinking that this was going to be a very interesting case. And he silently admitted he was glad the opportunity had come his way.

He put his feet back on the ground and rolled the chair into the desk. He opened the dossier again, reading the personal information section. Even after a weekend of review, he seemed to have missed the fact that he and Dawn shared the same birthday, September 4th, right down to the year. He exclaimed out loud, "Whoa, she was right on with that one!"

Browsing further, he stopped at the word "watchers." He thought *But who's watching who and what the hell does that mean?* He'd heard the word watchers used in UFO terms and in movies, but not in any governmental agencies. *Maybe there really is a secret governmental department researching this stuff. Maybe it's not the government. Huh. Is it the T-HE-RE?*

Dr. Kaplan's thoughts drifted to his patient, Mr. Brown, whom he had been psychoanalyzing for six months now. This case was his first exposure to anything UFO-related. Of course, he never really believed Mr. Brown was an alien being. That's when he realized his research into the possibility of UFOs was limited, but wondered *Was my new client's?*

Dawn mentioned she was under surveillance. but didn't seem alarmed by the fact. *More inquisitive maybe*, he thought. He was drawn to a few pages where Dawn was described as, "Communicating with strangers, but they are not moving their lips." He whispered to himself, "Why is the T-HE-RE interested in knowing she can telecommunicate?"

A few pictures when she was around age twelve showed her standing outside a library handing out pamphlets to a large crowd of people. She was observed attending a political rally as far away as Oregon at the age of fifteen.

She had a brush with the law at age seventeen, a drug bust, but was able to prove she was there trying to stop the exchange.

There appeared to be around fifty pictures of her at rallies across the US as recently as two months ago.

Okay, so she's a little radical. That doesn't make her extraordinary, he pondered. *Her intelligence was obvious, and it's only our first session. So, maybe her activities are only causing concern in certain circles? What circles?*

He was going to have to check the newspapers and online information sources to see if her name was out there. No, he won't check, he'll let Linda do that. Oh, and while she's at it, she can try to find out any information on this T-HE-RE group.

Knowing he was under pressure to evaluate Dawn, and, given his method of working with patients from their childhood, in this case, he'd love to jump ahead to what was going on with her today. Could he? Should he? No. He was probably chosen because of his methods. Perhaps Dawn's mother Lilly, and her sister Carole, could shed light on this time in Dawn's life. They were both scheduled to come in soon.

∞

Went to my writing club again and was surprised my book came up for discussion. A newer member stated my book was written in three parts, and felt it would be difficult to get the story published in that format. She's right, it is in three sections: the writer describing the story, the verbal accounts between the characters, and me writing to you!

So, where do I go from here? Some said keep it the way it was written, as it will cause a following—those that truly enjoy reading a different book style. Some said try taking out my writing to my readers and see how it feels. I tried taking it out, and no, I'm leaving it the way it is. Too much information on my research is in my communication to you.

A friend offered that anyone who doesn't like the personal format can just skip over it and reference it later.

I was told recently that one should consider this on critiquing—take what you want and leave the rest. So, the worst scenario would be no one will want to publish this story, but it's okay, I'm completing a bucket list project and truly enjoying this personal journey into the world of writing and learning who I am!

6

∞

So, my filled coffee cup is sitting on a warmer, I don't have to go to the bathroom, Snooky is behaving...okay, it's a go!

∞

Dawn was walking out of the building when she noticed the same Uber car and driver pull up to the curb. She didn't think much about it and entered the car. No words were spoken. He just acknowledged her with a nod.

As they pulled away, Dawn immediately started reading her cell phone messages and wasn't paying attention to where the driver was headed. Too late. He pulled off on a side road not even a mile from Dr. Kaplan's office. Dawn looked up and realized that wasn't the route to her home. She looked at the driver through his rearview mirror, but he paid her no mind. Dawn said, "Ahh, excuse me, sir. I don't think this is the right road." No reply. "Sir?" No reply.

Dawn tried not to panic, as all her life, weird situations would arise that she couldn't immediately explain. She sensed this as one of her déjà vu moments and figured the reason would be revealed. She decided to stay calm.

He drove a short distance, when suddenly the car veered off into what looked like an abandoned industrial park. *Wait, this isn't right,* she thought. "Excuse me, sir. Can you stop please and answer me?" No reply.

Okay, he's not going to listen to me. What are my options? I'm in the backseat of a car alone with this man. If I open the door... Dawn was getting scared. She could feel her heart pounding. She attempted to open the door. It was locked. She tried to roll down the window but that too was locked.

Panic set in fast. "Stop this car, stop it now," she cried. Still, no answer. In frustration, Dawn jerked back in her seat and again looked at the Uber driver through his mirror. He was intent on his driving. Dawn sat up and grabbed the driver's headrest, shaking it profusely. No reaction. All she could do was watch as the car kept speeding up. "Please, please..." was all she could say.

She opened her mouth to scream, but started feeling weird as if her movements inside the car were happening in slow motion while the car and the scene outside the window were whizzing by. She felt the car pick up tremendous speed as it drove through an open warehouse garage. She held onto the driver's headrest with all her might. Dawn's throat tightened as if she were screaming, but no sound could be heard. She realized they were going to crash into the approaching wall. She tried to close her eyes but couldn't. What she witnessed next was hard for her to decipher—a squishing sound, just as the car hit the wall.

No jerking occurred and no other sound was heard. Dawn felt as though the car was floating through air, enveloped in a brilliant white light. She sensed it tilt forward in a downward motion. A few seconds later she felt the car driving on a level surface. Soon, the light was transformed, and what she noticed next rather surprised her: an enormous room that one would recognize as a hangar for airplanes, but in the corner was a laboratory, which appeared to be in full operation. Dawn looked down at her hands and realized she was still gripping tightly to the headrest.

The driver stopped the car, and she heard the door lock rise. He got out and attempted to assist Dawn, but she already had the door opened and one foot on the ground. She took a close look at her abductor, who, for the first time, seemed so robotic. His movements were jerky at best. The feeling of being in similar situations raced through her mind. So familiar, yet...

At this point her inquisitive nature took over, surpassing her fear. She reacted on a simple knowing; she'd been through this kind of ordeal before and hadn't been harmed.

The driver reached down to help her the rest of the way out of the car, but she tilted her head up towards him and said, "Thank you." He bowed, turned and started walking away. She thought *That's strange; why did he walk away, and why did he bow to me?*

Dawn's mind was struggling to assess what just happened. She stood still by the side of the car, and for a whole minute took inventory of her surroundings. *Okay. I'm not in immediate danger. I'm really standing inside an airplane hangar! Why? There doesn't seem to be anyone here to greet me.* It was completely painted in a basic gray army color. Other than the laboratory area, the inside appeared like it hadn't been used in years. *Wait, what would an airplane hangar be doing in an industrial park in Brooklyn? That should be my question!*

She looked left towards the laboratory. There were people. *Wait, people? Whoa.* Their backs were to her, she couldn't really see much, the glass windows were so dirty. They looked so strange, even though their shape was that of a human, with a head, neck, torso and arms. They were very tall, though, with no hair. Their skin color was like a light shade of blue. They were wearing clothes but something...

At that moment, one turned around sharply, looked straight at her and then turned away. Dawn inhaled so deeply she lost her breath. She inadvertently placed both hands on her chest. Gone was her ability to keep calm.

She backed herself against the side of the car for support. Those eyes! Those eyes! She instinctively knew this wasn't the first time she'd seen those cylindrical shaped eyes.

Dawn turned and tried to get back into the car. She pulled on the door handle but it wouldn't budge. She started yanking harder but still it didn't budge. Her mind was so intent on getting into the car that she didn't notice a figure coming toward her. When she realized she couldn't get into the car, she started to turn around. In that very moment she heard the words, "Hello, Dawn."

Dawn slammed her back up against the car with such force she almost fell to the ground. She caught herself, using her hands and hips. She stood up and faced...a creature so human-like and yet...

This strikingly beautiful figure stood a few feet from her, bowing! It was so human in stature, but was quite tall, thin, and had light blue-gray skin; but when it moved a foot closer, the skin took on a glow, an almost crystalline azure blue.

Dawn felt her heart beating wildly, and as a means of defense, again placed her hands on her chest. She felt unable to move her legs. Her whole body stiffened. All she could do was stare at this figure, powerless to remove her gaze.

This creature stood still, bowing a few times in an effort to relieve Dawn's anxiety.

The eyes were somewhat slanted with large aqua green irises. He had a thin but nicely shaped nose. She noticed five fingers on each hand. Unlike the laboratory workers, he had very long, thin, platinum hair, down to the end of his back. Dawn couldn't help but feel surprised he was so human, and was unnerved by the thought of how handsome he was.

The creature took another step closer to Dawn. He was wearing a white tunic shirt down to the knees with a pair of tight black pants. She noticed a beautiful four-pointed star symbol on the shirt. It looked familiar...

As the being stepped closer, she watched as he became even more human-like in his features. The eye color softened, the nose stretched, and the cheeks filled in. He certainly didn't look robotic like her Uber driver. She thought *How can he do that?*

Dawn's hips were still leaning against the car but she straightened up enough to hold her own. The being didn't move again, giving more time for her to acclimate. "Hello, Dawn, Bringer of Light." Dawn was mesmerized as she stared into its eyes. *Did it just speak to me? No, it's telepathy!*

The entity stared into Dawn's eyes and through their minds it said, "My name is Actok, Dawn. Please don't be frightened—we're actually very close friends. For your safety, we have shielded your memories of us and our encounters, until now. Your unfortunate notoriety has moved up the timeline in which we planned to make contact. We feel it's time to explain your many unanswered questions.

"We understand how difficult it has been for you since your first encounter, the bus accident." Dawn knew what Actok meant, that bubble, the enclosure that pushed her through the water.

"We understand you are confused right now. Know this...we are here to assist you, Dawn."

It was at this point Actok bowed, paying homage yet again. Dawn wondered *This bowing to me, why? Why did the driver? My true self? What is happening?*

Actok took a few steps closer. "If I may, I would like to touch your forehead, as it is here that we can start the process of your remembering."

There were no real options at her disposal. She didn't feel threatened and her curiosity was piqued. "Uh huh" was all she could muster. Actok reached with his right arm and touched her forehead with his middle finger and backed away. Dawn felt a small but very cold jolt, which stiffened her body where she stood. Immediately, her mind revealed a vision—the day of her bus accident.

What she thought was a bubble or enclosure was actually a tubular capsule used to prepare someone for transport. A flash of memory revealed she had seen these capsules numerous times in her dealings with these beings.

Dawn's vision depicted a male, lying still, as a liquid tracking device seeped into his eyes. This liquid, once infused, afforded him the ability to hypnotize and telecommunicate (interface & telepathy); but more importantly, the skill to utilize a sixth sense, ESP (extrasensory perception) was introduced.

The next two flashes were more personal. Dawn was shown how she drove everyone crazy with questions as a young child, including a scene where she first learned how to obtain information without being obvious—by not filling the silence. Then, she was given insight as to what caused her migraines—her curiosity!

Another flash displayed Dawn's current predicament: using her telepathic ability had gained her notoriety.

Then, in her last vision she and Actok were speaking in a very strange room devoid of color. She was holding a piece of paper that kept changing its property. One minute it was a sheet of paper, perhaps five inches by five inches, then it projected itself to look like an ancient cuneiform tablet, a tome.

Dawn felt a warmth rising from her legs and soon came out of the stupor Actok had imposed. The visions subsided, and she thought *I'm not afraid now. Strange.*

"How do you feel, Dawn?"

"I'm okay. The heat felt very good. Like it energized me somehow."

Actok said, "Understand, Dawn, that all you have experienced and could not explain will come to your consciousness through our meetings. You remember me somewhat now, yes?"

"Well, yes...a little...actually. Wow, yes, I think I do!" Dawn, feeling totally unafraid, walked toward Actok in an attempt to shake his hand, but he stepped back out of her reach.

"Dawn, I cannot commune with you this way. Our frequency levels are such that I would bring you intense pain, much more than the jolt you felt. It would feel like an electric shock going through your body. You will come to remember this and much more. Till then trust me that you will be Awakened to your full potential and realize the bond of our friendship.

"I am leaving you now, but know this, Dr. Kaplan is a good man. You are free to mention this meeting and tell him all you know. He has been chosen to help you on your life-journey."

Actok and Dawn stared at each other for a brief moment. Dawn had a hundred questions to ask but realized this was the end of their meeting. As Actok turned, Dawn made a mental note to research the symbol on his cloak. She watched as Actok slowly walked toward the laboratory.

Dawn turned at the sound of a car beeping. The Uber driver appeared again and motioned Dawn to get into the car. As she walked over to the side door and got in, they exchanged a smile.

In the car, Dawn leaned her head back and immediately her mind went to the encounter with Actok. *He knows me! I'm a Bringer of Light? I feel so honored yet scared of what's coming next.*

7

∞

Well readers, now you know, yes, my story is sci-fi but not a thriller. I'm leaning more toward what man's future could actually entail.

I feel I haven't been "at home." Also, I've always been curious as to why I'm on planet Earth during this particular cycle.

The last few days were busy, yet I found time to watch some alien shows, and took copious notes. I love the show Ancient Aliens and actually bought their book last year, way before considering writing this story! Funny how things are coming together...

The house is again quiet. I'm in the bedroom and my hubby is in the living room watching a show, *Area 51*.

This is my fifth day attempting to write. So far, I've had to inform my granddaughter I cannot watch the three kids so she could go Christmas shopping. Then again when she asked if I could keep just one while she did more shopping. Turning her down didn't feel good. Felt selfish, actually. I know that writing is demanding of my time and apparently, I'm sticking to this. Hope the guilty feeling goes away. Does it?

∞

Dawn walked up to her apartment building feeling nothing but an overwhelming urge to sleep. She put the key in her door...

∞

She put the key in her door, she put the key in her door...and what? OMG, Am I stuck? Is this writer's block? No, I want to write something...

∞

...and thought she heard shuffling noises. She hesitated but someone jerked the door open. A man appeared, stuck his head out the door, looked both ways, turned to her and whispered, "Where is it?"

To her surprise, she rushed past him and into her living room yelling, "Who are you? How did you get in here?" She turned to see him coming toward her with his hand at an upward angle. She felt he was going to grab her. Dawn instinctively grasped his arm, started twisting and...an enormous shock ran through her body. On instinct, she immediately jerked her hands off him and, stumbling, ran into the kitchen and grabbed one of the knives from its holder. He saw the knife, stood still, put both hands up in the air and said, "Oh, okay Dawn, I get it." He put his hands down, then walked over to the couch, rubbing his arm.

Still shaking, Dawn watched as this intruder moved away from her and sat on the couch. With the knife still in her hands and at a safe distance, she repeated, "Who are you? How did you get in here?"

A look of hurt could be seen on his face. "You're not going to believe it if I tell you. Well, maybe you will."

He looked down for what felt like an eternity, then looked at her and said, "Dawn, I'm Khacee. Khacee."

He looked up just as Dawn's mouth opened. She was intently staring at him. When they locked eyes, immediately she felt an affiliation, like she might know him, but she couldn't remember how.

"Dawn, I'm wasn't going to hurt you. What you took as an attack was actually me raising my arm to say hi. You know, I can get near you but we can't touch. Well, it's obvious now...you didn't know."

Dawn intuitively trusted his words. As she started walking toward the couch, she placed the knife on the side table. She felt depleted of energy. She sat down next to Khacee, but quickly realized she might be too close and moved over. Khacee was rubbing his arm. "Haven't lost your reflex reactions though, that's good. I was afraid coming back this time you'd gotten weak."

Dawn gave Khacee a questioning look, "Coming back? Back from where? How do I know you?"

Khacee looked sadly at his star life soulmate and said, "Perhaps I shouldn't have come, Dawn. Apparently, you're not Awakened and here I am screwing up the process."

Feel it's important that you have a sense of what it is to be Awakened, as I make reference to the word throughout my story. I'll use my own verbiage so as not to be considered plagiarizing.

As human beings, we live in a physical dimension using our senses to support us. We sustain life through our ego— our perception of who we are. We unknowingly set boundaries around our personalities to "fit in."

An Awakening is a submission of the ego to higher planes of your reality by implementing faith. The perception of who you are expands, as does the level of your consciousness. You start to trust in the new reality presenting itself before you. This "knowing" ultimately aligns you closer with what you perceive is your ultimate Creator.

∞

Dawn's head was throbbing and she was too confused to decipher what he meant. The whole day's drama was just too much. Khacee looked closely at Dawn and said, "But I think I should warn you."

With this statement, Dawn positioned her body as she always did when she got into these conflicted states—she folded her arms around her chest and stared down at the floor. She never felt so tired. It was too much energy for her to continue and Khacee felt that too. He'd been privy to these episodes for eons.

"I'm going to go. I know you need to rest. Let me just say be careful, Dawn."

"Wait, warn me? Warn me about what?"

Khacee hesitantly replied, "You have a...well...like a book that's very valuable to the Council of...well, you know. Oh, maybe you don't. Sorry. The Council of Cosmic Light. It's kind of like an intergalactic library, accessible only to the upper stratum leaders of each planet. If in the wrong hands, this...book, this cuneiform...well...it can change the course of Earth's...timeline. I was hoping to review the timeline together, and well...have some private uhm...private..."

Watching Dawn contemplating this information, Khacee realized his star mate was unaware of their relationship and that she had anything of importance. Knowing her as he did, he allowed Dawn to withdraw into herself, and they both just stared at the floor.

Three full minutes went by when Khacee announced, "I have to say seeing you again was...." Dawn slowly looked over at Khacee. Did she want to know what he was about to say? His presence was disturbing her in a way she couldn't comprehend. Khacee stood up but hesitated saying anything. He wanted to tell her so much more but whispered, "Oh, Dawn, I..." He realized he shouldn't say another word, the timing was not right. After yet another long gazing into each other's eyes, Khacee just...disappeared. Dawn's eyes widened in shock. *Did he just vanish? What's going on?*

It took a few seconds before Dawn realized she was really alone. Questions, so many questions filled her mind. *Okay, first, how did he get into my apartment? And where did I get the nerve to walk right past him? He shocked me. Why? Is he human? He looked human. Very handsome for an...an alien?*

Did I really meet aliens today? From my future?

I'm not Awakened? What does that mean?

Actok. He's so beautiful. He says he knows me, how?

What book? Dawn scanned the apartment from where she was sitting. *A cosmic library? Intergalactic...what?* Frustrated she yelled, "This is insane!" Yet another question arose. *So, when I was told I'd been gone for hours, then later for days, was I...abducted?*

Dawn didn't understand a feeling creeping up into her psyche, a longing since Khacee left. *But what does that mean?* Her head was pounding. She felt a migraine coming on.

Dawn walked to the kitchen in a daze. She put water in the kettle and turned on the burner. She reached for her favorite cup and put a tea bag in it with some cane sugar. She went into the fridge for the Coffee mate then just stood there with it in her hands. Staring at the kitchen table, the thought came to her *What a day. I think I've led another existence!*

Even as a young child, Dawn had realized she had some uncanny abilities. Like knowing what someone was about to say, knew if they were coming down with a cold, and could tell if it was going to rain.

As a teenager, Dawn had little problem speaking her mind

and could hold a conversation with the best of them. Politics made her angry. She always chanted, "The tug of war for power at the people's expense."

Joining social causes and holding two jobs to attend rallies all over the US didn't help with keeping a low profile. Even after losing friendships due to her dabbling in Wicca, she never wavered in her desire to learn. Thinking back, she noted in her early twenties her innate capabilities expanded to include an increase in her auditory perception, being in the right place at just the right time, and all too frequently, knowing a person was terminally ill before they did.

Dawn looked down at the Coffee mate still in her hands and thought *Wait, will the tea keep me up? Perhaps coffee, I don't use sugar in that. No, it too has caffeine. Better just go to bed.* She put the creamer back in the fridge, turned off the kettle, and walked into her bedroom. It was 5:30 p.m.

8

∞

I believe in the existence of aliens. In today's world we are exposed to the likelihood all the time. Sci-fi movies help dramatize their existence. Shows like *Ancient Aliens* offer a plethora of ideas, which they back up with artifacts, historical accounts, and a different explanation for what was witnessed. Cameras and highly advanced equipment are spotting objects in the skies and under our seas on a daily basis. Bring into the fold mankind's unexplained history, and you start to question this concept—or should!

I fervently believe the powers that be on Earth are well aware that aliens exist and are amongst us. So as not to cause world panic, they have slowly and methodically leaked this information into our psyche.

I would venture so far as to say we have made deals with beings from other worlds, perhaps a trade-off—their technology for our...humans.

My research points to dimensions and frequency levels being the real issues dealing with beings from other worlds. I believe this is the crux of our "new existence" as humans on Earth. We might be in our physical form, but soon will exist through our consciousness, requiring our bodies less and less.

Nikola Tesla stated, "To understand the true universe, one

must think of energy, frequency, and vibration." Hmmm. Have you ever stood still and heard your body vibrate?

I'm finding that my exploration into what alien beings look like is so diverse that I could enhance their features in my story. I'm trying not to though, which requires a lot of research. Well, I might augment them a little...

The changes, the adaptations for some beings to be here on Earth are very challenging. They must be willing to cope with the lower frequency levels of our planet. Not an easy task.

Traveling is also an issue. To travel to our planet could take some species a week while it would take us five years to get to their home planet. It's the entering of our solar system that causes their problems. (Apparently, many have found a way).

When here, some feel they are walking in mud—every step is exertive. Their breathing has to be adapted to our heavy dense atmosphere. Others don't have such a hard time of it.

Ever hear of shapeshifters? They can change everything about themselves, and can walk through walls and survive here permanently if they choose. Did you know humans can do that? Yep. It's all about advancing our frequencies. I'm sure you've heard that we only exercise about ten percent of our brain's capacity...

Oh, yeah, I believe many alien species are living among us today and have been genetically, technologically, and politically manipulating us for eons.

I have a sign on my fridge WE ARE IMMORTAL SPIRITUAL BEINGS LIVING A TEMPORARY HUMAN EXPERIENCE. If this is true, where did I come FROM?

I wonder how many readers will slam the book down and say, "She's crazy!"?

My view is if you don't believe, you've got your head in the sand!

Well, that's my story and I'm stickin' to it!

∞

9

Dawn woke up and realized her migraine was gone. *What a break,* she thought, as usually they lasted for days. She looked up at the ceiling and wondered if what she had just gone through was a reality or a truly weird dream.

Dawn sat up, clasped her hands together, stretched her arms out in front of her and wondered, *What the hell happened after my session with Dr. Kaplan? Well, I was...abducted...in a sense.* After a few quiet minutes reliving her day, Dawn thought *True, neither tried to hurt me. Actually, they were warning me; no that was Khacee. Actok wasn't warning me but he was saying some crazy stuff. So, am I to believe I'm not from Earth? Oh, and why did the Uber driver and Actok bow to me but Khacee didn't?*

Time for coffee. Dawn got up, put on her favorite slippers, and walked over to her kitchenette. The apartment was too small to call the area a real kitchen. Actually, the whole apartment was too small. But the rents were so high all over Brooklyn.

She felt lucky she had found this little place on Avenue U. She decorated the apartment in light colors, mostly aqua; that was her favorite. Yet, if truth be known, walking through the tiny hallway to her empty bedroom always felt depressingly lonely.

Still, it was convenient to get groceries, jog in Marine Park, or visit with her best friend, Skyann, who lived a few minutes away on Bragg Street.

And she Uber-ed all the time; didn't see the need for a car expense.

Dawn put on the coffee and looked in the fridge for something to munch on. She picked up the leftover buttered croissant, got out the Coffee mate and turned to place the creamer on the table. It was then she noticed the tea bag was still in her favorite mug. She didn't pay much attention to it, as her mind was whirling around, trying to understand what had just happened to her.

Naturally I want answers to the things I'm able to do, but this? Entities from other planets visiting me? Deep in thought, she questioned *Do I get my telepathic skills from...them? This is scary.*

Dawn felt her abilities started after the bus accident—the trauma of hitting her head during impact with the water. She figured it jostled her brain and gave her abilities like the skill to hypnotize, being sensitive to the sick, and this knack of clairvoyance.

Now, she had lots to think about. She was comforted by the thought that at least a few things were coming to light. She said out loud, "But not today. I can't let all this interfere with my interview, I just can't. I've got to get this job. It's everything."

Dawn heard the beep indicating the coffee was ready, and poured the coffee into her favorite mug. It wasn't until the tea bag began floating around that she realized what she had done.

"Geez!" she exclaimed. She stared as the tea bag swirled around in the coffee. She took out the tea bag, looked inside the mug, and decided to pour the Coffee mate into the cup anyway. She took a sip, lingered, then took another.

Satisfied, Dawn walked toward her bedroom with the

coffee and the croissant. She took a gulp and a quick bite. Browsing through her wardrobe, she decided on the same outfit she had worn for her last interview, a light green suit she found at a Goodwill store. Practical. That was her.

Dawn's thoughts drifted to Dr. Kaplan. *He sure is handsome. So tall, what? Six feet five? His big green eyes are mesmerizing. I like his blonde hair; the cut makes him look like a scholarly professor, styled by messy. Oh no. Too much time reflecting on all this!* She took another swig of her coffee and another bite of the croissant, then scheduled an Uber.

10

Brian Rivers rolled over to face yet another young naïve woman so willing to join him for a night of inconsequential sex. This beauty beside him this morning was not an escort nor a high-priced call girl. Oh no, he had seduced his way into the upper echelon of politics and high society. His main course of splendid young beauties was provided from the wealthiest of men, who, without hesitation, offer him their daughters.

It's easy for a man with his charisma and good looks to charm anyone out of their wealth or self-respect. He's acutely aware of his assets and how to utilize them to the fullest. Flaunting pitch-black curly hair, seductive baby blue eyes, a tall slender body, and a captivating face with absolutely no flaws, he seduced everyone in his path.

It was true; this was a man with power, persuasiveness, financial acclamation, and to those who thought they knew him, a heart. Truth be known, he didn't have a heart, only a muscle that beats inside his breast.

What was also true about Brian Rivers was that he was about to become the head of what is believed by many to be the most secretive, elusive society on the planet—the Illuminati.

This man abhorred anything and anyone associated with

Almighty God. His master was Satan. He was under a time constraint, but, most importantly, the frequency levels, although they might vary, drained his strength. He had to survive by taking a strict regimen of vitamin boosters and oxygen.

Brian Rivers had numerous titles of which he enjoyed the benefits, but the one most savored, most coveted was...the Antichrist.

$$\infty$$

Did ya see that coming?

$$\infty$$

Brian Rivers had two missions: first, seek out a human female named Dawn Coleman prior to her Awakening. She was the highest threat to Satan's plan to seize the planet. Mr. Rivers was not commissioned to kill Dawn; that was his master's pleasure. He needed to compromise her, discredit her, before she came into her full "knowing." Before she could Awaken millions of souls to their full consciousness.

Then the plan was to annihilate all inhabitants who refuse to conform, and establish a colony of cyborg slaves.

The opportunity of confronting Dawn presented itself when his sources found her in Brooklyn, NY in early September working at a newspaper. She was in the cafeteria, showing some coworkers exercises to expand the mind using telepathy. He stood in front of the coffee machines and watched. After a few minutes, they started harassing her. He immediately walked over to her and pulled her aside. He introduced himself as Brian Rivers and said he was a salesman visiting for the day.

He told Dawn that her anxiety was palpable, and charmed

her into thinking counselling would help, that she would learn mental exercises to deal with the stress. He then offered it to her, free of charge! How simple it was to draw her into his web.

His sources informed that she was interviewing for another job. Soon, he would befriend Daniel Katz, Publisher at the *Brooklyn Gazette*—Dawn's new job!

11

Lilly was impressed with Dr. Kaplan the minute she set eyes on him. She just knew he was going to help them. He told of his intent to have her discuss only her daughter's childhood today and she was fine with that.

Dr. Kaplan could tell Lilly was the anxious type. She kept rubbing her hands together, fidgeting in her chair. She looked a lot like Dawn: small frame, blonde hair, and pretty eyes—but not the color of Dawn's, not that spectacular sapphire—more like a soft brown. He asked if he could record their meetings.

Lilly said, "Yes. Sure. I want to help in any way I can."

Dr. Kaplan turned on the recorder and said...

"Lilly Coleman: Session 1, September 13, 2018"

After a few preliminaries, Lilly began discussing Dawn's bus accident.

"She was only seven. I guess you could say she was a normal child up to that point. I never had any major problems with Dawn. But what you want to know is how she was after the first incident.

"When Carole, that's my older daughter, and I arrived at the hospital, the doctors told us Dawn was in a semiconscious state, but they felt she would come around soon. Physically, she looked like nothing serious had happened to her. Her face was not bruised, even though she had suffered a head injury.

The preliminary tests were negative. She had a band around her head, which the doctors said was a precaution, that she needed the tension around the forehead to keep the swelling down. They were surprised she didn't have more serious injuries since the bus hit a cement railing and then slammed into the water.

"Two days into her hospital stay, let's see, it was around eight o'clock at night, when Carole and I heard Dawn scream. We ran to her side. We were so happy she woke up. She was tugging at the intravenous tube so I stopped her. We were both trying to explain to her that she's in a hospital, but everything was going to be fine. She looked at us and asked, 'Then, why are you both crying?' I quickly mentioned they were tears of joy.

"Carole and I looked at each other and we instinctively knew we shouldn't say too much, but I mentioned she was in a bus accident. It was at this point I looked at Carole and we realized we better stop crying. Dawn is a sensitive girl and we didn't want to upset her while trying to explain what happened.

"I was so glad that the next question, 'How are the other kids?' was interrupted by the nurse telling us Dawn needed her rest. Carole and I were grateful we were spared having to answer that question.

"Dawn was released the following morning. They said they couldn't see any residual indications of trauma. We were to watch her carefully though for the next few days.

"Well, the car ride home was stressful. The questions started, oh boy, the questions. How do you tell a seven-year-old the details of a horrific bus accident in which she was the only survivor? Carole, bless her soul, was attempting to console Dawn in the back seat by providing evasive answers. This approach wasn't working. So, I briefly said, 'Your bus lost control and fell into the river.' No reply, silence, as though she were trying to enact the scene in her head. I turned the radio on hoping to distract her. This tactic didn't work. I could tell that all we were doing was raising her frustration levels.

"Then she asked, 'Where is Megan? Miss Trexler, is she okay?' One thing about Dawn, she's persistent. I told her I'd explain more when we got home, that I should be watching the road.

"When we settled in at home, I told Carole to go do her homework. I sat on the couch with Dawn and started to explain. 'Dawn, you know me, I'm pretty much to the point, so I'm just going to come out and tell you, you were the only person that didn't die on that bus.'

"Dawn lowered her head for a few seconds then looked up at me and said, 'This is what I remember. I didn't see anyone from the bus on the rocks when I first woke up.'

"Now of course, this story drew attention and was considered important enough that the local newspapers picked it up. When they started coming to our house with their vans and cameras, I just said Dawn was too young to be interviewed. That was easy. But when family and friends came by and asked Dawn what happened she would just tell them that 'something' saved her. I attributed that 'something' to two things: good luck, in that she was sitting near the opened window, and the fact that she was an avid swimmer, having taken lessons since she was two.

"After a while, things got back to a semi-normal state, as the interest of the public waned. At least to the outside world."

END OF SESSION

∞

Know what I find cool? The Alexa or Google Mini. Imagine, hands-free, I just ask out loud for a machine to find a reference for me. Can I give it an Irish accent? How much are they?

∞

12

Dawn had money saved if her interview at the *Brooklyn Gazette* didn't go well, but it did; Daniel Katz was interested. He knew of her tenacious reputation through her previous boss, his golf buddy. And he had concerns over these telepathic abilities he'd heard about, which of course, were not listed on her resume. He figured it could be an asset; she might get insight another reporter wouldn't be privy to. Throw in her good looks...

He couldn't tell her he knew all this though. She might up the price beyond what he was willing to pay.

Dan Katz had that kind of face that got lost in a crowd. It was so non-worthy of a second look you'd pass him by without a thought. He was tall, perhaps six feet five, but he had terrible posture making him appear shorter. His skin looked aged and pale, the product of never going outdoors. His hair was turning gray, what was left of it. He was teased a lot that perhaps he should just shave it all off.

He never married or had kids. Like Dr. Kaplan, his love was his work.

They decided on a starting salary, and she'd start work on Monday.

Dawn arrived for her second session with Dr. Kaplan. She

was grateful she didn't run into Linda, but wondered why she felt that way. Teresa welcomed and escorted her to the doctor's office.

Dawn Coleman: Session 2, September 14, 2018

"It wasn't easy for me at school. It was the beginning of a new school year, my third grade. I had decided to keep a low profile but that wasn't going to work.

"A lot of kids seemed angry that I was the only survivor of the bus accident. They kept away from me, didn't include me in things. Needless to say, I didn't have friends, per se. Just a few kids who would say hi and sit with me at lunch, that sort of thing.

"Didn't take long to know that Skyann was the class bully. Our introduction wasn't an easy one. No way. Mom was called to the school. She wasn't happy.

"Skyann was seated right behind me. I felt a tugging on my hair, then another. I knew it was her but I also knew...somehow, that retaliation wasn't going to work. So, I turned around and smiled. This naturally irritated her and she kept tugging, but I kept turning around, smiling.

"Then, I'm at lunch standing in the food line, when Skyann walked in front of me and wouldn't move. I didn't do anything, which really maddened her. She wouldn't move along with the line. She just stood still and the kids started telling her to move. She yelled it was my fault. Then the kids got loud and the school aide came over and asked, 'What's holding everything up?' I don't believe she was expecting an answer and she didn't get one, either.

"Skyann was told to move along. She got behind me at this point and started shoving me. She was really being a bully. I guess I'd had enough. Turning fast, I stared right into her eyes. She started to say something but just froze. She gazed into my eyes for the longest time, then screamed really loud. Everyone started looking at us, but she kept screaming. At that point I backed off.

"Some kids started to shake her to quiet her down but the school aide came running back over. The aide looked at me but hugged her and they started walking away. The kids stared at me and when I looked up at them, they looked so frightened. One by one they got back in line. I didn't care if I got in trouble at that point, so I just left the cafeteria and went outside and sat on a bench.

"After a while a teacher walked over and asked if I would go with her to the principal's office. She held out her hand and I took it and she seemed to know I didn't want to talk, so we didn't. We walked to the outside door of the principal's office. The principal, Mrs. Taylor, greeted us and excused the teacher.

"Mrs. Taylor brought me into her office and motioned I take a seat. She explained that she already heard Skyann's side of the story and asked for mine. I told her, but I don't think she believed me. She asked me why I thought Skyann screamed like that. I said, 'I don't know.' I couldn't tell her that I seem to do that to people who aggravate me; if I stare, they usually stop.

"My mother arrived. She came and sat down next to me. Then Skyann and her mother walked into the office. We were seated across from them. Skyann wouldn't look at me. I could tell her mother was very concerned. She told us that her daughter said she's so scared of me, but when she asked her why, she couldn't answer. Then, my mother was getting defensive, and it felt like the whole room started talking at once.

"Through this fiasco, I got up, walked over to Skyann, and quickly leaned down to hug her. She looked up into my eyes. She reached her arms around me and we just hugged. Finally, everyone noticed what we were doing and the room became silent. Skyann said, 'It's okay now.' Mrs. Taylor finally said, 'Well, if everyone is in agreement...' And that was that."

END OF SESSION

∞

Another milestone. All my notes are typed into this program! Hey, I'm DOING THIS!!!

∞

13

∞

I've always enjoyed research. At around age eleven, I started to walk two miles to the library at least twice a month. I enjoyed reading and even browsing through all the books on display. Soon I realized the walk home was harder, what with all the books I was checking out. Then, after years of this scenario, I obtained a car, and soon after that, the internet gave way to instant access.

Been at this for hours it seems. Think I'll stop now. But what will I do? Clean house? Eh. Don't need to shower. I am having a small party tomorrow night. Got to get some stuff at Walmart. I don't hate Walmart, I hate GOING to Walmart. But it has everything, what are you going to do?

Had quite the fiasco on Christmas Eve Day. It was my husband's birthday, so I was very busy planning for the party. My granddaughter called to say her hubby got a piece of metal in his eye and he needed to go to the hospital, which turned into a two-day stay. Oh, and the hospital he needed was a two-hour drive one way! We still managed to enjoy the party. We Face-Timed him, so he could see we all prayed around the table for him. Ah, technology.

The rest of us exchanged gifts and got down to what I love

best, Texas Hold 'Em, of which I came in second to my grandson. Guess I taught him too well!

Due to all the family upheaval, not much writing got done.

It's three days after Christmas and I purposely packed up all the Christmas stuff and got the house back in order. I'm hoping to spend all day tomorrow at the keyboard. But it is the weekend. We'll see. I'm trying to be disciplined.

I am proud to say that this is becoming a serious project. When not writing I'm thinking about writing. A section of my bedroom has become a small office space.

I'm using some character names from real people in my life. Is that a good practice? I worry that IF this book should ever get published, the family member or friend will think I identify them with the character and that's not true.

I took the advice from my friend's book and purchased a diffuser and it's fantastic. It's very quiet and changes colors and I enjoy the eucalyptus oil a lot. Sometimes I stare at the emitting smoke and a story line comes into my head.

A few of my family and friends have been told my daughter and I are writing. Now, if I can just get this book done... How long does it take to write a book...normally? It's taken me thirty-two years to get serious!

14

Dawn's sister Carole was glad that her first session with Dr. Kaplan was on a different day than her mother's. She didn't want to be influenced by the anxiety her mother conveyed whenever confronted about Dawn and her "problem."

While getting dressed for her appointment with Dr. Kaplan, Carole took time to reflect on what she would discuss. *Well, I'm thirty-nine now and have had a long time to adjust to my sister's weird behavioral changes over the years. I love Dawn and would protect her always. I hope I don't get defensive with this doctor, just not sure what to discuss, being I never spoke with a psychologist before.*

Carole walked into the waiting area, where Teresa greeted her from her desk. "Hello. You must be Dawn's sister Carole, how nice to meet you. I'm Teresa Del."

"Hi Teresa. Nice to meet you, too. Is the doctor in?"

"Yes, please follow me, I'll take you back to his office."

As she was rising from her seat, Linda walked in and announced, "I'll take it from here, Teresa. Thank you." Teresa was embarrassed; no, humiliated. She knew for sure, now, that Linda had initiated a practice of only allowing her to go so far with the patients. She wondered how she had allowed this to happen. How did she lose control of the office as soon as Linda arrived?

Carole turned to see Linda walking over to greet her and immediately felt uncomfortable. Oh wow, she thought. Her eyes, they're so different—are they red?

Linda said, "Hello, Ms. Coleman, I'm Linda Chalmers, Dr. Kaplan's assistant. Can I get you a cup of coffee or a glass of herbal tea?"

"No, no thanks," Carole replied.

"Well then, would you follow me to Dr. Kaplan's office? He's waiting for you."

∞

Wow, I'm on a roll...

∞

Dr. Kaplan stood up from his desk and walked over to greet Carole. "Hello Ms. Coleman, I'm Dr. Kaplan, glad to meet you."

Carole said, "Yes, glad to meet you, too. I sure hope you can help us."

Linda excused herself. Dr. Kaplan motioned for his new client to lie down on the lounger. He couldn't help but notice Carole's tall stature and the blunt blonde haircut that perfectly accented her blue eyes and little pointed nose. A few freckles dotted her cheeks, making her appear younger than her age.

He pulled his chair alongside her. "Carole...can I call you Carole? I like my sessions as informal as possible."

Carole answered, "Sure, doc."

At this point Dr. Kaplan explained his methodology and Carole was surprised, but nodded her head in acknowledgement.

He said, "Do you mind if I record our sessions?"

Carole hesitated a moment and then said, "No, you go ahead."

Dr. Kaplan positioned his chair in his usual way, to the right and behind Carole's head, then leaned over and turned on the recorder...

Carole Coleman: Session 1, September 17, 2018

"Let's start with when Dawn was young, say around two or three, okay?"

Carole stated, "I like where you're going, doc. I'm quite a..." Carole put her hands up in a gesture indicating quotes, "...let's cut-to-the-chase kind of gal. So, to answer your question, she was a pretty normal kid. We were always close. We liked playing together despite our age difference of six years. I always wanted to protect her.

"So, nothing comes to mind, nothing out of the ordinary until she was around seven. She was in a horrific bus accident and was the only survivor. I think that trauma affected her brain somehow. She sees things, has abilities that most of us don't have. It's scary. I think you know about the bus accident, right? Do you need my version?"

Dr. Kaplan said, "I have two versions now, your mother's and Dawn's. I would like to have your version. Sometimes you can offer a different insight..."

Carole said, "No, seriously. You don't need mine. Mom and I experienced the same event. We've talked about it so much." There was a moment of silence. Carole chimed, "I'm thinking of what else I can offer at that young time in my sister's life, but regrettably, I can't stay in the period of time you'd like, doc, because it was just small things that happened. So, I'll just go ahead and talk about when I started noticing changes in her."

Before Dr. Kaplan could stop her, Carole continued, "Let me see...I'll give you an example of when she was around ten, she started talking to strangers. She'd stop them on the street and just talk. It scared the hell of out my mother. I'd watch her and wonder how did she know they wouldn't hurt her or get nasty? The conversations were strange, too. They'd talk about current affairs and always, always about the future. Current affairs, you know? Jesus, she was only ten!

"And then, when she was around eleven, she constantly found excuses to stay after school. She'd sit with teachers or other students who were interested in world events or...okay, I'm gonna say it, alien stuff. Should I stop here?" Carole's voice was cracking. She felt angry.

Dr. Kaplan's attention heightened with the word alien. He also felt the conversation was jumping too far into Dawn's older years. Still, his curiosity got the better of him. "Well...are you okay with talking about it? You seem upset." Carole's mood was changing. "This whole thing's got me upset, doc. I've always been able to protect my sister, but now, I feel I'm out of my element, fighting something I don't understand, ya know?"

Dr. Kaplan was very concerned. Just a few minutes into their session and already Carole was getting agitated. He said, "Carole, if you're uncomfortable, we'll stop here for today." He needed to gain her trust.

Carole sighed, "Nah, I'll keep going. Well, when Dawn was around twelve, she started to get migraine headaches. Bad ones."

Again, Dr. Kaplan wanted to interject, but couldn't ...or wouldn't...

"She'd stay home in her bedroom with the curtains closed. She didn't like any noise. Usually, she was outgoing, so this freaked me out.

"I stayed close to her. We used to go shopping a lot, but now it was mostly just being in the same house. I have to admit I had a friend who was starting to take up a lot of my time. That, along with school and my part-time job, made it stressful to keep everything in check. Then I moved out of the house when Dawn was fourteen, as that friend and I got a place together. Yeah, I know. I was young and in love. But it didn't work out. She was, quote, finding herself, and I just got in the way.

"I don't want to jump the gun here, doc, but I want to mention that my sister had an episode that made me almost want to move back home. She went MIA. You know, missing in action? She had to be almost sixteen, so it scared the hell out of mom and me. We called around but Dawn wasn't at any of her usual hangouts. Even Skyann, her best friend, said she didn't know where she was. We panicked and went to the police after those twenty-four hours you gotta wait, you know? They put out an APB and then we played the waiting game.

"It was two whole days when we got a call from Dawn. She didn't sound herself, said she was in Coney Island, and could we please come get her. Coney Island! Imagine. Said she was at an old bus stop near the huge roller coaster. I knew where she meant, me and a few friends used to hang out around there when we were teenagers. Well, that's only a twenty-minute ride from Gerritsen Beach, so mom and I picked up Skyann, who really wanted to come with us, and off we went.

"In the car we discussed whether to act mad or just be glad she's okay. Oh boy, she was a mess. Her expression was blank, you know? Like she was in shock.

"It was raining out and her clothes were wet, but there was some slimy stuff on them too, and her hair was full of sand like she'd been lying on the beach. Mom grabbed her and started crying. I was so upset and I remember screaming at her to answer me 'Where have you been?' She didn't reply. I thought she's got to be in shock. But then she released my mother's embrace and walked over to Skyann and yelled, 'Don't ever leave me again.' What? What did she mean again? I thought Skyann said she didn't know where Dawn was."

Carole was looking down at the floor. She got quiet. Dr.

Kaplan allowed the silence. Carole looked at Dr. Kaplan. "You should have seen Skyann. Her eyes widened, she stepped back, and then looked at Dawn. She put her arms around herself and bent over and started crying. She said, 'I was scared, Dawn. I peed my pants. I didn't know where you went.' Dawn looked at mom then me. I got the impression she thought Skyann said too much. She grabbed Skyann, hugged her tight and said, 'It's all right. It's all right, Skyann.' Mom and I just looked at each other. I thought, what the hell is going on?

"When we got back home, we notified the cops we found Dawn. But then, more of these missing days started happening."

Carole's demeanor and facial expression changed when she said this. Because of that and the fact the information Carole was providing was moving way too fast into Dawn's older time frame, Dr. Kaplan thought it best to stop.

"Carole, we're going to stop here for now. I am impressed with this, our first session and you so forthcoming. Let's take time to assess what you've been able to remember and we'll review and pick up at our next session, okay?"

Carole shook her head in acknowledgement. She felt physically exhausted.

END OF SESSION

∞

Writing now for about four hours. I'm finding I need to do research on a question haunting me since I thought about doing this book; do you need a beginning and an end before you write one? I was told what the teacher in that writing class said to me was not true. You don't necessarily have to have an ending when you start to write a story. So, I'll stop writing and check this out.

OK, the verdict is in. It's a good idea. It isn't written in stone, but still, it's good to know where your characters are finishing up. Some authors just don't believe in that ideology.

Since my book is fictional, and the embodiment of the text is definitely debatable, I have flexibility here. So, I'm thinking of an ending, but it just might change!

15

∞

My daughter accompanied me to my first writing—no author's club meeting. "I'm learning." There were about twelve of us. I felt comfortable right away. And no, my age wasn't an issue.

I was surprised they didn't read an excerpt from their stories but apparently, it's done online now. It's a sharing concept, but you don't have to share your work with everyone. Cool.

They asked Linda if she was writing anything. She said no, that she was there to give me support. A few suggested she should try to write something. Linda was so impressed with the group and the idea of writing something herself that she went home and started to do just that! The truth is this group is contagious!

She called me to read what she had just written. I told her I wanted more! We will support each other, as we now have a buddy system. We both can't wait for the next meeting.

I'm into week three and I have fifty-four pages written. That doesn't seem like I'm serious enough, but in my defense, proofreading is constant.

I am finding it hard to sit at the computer and just write when a plethora of games are available too. I have to be serious enough to break that habit and only allow myself so much time playing, or figure out a good time slot to write and don't play at all!!

16

∞

I'd like to share with you some information not related to my story line but of interest to anyone seeking answers⋯like me.

What is a hybrid? It's a species whose DNA was genetically engineered to merge with that of other species. There is a theory I relate to. It just explains in more detail anything I've learned by any person, church, or movie. To me the following makes sense.

[Just a note: I use the title Almighty God while other species call Him their Prime Creator.]

Here's an excerpt from "The Pleiadian Message—A Wake Up Call for the Family of Light." I have created a synopsis of the video, mixing my interpretations in parenthesis.

A Prime Creator, along with His master geneticists and engineers, were looking for a planet to perform an experiment. They decided on Earth, an uninhabited planet at the end of a galaxy, but it was easily accessible. They wanted to explore how the humans they were going to create would store information through frequencies and the genetic process. (To me, this means our minds intake the knowledge we experience through levels of vibrations we can withstand or manipulate. The genetic process is our ability to procreate.)

The Prime Creator chose planet Earth to create an oasis that all in the galaxies of the universe could portal to, exchange knowledge, explore, and create with a free will.

He designed humans to have the ability for self-exploration, gratification, and expression. He gave them part of His energy and essence of life, so they could be extensions of Him, stating, "Go out and create and bring everything back to me."

The Prime Creator wanted Earth to be a cosmic library and the inhabitants His Family of Light. They were, in the beginning. Thousands of species visited planet Earth, and many decided to coexist. His plan was for all to use free will, but this free will policy in and of itself allowed that if your desire was to conquer Earth, you could. Of course, that wasn't His vision, but that's what happened.

(I know what you're thinking...why can't Almighty God stop something He doesn't want, right? Well, the free will policy meant no interference.)

Some species desired Earth for its beauty and energy, and had expressions of love as their prime focus. Others saw Earth for its resources; gold, copper, and other raw materials. Their planets were dying and needed these goods to survive.

The Anunnaki were such a race. They're shapeshifters, and can appear like giant humans or can display their true primary origin—reptilian.

The Anunnaki did not care for the humans that the Prime Creator had made. Their main objective was to get Earth's gold back to their planet, Nibiru, to save it. They needed the minerals Earth could provide them, especially gold, but also copper. They brought their own slaves to do this laborious work.

Other Anunnaki wanted Earth for themselves. The humans on Earth rebelled. Other races, some living on Earth, some visiting, were also willing to compete for control. Horrific battles took place in the skies above Earth.

The Anunnaki won, but the cost was high. They created

and dropped a neutron bomb on Earth to win the war. They had no knowledge of how powerful a weapon it was; it inadvertently wiped out so much of life on Earth. Most of their slaves were annihilated, as were thousands of other species, both indigenous and established from other galaxies. The greatest noted loss, of course was the dinosaurs. Does this story sound familiar?

The fallout took two hundred years to recover.

The Anunnaki and humans that were still alive hated each other. Now that the Anunnaki lost their slaves, they looked to the humans to do the mining. Ah...but there was a problem. They couldn't allow humans to remember their Family of Light, as control would be easier if humans lived in spiritual darkness, separated from the knowledge of their Creator.

So, the Anunnaki rearranged their DNA, thus keeping them existing on a certain limited frequency band. The Prime Creator designed us with a helix of two strands of DNA. When the Anunnaki severed the helix, they separated the spiritual sense from the physical, leaving our species in spiritual darkness.

They left the dead strands in us, and that's why some of us are more aware of a Prime Creator and can "feel" closer to our non-physical side. There are those that recognize psychic anomalies and some that feel a closeness with deities.

This ends the account.

I'd like to share with you some further research on this particular alien race.

Many believe that millions of Anunnaki are on Earth, controlling us in a certain vibrational frequency. They absorb their strength by "feeding" off these frequencies. How does one feed on a frequency? I would think through absorption of energy. If they can keep chaos on the planet at high levels, e.g., wars, hatred, etc., they "feed" off that energy. So, could the hatred and chaos surrounding a president, Donald Trump, be a feeding frenzy for them? A banquet of frequencies; the more they divide us humans, the more active they are? So...the more we allow this, the more control they have over us? Hmmm.

Can you believe this?

I found the story of two Anunnaki brothers, Enlil and Enki, extremely impressive, and hope you take time to discover this for yourselves.

Research indicates that we are living on the third dimensional frequency level and must, to save ourselves, transition into the fourth. Our Earth is changing; some say dying. It's a fact Earth is spinning on its axis faster, making our days a little shorter.

In the near future, it's predicted we won't be able to sustain our way of life here, or in other words, live on the frequency level we are functioning on now. That's why we keep hearing about us moving to Mars!

Time is not the same on Earth as on other planets or solar systems. Scientific studies indicate it's there, but not functioning like we use it here. And there are at least ten billion stars in our galaxy alone. So, time and distance make it impossible to gauge when this transition might occur. A lot of scientific research leans towards the next fifty years. Spiritually, it's easier to accept and adjust to this new reality, to find our innovative place in the system of things.

Now, there is a benevolent, loving species, the Pleiadians, who are extremely spiritual beings that perform the will of the Prime Creator. They have been following us since our inception. Some say they are us, but in our future. This is where the time element gets involved. How far into our future? How old are they?

This theory, and I'm inclined to believe it, indicates our future selves decided Earth was worth more than all other planets combined. Our future selves grouped and journeyed far and wide to other galaxies to gather support to assist in waking us up consciously from the darkness back into the light.

Still, I question, if we are Pleiadians and are alive in the future, then why wouldn't we know the outcome of humankind? Why would we need to travel back in time to assist...us? More research IS needed.

I'm mentioning these particular races as they appear to be responsible for so much of our history! Knowing this, how do you feel?

Are you starting to re-think what you've been taught?

17

Linda was a genetically engineered reptilian female closely related in features to that of the Anunnaki. Her home planet is Lacerta. She was a Terran. Her race was one of the oldest recorded that lived on Earth. These beings are the snakes mentioned in the Bible. The Egyptians and Incas worshipped them. But some ancient Christian religions labeled them as the evil serpents. They were manipulated right from their beginning.

Linda went through horrific mutational changes to reach the physical form necessary to live on planet Earth. Her reptilian features, structural form, and the method in which she eats and takes in breath, all were manipulated, but produced a very human hybrid.

Linda had created a beautiful human manifestation. She had everyone duped, especially Dr. Kaplan.

The internet is a fabulous reference and YouTube a great source. My research so far has shown that the creation story line stays true, no matter what species you get the info from.

The Lacerta race tells just a slightly different story of

human creation, very interesting and worth noting.

They say that an asteroid did not destroy the planet, but a nuclear fusion bomb engaged by the Anunnaki. This resulted in a nuclear winter on Earth wherein most humans, along with Anunnaki slaves were annihilated. Their account indicates it took over twenty years for the dinosaurs to die off.

Due to their catastrophic mistake, the Anunnaki found it extremely difficult to continue mining here. Perhaps too because all the animals died off and their main staple of food was flesh (but apparently not human flesh). The climate also became very cold and their reptilian-based race could not sustain life here.

Here's another theory—that the Anunnaki were at war to prevent an Anunnaki God named Marduk (son of Enki) from destroying their Spaceport in the Sinai Peninsula. Great story—look it up!

It's important to mention that if you rely on the scientists that state rock layer studies indicate a meteorite (or asteroid) killed off the dinosaurs, keep in mind they probably wouldn't put any credence to alien races ever having been here.

Just discovered yet another theory: The Prime Creator (I, who am), created a conscious enlightened body of beings called the Pleiadians. They, after many eons, wanted to experience the "form," so a holographic Earth was created for them. The Pleiadians knew these beings had no spirit (long story), and entered them. They infused their DNA into these beings (apparently Enki's doing!), making them function the way they wanted to exist. I would say that makes me understand more why they are so interested in our race as we go through this spiritual Awakening.

But, is this theory true? Are we really living out an existence on a holographic planet where nothing is real but the challenges we accepted before we came here? Have you ever heard of Entropy Trauma Reduction of Souls? I suggest you watch "The Holographic Universe: Living in a Simulated Reality," a show on Gaia—the *Beyond Belief* series. Fantastic!

Is this new information for you? Have you felt you weren't told enough or have been downright lied to? Is all this information I'm writing to you also a lie?

What if it were true?

18

Khacee materialized through a portal from his home in Schedar, the brightest star in the Cassiopeia galaxy, which is the closest galaxy to Earth's. This certainly wasn't his first trip to Earth but he never enjoyed the process. Earth's atmosphere was heavier than on his planet. His body was less dense. Coming to Earth required modifications in his appearance, his method of function and communication. The transition always left him feeling weak.

Khacee was a free-willed hybrid experiment, or creation, depending on who you ask. He was aware he had a Creator; they don't call them gods. This Creator allowed these beings to travel through the universes, intermingling with other creations. But they had a purpose: to share their advanced knowledge through love. On Schedar, as with millions of other worlds in the cosmos, with living through love there was no war, conflicts or hatred.

When they visited planets like Earth with humanoid beings, they were allowed to watch and commune, knowing these worlds create wars, and the occupants thrived in it. If one chose to enter worlds with conflict, they might warn but must not intervene...too much.

Khacee and Dawn have devoted themselves to the will of

the Prime Creator and have, through many eons, traversed the universe in His company. They both have witnessed firsthand the devastating effects of a planet not willing to commune in love. Khacee is honored to be serving on the Ministry of Enlightenment.

19

∞

Sad news. Our sweet little dog, Snooky—we had to put her down. She just got too old, almost eighteen, and her quality of life was dwindling. Talk about being part of the family. You could raise a kid in that amount of time. She is going to be missed forever.

∞

Lilly Coleman: Session 2, September 17, 2018

"Dawn was never the same after the bus incident. Although no one outside the family really noticed any change—yet. The TV reporters and magazine interviewers parked themselves outside our house for a few days even though I was telling them there was no story to be told here. About a week later the public's demand for a story died down, well, was overshadowed by the front-page headline of Mayor Borski's alleged affair with Senator Joan Frisk. Remember that?"

Dr. Kaplan said, "Oh, yes I do."

"But, try as I would, I couldn't restore Dawn to the way she was, you know, a little girl. Subtle changes were taking place. I work, so with Dawn in school and me at work, it was at night that I'd notice the changes. She didn't want to play with her electronics or ask to play a game with us. She'd just sit in front of the TV as if mesmerized. At dinner, and before bed, and again in the morning before school.

"I'd have to say the hardest thing for me to deal with were the constant barrage of questions that I couldn't believe were coming from my little girl. Disturbing questions I didn't know how to answer."

Dr. Kaplan interjected, "Let me stop you there, Lilly. Can you be more specific? What kind of questions?"

"Well, the worst one was about whether I was her real mother. This was a day or two after she got out of the hospital. I was walking over to her bed with some lunch on a tray when she asked, 'Why won't you tell me why I'm here with you and not my real home?' Well, I can tell you, Doctor, it took all I had not to drop the tray right out of my hands. I got to her bedside and bent down to put the tray on her lap when she looked up at me...accusingly!! I stared into her eyes and for the first time I felt afraid. Afraid of my own daughter!

"I was starting to stand straight up again when she grabbed my arm! We didn't talk, I couldn't. We were locked in a gaze. I felt this wasn't my daughter, this was...this was...someone else."

"I see. You're saying when you were locked in a gaze you felt afraid. Did you think she would get physical with you?"

"Oh yes! Yes, I did. Her eyes, they seemed to change color as I got drawn into that gaze. I felt helpless, weak, like all my energy was drained in that moment. Yet..."

"She didn't hurt you?" Dr. Kaplan inquired.

"No, well...no. I was more afraid. That was just one incident. The next day she was sitting up in her bed and when I walked in, she turned off the TV and said, 'I can't stay here long, there's too much to do.'

"Then, later that same day she begged me to drive her over to her friend Skyann's house. On the way, she asked me if I knew if there were aliens on the planet. I told her I didn't think so. She said, 'Well, I do.' Just like that!

"What amazed me was when she asked me these questions there was no shyness, just an accusing look on her face. I became uneasy, so with the excuse, 'You're watching too much TV, it's not healthy for you,' I monitored her time.

"Well, she adapted just fine to the new arrangement, but I noticed she'd become more selective. She stopped talking about aliens, too. It seemed her preferences were for as many news shows she could cram into a time slot. No more *Sesame Street* before school. What surprised me was she showed no remorse for the loss of this show that she watched daily." Lilly got quiet.

Dr. Kaplan looked up from his notes and asked, "Lilly, was there any specific incident that happened to Dawn around the age of eleven or twelve that made you realize her personality changed? Go back, think of her at home, was she becoming a hermit? Did you feel a separation from her? What was going on in your mind?"

Lilly raised her voice, "Oh no! Not a hermit. She loved talking with people. Anybody. She enjoyed the library, I remember that. She'd bring home way too many books and of course I had to keep track of when they were due, so naturally I had access to what books she was interested in. Well, that's what got my attention. Then...it's so hard for me to stay in this time period. I want to jump ahead..."

"I know Lilly, but let's try to stay focused on Dawn and the changes during this period in her life."

"Okay. For instance, Edgar Cayce. You know, the Sleeping Prophet? She would check out lots of his books. She'd sit at the dinner table and tell us about his abilities like, 'Did you know Mr. Cayce slept with a book under his pillow? Then the next day he knew everything in it? It's true.'

"Once she told us that Mr. Cayce could help people who were sick. He'd ask them what was wrong then go to sleep and wake up with the answer! I didn't know at the time if this was true or not but I was surprised she was interested in that stuff.

"She even tried experimenting with Carole and me. It was so funny...at first. She'd ask us where it hurt or what are we feeling. Then she'd go to sleep, wake up, and tell us what was wrong. You know like, 'You're coming down with the flu.' Or, 'Don't worry. It's just a stomachache.' We just went along with it...in the beginning, because usually she was wrong, in the beginning."

Dr. Kaplan's alarm prompted an end to the session.

END OF SESSION

My daughter and I went to our second authors club meeting and were not disappointed. We met writers who were published, writers who were brand new like us, and a woman who had her own publishing company. They really enjoyed my daughter's excerpt from her story. I was so happy she received that response and I'm sure it has encouraged her to continue. This whole experience has been rewarding for both of us.

∞

20

Dr. Kaplan was waiting for his next patient, Mr. Brown. As usual, he was late again. *This is good, it gives me time to ponder.*

Applying his usual pondering routine, his thoughts immediately drifted to Dawn Coleman. *What would cause her to be such a different person after the bus accident? It's like she lost her childhood.* He finds that sad, but lots of children have experienced that lifestyle. If truth be told, so had he! Of course, in his case there was no real drama. Just a need to constantly better himself, engrained in him by his parents.

Then there's Lilly's comments that she felt afraid of her daughter. This brings new light...what happened to Dawn that she'd question her reality at such a young age?

He scanned the degrees hanging on the walls, culminating in twenty years of accomplishment. The consequence of his lost childhood, and the sacrifices made to attain that level of success were displayed right there, on his wall.

His thoughts drifted to that haunting question of why he hadn't married. It's the same answer: *No time to devote to another person.* The result of all that education had given him a lover, a jealous lover—his lucrative business.

Dr. Kaplan had lived in Brooklyn all thirty-five years of his life. He felt a rhythm of life here, fast-paced yet homey. He was loving the move to Gerritsen Beach. The house on Gotham Avenue needed renovations but he just had to have it. His residence was less than a half hour drive to Nostrand Avenue, so no sacrifice there. Gerritsen Beach was up-and-coming, and he liked being a part of the transition.

That homey feeling came when he visited with his mom. His parents only lived a few blocks away on Knapp Street. Mom always knew what to cook and made the visits so special with talk of the old days. She never brought up work or why he wasn't married. She loved his ideas of decorating the house, but she did wonder where all this Egyptian influence generated from. She believed in reincarnation so maybe....

When Dr. Kaplan visited his sister Gail's house there was usually a party going on. So, the drive to Queens was always worth the trip. The house, stunningly modern, projected an energized atmosphere. Here was where David socialized and meets his... well...acquaintances.

Gail opened her own boutique store in Manhattan and could be found there most of the time. She had no intention of joining her parent's real estate business. She liked being in control. No kids, she hasn't got time. Her husband Jim ran a huge construction company and his work took him as far away as Pennsylvania so Gail wallowed being on her own. They seem to have it all together and David really enjoyed his time with them.

Dr. Kaplan's eyes drifted to the picture that Dawn and he discussed at their first meeting. No other patient ever mentioned it. It brought him back to the day Gail took them to an auction. One look at the picture and it was love at first sight. The bid was high but that didn't matter. He had to have it. *Should it be hung in the house or the office?* Well, where did he spend the most time? Whenever he looked at it, Egypt beckoned.

∞

I am feeling proud of myself. It's February 2019 and I'm doing this. Even suffering through a horrific cold, thanks to my darling husband. But the tea and hot soups he brings make up for it!

Blessed is the only word to describe how lucky it is to be left alone to do this story. So, I'll take the cold and revel in my peace.

∞

Dr. Kaplan went back to his thoughts of Dawn. He opened the dossier to the part where Dawn was gaining too much attention. His thoughts were coming fast. *It didn't mention from whom Dawn was drawing attention, just that she had been seen hobnobbing with some elite group and telecommunicating with them. So, what happened between then and the time I received this dossier? What could this group want from her?*

The sessions are going well. I get a feeling from Dawn's sister that she was frightened for her. I want to pursue Lilly's feelings for Dawn.

Dawn's forthcoming. I like our rapport but there is something, something I need to find out...what prompted her to change so drastically? If I can keep the sessions at this level, I know I can get to Dawn's real problem. I'm leaning toward a psychotic nature but it's too early to diagnose.

The intercom snapped him out of his reverie. "Dr. Kaplan, Mr. Brown is here," Teresa said.

21

∞

Research excites me. I am particularly comforted when my belief system I've questioned most of my life is presenting itself, right there, on the computer screen. Let me give you an example. How does a Rapture happen? Well, on a pre-determined day, Almighty God and his entourage (for lack of a better word) beam you off the planet in one fell swoop. What would be your first thought? That all those that were taken were accepted as true believers, proving that Almighty God does exist? That you were left behind to spend the rest of your life giving more effort in developing your spiritual self?

Or, because you weren't "taken," you must suffer through a period called the Tribulation: a horrific time on Earth to include famine, wars, plagues and millions of deaths?

Have you seen the movie or read the story *Left Behind*? I truly recommend you do. Two men create a story line explaining what the Bible is saying to us, modern man.

There is much ado regarding the theory of living a holographic life on Earth. So, I question—if we, as spiritual beings are here to experience the human form wherein the outcome relies on one's faith-based choices, then is this existence you and I are living through every day really a holographic experiment? Wish I could read YOUR thoughts!

∞

Actok's home planet was within a seven-star cluster located in the constellation of Taurus. He lived on the major star, Pleaides. He was almost six hundred years old in Earth time, and had tirelessly, and with great respect, held the position of Most-High Unifier for two hundred and forty years in the Ministry of Enlightenment.

The Pleiadians were known to be a race of highly advanced spiritual and knowledgeable beings. Their race was the most similar to Earthlings; their form was very human, and one could walk past them never realizing their true nature.

Actok's first priority when he arrived back on his planet was to assemble with his top advisors, all members of the Ministry. Khacee had arrived the day before, and was glad he could attend the meeting.

Actok was awaiting his ambassadors in the middle of the Isolytic Chamber. He was standing at the most prominent position, the top point of a triangle symbol carved on the floor.

His advisors greeted him one by one and took their place along the triangle. Nocren arrived last, and Actok could see he was already in a grumpy mood.

Actok called the meeting to order. "The Awakening has begun. Our Light Warriors are gathering their Starseeds in the most massive spiritual movement on Earth.

"My communication with the American President Robert Fredericks was very productive. He has aligned himself with our vision. He has given us carte blanche to their military, FBI, and CIA.

"The United States has covertly planted agents in four of the most secretive organizations: the Common Purpose,

Freemasons, the Bohemian Club, and the Illuminati. Without hesitation the president offered to share all their findings with us.

Their intelligence agencies have been able to prove Brian Rivers is actually Vasile, Satan's counterpart...or creation! Vasile is preparing to position himself as the head of the Illuminati. Biblically, they are correlating him as the long-anticipated Antichrist.

"President Fredericks is rightfully frightened, as these groups are gaining political and influential members. I saw firsthand how they are creating havoc and feeding off the negativity they are causing on Earth.

"Vasile's movements indicate he is residing in America at the moment. We know not where—yet.

"We created a situation wherein he would meet up with our David Kaplan. Vasile went to the doctor on the pretense of high anxiety. We knew his true mission was to seek out a career-oriented psychiatrist who he felt would do his bidding if the price was right. We allowed and monitored his few visits.

"Vasile has sought out our most honorary emissary, Dawn, the Bringer of Light. He has manipulated her into receiving private psychiatric therapy with our David. Unbeknownst to Vasile, David is one of our emissaries. David is not Awakened yet, so he doesn't realize he has purposely been positioned to guide Dawn during her sessions. All this is working as we had anticipated.

"Our intel suggests these groups have not yet approached David personally. They're only interested in his reputation, of which we embellished. We have created that illusion and we have choreographed that scenario. So far, so good.

"This situation has prompted us to start David's Awakening prior to his timeline and prior to any organization having influence over him.

"France, Germany, Israel, Norway, Iraq, and Egypt are reviewing their options to assist us. Iran, Spain, England, and

Switzerland have been influenced by the Draconians, our most challenging adversaries. America, Ireland, Africa, Turkey, Greece, and Italy have all affiliated themselves to work unilaterally with us, and are working diligently to lobby other nations to do the same.

"As you are aware, these main countries affect the decisions of many others, including Russia, and therefore much work is needed.

"Emissary Renu has worked diligently to establish underground bases in Japan and China. She is in the process of building the largest base on Earth in Jerusalem. The current changes in Earth's events have mandated this action.

"We have put in place the timeline to assist her congregation of Starseeds to Awaken. Therefore, her charge requires a higher level of secrecy. She is gaining influence and her following is in the millions.

"My visit to our emissary Dawn was successful. The hundreds of reincarnation scenarios from her home planet to Earth has weakened her spiritually. She will need to be integrated on a slower level. If everything stays on course, she will be meeting with Renu very soon. We expect Dawn's abilities to come forth rapidly after that encounter.

"Renu and Dawn had an arrangement of protecting the tablet until Dawn was Awakened: a coded lock was placed over the area of the tome. Emissary Khacee..." Actok looked over at Khacee and bowed "...well, let's just say when he went to secure the cuneiform, he was surprised to realize she didn't recognize him."

Actok looked down and with a very sad sigh said, "Without this reference..." Then he looked over to his friend Nocren, "If we could only slow down Earth's..."

Nocren spoke up, "No, Actok, no. We cannot interfere, only advise, unless specifically ordered by our Prime Creator! You know this."

Actok looked over at his friend then slowly lowered his

head. "Yes, I understand. But Earth...our mission, Nocren. Can we not do more?"

"No, we cannot interfere at that level. Let us be reminded of the mistakes our forefathers have made. They too loved Earth, especially the concept of free will. But look at the outcome of their interference.

Nocren continued, "Our Prime Creator has His strategy in place. We will obtain the cuneiform and return it to Dawn for her reference when she Awakens. We must stay on course with His plan."

Nocren looked at Actok but said no more.

Actok slowly glanced around at the ambassadors, looking at their faces, faces he has worked alongside for hundreds of Earth years. "Do you have any questions?" he asked. All shook their heads no.

"Let us commune." At that moment all in attendance bowed their heads and closed their eyes. A soft humming noise could be heard. All present were consumed in a ritual of mind and spirit. An energy, that of brilliant light, emanated from each participant. Their light moved in front of their bodies, all creating individual glowing orbs. The orbs then moved slowly in unison toward the middle of the triangle. Then swirling, with a rhythmic musical element, the orbs stayed atop of the triangle for several minutes. The light was wondrous, pacifying. If one could feel the presence of a pure and unadulterated love, this would be the moment.

A few minutes passed and the swirling motion slowed. One would almost feel a sadness, a loss as the orbs filled with light energy separated and made way to bond with their own hosts.

All raised their heads and opened their eyes simultaneously. The light dissipated and Actok said, "It is done. We are all in unison to continue with the mission on its adopted course. I will commune with the Prime Creator now."

All but Nocren left the room. He closed the door and looked

over at his friend. "Actok, please, know I meant no disrespect."

Actok walked over to his friend and said, "I thought you came in here today to disrupt but instead you clarified. For that I am very grateful. Now go. I must commune yet again." Nocren opened the door, hesitated, then saw Actok nod his head. He knew all was well between them, for now.

There is nothing, other than his wife Saghi, that Nocren loves more than his involvement with the Ministry of Enlightenment. This organization is the oldest and most productive of its kind and has been since its inception, four thousand three hundred years ago, Earth time.

Nocren recognized his position as The Noble Elder, but he was not complacent; no, his goal was to become the Most-High Unifier, the highest level of achievement, the position his friend Actok retains.

Nocren had no justification to think Actok had lost his ability to make decisions. Yet...he thought *If it were me in the position of the Most-High Unifier, there would be no need to bother council with so much detail as Actok did today. The approach of immediate action would demonstrate my position!*

Nocren's ancestors were from Alcyone, the largest and closest star in the Pleiades. The Alcyones were a race almost identical to the Pleiadians in their beliefs and way of life. His race had pledged their loyalty to the Pleiadians. This merging has been beneficial to both societies for over four thousand years.

Nocren's skin color was a pale white. He was well-built, with striking long blonde hair down to his waist. His face was human, with features comparable to those of the inhabitants of Scandinavia. A battle scar, a long, indented slash starting above the left side of his nose down to right below his cheek, dramatized his persona. No one would doubt his loyalty to the Ministry.

His eyes were the focal point of his face, slanted with the effect of seeing a prism of color swirling in them. Many Earthlings would consider him albino. No one would believe he was five hundred and two years old.

He never knew his mother, she died giving birth to him. Nocren's father, Buli-nasa, was a famous warrior, not for how many lives he had slaughtered, but for how many he was able to save. He was the leader in an undertaking to help planet Earth against an invasion over three hundred years ago, Earth time. The inhabitants of Earth at the time weren't even aware they were so close to annihilation. When the threat was revealed, Buli-nasa took Nocren, then one hundred and six years old, to recruit help from nearby galaxies. Nocren was a natural in the art of communication and soon a total of six thousand ships were at their command.

Buli-nasa's fleet, along with Nocren in his own command vessel, met the enemy when they were entering the Milky Way. Their cloaking devices were removed when they neared the enemy's two thousand ten ships. This tactic totally took the enemy by surprise. The defeat was swift; no need for warfare. The enemy realized they were outnumbered three to one, so they turned themselves around and went back to their home planet.

Buli-Nasa was buried on the sacred hill, Tuam, next to his father, as was their custom. Thousands came to Alcyone for the ceremony to honor him and his family. Stories of his bravery and wit were still heralded throughout the galaxies.

Nocren proudly wore his white tunic with the Ministry of Enlightenment's symbol: a Pleiadian symbol displaying a four-pointed star in the middle of wispy flowing lights of energy. All wore the same white garment displaying this symbol when in the Isolytic Chamber, and while performing rituals or other important duties requiring a show of unity. This was the same symbol Dawn recognized when she met Actok.

A psychic (yes, I've had readings throughout my life) told me that during this life I should rest, it's meant to be a pretty easy duration. She said, "You have reincarnated many times as a healer, and were a highly acclaimed shaman in your last incarnation. If you choose to return, you will be at the center of chaos, where mankind chooses their future existence, when healers will be needed to risk their very lives." Okay, words along those lines. lol

Whoa! So...am I a Light Warrior, a real Avatar? With those titles comes responsibilities...

22

∞

Oh boy! This is going to be hell to write, then re-write and re-write again. How do you describe an incident happening to a character without using the words he or his or she or hers a thousand times? One woman in my authors group suggested I use action words to describe the visual instead of those words. NOT EASY FOLKS!!

∞

Dr. Kaplan woke up gasping for air. When air finally entered the lungs, he sat up immediately and realized his whole body felt wet. The middle of the stomach felt slimy, cold. He jumped out of bed and looked back down. The bed was very wet. *What the hell*! he thought. He leaned down and touched the slimy substance and smelled it. Nothing.

He hurried over to the full-length mirror, slime dripping down his legs. He could feel the blood flowing through his heart, his throat felt raspy and dry. The sight standing before that mirror frightened him to the core. The hair was matted, almost pasted to the scalp. Some sort of slime was covering his entire body. Even his back, as much as he could tell, was covered with it.

Dr. Kaplan took note that he felt no pain associated with this...whatever this was. Then, in a high-pitched voice he didn't recognize, said, "Okay, okay, let's just figure this out."

∞

I eliminated eight *he*, *he's*, or *his* words in the above three paragraphs. It works!

∞

Dr. Kaplan ran to the bathroom and turned on the shower. A quick look in the mirror identified stubble on the face and very puffy eyes.

As the water was heating up, he once again looked at his body. No blood, no vomit. He screamed, "What the hell?" and started stomping his feet up and down. Bad move. Globs of slime started sliding off onto the floor.

He quickly got into the shower. The water pressure allowed the gunk to slide off easily leaving no telltale evidence. After washing his hair, he felt a little dizzy and was shaking. He just stayed in the shower letting the heat and water do its best to calm him down.

Once dry, Dr. Kaplan wrapped the towel around his waist and tied it. Then he removed the shaver from the cabinet and plugged it in. He looked in the mirror and with the right hand took hold of his chin. Twisting the head side to side, he wondered. *How did I get stubble on my face?* He'd never allow that to happen, even if off work for a few days.

Turning on the electric shaver, he thought *It better do its job*, when the phone rang. He walked over to the bedside table and noticed the time, 8:56 a.m., and picked up his cell. The screen indicated "IT'S MOM." He thought *Damn, what do I tell her? I don't know what just happened.* He decided not to answer. While waiting for the ringing to stop, he noticed the date: September 21, 2018. *Whoa, I thought it was September 19th. Where did two days go?*

Back in the bathroom, the shaver performed the task of removing stubble while Dr. Kaplan's mind was still trying to absorb what had just happened. He stared at the finished product. He was satisfied with his reflection.

While still in his towel, Dr. Kaplan grabbed another and cleaned up the bathroom floor. He left the towel on the floor and walked over and placed both hands on the bathroom door frame and scanned the perimeter of the bedroom. No broken windows or signs of a scuffle. Nothing strewn around or anything amiss.

He walked over to the bed again and looked down at the sheets. Suddenly, he couldn't move. A vision appeared on the sheets—his body floating in a pod. His knees went weak and he whispered, "I've been abducted."

Dr. Kaplan started moving around his bed in a trance-like state. He was aware his body was shivering. As quickly as the vision started, it stopped. He looked up and just stood for a moment, trying to still the reflex of shaking.

With the passing of a few minutes and using a breathing technique, Dr. Kaplan felt he had control of his physical condition. Carefully, he removed the sheets. He walked back into the bathroom and retrieved the towels and put all of it in the washing machine. Somehow, he instinctively knew the housekeeper shouldn't see them. After the washing machine started running, he turned, then stopped.

Staring at the floor, another vision—cavorting with friends, in a very familiar room, the Assemblage. Visions were flowing faster now. He was being shown he's not an Earthling but from the planet Sirius. They were his true family.

Suddenly he felt a longing. His heart hurt. He put his hands through his hair. He looked up at the ceiling and thought *Is this really true?*

His head was swimming with visions. All his research to learn more about the world and the universe had not been a waste of time. The determination to be a psychiatrist. His drive. Even the loneliness; it had been a planned lifestyle from the beginning. No, not from his Earthling parents, but from his family on Sirius. In that instant, he "knew" he had a mission: to fulfill his duty in helping the most valuable planet in all the galaxies transition into its new reality.

Back in his bedroom, the visions were slower but more intense. He walked to his closet, picked out a pair of pants and as he was leaning down to put them on, another vision appeared on the floor. He saw his friends, his real parents, then someone familiar came into view. *What? That's...that's Dawn. Dawn Coleman!*

23

Dr. Kaplan walked into his fully equipped kitchen with all up-to-date appliances. Stone floors. Gorgeous countertops with a beautiful backsplash depicting Egyptian symbols. The table set was wrought iron with custom-made seat covers detailing yet another Egyptian symbol.

He called his mom. He comforted her by saying he had to go away on a special case he wasn't allowed to discuss. She said, "Well, that's fine if you have to go away, sweetie, but next time, let us know, will you? We went half crazy." He promised her it would never happen again.

Next, he called the office. Linda picked up. "Sorry Linda, you must have gone nuts wondering where I was. I just had to get away. I know we were in between patients so I just grabbed the time. Funny how that worked out."

Linda replied, "Oh sure. I understand. No problem, Doctor, it's been quiet here." He was grateful she didn't ask any questions and told her he'd be in Monday.

Then he called his sister and got her answering machine. "Hi, Gail. Sorry I didn't get back to you. Been away on a quick trip I can't discuss. You know, it's confidential. Hope you're over being mad at me. Love ya."

Dr. Kaplan reviewed the rest of his calls. Realizing they

were not urgent, they were deleted.

Then he took one last look around the house for any slime residue. Confident that all was in order, he wanted to reflect. He made himself some coffee, got out the Coffee mate, put in a teaspoon of cane sugar, stirred it up, and sat down at the kitchen table.

Dr. Kaplan realized he had just experienced the most exciting of adventures. It wasn't all understood, but his association with Dawn Coleman was no accident. "It can't be!" he exclaimed. He inwardly felt she would be able to explain what had just happened...and possibly why.

He fervently believed, after all—everything happens for a reason!

24

∞

Was writing when the song "Silk Road" by Kitarō came on. It's a beautiful song, so I sat back to listen. With arms behind my head, I started browsing the desk area. You can notice a lot about a person by observing with what they surround themselves. I applied the methods of my favorite sleuth, Sherlock Holmes, and started detailing my surroundings!

A new light-gray desk encompasses a corner of the bedroom. To type, I place a hand on a mouse pad with the picture of an alien standing on Earth with his ship above him.

At first glance, one couldn't help but notice a pole lamp directly behind the desk, offering me a bulbous light fixture over the computer. Then I would suppose you'd notice a plethora of notes, handwritten and typed, directly on the left side of the computer. Two aroma-scented deco pieces are found on the left behind the paperwork. A pair of black speakers are emanating soft music on the right side of the computer. A rum and coke, sitting on my right, tempts me to finish it.

A clipboard is hung precariously on my left, unsteadily supporting even more reference paperwork.

While "Dervish Dream" by Karunesh starts playing, I allow

my eyes to roam a little longer. Next to the clipboard are a few photos placed on one sheet showing my father and mother when they were very early into their very short marriage. My grandmother and one of my most favorite people, Uncle Louie, are there, too.

Above the clipboard and spread all over the wall are metal and plastic ocean creatures. Waking up, I'm always comforted by the peaceful scene spread before me. Oh, what I wouldn't do for an artist to draw me a background wherein my creatures are in an underground cave! Anybody got $600?

Well, what did you learn about me?

Skyann might have been thirty-five years old, but at first glance, one would say she was twenty-seven at most. If one passed her on the street, they'd make the assumption she was a model: too thin, maybe a size six, deep brown eyes and an oval-shaped face. Her red hair was cut in flowing layers down her shoulders. It's the nose that really complimented the face though—slightly turned upward at the peak. It was definitely her prominent feature. All too often people commented she looked like the actress Amy Adams.

Skyann's dress code enhanced that model image she carried. Not one for conventionalism, she could go from sneakers with a dress to high heels with shorts.

When her parents died, Skyann was the sole heir, and with that money she decided to stay in their home and do major renovations. It was a big house with four bedrooms and two and a half baths.

The money left over after the renovations was still enough for Skyann to dabble in her life's fantasy, writing. Her very first book, a Celtic thriller entitled *The Black Velvet Band*, was successful enough that her agent encouraged her to write a series. In this sequel, the heroine takes on a few of Dawn's traits, a similarity Skyann wondered if Dawn would notice!

Never married, and never seriously thought of having children, one could conclude Skyann's quite settled in her ways.

Lately, she'd had an uneasy feeling of being watched. This constant state of panic made her question...*Am I getting paranoid?*

Skyann jumped when a car door slammed. She ran to the window. It was Dawn. She hurried downstairs and opened the door. Dawn put her finger to her lips, expressing that Skyann should not talk. She whispered, "We've got to talk." Skyann closed the door very quietly and they both stood still for a few moments.

Dawn started scanning the living room. She looked under lamps, behind the TV, behind the picture on the wall, and under the furniture.

Dawn tiptoed into the kitchen and went through the drawers and cabinets. She used the small stepstool against the wall to look on top of the fridge. She checked under all the granite countertops. She looked up at Skyann and shook her head no. She went to the first-floor bathroom and searched the room as best she could. Nothing. She found nothing.

Still, Dawn felt it better that they go outside. Signaling Skyann to follow, Dawn quietly opened the door and stepped onto the deck. Skyann motioned to the lounger. Dawn shook her head no and stepped off the deck towards the trees with the swings on them.

As soon as they sat on their swings, Dawn stood back up to check underneath their seats. Nothing. She sat down but looked forward. She said, "Listen, sorry for all this. But something has happened to me that might explain what's been going on all my life."

Skyann leaned over to see her friend's face. She noticed the stress and could tell she was agitated. Dawn turned her head toward Skyann. "I'm just going to come out and say it.

I'm beginning to feel I have been abducted by aliens since I was a little girl."

Flashbacks of events and time loss episodes ran through Skyann's mind. *So, that's it. That's where she goes. That's why she comes back in a daze for weeks on end.*

Dawn watched her friend as she processed the information.

Skyann finally spoke, "Geez, Dawn, that's a lot to take in, you know? Yet it does explain some things I only remember bits and pieces of. I was with you so many times when you'd just...disappear. And those times I saw when you were being taken...it's real...it wasn't a dream."

Dawn said, "Wait, I remember when you told me that once. But, like you, I just brushed it off as a bad dream."

They both sat in their swings rocking back and forth. Now...they knew.

25

Dr. Kaplan walked around his kitchen in a daze. *Could I really have been abducted? Yes, yes, I have.* He's never felt anything like that had ever happened to him. So why now? He looked over at the coffee he had made ten minutes ago and realized it had gotten cold. He put the cup in the microwave and heated it.

He wondered if what just happened to him, the visions, were real. *Why is Dawn Coleman in my vision? Why has all this happened since I met her?*

He only knew she had had a terrible accident and hit her head. The hospital report did not indicate any permanent brain damage, and she showed no side effects to indicate there was.

And then there was this dossier and possible secret agency watching her. *Why? Telepathy? With whom?*

Dr. Kaplan sat down in his chair, and with his coffee cup in both hands, wondered if perhaps he should call Dawn. But that was strictly against his own procedural policy. Who could he call to talk to then? He thought hard. Nobody. Absolutely nobody. Then the sense of helplessness crept into his psyche. *I'm going to be labeled crazy if I admit to being abducted. Besides, my colleagues might stop dealing with me.*

He looked over at the clock on the stove. It's 9:10 a.m. He called the office again. "Hi, Linda, isn't Dawn Coleman on the schedule for Monday?"

"Good morning, Doctor. Yes, at four o'clock."

"Great, do me a favor. Spend some time on the internet and find out what you can about her, you know, Facebook, newspapers, things like that."

Linda responded, "I already have, Doctor. She doesn't use social media but there's an article about her demonstrating telepathy at a party. The information is on your desk."

How does she do that? he thinks. *How does she know just what I need?*

"Wow, Linda, that's great. See you Monday then."

Linda sat at her desk and smiled. Her mission was running smoothly. She thought *How easy he can be manipulated. Never even questioned the coincidence that Dr. Jessup just happened to have an assistant he could...borrow? Never questioning did he really need one? He had Teresa.*

Just then Linda realized *What did I expect? He's just a human and not Awakened yet.*

Linda's assignment was not to interfere directly, but to report any and all communications between Dr. Kaplan, Dawn, and any of her acquaintances to a private organization, the T-HE-RE. Since she transcribed all the recordings...

26

Skyann and Dawn decide to get something to eat. They went in Skyann's car to the Mirage Diner and took a booth in the back. They ordered and Skyann reached for Dawn's hands. They were quiet for a minute.

Dawn said, "I hope we weren't followed."

Skyann shook her head. "I don't think so. I kept looking in the rearview mirror. I think we're in the clear. Oh geez, listen to us."

Skyann could feel Dawn was shaking. She held her hands tighter. Dawn started, "I've got so much to say but I'd better start with the letter. You know I was disappointed with my last job. It got so that they were making side jokes about my abilities and weren't taking me seriously as a journalist. Every time I presented an article my boss would say, 'Ooh, so did you have outside influences help you write this, Dawn?' You know, things like that."

The waitress walked over with a pot of coffee. While pouring the coffee, she noticed the two were holding hands. Dawn looked up and realized what the waitress was staring at. Dawn let go of Skyann's hands and sat back in her seat. While the waitress was walking away, Dawn and Skyann looked at each other and quietly laughed.

Dawn sat back up with her elbows on the table. "Well, one day a man came into the office and watched as I was being harassed about my abilities. He asked if I wanted this to end, said he could help. I looked into his eyes and immediately I was able to realize what he was talking about and how serious he was. I could read him Skyann. And he could read me.

"I started to talk with him when I noticed a few people were slowly walking toward us. So, I just shrugged my shoulders as if I wasn't interested. He smiled and whispered, 'You'll be hearing from me. Name's Brian Rivers.'

"A few days later I found a letter from him on my work desk, no forwarding address, naturally. I'll bet that isn't his real name, either. But anyway, it stated he had also grown up with unexplainable abilities. Unfortunately, his were exploited and resulted in a confusing, difficult childhood. He said I have a natural gift and it shouldn't be exploited, but nurtured. He found therapy very helpful and knew of a very good psychologist, a Dr. Kaplan.

"Well, that got my interest. I read further and he said not to let money be the reason I don't go see this doctor. He said it's a genuine offer from one who wants to help another..." Dawn's fingers gestured the quotes— "...special person. I thought a lot about taking him up on his offer. I was hesitant; you know me, I don't like owing anybody anything. And, why would a total stranger pay for therapy sessions? Yet, you of all people know what I'm going through, and not having the answers is killing me."

Skyann looked sadly at her dearest friend. She couldn't find any words to console her. She waited till Dawn felt like talking again. After a minute or two...

"Dr. Kaplan seems to employ a particular method with his patients. Well, I have always felt everything started with the bus accident so I called him. I've seen him twice now. I'm skeptical but if this therapy could help me..."

"Did you do some research on this Rivers guy?"

Dawn replied, "I tried. Not enough info to look up. I have to realize of course how limited my access is."

"So, what made you comprehend you've been abducted, Dawn?"

"The only answer I can come up with is that I was allowed to remember this time." Dawn looked at her friend. She felt a warmth, a comfort, knowing Skyann wouldn't laugh or tell her that what she was saying was impossible.

Skyann just kept quiet, even though she felt her whole body tensing up.

"I met an alien...being named Actok, I think. Yes. Actok. He was...well, I say he but..." Dawn's mind drifted off. Skyann started to feel herself shake, but controlled it, not wanting to frighten Dawn, knowing her friend needed time to reflect on her experience.

Skyann pushed Dawn's coffee cup towards her. "Here, drink this, you need it." Dawn took a sip and seemed to drift back into thinking mode. Skyann sat quietly.

The waitress walked over with their food. For the next few minutes, they busied themselves preparing it. After about two minutes of total silence, Dawn said, "I know how strange it all sounds, Skyann, but you were with me for so many of these visits...no...abductions. I wonder if they ever took you, or why you never questioned me as to where I went?"

Skyann replied, "Well, maybe it's like in the sci-fi movies, they put a spell on me and I'm not allowed to remember. Other than that, I can't give you an answer."

Skyann looked around. She said, "Look at us Dawn. Sitting in a diner in a reality that we're so used to. But apparently, we've been through some ordeals that have taken us into a different reality, one we can't explain yet."

"I know. Let's just sit here and figure this out. What did you think was happening to me all those times?"

Skyann swirled her fingers around the top of her coffee cup and replied, "I do remember a few times when we would go shopping or clubbing back in the day. I'd be talking to you and you'd just...disappear. It's then that my memory gets clouded. Like how did I get home? Sometimes I remember lying to your mom saying you were with me the whole time. I didn't like that, but hey." Skyann hesitated then admitted, "Dawn, I'm scared for you."

Before Skyann could say anything else, Dawn motioned to her with her head to look at the doorway. A man dressed all in black was walking in and was keeping his head down.

"O-M-G, Dawn, do ya think..."

"Don't stare. Look at me." Skyann turned toward Dawn. Dawn's view was better and she noticed the man take a seat. He didn't look over at them. She watched him for a few more seconds, and when he didn't seem to be observing them, Dawn turned to Skyann and asked, "Are we getting paranoid or what? Let's eat."

After a few bites Dawn said, "Listen, I'm scared too. I've been approached. A group of men looking just like that creep over there stopped me in the park last week while I was handing out brochures. They said they were taking a political survey and would I answer a few questions. I agreed. We sat down on a bench. There were a lot of people around, so I didn't feel afraid, just curious."

"There's that word again, Dawn, you're always curious."

"Yeah, right? Well anyway, the topic was politics and you know I love that subject. So, after about ten questions, one said something strange to me. He said 'We're doing a separate poll on your age group. There's been a lot of UFO sightings this past year and we were wondering what your feelings are on the subject. Do you have any?' I said I didn't.

"He asked if I had any weird dreams or time lapses. Well, at this point I got suspicious. I hesitated and looked over at the guy's lapel. He had an insignia with the letters T-HE-RE on it. I didn't know what that meant. I asked him if he could tell me. He said, 'Oh this? It indicates we're a poll-taking agency representing the five boroughs.' I didn't believe him. I'm sure he realized that when I got up and just walked away."

"So, do you think that guy over there is from the same group?"

Dawn thought a minute, "Yeah, yeah I do. So, we've got two alternatives here; either they are a group of polltakers, nothing more, or that's a front they use and they're really watching me. Either way it stinks." Dawn could see Skyann was doing her best not to look over at the guy dressed all in black.

Skyann said, "Let's leave and see if he follows us."

Dawn was surprised at this suggestion but answered, "Okay, let's see." They called over the waitress, paid the bill, and got up to leave, trying desperately to act normal and not look over at the man. Still, they both stole quick glances and noticed he didn't seem a bit interested in them.

Walking towards the car, Skyann tried to break the tenseness both were feeling. "Oh, Dawn, look at those beautiful colors coming through the clouds, that gorgeous lavender and gray color. Want go back to my house and sit on the swings again?"

Dawn instinctively knew it was going to rain. She shook her head no, then said, "We have to be smart now. Anything we do has to have a backup plan. They know we know, whoever—they are."

As Dawn was getting into the car she mentioned, "Another thing, I'm not comfortable involving you in all this." Skyann didn't reply. They put on the seat belts, but just sat for a few minutes to see if the guy inside came out. Nothing. They drove away.

The man in black looked out a window as he walked to the front of the diner and texted, "They just left."

27

Carole wanted so much to tell Dr. Kaplan all about Dawn during her first visit, but he kept preventing her. She was a little skeptical that his method wouldn't work in this case. Didn't he want to know how many times she'd go away for days, why she didn't date seriously, why she was so involved in politics and was trying desperately to get into a more serious newspaper business? Fact was, Carole wondered these things and for too long has had no one to ask.

Carole worked at Fuchs & Kline on Court Street in Brooklyn. She loved her job. It was long, hard hours but tremendously satisfying. She enjoyed her friends and loved the new home on Avenue T she purchased last year with her partner, Kate. She was close with Dawn and her mother, and made it a point to call almost every day and tried to see them often. She didn't remember her father. She was very young when he left.

When her mind drifted to her sister's behavior, she had to admit it was troubling. She found Dawn's ability to telecommunicate really scary because she was doing it more often, and that was drawing attention. Friends of friends were inviting her over to their house on the pretense of a party, but it inevitably led to her telepathically trying to communicate with someone there. Dawn's intuition forced her to realize this and it hurt.

Her mother often asked her girls why they never married. It was driving her crazy, she wanted grandkids. Carole couldn't speak for Dawn, but knew why she didn't...

28

Dawn Coleman: Session 3, September 24, 2018

Dr. Kaplan was different today. She couldn't wrap her mind around it; but almost standoffish. He wouldn't look at her in front of Linda and he didn't greet her with his usual big smile. Dawn wondered what this session was going to bring. She had so much to tell him but felt somewhat apprehensive.

After they both took their usual positions, and he turned on the recorder, Dr. Kaplan looked up at Dawn and they just stared. Dawn sensed something...

A whole minute passed between them. No words were spoken. Then he reached over and turned off the recorder. He wanted answers to what happened with him. *But what if she has nothing to do with it? Why did I have a vision of her? She didn't mention being abducted. But all this mystery around her. What if asking her questions along those lines will make her think I don't understand her? What if...*

Dawn spoke first. "Let's talk about the elephant in the room, Doctor." Dawn stood up and started walking around the room, checking light fixtures, looking behind pictures and under furniture. He just watched her in awe. When she felt comfortable the room was not bugged, she said, "I think it's time we talk about the stuff going on in my life right now. I don't care if you record me or not."

Dr. Kaplan motioned to Dawn, "Let's sit down. Let's discuss what's on our minds. Then, maybe, we'll record this session. Okay?"

Dawn walked back over to the lounger but sat upright. He positioned his chair so he was facing her. He could see she was agitated. "So, who goes first?"

"I will. I think it'll make what you have to say a little easier," Dawn replied. She looked down, stared at her folded hands on her lap, then said, "I am an abductee." The room became so still, like all the air was sucked out of it. For a second neither felt they could breathe.

"Uhm..." was all he could muster.

Shaking, Dawn looked straight into Dr. Kaplan's eyes. "I didn't know it until I left your office on my first visit. But before I say any more, I want you to know it's not a matter of trust but of your security that I worry. I don't know where these sessions may lead. You would be deeply involved.

"Also, the person I believe is paying you, Brian Rivers, I don't know what his agenda is, but now I know it's on a bigger scale than I imagined."

At hearing the name Brian Rivers, Dr. Kaplan looked up at Dawn and said "Uhm, Rivers?" *So, she knows he's a patient of mine. What does he have to do with this? Unless...*

Dr. Kaplan took a leap of faith. "Dawn, do you know about the T-HE-RE?"

Dawn shook her head no, then remembered, "I noticed those letters on some guys who were taking surveys in the park."

Dr. Kaplan mentioned, "Apparently, that's the organization paying me for your sessions. They asked me to report your sessions, which I have. I let myself believe I was helping a governmental agency. I even had Linda check it out but she found nothing on those acronyms."

Dawn inquired, "So, what's Brian Rivers's part in all this

and what did he hope to gain from us having sessions? Now, I'm wondering if that's even his real name!"

"Dawn, I wasn't sure why these people were sending you here to see me. I'm still not sure. Then I got to know you a little...wait, even telling you this...gee, what do I say?"

Dawn questioned, "Wait, people? You say it's a group of people paying you? No, I know nothing of them."

"Well Dawn, I would consider this a possibility, that this is a group, an organization, if you will. Now I wonder if Rivers was involved in all this."

They both stopped talking and were trying to process the information. A minute passed when Dr. Kaplan said, "I have something else to tell you, Dawn." He stared at her, took a deep breath, and announced, "I think I've been abducted, too."

Dawn's mouth dropped and she couldn't speak. Dr. Kaplan sat perfectly still. They both needed time to think. After a few moments, "Do you think it's been on a regular basis, too?" she asked.

"Not sure. Hell, I'm not sure of anything right now. Just once...I think. Since I've met you."

Dawn asked, "Since you...oh no!" Again, silence. Then Dawn questioned, "Do you remember ever meeting anyone named Actok?"

"Actok. Actok. Not really, why?"

Dawn replied, "Well, this is who I met during the abduction. He said it's okay to tell you what's happening to me and that I can trust you."

Dr. Kaplan squirmed in his chair. "Okay, this is getting weird. Was he an alien being? What did he look like? When did you see him? Wait, too many questions and time is going by and we're not recording anything."

They both agreed not to record their session. He then told her of his experience waking up on his bed. She told him she remembered being enveloped in the same substance when she was saved from the bus accident. He asked if she believed it was the liquid slime in the capsule that gave her the ability to telecommunicate.

"I believe so," she replied.

They stopped speaking, immersed in their own thoughts. Then Dr. Kaplan asked, "Do you think I'll get abilities now, too?"

"Not sure. Perhaps. I was young and didn't realize I was changing. It might happen faster for you."

What they came to realize was they had experienced a phenomenon leaving them with more questions than answers. They agreed to meet outside his office that night, in the park around nine. He told Dawn he'd make up some excuse about the session not being recorded.

As Dawn was leaving his office, she said, "Oh, by the way, better check your kidneys, you're developing a stone."

29

∞

My story line has grown since I first thought of what I would write. Research has played a huge part. Affirming my belief that I'm a visitor here and that I have a mission has led me to wanting more insight, a clearer understanding. The question of where I am going is driving me onward. Hope you're learning too!

∞

Dr. Kaplan was kept busy with appointments until five o'clock. He went to the bathroom, then walked into Linda's office to say good night but found the room empty. He looked in his office and found her rummaging through the tape recordings of the day's sessions. He said, "Good night, Linda."

Linda looked up. "Oh, Dr. Kaplan, you seem to be missing the session with Dawn Coleman."

He hesitated, then said, "Oh, yeah. I was having difficulty with the machine so I took notes, but I want to review them before I have you type 'em up. Can you look into getting that fixed? I might even need a new one."

Linda stood up and stared at him. It made him uncomfortable, almost like a little boy who got caught telling a lie.

She hesitantly said, "Sure. I'll take care of it."

"Thanks, goodnight, Linda." He didn't wait for her reply. He hurriedly closed the door behind him.

When Linda checked the recorder, she knew the doctor was lying. It was working perfectly! She stood over the doctor's desk and her fire-red eyes began to sear. She started questioning what could have happened. *Why was he lying? How come he didn't offer me his written notes? I've always deciphered them before! How can I report Dawn's progress if I haven't got the information to send? Maybe it's a fluke. I'll play this one off. But if anything's amiss at the next session, I'll know.*

30

Dawn went straight home. She drew her shades and locked her doors. She checked her house for wiretaps, as had become her custom. *Is it safe to use my cell phone? Oh my, am I paranoid!*

After Dawn checked for bugs, she took the chance and called Skyann. "Skyann, listen. Try to read between the lines. I just told my... new friend what's been happening. Guess what? He's had the same experience!"

"No. Really?" Skyann exclaimed.

"Yes, and we thought we'd better meet somewhere to continue figuring out what's happening to us. There is clarity in learning the truth, so what I told you before? Now I have someone to help me figure this out."

Skyann understood she meant Dr. Kaplan. She also heard the frustration in Dawn's voice. "Dawn, why don't you lie down for a while and call me later. After you get back, okay?"

"Sure, but before I go, how are you doing? I'm so sorry to get you involved in all this," Dawn expressed.

Skyann didn't want to say she felt she was being watched. She didn't want to say she hasn't slept well lately or mention the haunting question she'd been asking herself...*Have I been abducted?*

"Dawn, I'm fine, don't worry about me. We'll talk later," was all she offered.

31

Dawn had seen too many movies wherein the bad guys get ahold of your computer and you're screwed. She wanted to reference what she remembered Actok had told her. She knew her computer abilities were limited. She needed to hide this experience, yet document it. As she was lying in her bed, she figured out who could help her—Henry.

Henry Jackson was a geek; no other word described him. They met when she was rallying in Manhattan three years ago. He was a friend of a friend.

They started a conversation at a diner after the rally. The place was so noisy it was difficult for them to hear each other. After a few attempts at, "What? What did you say?" they instinctively stopped speaking and looked into each other's eyes. The noise drifted away. Then, without a word, they started to relate. Henry and Dawn communicated with their minds as easily as one person speaking to another.

Dawn and Henry were relating this way for about five minutes when Henry felt a hand on his shoulder. Henry looked up at his friend and said, "Huh? What?"

His friend looked questionably and inquired, "Hey man, where did you go?" Everyone looked at Henry and Dawn but Henry just brushed his friend's hand off his shoulder and made a grumpy noise.

Henry and Dawn exchanged a knowing smile; one that communicated they were old souls. It was easy to see he was from New York, and she couldn't have been happier when he said Brooklyn. They also exchanged their cell phone numbers.

Dawn knew that Henry was going to be a good friend. She liked a few qualities right off the bat: he was opinionated and up on current events; he was a fan of ufology and wasn't afraid to admit it and, he had the reputation of being a high-powered computer tech.

Dawn also appreciated that Henry had a kind face, one that put you at ease. His hair was thick and black, and he had a habit of always putting his hands through it. He was very tall and sort of lanky. Perhaps his face could get lost in a crowd, but he did have soulful brown eyes.

The minute Henry met Dawn he instinctively felt she needed protection. *From what, though?* Henry certainly wasn't built like a bodyguard but the reaction he felt was so real. Even though they talked at least four times a week, Henry felt he needed to stay close, real close.

32

It was ten to nine when Dawn arrived at Marine Park and walked to the bench previously designated for the meeting. She was glad the sudden heavy downfall of rain earlier had stopped and the bench was dry. The pole lamp above the bench emanated just enough light. There were only a few scattered people, being it a Monday night, but no one was near their area. She felt confident she wasn't followed. *I hope David took precautions, too. David. I'm calling him David!*

Dawn noticed Dr. Kaplan when he rounded the bend. She saw he was hurrying and looked like he was carrying two very hot cups of coffee. When they neared each other, he quickly bent down to put the cups on the bench. Then he stood up, shook his hands in a gesture that indicated the coffee cups were hot, and realized Dawn was smiling at him. For a moment he lost his breath. She started staring into his eyes. David felt an overwhelming sensation of calm, then his eyes locked with hers. They stood in this trance-like state for about a minute. Then Dawn broke the mood and motioned with her hand for David to sit. David picked up the coffee cups, handed Dawn one, and they both sat down.

Their heads turned toward each other and, again, Dawn stared into David's eyes. Immediately both started to telepathically communicate. Soon David realized he could look straight ahead and it wouldn't break their level of communion. He closed his eyes and realized that didn't affect his newfound ability either. He thought for a moment and transmitted, "Oh my gawd, I'm doing this! Okay, let me just have a minute to realize this is actually happening to me."

Dawn conveyed, "Sure. I know the first time feels like it's not real. Take a few minutes."

It was very quiet sitting there on the bench. He watched as Dawn took a sip of her coffee and was surprised that he too could perform that function without losing their psychic connection. Dawn had a very serious expression on her face. "I have so much to tell you, Dave...Dr. Kaplan."

He interjected, "Dawn, start calling me David outside the office, okay?" Dawn smiled and said, "Sure." She was glad he wanted that level of familiarity.

Dawn continued, "Now that we can commune this way, we are safer. We can have sensitive discussions just between us. There are problems for you, though, with this level of understanding. One, your duty to your profession. Two, you're supposed to report what you are learning to whomever is paying you..."

Dr. Kaplan tried to interrupt, but Dawn held out her hand and said, "Please, realize I am just as much at a loss as you at this point. Knowing you have had this abduction and can now communicate telepathically allows us to explore what's happening more privately. I am very concerned what this new development will cause you going forward. The recordings will be jeopardized. Perhaps your career." Dr. Kaplan didn't speak. He was deep in thought.

It was getting darker out and there were even fewer people around. While Dr. Kaplan was thinking, Dawn took the opportunity to do a quick survey of the area and felt they were safe. She wasn't sure how she knew that, but she accepted it as fact.

Dawn totally did not expect his reply. "Do you think I'll get other powers, like healing the sick? Wouldn't that be great? What if I could just touch a patient and heal their mental ailments?" He hesitated, "What if I could go to other planets? In one of my visions, I saw a family. I supposed it was mine."

Dawn gave a little laugh and said, "Okay Doc...David. Enough. You can fantasize all that at a future time. It's getting late and we have to focus, at least cover our next few moves. We'll have time to discuss what we're going through later. Okay?" They both looked at each other and realized the seriousness of their meeting.

"Listen, don't worry about me. I'll figure this out. I want to help you, Dawn. I'm here, I'm in. Now that this has happened to me, I have to get around it in my head. It's given me a deeper understanding of what you are going through. I was actually starting to misdiagnose you. I don't think my method would have worked in your case."

Dr. Kaplan continued, "The recorder, that's going to be the problem. Your mother is coming in tomorrow, right?"

Dawn nodded her head in the affirmative.

"Well, I've already put myself in hot water with the last session. I told Linda I was having problems with the machine and couldn't record on it. I don't think she believed me. That means we definitely have to record tomorrow's session or the group paying me will get suspicious!"

Dawn said, "Well, because your method keeps my timeline in the past, I think we're safe with my mother's and Carole's sessions. It's mine we'll have to work on. At my next appointment, how about I fabricate a story of how surprised people were of my ability to talk politics at such a young age? Then I can mention the rallies, you know, stuff like that. Just don't ask any leading questions and I think we'll be all right."

"Okay, that's feasible," he said. "There is something else, Dawn. Linda. I know I shouldn't change my routine around her, but she's so good at reading me. Hope I can act normal and she doesn't pick up on anything."

That thought made Dawn shudder. Just the mention of Linda's name made her edgy.

Dawn noticed David staring at her. She didn't want him to react on her tenseness nor make him anymore hyper than he already was. To put his psyche at rest, she didn't let on her feelings about Linda.

Dawn allowed him time to fully reenter his reality. They both sat and drank their coffee, which was by now at a perfect temperature. About a minute went by when Dawn commented, "Try drinking less beverages with caffeine in them, okay? Get that checked before it becomes an issue."

David stared at Dawn and smiled, then said, "Yeah, I'll get on that right away."

In the shadows, just a few feet away, was Henry.

33

Proofreading. I've been on the same hundred and twenty-seven pages for a week now. Proofreading. Apparently editors are costly, but I am not ready to purchase a big grammatical program just yet.

I am getting serious now, though!

Lilly Coleman: Session 3, September 18, 2018
"My daughter was starting to converse more with my friends and a few neighbors than with her best friend down the street, Skyann. She seemed to get bored quickly when Skyann didn't understand her. Even Carole was starting to give me looks like 'What's happening?'

"To notice some form of frustration or anger in Dawn would have been helpful, because then I could reach out to her. But with no outward signs...

"Deep inside, there was the feeling she needed help but who could I go to? She was only a little girl. What if I went to a psychologist and she got misdiagnosed as a schizophrenic or worse a child prodigy of some kind? I didn't understand what was happening to my own child.

"I never considered myself a religious woman, but I found myself praying when I was alone. Well, maybe not praying, but talking out loud to the forces that be, you know? I was so afraid that others would start to notice the changes in Dawn. And notice they did!

"First, the school called. A meeting was set up with Ms. Lyons to meet in Dawn's classroom. I'd met Ms. Lyons once before, on Orientation Day. While I was walking towards Dawn's seat, I noticed Dawn's work pinned on the wallboard. I was impressed with the hundred marks on both sheets but also surprised as she didn't usually get those kinds of grades.

"Ms. Lyons pulled up a chair and sat next to me and said, 'Mrs. Coleman, I'm sorry to have called you here for this meeting, but I thought you and I should talk. Dawn, who is usually a very quiet child, is now the most outgoing student in my class! She is showing signs of restlessness and, at times, challenges me on any subject, especially religious ones. This being a Catholic school, we encourage our students to question us. I was discussing angels and their presence throughout history. I mentioned their impact on our art and music. That's when Dawn raised her hand and asked, 'Are angel spirits, or are we the angels?' I almost fell over. What a question for a child so young.

"I remember Ms. Lyons asking me, 'Are you all right, Ms. Coleman?', but I wasn't listening. My mind was reliving the ceaseless questions Dawn was asking me lately. I looked up at Ms. Lyons and I remember saying, 'Huh, oh yeah, what were you saying?' I must have looked like a mother on drugs or something.

"Then she pulled her chair in closer and tilted her head slightly and looked straight into my eyes and said, 'I have to tell you Dawn has changed a lot and in a short time.' Then she asked me straight out, 'Is everything okay at home? Please don't think of me as prying, I'm just truly concerned. She's such a good little girl, but lately there is a noticeable difference in her attitude, not only in her academics but socially. She is up on current affairs. I don't know where she's getting her information because we don't cover anywhere near what she can discuss in class. Do you assist her with this? Does she have relatives who are influencing her in this area?'

"When I didn't—couldn't—answer, she said, 'Is there anything I can do to help?'

"Let me tell you I was tired. Tired of shielding, making excuses, tired of trying to believe nothing had really changed. I remember raising my head to the ceiling, and saying, 'I don't know what's going on. I just know my Dawn is not the same little girl anymore.' Then I realized what I had just said to a teacher. What if she told the others? I felt so vulnerable.

"I stood up, got my pocketbook and said, 'Please keep me posted, Ms. Lyons. I'm sure that with time everything will get back to normal. She's had a very traumatic experience, and this is probably just the aftershock of it all. Thank you so much for your concern, though.'

"Ms. Lyons stood up and said, 'I think it would be a good idea if the school guidance counsellor, the principal, and you and I get together soon, okay?' I didn't want to look nervous, so I just nodded my head. We shook hands and said goodbye and I remember the long walk down the corridor to the exit door."

END OF SESSION

34

∞

Oh geez, sometimes I feel I'm in way over my head. The research needed to continue this story, yikes.

∞

With all the movies, TV shows, and specials watched since childhood, Henry had no doubt aliens existed. In his mind, it was a fact that thousands of species were thriving on other galaxies. Some have visited numerous times while some have decided to live among us. His obsession with ufology, visiting as many as eighteen sightings, and being a member of four online alien groups has convinced all his friends and family that he's serious on the matter.

So, when he awoke from an abduction...

Henry opened his eyes to a blinding white light that faded immediately. He found he was right where he usually liked to be—lying down on the couch. He listened. The house was quiet. He felt weird though. No, he felt something weird. He listened again; this time confident no one was in the house. He moved and heard a sloshing sound. He bent his head forward and noticed the blanket he'd been lying on was wet. Had he peed in his sleep?

He tried to sit up and realized his whole body was slimy. He screamed, "Ahh," and jumped up from the couch, frantically brushing the slime off himself. Unconsciously, he swept his hands through his hair, as was his habit. Bad move. Slime came pouring down the back of his head. Stomping frantically to the bathroom, he jumped in the shower. While the water was washing away the slime, he tried to comprehend what had just happened.

Henry had a disciplined mind, so deciphering a problem in its proper perspective was a routine practice. First, he allowed the pelting of the water to soothe his nerves. Next, he examined his body. *Well, I'm not melting or burning from this stuff.* He put two hands in front of his face and smelled. *Nothing. Okay, safe for now. What the heck is this stuff? How did I get it all over me? A prank? Nah, I don't know anybody that would pull a stunt like that.*

After his shower, he hurriedly dressed. He went over to his cell phone and was shocked to see two days had gone by. It was September 23rd! He saw two calls from work and two from a friend.

Picking up his clothing, Henry walked back to the couch and carefully lifted up the blanket. He walked over and dropped the clothing into the washing machine, added detergent, then ran the load. He walked to the kitchen, picked up a washrag and a measuring cup, and went back to the couch and cleaned up the slime, leaving a sample of it in the cup for a later inspection. After all, he considered himself a scientist...of sorts.

Henry was drawn back to his bed. In the few steps it took to get there, the obvious, and only, conclusion came—*I've been abducted!*

Henry plopped down on the bed and closed his eyes. His

mind was empty of thought. Upon opening his eyes, a vision...on the ceiling...*What? That's my recurrent nightmare! That's me with...with beings abducting me onto their ship.* Henry looked away and closed his eyes again. Immediately his ears began to ring. He couldn't stop hearing the noise...until he opened his eyes and stared at the ceiling again. He was being forced to watch...watch his abduction!

His abductors were very tall, and very humanoid. They were standing together in a room and smiling at each other. He got the feeling this scenario had happened recently. One of the aliens looked familiar to him...It was Actok.

Actok related telepathically, "Henry, my friend, soon you will come to know your purpose. You will remember everything." Henry tilted his head, as if trying to decipher where the voice was coming from.

Another vision appeared on the ceiling. The projection showed Henry in a very white, very bright room. He was three years old. He saw himself sitting in a chair with a special handheld machine. The purpose was to figure out how to use it. Henry did, in less than a minute.

He noticed again that it was Actok standing alongside him.

The flow of his lifeline moved on to when he was ten. Once more, sitting in the same chair, but this time with a computer and desk in front of him. Henry was given a task to solve an encryption in less than ten minutes. Actok congratulated him when he finished in six.

When he was nineteen, he was recruited. There was quite the celebration apparently, but until now he had no memory of it. He realized that in all his visions, Actok was with him. They were very good friends.

Henry viewed a series of visions wherein he was given instruction. He followed, and with no intervention, solved the problems. Henry's major coup to date was the ability to decode a scientific method using an elaborate formula with symbols. Quite the challenge. He wasn't privy to why it was important to solve, just that they needed to know what it entailed.

His next vision showed Actok interviewing four other trainees besides himself. He realized they were the remnant of thousands, but Actok's ministry choose him.

Henry recognized what he had always felt was true; aliens did exist.

Sitting up, a vivid scene came into his mind. He knew Dawn, and has, through many incarnations, protected her on missions!

Henry came to realize something else, something much more important; his obsession with science and technology had a purpose. *I've been trained to be a warrior...a geek warrior!* This was all the catalyst Henry needed to become fully Awakened!

The idea that abductees wake up and find themselves in slime is not mine, but I've found it a good vehicle for Dawn's, David's, and Henry's abductions.

35

Put together a small-framed, brown-eyed, round-faced, Hispanic young woman with auburn hair flowing down past her back and you had Teresa Del. She looked to be about twenty-two, certainly not her real age of twenty-seven. She dressed neatly, but not in the most recent of styles. Her hair usually needed trimming but it sure was her focal point.

Why did Dr. Kaplan feel a need for an assistant? Teresa pondered. *Wasn't I doing a good job running his office? Is it that he wanted his practice to look more impressive? I know he's a man hungry for advancement. Guess Dr. Jessup's offer to "loan" out Linda was too good to turn down. Still, I didn't believe his comment to me that, "It's just for a little while, just to see how it works."*

Dr. Kaplan tried to soften the blow by saying what a fabulous job she was doing but that maybe having Linda would lighten her load. He even explained it wasn't her work ethic, but she knew it was really to hide his guilt.

Teresa didn't like Linda right off. When they first met, Linda gave her a smile that she could only read as, "Don't mess with me." Her eyes were intense, staring her down. *Were they...red?* She felt startled when they shook hands.

The first change Linda made was to direct Teresa to the

reception desk, advising this would be her new office. That stung, but she dealt with it. The second was informing her she would no longer be transcribing the patients' sessions. That hurt. That was her favorite part of working there.

She was still given the task of welcoming patients and doing the daily schedule, but each new day was becoming more demeaning. She even stopped introducing herself to the clients as Dr. Kaplan's assistant; she just avoided announcing her title. Teresa felt it was only a matter of time before Linda would take over all her duties. *Why should Dr. Kaplan pay two to do the job of one?*

I need this job, she thought. Teresa was recently separated and raising her son Juan alone. The paycheck barely met her needs, just enough to keep her head above water. Her deadbeat husband went back to Ecuador, back to his family. She had a claim in for support and a court order for divorce, but was told it was very difficult to track a person when they left the country.

Teresa now resided with her father, who everyone just called Poppy. Her mother had died of cancer six years ago. Poppy adored Juan, and loved caring for him while his daughter worked. It was fortunate for Teresa that he only lived a few blocks from her job on Nostrand Avenue.

Teresa's work schedule didn't allow much of a social life. Her father was in a relationship, so when Juan went to sleep, the house was quiet and the loneliness would take hold. Her so-called "friends" were mostly people she had known while married. They dropped out of her life soon after he had left.

The only security Teresa had was from a recent life insurance policy she purchased for little Juan. Her sister, Angelicia, was named beneficiary. Even though she wasn't paying rent, there was very little left to enjoy a decent lifestyle.

Angelicia Rojas was a widow; her husband had died in Afghanistan two years before. She had no children. She held a Black Belt Level Two and could certainly fend for herself. If you ever wanted to find her, she'd be at work or the dojo.

Angelicia was rough around the edges. Visualize a woman around five feet, with a muscular body and a two-toned black and blonde spiky haircut, then add in her stark glare—would you mess with that? Her attractive feature was her pretty round face that complemented beautiful dark brown eyes. Like Teresa, her appearance was deceptive; she was thirty-four but looked around twenty-eight.

She visited with Teresa at least three times a week. Lately, Angelicia had noticed her becoming despondent. Now, knowing she was losing her job, it was time for the talk. She'd always protected her little sister and felt she had to do something to lighten her load.

They sat down together at a quiet table in the Brooklyn Public Library. It was after one on a Saturday. Juan was happily yanking large amounts of books off the shelves. Angelicia asked, "Teresa, how sure are you that you are going to be relieved of your job?"

Teresa replied, "Oh, quite sure. Linda's slowly but methodically making my position there pointless!"

"Listen, Teresa, I can probably get you into my store. They always need people and the holidays are right around the corner. You can come in as a temp and advance to a full-time position."

Teresa thought for a moment. "Yeah? Well at least that's something to consider. Wow. You know I haven't time to read so I'm not up on the latest bestsellers, but I'll think about it. You're the assistant, so maybe you can show me the ropes. Even if it doesn't pan out, thanks for the offer."

Juan was attempting to pull a page from one of the books. Teresa ran over to stop him. She picked him up and walked back over to her seat. Juan was fidgety but most two-year old kids were. She knew Juan wouldn't stay quiet much longer and was overdue for his nap.

Teresa looked seriously at her sister, "Ang, I want to tell

you something, but you have to promise not to ask questions as I don't know the answers, okay?"

"Sure, what?"

Teresa looked solemn. "I'm a little scared of Linda. She has this look, you know? I don't trust her. It wouldn't surprise me if she was a plant. Like there's a bigger picture as to why she's at our office. Why would she try to get rid of me? Why is she always there? It doesn't matter what time I show up, she's there. It's weird."

Angelicia respected Teresa's request and didn't ask a question. She just said "Huh." She knew Teresa would tell her more if she just waited.

Teresa stood up, holding Juan in her arms. He started arching his back and pulling his pacifier out of his mouth. She knew he was hungry and tired. She offered, "Listen, it's probably just my nerves, but I'd swear that woman is not natural. She's so...robotic. I can't get her engaged in a conversation to save my life. She acts like I'm not around sometimes. I don't get it."

Teresa handed Juan to her sister and walked over to the mess on the floor. She put the books back on the shelves. They were walking out of the library when the rain started. Angelicia kissed Juan goodbye. The sisters hugged at the door. Teresa promised her sister she'd think hard about the position at the bookstore. They rushed toward their cars.

Angelicia couldn't get her sister's words out of her mind. Not natural? Robotic? What answer could she give?

36

Dawn was at the *Brooklyn Gazette* in City Point on DeKalb Avenue, sitting at her new desk. She liked where it was positioned in the huge newsroom. Lots of sunlight was coming through her cubby and it was right in front of the boss's office. Some of her coworkers had introduced themselves, and two had invited her to join them for lunch in the cafeteria. So far, so good.

Her boss wasn't in yet, so Dawn took the time to set up her work station. After half an hour, she thought she'd find the cafeteria for a cup of coffee. Just as she walked out of the cubby, she made a left and bumped full force into someone. "Oh, I'm so sorry. I didn't see..." She looked up and realized it was Henry, Henry Jackson!

"Hey, Dawn, how's it going?"

Dawn yelped, "Henry, what a surprise. Are you working here?" She looked at his name badge and said, "Well, I guess so. I didn't know you left your other job. We just talked two days ago."

A smile spread over Henry's face "Yeah, well, they didn't appreciate me. This job opened up, so I grabbed it."

"So, what department was lucky to get you?" she asked.

"Where else? I'm the Senior Systems Administrator

around here now, so if ya got any problems with your computer, just dial 266. Do you want to get a coffee? I was just heading over that way."

"Sure, and we don't have to communicate telepathically here!" They both laughed as they walked down the hall. Dawn felt elated. Not only did she like her first day at work but her friend Henry was here, too.

They enjoyed a quick cup of coffee in the cafeteria. Then Dawn asked, "Listen Henry, I do need help securing stuff on my personal computer. Do you think you could come over to my place sometime and assist me with that?"

"Sure, I can do that."

"Gee, that's great. Thanks, Henry."

Henry talked of his position and wished Dawn good luck, then said he'd better get back to work. Henry walked Dawn back to her cubicle. He didn't say anything in particular, but Dawn sensed he had something on his mind.

It was quiet in the newsroom; most of the staff were out in the field. Dawn sat back in her chair and started up the computer. While it quietly loaded, her mind drifted back over the last few days. She'd accepted her reality but wished she knew more. She closed her eyes, and naturally her thoughts drifted to her session earlier that morning with Dr. Kaplan. Now that a closer bond had developed between them, she feared for him and wondered why she didn't fear for herself as well? She was anxious for their next meeting.

Khacee. Khacee. Usually Dawn could read a person, but he was a strong personality and she couldn't get a clue. Dawn wondered *Why did he visit me? How did he get in to my apartment and then just vanish right in front of me? He mentioned a book. I can't remember anything about a book. Perhaps I know him from when I had these abductions...*

"Why am I so calm? Actok. That's why," she whispered. She couldn't wait to visit with him again. He'd promised to clarify more of her lifelong mysteries.

Dawn's thoughts then turned to her mother and Carole. What would she tell them? What were they saying during their sessions? She sensed her mother was sad and decided that soon she'd console her with a heart-to-heart conversation and some shopping.

Then she wondered how Skyann was going to adapt to this new situation. Her best friend. How much should she involve her? *Well, Skyann wouldn't leave me now, so the question is moot. Still...*

What about Henry? She could tell him anything but she had to make sure she didn't put him in harm's way. *Harm's way...from whom?* she pondered.

37

∞

My research has led me to want to write about three main alien races, the Pleiadians, the Anunnaki, and the Draconians.

The Pleiadians (already introduced) reside in the constellation of Taurus, within a seven-star cluster called Pleiades. They have a life span of around seven hundred years. Some research indicates they are us, but in the future.

They are spiritually enlightened and very advanced hybrid beings of light. Their bodies can shapeshift and made to look very much like a humans. Their planet is not in conflict. Their devotion is to the Prime Creator, the same deity we call Almighty God or God. They believe He is responsible for all life, and serve Him throughout their galaxy and beyond. They love our planet Earth and its inhabitants. They speak to us through mediums and dreams.

It is believed the Pleiadians are preparing us for the coming changes humans will be facing, but cannot interfere until we have "passed the test." I would assume that means choose whose side you're on and prove it!

Ah, the Anunnaki. I have already mentioned their race in the creation story, but I'll add a little history here. They are believed to be the oldest species to have lived on Earth (around 433,000 years ago). Their life span is around twelve hundred years. Samarian pictures from Mesopotamia describe these beings as winged humans while others depict their reptilian nature. They settled in Mesopotamia, Sumeria, Babylon, South Africa, and Egypt.

This specific research led me to this fascinating fact—the Anunnaki race are mentioned in the Bible! In Genesis 6:1 and Genesis 6:4! It talks about tall beings, the Nephilim, (another name for the Anunnaki and the planet they are from—Nibiru), intermingled with the daughters of man. The Bible doesn't explain that but the story of the Anunnaki does. Huh.

In Corinthians, a race called Elohim are also believed to be the Anunnaki.

Another great surprise is how many other alien species can look or function like we do. They may have some characteristic differences, like how they eat or excrete their bodily waste. Some cannot function on our planet; our third dimensional plane is too dense for them. Yet, the Anunnaki have abilities far greater than just functioning; they are one of the races that can go through walls and commit very scary abduction scenarios.

I haven't found any reference to infer the Pleiadians are other than enlightened spiritual beings, unlike the info one can obtain on the Anunnaki!

The Draconians are sometimes referred to as the Royal Draco race. They are one of the most feared superpowers, constantly asserting themselves throughout the universe. They're experts at evolving wherever they go. Their true nature is that of the reptilian, with the common green, scaly skin, three long fingers, a weird thumb with talons on the ends, holes for ears, and they are very tall with muscular appendages. Oh, and they can weigh up to two thousand pounds!

They're noted to be in close association with Satan and the Illuminati, and are considered responsible for secretly manipulating mind control over the media on Earth.

Their only desire is to dominate Earth for themselves, eliminating every other species on it.

"*Your ancestors called them demons. Today, you call them*

aliens. Where I come from, they are one and the same."
 – Unknown
 My hope is at this point, you may want to do some initial research on these races to enjoy the story line a little deeper.

38

Skyann knew it was just a matter of time before she would have to see Dr. Kaplan on Dawn's behalf, but that didn't mean she liked the idea! Helping her best friend was one thing, but how to explain what she might have witnessed was another! What if he found her crazy and wanted to see her as a patient? What if she said something that would jeopardize Dawn?

These thoughts and more were swimming around in her brain while getting dressed for the appointment. She was strengthened by the fact Dawn told her the doctor was an abductee. Her concern was, *Will he try to hypnotize me to see if I've been abducted? Does he do that?* Part of her wanted him to, the other was terrified of knowing.

Skyann walked into the reception area of Dr. Kaplan's office. Teresa looked up and walked over to Skyann. "Hello. You must be Skyann Peters."

"Yes, I am," Skyann said.

"Skyann, what a beautiful..." Teresa's attention was diverted when Linda walked into the room and over to Skyann. "Hello. My name is Linda Chalmers. I'm Dr. Kaplan's assistant. She shook Skyann's hand. You must be Skyann Peters." Teresa was taken back that Linda disrupted her conversation. Linda seemed uncaring of Teresa's feelings.

Again, Skyann repeated, "Yes, I am." She thought, *She's beautiful yet scary.*

Teresa gave Linda a look of aversion, which didn't go unnoticed. Linda said to Skyann, "Won't you follow me? Dr. Kaplan is waiting."

Skyann turned to Teresa, "It was nice meeting you, Teresa."

Teresa said, "Yes, you too, Ms. Peters."

The walk to Dr. Kaplan's office was a quiet one, giving Skyann time to process what she had felt between Teresa and Linda—tension; you could cut it with a knife!

Dr. Kaplan got up from his chair and greeted Skyann. He felt as if he'd met her before.

Linda excused herself and closed the door.

When they met in the middle of the room, he was a little hesitant to shake her hand...

Skyann was thinking how handsome he was and how Dawn forgot to tell her that! He reached for her outstretched hand and was glad he didn't get a reaction. Staring, he stopped talking and then realized he was holding her hand a little too long. Skyann looked up at him questioningly. He pulled his hand away.

Dumbfounded as to why he had done that, he tried to shrug it off by saying, "Skyann, what a beautiful name. Kind of makes you take pause and think of the universe."

Skyann blushed at the compliment but pretended she didn't notice his uneasiness. She just sarcastically stated, "Well, I must say, Doctor, that's a new one."

It was Dr. Kaplan's turn to blush. He was thinking of what to say next. He didn't usually feel flustered when he met someone new. So, with as much muster as he could, he changed the subject. "So, Dawn tells me you're her best friend."

"Yes, that's true. School buddies. We go way back," she replied.

The room got quiet. To end the uncomfortable silence between them, Dr. Kaplan said, "Please, have a seat on the lounger. Uhm, I want to take a few minutes to explain how I run my sessions."

Skyann walked over to the lounger, put her pocketbook to the side, and as she made herself comfortable, replied, "Yes, that would be helpful."

Dr. Kaplan went into explaining his modus operandi and soon they both became a little more relaxed. He said, "I'm going to start recording now, okay?"

Skyann nodded her head yes.

Skyann Peters: Session 1, September 25, 2018

Dr. Kaplan was introducing Skyann and the recorder was taping. Skyann sat up quickly and stated, "Wait, I think you should know I know."

Dr. Kaplan was hesitant to ask but said, "Know? I don't follow."

Skyann looked over at the tape recorder. Dr. Kaplan realized she wanted to say something that perhaps shouldn't be recorded. He pressed the stop button and looked at Skyann. "Okay, what do you think I should know, Skyann?"

"That I know you've been abducted," she said.

Dr. Kaplan's facial expression said it all—he was astounded! He felt so out of his element. He couldn't get the abduction out of his mind now. It was all racing back into his thoughts.

He stared down at the floor. That's when Skyann realized, *He's reliving the event in his mind. I'll just wait.* It seemed a long time, perhaps two minutes of silence. *This is getting awkward*, Skyann thought.

All the while, his silent timer was ticking away precious moments of Skyann's session.

Finally, Dr. Kaplan announced, "Okay, so Dawn must have told you about that. Let me think a minute, Skyann. We've got to get this recorder back on and soon. I don't want to raise any flags just now."

Skyann suggested, "Let's just keep with the way you were going to do this recording and we'll talk later...someplace else. Or I can say I got sick."

"Let me think," he repeated. They got very quiet.

Two full minutes passed. Skyann coughed and Dr. Kaplan turned his face to her. He tried to get his composure. "Okay, let's do this. I don't know how much you know, and for the sanctity of doctor/patient privilege I won't offer any information. But, for the sake of this meeting and to put something on this recorder, let's just say you know Dawn has the ability to telecommunicate. Yes. Let's try that."

"Okay. That sounds feasible," Skyann replied.

Dr. Kaplan put the tape back on.

The conversations stayed in the early stages of Dawn's life, so other than the preliminary questions, all that was mentioned was that Skyann wanted the doctor to know Dawn can telecommunicate, and she was concerned about her sudden notoriety.

39

Dawn enjoyed her new job. Her coworkers were pleasant and she found the work exciting. Her new assignment, interviewing witnesses to a shooting in downtown Brooklyn, gave her access to being out in the field. She was beginning to feel good about her life choices.

On arrival, Dawn flashed her ID card to the police officer and he allowed her through the yellow guard tape. She started to walk over to the tenement building, hoping to find a witness. She spotted a young woman who looked badly shaken up. She was sitting on the steps of the building with her knees up to her chin. Dawn walked over, hoping to get her statement. When she was a few feet away from the witness, Dawn realized she had been crying, and figured it was someone she knew that gotten shot.

She sat down next to the woman. "Hi, my name is Dawn. Are you okay?" There was no reply, Dawn continued, "I'm with the *Brooklyn Gazette*. I'm here to take statements from any witnesses...."

The woman grabbed Dawn's right arm and stared into her eyes. Telepathically she stated, "Danger, you are in danger. Protect. Seek Henry." The woman immediately released Dawn's arm, went back into her seated position, stared straight ahead, and gave Dawn no acknowledgement at all.

Dawn was trying to process what just occurred. *Danger?* she thought. When she stood up, she noticed the woman didn't move. It was as if Dawn wasn't standing near her at all.

Visibly shaken, Dawn kept looking back at the woman as she walked over to her car. She thought, *Danger? What, is my car going to blow up? What if I have an accident on my way home? What if someone's at my apartment waiting for me?* She looked back over to the woman. She was still seated in the same position. She honestly didn't know what her next move should be. *Well, thank goodness for cell phones,* she thought.

Henry was at his work desk when he answered his cell on the first ring. "Henry Jackson here."

"Henry? It's Dawn. Listen, are you busy? I'm nervous and need a ride."

Henry realized that was the nervous feeling he was having; Dawn needed him. "No, where are you? I can come get you right now."

Dawn said, "I'm on the corner of Flatbush and DeKalb Avenue. I'll just stand here, okay? You won't get in trouble at work if you leave, will you? They know I'm out in the field."

Henry could hear the strain in her voice and as he picked up his keys exclaimed, "Heck no. On my way."

Dawn was around a hundred yards from where the woman was sitting. It made her feel eerie. *She isn't moving at all.* Dawn thought of going back over to talk to her again, but was too frightened. She started walking away.

It took Henry about fifteen minutes to get to Flatbush Avenue and notice Dawn standing next to a building. He pulled his car over and she got in. She was visibly shaking. He turned off the car and they sat together in total quiet for a few seconds. Then he leaned over and hugged her.

Dawn said, "I'm in danger, Henry, and I don't know why. Not really. But we've got to talk. I have stuff to tell you."

Henry looked at Dawn and quietly said, "Yeah. I've got

stuff to tell you too. Let's go get a coffee, okay?"

Dawn nodded her head in agreement. She glanced over to look at the strange woman, but she wasn't there anymore.

Henry drove to a coffee shop on DeKalb. They took a small table in the back. Henry ordered them coffee and sat down. Dawn looked scared. He said, "Listen Dawn. I have great news but I'm not sure how you're going to handle it. I'm worried about you..."

Dawn leaned into the table to get closer to Henry and softly stated, "I'm an abductee, Henry."

Henry just stared at her with a wide grin. "I know, Dawn, and wow am I glad you know. But, there's more; I've been Awakened."

"What? Awakened? What does that mean?"

"It means I'm fully aware of why I'm on this planet, what my purpose is for coming here, and where I'm going when I go home." Henry thought it best not to mention his previous associations with her at this point.

Dawn's mouth dropped. She wondered if he knew Actok. She asked, "So you know Actok?"

"Yeah, pretty cool, huh? Everything's coming back to me. Like I've led other lives. But wait...do you remember him? He's abducted you? That's not his normal..."

"Well, I wasn't taken up on a ship. I was in an Uber car and it took me to this place...I don't know, it looked like an airplane hangar. We met there. I only vaguely recognized him. He said I'm an important person...wait, what did he call me? A Bringer of Light. He said I have to meet with him a few times to regain all my memory. I've been thinking of little else since I met him. I've been trying to figure out what he meant by saying I have an important role here on Earth." After a few sips of coffee, she confessed, "I'm scared yet excited."

"Well, Dawn, have I got news for you. Good news. I'm here to protect you, I know that for sure. I'm fully aware of who you are now. So, try to relax. I don't want you to get one of those migraines you suffer while you're here. Now, tell me, why do you think you're in danger?"

Dawn asked, "So, you know me...in another reality?"

Henry smiled and said, "Yes, Dawn, Bringer of Light. I'd bow, but it's a little hard doing that in here."

Dawn laughed. She couldn't help it. Henry was so easy to be with and she needed to let go of the anxiety she felt. "Okay, Henry, out with it! Why am I here if I'm from somewhere else? Why would I come to this planet, at this time, and go through this...process? How come people are bowing to me?"

"I'm going to let Actok handle your Awakening timeline. We'll talk more later on that subject, but tell me, why are you in danger?"

Dawn lowered her voice again, "I went on an assignment to gather witness statements for this shooting that occurred yesterday. I walked up to a potential witness and she... telecommunicated that I'm in danger. She told me to seek you out. She scared the hell out of me, Henry. That's when I called you."

Henry took Dawn's hand and said, "And you did seek me out, good. Would you recognize her if you ran into her again? Want to go back there?"

"No! She left the scene after you arrived. I took my eyes off her when I saw you, looked back and she was gone."

Henry said, "Listen Dawn, we're in this together. You keep yourself focused on what Actok is telling you and I'll worry about your protection, okay? We'll figure this out. Can you fill me in on anyone you think needs watching?"

Without hesitation Dawn said, "Let me start with this guy, Brian Rivers. There's more to him than I realized!" She mentioned it was Rivers who suggested that she see a psychologist named Dr. Kaplan and that he would pay for the sessions.

She also told Henry, "Dr. Kaplan confided that he had recently been abducted—since meeting me! He said he'll assist me to get to the bottom of what's happening. Oh, and when I met Actok he knew of Dr. Kaplan and he said he's a good man and I can trust him."

Then Dawn mentioned her friend Skyann, informing Henry she wasn't sure how involved her best friend was in the abductions or if she herself was an abductee.

"I'm worried for everyone around me. So far my sister and mom seem safe but what if..."

"Dawn, Dawn, stop. I'm here," Henry stated.

"And you, Henry. I'd be so upset if anything happened to you!"

Henry shrugged his shoulders and almost whispered, "Stop getting yourself so excited. All this happening to us now is just proof that the Prime Creator has everything under control. His plan is in operation."

Dawn questioned, "Who?"

"Our Prime Creator, Dawn. You know, Almighty God. He's got his Starseeds in place now ready to become..."

"Oh Henry," she said. "I have so much to learn. Starseeds?"

Henry leaned back on his chair and put his hands behind his head. "You know what? Let's just wait for your Awakening and you'll remember all on your own."

They both stopped talking for about a half a minute. That's when Dawn thought of the whole Khacee scenario. "Oh Henry, I've got to tell you about this guy that showed up in my apartment..."

∞

Starseeds, Light Warriors. In the spiritual community, these words were adopted to explain positions in this realm. Starseeds are us, un-Awakened. Light Warriors or Light Workers are us, Awakened. I like the word Avatar vs Light Warriors, personally.

Starseeds are comprised of beings, spirits, and souls that have come from all over the universe to live a physical experience on Earth. Their purpose is to assist us with lessons they have learned on other worlds. They are aware that we are all connected.

Light Warriors are defenders of the light; blocking curses or other obstacles that withhold spiritual Starseeds from learning universal truths.

They are protestors, speakers, and advocates for the human race.

40

It was the end of the day, Monday, and Dr. Kaplan was walking out of his office just as Linda was walking in. They almost bumped into each other at the door.

"Oh, excuse me, Linda," he said.

"No problem, Dr. Kaplan. Good night."

Dr. Kaplan kept walking, hoping she wasn't going to stop him, but sensed she was and said, "Good night." Sure enough...

Linda stated, "By the way, Doctor. The recorder? I had it serviced, but the technician didn't find anything wrong with it." She hesitated, "In any case, it should be working. Have you had any problems with it?"

Dr. Kaplan tried to keep an expressionless face. "Oh, I just assumed you had it repaired. It worked fine today. Thanks Linda. Good night."

"Good night," she answered.

Linda heard the doctor walk through the reception room door. She waited a few seconds, then walked over and locked it. Teresa had left for the day so the office was hers. She got a bottle of water from the fridge then walked over to her desk.

Ah, the best part of my day, she thought. She enjoyed transcribing the sessions on Dawn Coleman and anyone associated with her. So far, it hadn't been too prolific.

About a minute into the recording, she heard Skyann's words, "Wait, I think you should know I know."

Then she heard the doctor say, "Know? I don't follow."

She listened intently but only heard silence then a clicking sound, like someone turned off the recorder. She let the tape play but stopped typing. She heard the machine come back on and they were talking about Skyann knowing Dawn was telepathic.

Linda thought, *Something's not right.* She played back the recorder from the beginning and listened again. Same hesitation, same clicking noise. It was obvious. Dr. Kaplan had turned off the machine, but forgot to rewind before hitting the record button. Fortunately for Linda, she was privy to Skyann's verbiage.

Linda hesitated, then grabbed her bottle of water off the desk and started twisting the top open. With her hands on the bottle, she stared at the recorder. She thought *I've just caught the doctor trying to cover up the fact he turned the recorder off to find out what Skyann knew. Then, he turned it back on as if nothing were amiss.* She opened her bottle of water, took a few sips, then began the transcription again, knowing it had to typed even though she was positive it was orchestrated.

Linda, who has always felt the doctor a fool, had now caught him—not once, but twice—manipulating the information that should be on the recorder. So, it was no mistake that during Dawn's session they deliberately stopped recording. It wasn't a fault of the machine. And now? Now she knew Skyann told the doctor something they didn't want recorded. *What?*

Transcribing further Linda felt as if the session was forced, like both were trying to hide something. *And what is that giggling about?* She listened to Skyann explain Dawn's ability and thought *So what if Dawn telecommunicated?* Linda questioned. It couldn't be that. She planned to find out!

41

Henry drove Dawn to her apartment on Avenue U. He didn't know this side of town and was suspicious of everyone hanging in the street. He scanned them with his newfound ability to adjust his frequency levels. All was clear.

When Henry and Dawn got close to her door, they heard her house phone ringing. She hurried with her keys, opened the door, and rushed to the phone. It was Skyann. "Hey, girlfriend. Thought I'd try your house phone, just to be careful, you know?"

"Good idea, as I check for bugs daily." Dawn replied. "Listen, my friend Henry's here and..."

Skyann said, "Well, I've got to talk with you. I want you to think about something, just listen, then I'll hang up. Okay?"

Dawn looked over at Henry and he waved his hand as a sign to go ahead and talk. He walked over and sat at the kitchen table. "Okay, what's on your mind?"

Skyann got quiet then said, "I'm nervous about you living alone. I can't run over every day and with all that's going on, I want you closer to me. You know I've got this big house; come stay with me. Give this some serious thought. We can work out the details later. So, I'll let you go, but think about this carefully."

Skyann hung up and Dawn just stood there holding the phone in her hand. She looked over at Henry, and as she put the receiver into its cradle, she said, "Wow, Skyann just asked me to move in with her."

Henry just said, "Hmm."

"What's that mean, Henry? Hmm. She's my best friend and I'd trust her with my life!"

Henry quickly interjected, "Oh, no, uhm...if you think it's a good idea, go for it. It probably is better than you being here alone. I just wish I knew her."

"Well, that can be arranged," Dawn said.

Dawn took a seat at the table and asked, "Do you know Khacee? The one that visited me?"

Henry hesitated then replied, "Listen, Dawn, again, I'm going to let Actok explain all that to you, okay? I don't want to interfere with your Awakening timeline."

Dawn, looking off as if in her own world, uttered, "I'm wondering if I will see him pop up unexpectedly again. I have to admit he was quite a character."

"Yes, he is. Oh...sorry, you got me on that one. Yes, I know him. He probably won't come back again, though, not now. So, don't worry about that, okay?"

"Okay."

Henry sensed from Dawn's expression her affinity for Khacee, and he felt bad he couldn't just tell her, but he knew he was not in a position to do so.

Not sure but I'm hoping this problem is not new to writers...I've been proofreading and changing my work for over a week and have only added three pages!

Can't blame it on anyone, either. The family has offered so much support to this goal of mine. It's discipline. I'm trying...

42

Skyann and Dr. Kaplan were trying to act normal when they started the recorder again. It wasn't easy. They sort of knew what they would say, but now, for some reason, they were both in a silly mood. They kept making faces at each other and sometimes they had to suppress a laugh. Very unprofessional.

On cue, Skyann didn't detail anything that hadn't been said by Lilly or Carole. If Dr. Kaplan felt she was saying too much he would just shake his head and make a face.

After the recorder was turned off, Skyann gave a huge sigh of relief. Dr. Kaplan told her they would have to talk again prior to their next session. They exchanged cell phone numbers.

Skyann kept it together as she accepted her new appointment from Linda. They both offered a cordial good bye. Skyann waved at Teresa who waved back from her desk.

When Dr. Kaplan was alone in his office, he tried to figure out why he was so nervous about what was being said on tape. That's when he realized it wasn't the recordings, it was Linda. For the first time he thought about the timeline: how this Dr. Jessup called out of the blue and was offering an assistant. At the time he thought it was to help him in establishing a more upscale practice. He now thought *How vain!* Then he realized she started working for him right before Dawn's first session. *A coincidence?*

Wait. Is Linda only part of the picture? This group, this T-HE-RE, did they have anything to do with her being here? The thought made the hair on his arms rise.

For the first time, Dr. Kaplan realized he might have gotten himself way in over his head. He thought about all that had happened since finding that envelope on his desk: dealing with a woman who was under surveillance, a new assistant he really didn't ask for and, of course, *I've been abducted by an alien race!!* He'd realized and accepted for the first time that aliens were real. The puzzle pieces were coming together. *How naïve I've been!!*

Now, moving forward, Dr. Kaplan tried to get his thoughts in order. *Should I round up all of Dawn's family and associates that know of her situation? Uh, that might be dangerous on a lot of levels. And, it could potentially hurt her mom or sister, who don't seem too involved in this abduction scenario. Perhaps it's better to keep them out of the loop.*

I can't think of Dawn as my patient anymore, either. I'd better ask what she thinks about all the rest of us getting together to compare notes and create a plan to move forward.

43

∞

Writing this story is a very stimulating mind exercise. Perhaps it's my age, perhaps my imagination, or maybe both, but my mind is drawing out from its far recesses the movies, discussions, and books that have been stored up there. I don't seem to have a problem formatting that info into a scenario of my own. Making it realistic, now that's the trick.

When I started writing this, I knew I'd have to conjure up fantasy plots with visions of futuristic scenarios. And, usually, my brain would come up with ideas all on its own. But, (and I know I'm not supposed to use that word at the beginning of a sentence, BUT nothing else fits), if I get stuck, I have a lot of help at my disposal. I've mentioned the shows *Gaia* and *Ancient Aliens*, but I do reference YouTube and watch a lot of sci-fi movies also.

∞

44

It's Sunday and Dawn is at home. *What a week,* she thought. So much had been revealed to her; she'd met Dr. Kaplan, Actok and Khacee, didn't like Linda, started a new job, was told she was in danger, saw a man in black, and oh, been abducted!

The thought of Brian Rivers was foremost on her mind. Why would a guy she didn't even know offer to help her? His explanation that he'd been there, done that was realistic at the time the offer was made. She hadn't thought about the why's, only that she was desperate for answers. Yes, he had flirted, but he hadn't attempted contact.

Dawn sat on her bed and looked down at the floor. She started gazing at her monkey slippers—her favorite slippers ever, with real fluffy brown and yellow fur and a big monkey face staring up at her.

An idea crossed her mind; put this whole scenario into two categories: Explainable and Unexplainable. She grabbed her pen and a small notepad from her side table.

Funny, she started with Skyann. "Okay, let's see where this goes," she said out loud. On the Explainable side she wrote: "Best friend since childhood. Easily frightened. Just asked me to move in to help protect me. I'd have to wonder who's protecting who?"

Dawn looked back at her notepad, and again speaking out loud, "Okay, now on the Unexplainable side...hmmm, only that she was present comes to mind." She wrote: "Present during most abductions." This thought stopped her in her tracks. *Abductions? How many? Was Skyann always present?*

Dawn moved on to Henry. She listed under Explainable: "Good friend. Confidant. Geek." Under Unexplainable she listed: "Nothing." She erased "Nothing" and listed: "We both work at same office."

This process was making her excited, realizing it was a good way to put the pieces in perspective. "This feels right," she announced to no one.

Next, Dawn listed her mom and Carole. She thought about their relationship of late and saw nothing had changed, except she sensed a sadness in her mother lately. She knew they were concerned about her. She even knew that they would be very happy if she considered moving in with Skyann. Still, on both sides, she listed: "Nothing."

Dawn entered Dr. Kaplan's name next. On the Explainable side she wrote: "My psychiatrist. Seems kind and trusting. Actok knows of him. I believe his abduction story." She hesitated, smiled and entered "Cute." Under Unexplainable, another question: "T-HE-RE connection?"

Who's next? Oh, Brian Rivers. She was deep in thought on this one. Under Explainable she jotted: "Charismatic, but feeling I shouldn't trust him." Under Unexplainable: "Motive for helping me? Is this his real name?"

She then wrote the name Khacee, as she had no idea how to spell his real name. Under Explainable: "Nothing." Under Unexplainable: "Alien? Looking for a book. Disappeared in front of me. Seems to know me very well. Kind of miss him...do I know him?"

Dawn reviewed her list. She thought something...*no, someone was missing.* Who? She put her notepad down and stared again at her monkey face slippers. Out loud she asked her monkeys, "Who am I missing? There's nobody at work."

She...wait...she yelled, "What about that man in black and...Linda. Oh." Dawn looked down at her monkeys and exclaimed, "Thank you, guys!"

Dawn hurriedly picked up her notepad again and wrote: Man in Black. Under Explainable entered: "Nothing." Under Unexplainable: "Mysterious. Watching Me? UFO-related? Friend? Foe?"

Geez, I'm putting a lot under him. Now, one more. Linda! Why did Linda even come into my head as a possible... possible what? She stretched her imagination to try and give a positive entry for Linda but could only come up with: "Dr. Kaplan's Assistant." Under Unexplainable she wrote: "Frightens me. Reddish Eyes. Cold stares."

She placed her notepad on the side table and fell back on the bed. She had just landed when a thought came flashing across her mind. *Actok, now why didn't I think of him until now? How unbelievably strange.* She sat up, grabbed the notepad and opened her list. On the very bottom she wrote: Actok. Then hesitated. A minute went by. The pen hovered above the paper. Finally, under Explainable, she entered: "He's an alien being. Says I'm the Bringer of Light. Said I can trust Dr. Kaplan." Under Unexplainable she wrote: "Did I really encounter an alien being who told me I have a mission? Will he visit me until I can go through an Awakening—whatever that means! So far, the only info is what Henry tried to explain."

Dawn reviewed her finished product. She was glad she had done this. She would continue to enter or change information on everyone, and add anyone she would meet in the future.

45

Skyann's offer was real. She knew Dawn had been very lonely for a long time. That little apartment she called home wasn't conducive to entertaining. Actually, it emanated a depressive atmosphere, what with its dark hallway and super little kitchenette. Besides that, there was the safety issue; she should be around other people.

Skyann realized Dawn's hesitation to move in was the fact that she didn't want to place her in harm's way. That's why Skyann wouldn't mention her strong sense of being watched; it would only put more pressure on her. *Guess that's what friends do, they try to protect each other,* Skyann thought.

Skyann had another concern. She'd developed a super crush on Dr. Kaplan. She didn't want to jeopardize their reason for getting together, which of course was to help Dawn. She understood it was best to play coy, but those eyes...his funny, down-to-earth personality...he was so attractive on so many levels!

∞

As my characters are being developed, I can actually see them now! When they interact, especially. This is a revelation to me. It didn't occur in the beginning of my story. Geez, why doesn't everyone write???

46

Actok understood that Dawn would tell Skyann about him. He knew Skyann's mind would process the events and realize the truth—Dawn was an abductee. What Skyann would come to know was who Dawn really was and why there were so many abductions. Like Dawn, Skyann would soon comprehend that Dawn was the Bringer of Light to planet Earth!

Even though Dawn worked at a prominent newspaper, was somewhat radical in her beliefs, and had witnessed the loss of millions of people a few weeks earlier, she, in her world, had little time to assess that loss, since it didn't affect her personally. And, like ninety percent of the inhabitants of planet Earth, had little sense of the depth of changes taking place on it!

The factions behind the scenes were working through secretive dealings with the people who needed to know. Vasile and his massive entourage were manipulating governments all over the world, rising up the ranks, proposing a New World Order wherein there was one regime, one health program, one financial institution, and one leader—him. He could be this secretive; his position protected his identity. He wasn't ready to expose himself to the inhabitants of Earth...just yet. Even

Dawn had not seen Rivers as his true self.

Over three-quarters of the world's leaders were grateful he wanted to step up to the plate. Anyone in the know knew grave financial hardships were coming. Governments were falling, and people of power and wealth who had insight into this information were globally beginning to question their leaders. Demonstrating his fake façade, he pacified them to the point of total surrender. He took such pleasure in lulling his victims into his web.

47

I've created a few helpful folders in my computer, of which I can refer:

1) CHRONOLOGICAL DATES
2) REFERENCES
3) STORY LINE
4) LIST OF ORGANIZATIONS
5) ACKNOWLEDGEMENTS
6) BIO
7) DEDICATION
8) PHOTO

I think it's a good idea.

∞

48

The good news? A few weeks after the loss of millions on Earth, a Pleiadian Ascension Cycle had begun on Earth. Starseeds were beginning to realize the partnership between themselves and their precious planet. Frequency levels were rising within them, and utilizing their newfound consciousness, they worked alongside Light Warriors, who knew it was time to warn the masses that change was coming.

Actok had thousands of emissaries, trained Light Warriors, visiting every continent on Earth. They encompassed beings from hundreds of galaxies in the universe willing to assist the Prime Creator.

At the moment, Actok was in Matera, Italy, meeting up with old friends, emissaries Rosalee and Kristian, Awakened Light Warriors. They were volunteers from Arcturian, and very close friends with Nocren and him. He had missed them; it had been many eons. Through their efforts, millions of Starseed hybrids and humans were to be Awakened...tonight.

His visit would be quick: oversee the setup and reacquaint with friends.

Actok knew there was much to do to prepare Dawn for her mission. Therefore, he relied heavily on his family of spiritually enlightened beings to rouse as many souls as possible.

Kristian greeted Actok in an underground cave not yet known to even the locals of the area. It was perfect to hold a massive crowd of thousands, and thousands there were!

Kristian and his crew had worked day and night to fabricate this place for the Awakening without attracting any unwanted attention. Signs were posted to keep the noise down to a minimum.

Of course, with Actok's assistance and permission from the Prime Creator, a holographic image of indigenous stones and shrubbery were placed over and around the entire area.

The cave was situated near the sea, making a way for every attendee to arrive in small, local ships after dark. Here, another hologram was initiated at nightfall to appear as nothing more than a sea of water near the shore.

Yes, there was danger; not every plan was impenetrable, but not even an aerial view would suggest anything amiss!

Actok and Kristian walked over to where Rosalee was standing on the stage behind the curtains. She was getting ready to speak to the assemblage. She looked over and smiled at her friend. Actok bowed his head.

Rosalee's small frame and beautiful smile did little in comparison to her strikingly beautiful red hair. When she stepped out from behind the curtain, everyone turned to watch her walk toward the podium. The crowd, knowing not to create too much excess noise, waved their hands in the air for a full two minutes.

Rosalee stepped up onto a small box behind the podium: without it, no one would see her there! With a quick finger to her lips, Rosalee hushed the crowd. She held onto both sides of the podium, looked slowly all around the room, then said, "Greetings to all. We are honored to be among you and realize the risk you took in order to assemble here tonight. Every precaution was taken to shield this gathering from prying eyes.

"Kristian and I have been working with you, preparing you

for this very moment. We realize you may have invited friends or loved ones to come here tonight. We are in alignment with your decision. That being said, the information they hear may be new to them. They will not be on the same frequency levels as you, so be patient with them as they learn who they are and who you are becoming!

Rosalee looked out and stretched her arms to the crowd. "You are the conception of the Prime Creator, His experiment of love and knowledge. Do not take the word experiment to heart—in English it's hard to find the term. Know you were created in His image.

"Each and every one of you have come from somewhere else. Each one of you. Okay. Still with me? I didn't see anyone walk out. That's good." People were smiling, trying not to laugh too loud.

"For those here that might not fully understand what is happening on our planet now, let me take a few minutes to explain. The world is in total chaos. It happened so quickly. We're experiencing a viral plague, COVID-19. A new leader is emerging behind the scenes promising a New World Order. Soon, he will expose himself to you as your savior. He'll seem to have all the answers.

"The streets of many big cities are full of anarchists, totally focused on the destruction of our values. We are being introduced to the idea of an embedded chip in our hand in order to eat or purchase anything. Daily there is some new movement to bring down our precious way of living. You're witnessing catastrophes on this planet like never before. There is talk of yet another plague...

"Most of you will survive by living underground or in communities so small they can barely function.

"In light of all I've just said, do you think you're alone? No! It is now time to awaken to who you really are and why you are here on planet Earth. Tonight, your questions will be answered. Tonight, my loved ones, you will know!

"Each one of you is an individual, true, but in reality, a whole consciousness. While here, the memory of your true identity was hidden, on purpose. You see, Earth was fashioned by the Prime Creator to allowed free will to all who inhabited or visited. He created Earth as a cosmic library for all beings from all galaxies to come share their knowledge and exchange ideas and all with the ability to act upon their decisions.

"I realize some of you are hearing this information for the first time. Take heart. You are exactly where you're supposed to be! Tonight, you came here a Starseed, a seeker, but you will leave an enlightened human being!

"Everyone here...everyone, has volunteered to incarnate for this mission, a tour of duty, you might say. And inwardly you sense you have something to offer, right?" The crowd bowed in agreement. "You've just never been able to find a way." Some in the crowd started whispering to each other, while others just stood in awe.

"Kristian and I are so proud to have led you to this moment. Your special talent will be realized...tonight. You might be a healer, a grid worker (a human vessel who helps one channel energies), or maybe a lightkeeper (a human who helps direct Starseeds), just to name a few. Know you are all here for the same common interest: to advance your spiritual consciousness."

Rosalee stood aside as she welcomed Kristian to the podium. The crowd went wild. They waved their hands in the air back and forth for over two minutes, two minutes during which Kristian turned red with embarrassment, and deep love welled from his bosom.

Kristian looked out at the crowd and put his hands to his mouth and coughed. This was his trademark. His way of acclimating himself to speak in front of such a large audience. The arena grew silent. Then, Kristian said, "Starseeds, you have waited, suffered, endured long enough. Tonight, you are ready. Do not be afraid, dear ones, as tonight you will reach nirvana. You will be in close union with your Prime Creator once again."

During a quick break, Actok reunited with his friends but time constraints deemed he limit their visit. He did inform them however that he felt the program was in good hands.

∞

Readers, you have been given insight as to Dawn's predicament, but nothing regarding how she will be Awakened. Or, what happens when she is.

You have been exposed to the fact that alien entities, good and bad, are a staple of this story. Abductions have occurred.

I've mentioned a few groups, the Antichrist has been introduced, and you've learned of an organization I created on Pleiades, the Ministry of Enlightenment. I'm hoping you did some research on the alien races I've mentioned, and perhaps have reflected on why you believe the way you do.

If you feel you know the story so far and you'd enjoy stepping out of the box somewhat then...prepare now as we journey down the black hole... Okay, theoretically you would not survive a trip down a black hole, but who do you know who ever ventured down a rabbit hole? Let's go···

∞

49

It's Wednesday, October 3rd, and, despite the fact it was a newspaper business, you could hear a pin drop. Dawn was at her desk thinking of the woman who had warned her she was in danger. *How did she grab my arm, tell me something so important, then turn around and act like she didn't even see me standing there?*

Maybe I should go back to that area again and seek her out. But what are the chances I'd find her? Or, that she'd talk to me? If she was there and willing to talk, she'd probably say she doesn't remember the incident at all.

Then, there's the fact I'd have to hire an Uber driver who'd have to be willing to wait as I searched the area.

These thoughts were going through her mind when she felt someone was watching her. She looked to her right but saw no one. She turned to her left and immediately felt startled—there was a man standing outside her cubicle.

Dawn couldn't move. She felt paralyzed. "Hi there, Dawn. Remember me? Brian...Brian Rivers." He walked into her workspace. Dawn still couldn't move or catch her breath. His presence was so unexpected, alarming.

The look on her face expressed her physical condition. He eyed her up and down, then chuckled, "Well, I must say, I didn't expect such a welcome. Sorry to have frightened you."

Finally, Dawn felt she had her senses back. She realized how stupid she must have looked. "Oh, Mr. Rivers, you did, sorry. Didn't expect to see you here."

"Just Brian, Dawn. So, are you saying you're happy to see me?"

"Sure, sure. How are you? I'd offer you a seat but…"

"I'm fine, Dawn. I was, as they say, in the area and Dan…Mr. Katz filled me in on your employment here. Says he's very happy to have you. How do you like it? Different, huh?" He leaned in to her and whispered, "Nobody around to make you feel uncomfortable about your…abilities, huh?"

Dawn grasped his underlying meaning. She looked up at him, "Yes, I've been hoping to talk with you about that, you know, the sessions you're paying for. I…"

Dawn saw an opportunity to dismiss herself from the sessions and she took it. "Yes. It has helped, tremendously. That's what I want to tell you. I'm going to stop going to him now. I feel he's made me aware that I'm not so different after all. I just have to process the experience when a scenario presents itself."

He stared at Dawn but didn't speak. She was very uncomfortable, and felt the back of her neck tense up. Then he smiled, a smile that Dawn took as malicious. "Really? That IS quick, Dawn. Are you sure? I know he's good but…"

"Listen, I'll stop for a while and let a situation happen and if I can't control my…my abilities, then I'll go back to him. Okay? Seriously, I want to stop them for now. And thank you so much, Mr. …ah, Brian. It has truly helped me."

Again, Brian Rivers stared at Dawn. "Sure Dawn. Sure." He got quiet. He walked out of the cubicle, then leaned back and looked at Dawn once more. It took all her reserve not to say any more. He said, "So, till we meet again?"

Dawn faked a smile, "Yes, and thank you so much." She wondered how this man got around: was he really a salesperson? He had called Katz "Dan".

He smiled at Dawn, hesitated, then turned to leave. When out of Dawn's view, his teeth began to gnaw, his neck muscles became taut, and it took every ounce of his control to not go back into Dawn's vestibule and crush the life out of her!

He certainly hadn't expected this! An invitation to dinner was what he'd hoped to achieve. Get her comfortable, then drug her. Take her back to his place and get the truth out of her, on tape! He knew he couldn't kill her, but he couldn't wait to discredit her in front of the whole world.

50

Henry was uneasy. Wasn't sure why, but uneasy. He fussed all morning around his office. Must have made three trips to the cafeteria, and four cups of coffee. He mumbled, "It's only Wednesday. Gotta get a grip."

He kept trying to find excuses to walk over to Dawn's cubicle. Every time he got close, he noticed she was fine.

Around eleven thirty, Henry just couldn't stand it any longer. He hadn't been to Dawn's area in over an hour. He walked over and right into Dawn's work space. That's when he noticed she was crying.

Dawn was startled at someone entering her cubicle. Her immediate thought was that it had to be Brian returning, but then she noticed it was Henry. She stood up and put her shaking arms around him.

The guilt Henry felt was overwhelming. He had known something wasn't right, but couldn't put a finger on it. He took out his handkerchief and wiped Dawn's tears away. Then they both walked to the cafeteria. Henry was attempting to down his fifth cup of coffee of the day, as Dawn explained her confrontation with Brian.

Henry said, "I don't trust him, Dawn. I'm sure he's the reason I was so distraught all morning. I sensed something...I should have trusted my instinct. Damn."

Dawn said, "Well, if I got out of those sessions, that's a relief. It'll make it easier on David now. I was afraid of him getting into some kind of trouble. By the way, did you hear from him? He wants to set up a meeting with us."

"David, huh? It's David now." Dawn could see the jealous reaction but didn't acknowledge it. With a noticeable hesitation he continued, "That's a great idea. The sooner the better, so tell him I'm in." Henry continued, "I'm going to check this Rivers guy, see what I can find." Then, on a more personal level, he said, "Listen, I think it's a good thing if you move in with Skyann. Have you given it any more thought?"

"Yes. I hired a van and started moving some big stuff in already. You know, some pieces of furniture. But I'm not there physically just yet. My main concern is that I hope I don't put her in harm's way. I would die if anything happened to her."

"Well, you know the old adage, Dawn, there's safety in numbers."

Dawn smiled, "True. True. Perhaps I should call David and make that meeting tonight. What do you think?"

"Go for it."

51

Teresa figured if she was soon being fired or laid off, she was going to get to the bottom of why Linda was hired in the first place. She did something so out of the ordinary; she purchased a recording device and placed it under Linda's desk. If she got caught, who cared?

It only took a few days to get enough information on Linda to tell Dr. Kaplan what was going on in his office. Teresa found out Linda was a plant. She was secretly calling someone named Vasile, a name she did not recognize, advising him of all transactions going on with the Dawn Coleman case.

Teresa got the affirmation she needed on day three. While getting ready to leave work, she noticed a man walking into Linda's office. He didn't see Teresa, but she thought he looked familiar. *That's Brian Rivers! He's come here a few times for counselling.*

So quiet were the two that she had to sneak down the hall to listen. Her anxiety was rising, but she didn't care at this point if they found her there. When she reached the door, the hallway felt extremely cold; enough to where she immediately folded her arms in towards her chest.

Teresa heard this man telling Linda that their game might be up and to drug Dawn with sodium thiopental. "I need something on tape, damn it. This stuff should make her talk. If not, find something that will. I want her credibility questioned. Now. Before she Awakens and it's too late."

That's when Teresa heard Linda say, "Yes, Vasile. Right away."

Vasile? Teresa silently questioned. *So, Brian Rivers is Vasile!*

Teresa wished she knew what the hell they wanted Dawn to talk about. She also wondered what Awakened meant. *Awakened from what? No wonder Linda took the transcriptions away from me; she was transcribing a recording for Dr. Kaplan then hand-delivering a private recording to this man!*

Teresa quietly walked backward toward the outside office door and then ran to her car to call Angelicia. Her sister said she'd leave work right away and that they could meet in Sheepshead Playground.

While Teresa pushed little Juan on the swing, Angelicia said, "I can't believe it. You actually did this? Bought a device and recorded this woman? And...my little sister listened in on their conversation? How brave!"

"Yep. Now what do I do? That's the question. I can't go to the police until I know Dr. Kaplan's involvement. What if he's in on this?"

"Well, you can't wait, either! What if she drugs Dawn?"

Teresa looked down at the ground and shuffled her feet. "What if I confront her? You could be there..." Teresa suggested.

Angelicia gave Teresa a look of encouragement, "Well, you're certainly not going to go through this alone! But confronting her? Not a good idea. I'm thinking that maybe you need a leap of faith here. Do you really think Dr. Kaplan could be in on this?"

"Ah...not really. He's a very driven man but I think a good one. He didn't just fire me, you know?"

"So, let's give him this information and see what he says.

If we're wrong, well..."

"Okay, Angie, sounds like a plan."

Teresa called Dr. Kaplan stating her sister suggested she tell him what she knows. He listened as Teresa explained she recorded Linda, and immediately he felt Dawn needed protection. He thanked Teresa for her bravery. Then he thought he'd invite them to the meeting they were trying to plan, but figured he'd better ask the group first. He thought *After all, they might have just saved Dawn's life!*

52

Dawn woke up, put on a frozen dinner and turned on the TV. Almost every channel were showing close-up shots of something unusual flying in the skies over New York and New Jersey. It wasn't one unexplained object, but five. They looked like ships, cigar-shaped, and were maneuvering in strange patterns. Then, they would jut up and shoot right through the clouds and come down again.

The reporter was keeping his cool, saying, "It's probably our government putting on a show with some new technology." Then he decided, for effect, he'd remind his listeners of the fact, "Still folks, it's not the first time, nor will it be the last, that alien ships have been reported hovering over big cities."

The cameraman was egging him on, so he continued, "And let's remember what is rumored to be happening at Area 51. I know, the first movement to infiltrate that building and its surrounding area failed, big time. But this new movement is gaining unprecedented attention. People all over the world are said to be coming to show strength and support. The people want to know the truth, and you know, it's out there!"

Dawn finished her meal and wondered why she wasn't alarmed hearing this news. Actok, that's why. Meeting Actok was helping her to understand. Brushing the thought aside, she headed toward the bedroom to retrieve the cell phone. That's when it hit her! While in the Uber car, she had turned it off to get a quick nap on the trip home. A quick review informed her that Dr. Kaplan had tried to call three times. Skyann had tried twice. Henry twice. *Oh, the meeting! That's why they were calling, I forgot to call everyone to set up a meeting. There's just too much on my mind, damn it, too much,* she thought.

Dawn called Dr. Kaplan first, who was in panic mode. He told her of what happened at the office and that he had told Skyann. The call was interrupted by Skyann. Dawn put them on speaker and got Henry on also. Dawn tried quickly to introduce Henry. Everyone was upset and talking at once. They were discussing the unexplained ships hovering over New York and New Jersey when Dawn yelled, "Stop guys. Stop. Let's get together at Skyann's in about an hour, all right? Is that all right, Skyann?"

"Yes, perfect."

"Dawn, I'm coming to pick you up," Henry exclaimed. Skyann didn't interject with a counteroffer, thinking they should have time alone to process this situation.

Dr. Kaplan mentioned Teresa's involvement, and asked if the group thought it a good idea that she and her sister come along. They agreed it was fine.

Around seven o'clock, all were in attendance. No formal introduction was made, as everyone was intent on watching the TV and asking what the hell was going on. Except Henry; his higher frequency levels were working overtime, enabling him to sense, then surmise something was about to happen. Since Awakening, he's had to adjust control of the onslaught of vibrations coming at him from all directions. A loud voice, a soft whisper, could all create a chasm of sound his body had to regulate. And no one to talk to about it. He knew soon enough it would be the norm, but for now...

In the interim, Dawn scanned the rooms for bugs. This action made the sisters apprehensive and a little scared, so Henry introduced himself and tried his best to pacify them. Henry wasn't sure, but wondered if the new feeling he had was meeting from Teresa for the first time.

Skyann was busy making drinks and putting coffee on. She felt she needed wine tonight. Lots of it. She still hadn't told Dawn anything about what she'd been feeling, this eerie sense of being watched.

Dr. Kaplan took hold of Teresa's arm and pulled her aside, "Glad you could make it. Where's your son? I thought he'd be here."

"My dad's home tonight so he said he'd watch him."

"Oh good, that worked out." He stood next to her a moment, then continued, hesitantly, "Listen, Teresa, I'm really sorry, I was such a jerk. I was so caught up, I didn't want to see what this was doing to you. Please, forgive me?"

Teresa said, "I understand...now. So, my job's secure?"

"You bet! I'm going to close the office for a week and delegate my clients to Dr. Stein. Except Mr. Brown, I'll personally call him and get him in for a session. You know, I'm going to have to change my diagnosis on him now!" Teresa gave him a questioning look. While typing Mr. Brown's sessions, she assumed that Mr. Brown was living in a fantasy world. What did the doctor mean?

Dr. Kaplan continued, "Teresa, how about you take that time off with pay?" Teresa smiled up at him, her first real smile in ages.

A few minutes later Skyann noticed Henry and Dr. Kaplan chatting in a corner and wished she were a fly on the wall.

Dawn was preparing to settle the group down, asking for help to place some chairs around in a circle. When all were seated, proper introductions were made. Henry and Teresa kept sneaking quick glances at each other. Dawn and Dr. Kaplan sat together. Angelicia sat in the middle of Teresa and Skyann.

The sisters were really in the dark, and had to be brought up to speed prior to any plans being made. Dawn began explaining to Teresa and Angelicia what had been happening, including meeting Actok. Angelicia smirked at the first few comments; her reaction when she was nervous. Then she noticed the seriousness of the group's demeanor.

When Linda's name was mentioned, Teresa felt the tension in the room. She said, "I never thought she was normal. So rigid. Like a robot. She would never hold a conversation with me."

Dawn exclaimed, "She frightens me. Those eyes."

Angelicia couldn't help it. She said, "So, you guys all think she's a planted alien, out to do the work of this Rivers guy? I wonder what planet she's from?" All eyes look at Angelicia, and she immediately felt uncomfortable. *Oh no, they do think that way,* she realized.

Dawn understood Angelicia's apprehension and overlooked her comment.

Before Dawn could say another word, Teresa interjected, "Please, may I say something? It's really important."

"Sure, go ahead," Dawn answered.

Teresa turned her head toward Dr. Kaplan and announced, "I told you, Dr. Kaplan, but I don't know if you had time to tell the others. Brian Rivers isn't who he seems to be. I overheard Linda and him having a conversation and she referred to him as Vasile. He said he wants Dawn injected immediately with a truth drug to get her to confess who she really is." Teresa then lowered her head and glanced at Dawn. "Whoever that may be." The room became quiet as all interpreted the seriousness of what Teresa had just announced.

Henry said, "Now that makes sense. Yeah, saw him at the Gazette a few days ago but I didn't recognize him. Then I saw him on TV. Wait...is that the guy who made you cry, Dawn? Yes, yes of course it is! Hold on, I'll do a little background referencing."

Skyann interjected, "Henry, the reception here is at best iffy lately."

Henry said, "No problem." He stood up and walked out to his car. He was glad he could fix any reception problem, and didn't have to explain he needed complete silence while immersing himself in research on his laptop.

Dawn started to feel shaky as she realized who she was dealing with, but valiantly hid it from the group. Now it made sense: he was setting her up!

Dawn continued "Let's move on." She looked over at Dr. Kaplan. "What about your practice? What if Linda's at the office when you show up? How would you fire her at this point? You know I already told Brian...ah Vasile I wasn't going to go for counseling anymore. So now Linda knows."

He looked over at her. "Those are the exact questions I've been asking myself. Linda's no dummy. I was thinking maybe she'll just disappear overnight, as we're onto her game. She hasn't tried to contact you, has she? You know, to see if you're coming in or not?" Dawn, still shaking, shook her head no.

Henry was back within minutes, leaving his laptop in the car. He announced, "I did inquiries on both Vasile and Linda Chalmers. Lots of people with the last name Vasile, but nothing fit with his bio. Linda's info was there, and all as it should be. Couldn't find anything out of the ordinary, no warrants, no jail time. Nothing."

Dawn sighed, "Well, at least you found something. I couldn't."

"Yeah, I guess my sources are a little more extensive." They both gave each other a quirky smile.

Henry continued, "But what I want to mention is that organization you and I were just discussing, Dr. Kaplan. The T-HE-RE."

Dr. Kaplan glanced around at the group, "Please, everyone, call me David, okay?" They either nodded their heads yes or mumbled in the affirmative.

Henry continued, "The T-HE-RE. I did an in-depth search and came up with nothing. I can't imagine what that stands for. Does anyone want to venture a guess?"

There was silence as everyone thought of what those letters could represent. Then Angelicia spoke up, "Well, the obvious would be...THEY'RE HERE!!!" The group couldn't help but laugh.

Dawn said, "Well, a guy I met in the park said it was an acronym for their political activist group but I didn't think to ask what it stood for."

Henry spoke next, "It's not in the usual coded programs I have access to. So, I looked it up under ancient organizations and found something...

"Bear with me here. Either the T-HE-RE is a collective term indicating an organization, or the breakdown of all five letters and that dash mean something of an individual nature. Knowing little of Vasile, it's hard to know what organizations he might be involved in, or the leader of! But get this, the name Vasile? Means king!" The group all expressed the same surprised look but no one commented.

Henry continued, "So, let's say he's bad, really bad. That would put him in a category with a real evil occult or perhaps some bad-ass aliens. The Illuminati comes to mind."

Everyone just looked at each other, but it was Angelicia who questioned, "Is this Illuminati an alien group?"

Henry looked around at the group and then back to Angelicia. "Uh, no, well, maybe, there's...sorry. I'm confusing you guys. The Illuminati was a very old, secretive, Earth-bound society that many believe still exists. What they really do now is a mystery, but rumors swirl all over the internet that they're alive and well and in charge of world events, but from behind the scenes. Just the kind of group this Vasile guy could hide himself in, hell, possibly be presiding over. He could be an alien himself, disguised as a human, and hiding himself within that organization. Another theory is that aliens are running that organization."

The room got quiet for a moment, then Henry continued, "I know all this information is weird to some of you, and I don't expect you to understand or believe all of what I'm saying. I study ufology, have always believed in UFOs and now, of course, have been Awakened."

Teresa and Angelicia both interrupted with, "What?"

Teresa leaned forward, "Awakened? I keep hearing that word. Awakened from what? And does this make Linda an alien plant, really? I've been working with an alien?" Sighing, Teresa folded her hands and sat back on the chair.

Henry continued, "You'll be hearing the word Awakened a lot, guys. As you learn, it will be explained in more detail. Now, my...other thought...well, this guy is perfect for what I'm about to tell you, you know, hide yourself in plain sight? In my book, he's a candidate for...The Antichrist." The room went crazy. Teresa's eyes bulged, Angelicia coughed on her wine, Dawn and Dr. Kaplan gazed over at each other and Skyann's mouth dropped wide open.

Henry ignored all the surprised facial expressions and continued, "It's a known fact with ufologists that some alien races are using the Illuminati as their..." Henry put his hands up and gestured a quote 'Earth-based camp,' if you will. While here, they thrive on negativity. It feeds them. And with the power of such a huge organization backing them, it's easy for them to spread negative information. Uhm..." Henry looked around at the group and noticed their questioning expressions. He added, "So...when the time comes, they'll expose themselves, and can trick you into thinking they have all the answers. Listen to them and all will be fine. That's their plan."

"Wait, it feeds them?" Angelicia asked.

"Yeah, sorry. Let me explain in real quick terms. We live in a physical world." Henry slightly lifted the skin on his arms. "Aliens either don't like or need this body. It's too dense for them. These aliens thrive more on a conscious level; their frequencies energize or "feeds" them. Another way to explain frequencies is dimensions. Levels of energy fields..."

"Okay. That's okay. Don't try to explain anymore," Angelicia said. Teresa shook her head in agreement. The sisters leaned back behind Skyann's head and exchanged a look between them indicating this information was way over their heads.

"Geez, sorry. Got carried away," Henry admitted. Teresa gave him a smile.

"Now, getting back to the T-HE-RE quandary. There's no identifiable format in this acronym, so my thought is it's got to relate to what the group is doing. Knowing what I know of the Illuminati, it could be a sub-branch or secretive alien-assisted group operating inside their assembly, perhaps the Anunnaki. Bad guys. Really bad guys! Well...that's debatable to some die-hard ufologists..." Henry noticed everyone in the room was staring at him, so he stopped talking.

Dawn's eyes scanned over each person slowly, watching their reactions. *Is any of this believable to them? To me?* Dawn asked, "Well, it helps to explain the mystery surrounding Vasile's part in this. Let's say he is a...an...Anunnaki. What does he want from me? I know Actok said I am important and that I'm not Awakened yet. But HOW important is what I want to know."

Dawn said, "Oh, which brings me to this. I thought I'd keep notes on what's happening and I brought them with me. It's just a list of...well, it includes you guys, except Teresa and Angelicia, I just met you two. But I had to get a grip on who was involved in what's going on with me. This list is just for us, as a guide. It's here if anyone wants to take a look after this meeting..." Dawn placed the notepad on a side table. It didn't go unnoticed that she was visibly shaking.

Dr. Kaplan said, "Great, Dawn and Henry, thanks. It helps to know what we are dealing with. So, let's get down to business, we have to decide what actions to take."

53

Linda was livid. She'd failed her mission. She understood Dawn wasn't coming back in for a session. How could she go back to Lacerta now? *Will Vasile even let me?*

Sitting at her desk and deep in thought, Linda twisted the cap off her water bottle. *How did this happen? Who tipped off who?* Before she could stop it, the cap fell and tumbled onto the floor. She watched as it rolled under the desk. She got off her chair and squatted down to find the cap. No luck. She placed her whole body on the floor and scrunched way under the desk and over to the cap when she noticed something; a torn piece of red tape, halfway stuck to the underneath of the desk. Nothing attached to it, just the tape...

What was this for? Looks like something was attached to this tape. Was there a recorder here? Could Dr. Kaplan be on to me? No, he's ignorant. Wait, was someone...Teresa? Could Teresa have planted a recorder under here? Could she be that smart? No. I wonder if she'll show up for work again. Maybe I'm jumping the gun here. I'm going to come into work tomorrow like nothing's happened and see who shows up. I'll take it from there.

54

No one was watching the TV, so the group was oblivious as to what was happening right outside the house. Dawn was summarizing what the group's next move would be. "First and foremost, keep checking your phones and house for bugs."

Skyann chimed in, "And I'm going to be more aware and not do anything alone for a while. I'm stopping classes for a few weeks. Also, Dawn's moving in. I'll keep busy with helping her."

Henry told Teresa and Angelicia to be super careful and not speak of what they have been witnessed to. They both agreed. Angelicia looked at Teresa, "I'll be watchful, and stay close to her."

The group heard a slight rumble outside, but no one got up to take a look. Henry's body was on high alert with an influx of vibrations only he could sense. He attributed that feeling to the excitement of the group...or meeting Teresa?

Dawn stated, "I'll keep a low profile. No walking up to strangers warning they have a medical issue, or publicly telecommunicate. I won't attend any rallies. I'll stay close to Skyann and the rest of the group."

It was at this point Dawn thought she'd bring up the pros and cons of involving her sister and mom. They might start asking questions. Concerned for their safety, the group agreed she should tell them nothing at this juncture.

Then, Dawn remembered what Khacee had said to her about a book. "Khacee said...Oh sorry, some of you don't know of him. I had a visitor named Khacee. Said he was from my future." The sisters looked wide eyed at Dawn who continued, "Yeah, right? Well, anyway, he said I have a book, or like a book. I've been keeping a close eye on what I've been packing, but no luck yet."

Dawn started to feel her body vibrate. This was beyond the shaking sensation she had felt since the beginning of the meeting.

Henry tried to act as if his body wasn't experiencing any movement also. "I'll stand guard on Dawn during work hours and be available at a moment's notice if she needs me. I was thinking of something else, too. Let's all exchange phone numbers before we leave." The group agreed. No sooner did Henry speak those words when his body started to shudder.

At the same moment, Dawn was turning her attention toward Dr. Kaplan and was just about to ask his plan of action when the floor started to shake. All around the room objects were sliding their way to the edge, then falling to the ground. Furniture was jostled, with the group feeling their seats jerking them up and down. The beverages were starting to bubble. Everyone looked questionably at each other. Realizing the noise was coming from outside the home, they all ran out onto the front porch to see what was happening.

It was a clear night, so the spaceship was plainly visible. The ship was shaped like a huge cigar, silver in body and surrounded by a vibrant array of colorful lights. The whirring noise it was emanating grew so loud it was like being up close to a helicopter. "What is that?" Teresa asked, while holding her hands to her ears.

Skyann cried out, "Whoa. Listen to that noise. What the hell..." Dawn yelled to Skyann to get her camera. Skyann ran into the house, followed by Dawn, who turned on the TV, flipping quickly through the channels. Every channel was showing live scenes from cell phone cameras. Dawn watched as one displayed a cluster of UFO ships breaking rank with a group, soaring hundreds of feet high in the sky and lowering, hovering over a house, then soaring high again, rejoining the group, and in an instant just disappeared.

Commentators were speaking words like, "Oh shit, what's happening? Where's the military when you need them? Perhaps now we'll believe? Believe now that aliens are...real." and, "Stay tuned folks, we have our team on the way. We're trying to obtain more video." One commentator had his microphone to his mouth, but just stared into the camera, speechless.

Dawn ran back out to announce what she saw on the news. That's when she instinctively realized the life she knew was behind her now.

Skyann grabbed her camera off the dining room table. She started rushing toward the door when she felt a desperate need to pee. She hesitated a split second, then decided to keep heading out to the porch. She was visibly shaking, and it took all her wits to hold the camera steady. The whirring sound seemed to be getting louder.

Henry instinctively ran to his car and grabbed his laptop and held it tight. He walked over to the edge of the porch, all the while looking up. He was beyond excited. His whole body was vibrating at a higher frequency level, and he was reveling in the sheer joy of it. He looked over at Angelicia and Teresa huddling near him and said softly, "Hey, don't be afraid. Seriously. Our friends are here!" The girls looked at him quizzically.

Dawn met up with Skyann, they looked at each other, then embraced. Teresa and Angelicia got closer to them and soon joined in on the hug; all the while Skyann was trying to focus on steadying the camera as she videotaped the scene above her.

Dr. Kaplan stepped off the porch, his head tilted all the way back. The craft was right above him. He was scared, but excited.

The group didn't take notice of all the neighbors coming out of their homes. Strange, but no one screamed, then no one moved. It was as if they were frozen where they stood.

All of a sudden, the whirring noise from the ship stopped and the whole area became deathly quiet. Everyone was looking up. Then, the ship beamed a bright light directly onto Skyann's porch. Still, the neighbors could not budge. All they were capable of doing was looking up in total horror.

The light was getting brighter. Teresa yelled for Dr. Kaplan, who ran up to the porch. Skyann tried to stop shaking long enough to make sure the video camera was still running, recording the event. The light continued to get brighter and soon no one could see anything but whiteness.

When the light beam turned off, all on the porch were gone. Skyann's camera floated in slow motion down to the ground.

A teenage boy was the first to regain his senses. A quick look around indicated the bright light was gone and the danger had passed. Yet, everyone around him was still looking upward, as if in a daze. It took a few minutes and a few shakes to rattle his neighbors into their reality once more.

That's when the chaos started. A few panicked and started screaming, some cried, some fainted, but the majority were staring at the porch in disbelief. Yet, not one of them was brave enough to venture over there.

Everyone scattered back to their homes, but not before the sound of police cars and ambulances were heard nearby.

Later, when questioned, the witnesses would swear a huge, cigar-shaped aircraft hovered right over Skyann Peters' property. They would all remember seeing six people on the porch, then light beamed down from the alien spaceship and engulfed them.

When questioned if anyone had their cell phone with them, all would reply, "No. I didn't even think about it."

The incident took less than ten minutes to occur. And, even though the chaos and disbelief happened, the aftermath would always be remembered as the Day of Truth.

55

When word reached the local police they responded, but not before someone leaked the news to the *Brooklyn Gazette*.

Dan Katz couldn't have been any happier. At last, a good story, a real story!

Katz knew his night shift would need help covering this story. He ordered his secretaries to schedule a teleconference with all their relevant employees. He didn't care if their families were in panic mode; he had a paper to run. They knew to drop everything and get on their phones or there wouldn't be a job for them come tomorrow. After an intense fifteen-minute conversation, the staff got moving. They had to be the first on the scene.

Katz also sprang into action. Just recently, he created a department at the *Gazette* he titled "The Source." He had at his disposal a young, gullible private investigator, Natalie Brown. Everything she did indicated she was itching for advancement. Katz called her right after the teleconference call, asking her to do "a possibly dangerous task." Natalie immediately stated, "Bring it on."

It was 8:30 p.m. when his staff arrived at the scene, and the police were already there. About ten minutes later, another major newspaper reporter was getting out of her van with two assistants and a truckload of equipment.

While Katz's crew was setting up cameras, the police were busy canvassing the neighborhood. One cop walked over to a *Gazette* anchorwoman, informing her they needed to secure the area fast. He said the word came in that only the *Gazette* crew had clearance to be close to the FBI, who were in transit. He said he would make sure the other newspaper crews would know they could only set up behind the *Gazette*'s working area.

That anchorwoman was Tina Woods, a reputed top-notch newshound at the paper. She was glad the *Gazette* had such preference and she took full advantage.

When the cameraman signaled it was a go, she said, "Good evening. This is Tina Woods from the *Brooklyn Gazette*. I...I hope you can hear what with the noise of the police sirens, the ambulances and of course all the people in the streets and on their porches behind me. And now, all this lighting from our equipment.

"What a night. We are here on Bragg Street in Brooklyn, New York, following up on an unbelievable story."

The camera turned when Tina pointed to Skyann Peter's house. "That six people have been abducted off that porch over there. Yes, I said abducted! I'm talking aliens...among us... tonight! Can it really be true? Are there really aliens from other planets, galaxies, abducting us right off our own porches? Are they responsible for the loss of so many of our family and friends? All that we've been hearing this past year about close encounters, the media playing it up, the new shows and movies, have they really been trying to...prepare us?"

"Let's walk right over here. The police have informed me that the man I'm about to talk with is a Mr. Martin Welsh, who lives only two doors away from where this apparent abduction happened!"

The cameraman turned his attention away from Tina and

onto a man sitting on his porch step with his body leaning on a railing. As Tina approached, she said, "Mr. Welsh? Excuse me, Mr. Welsh?"

The cameraman took a close-up of Mr. Welsh, a man who apparently was in shock. She bent over and said, "Mr. Welsh? This is Tina Woods. The paramedics are on their way, do you hear me?" No response from Mr. Welsh, he just stared down at the ground.

"Oh wow, I think he's in shock. Mr. Welsh, the ambulance is almost here. Hang in there."

As Tina straightened back up, she looked into the camera. "I'm sure there are many others waiting for help. Perhaps..."

Two people came running over to Tina when they noticed the microphone in her hand. They both started talking to her at once when one noticed Mr. Welsh and went to help him.

"Listen, you've got to believe us. It really happened," the one stranger yelled.

Tina motioned to her cameraman to turn his attention onto a very frightened young woman holding her baby. The woman instinctively put her free hand over her face to shield it from the camera's blinding light.

Tina and the cameraman got closer, as did the competing news reporter. Placing the handheld microphone near the witnesses' faces, Tina asked, "Go ahead, tell us what you witnessed; but first, what is your name, miss?"

It was hard for anyone to hear with the police yelling more brass were on their way, and the sirens of ambulances nearing, so Tina repeated, "I'm sorry, what is your name?"

The woman timidly lowered her head to speak into the microphone, but backed away quickly when she heard the flashing of cameras. She clutched her baby tightly and fell on her knees, staring right into the blinding, flashing lights. Tina reached down to try to help the woman stand back up but the woman didn't budge. She looked like she was paralyzed, frozen in time.

Tina's cameraman never stopped filming. When the paramedics arrived, they ran over to assist the woman and her baby. Knowing they were safe, Tina nodded to the cameraman, who understood she was ready to report again.

The camera was focused on Tina as she pointed to Skyann's house. "Our sources indicate there were six people on that porch." She turned and pointed toward the house again. "Over there, at around seven o'clock tonight. They say a huge ship was hovering above when a bright light just beamed them up." For effect, Tina just stared at the camera with her large blue eyes, then said, "Rest assured, our crew is here for the duration and we're going to get to the truth."

Tina indicated to the cameraman to turn his attention to the people coming out of their homes. "We are going to try to interview all these potential witnesses, and keep you up-to-date with any new developments."

Katz never mentioned to his crew Natalie Brown's involvement.

56

Katz arrived at the scene of the abduction at around quarter to ten. He watched as some of his employees were busy interviewing witnesses. One of his employees looked over at him and shrugged his shoulders in disbelief.

He spotted his friend, who had just walked out of the house next door to Skyann's. Detective Gary Aimes noticed Katz and waved him over.

Katz and Aimes didn't shake hands; no need, they've been friends for years. Katz whispered, "Listen, thanks for the tip. Our crew got here first."

Aimes asked, "Yeah, well, you didn't get that call from me, right?"

"Sure, Aimes. Can you tell me what the hell's happened since? What do you know?"

Aimes nudged Katz to follow him over to his car. "This is the real deal, Katz." Pointing to Skyann's house, Aimes continued, "It's been reported six people were standing on that porch right there while this spaceship...oh fuck, listen to me...spaceship just beamed them up!"

Katz wanted to tell Aimes that one of his reporters might be in that group, but he had no proof. He was really concerned, since his friend Brian Rivers had given him a heads-up that

Dawn Coleman mentioned she was moving in with her friend on that same street.

Katz had told Mr. Rivers that he was going there and he'd check it out. How was Katz to know Mr. Rivers had been keeping Dawn under surveillance, and noted her moving a few large items into Skyann's house over the weekend?

Katz asked Aimes, "So, do you know who owns the house? Who their friends are?"

Aimes said, "The house info we know. A woman named Skyann Peters owns it. Been in the family for years. As far as brass is concerned, I was told don't go into the house till they get here." Aimes looks closely at Katz, "Hey, know anything I should?"

"No. What? You, if anyone, know I'm a digger, always digging for the real scoop. Anything you can tell me?"

Aimes looked around then whispered, "Yeah, but off the record, okay? And I mean it, Katz, off the record. And don't ask me why I haven't done anything about this information, either. We both know, I'm too close to retirement to stick my neck out now."

"Mum's the word. What 'cha got?"

"I was walking by Lieutenant Mason's office just two days ago when I saw him talking with a guy I'd never seen before. They didn't notice me, but boy was I curious. So, I hung around outside Megan's desk, acting like I was waiting for her.

"This guy was dressed from top to bottom all in black. Didn't pay much attention to that detail...until fucking today. They were talking about the reports of UFO ships. This guy said, 'Well, expect more. What we want from you is to monitor these crafts. Our intel discovered they're interested in your particular sector, Brooklyn, for Christ's sake, but we don't have a clue as to why. And prepare a list of the businesses, stores and residents occupying the area they hover and report back to me.'

"It was words along those lines. Then Mason said, 'Yes, sir.

I'll do my best.'

"Then this guy said, 'Remember, Mason, this is real, and we've gotta get a hold on it.'

'Yes, sir. I understand,' was all Mason could say. Can you believe it? Mason saying fucking 'yes, sir' to somebody?"

Katz asked, "Do you have any idea who he was?"

"No, but why's this dude wearing all black? Do you think he's, you know, one of those men in black? You know, the secret government agency with all those employees only wearing black?"

Katz replied, "Perhaps they do exist as an agency. What do you know about any abductions? Besides this, have you been hearing about any...aliens?"

"Hey, I didn't say anybody was fucking abducted, but then again, I just got here!" Aimes gave Katz a questioning stare and said, "Come on, what do you know? Why did you personally come here tonight? Let's give."

Katz shook his shoulders and said, "What? Just that this is probably the biggest story ever! Just trying to get to the truth before anyone else, you know how this business goes."

Aimes looked around, and when he felt no one was watching, quietly said, "Ok, so I didn't just get here. I'd better tell ya. I did go inside the house, through the back. You know me! Anyway, I was in the living room when I realized I wasn't alone. Heard like glass breaking. I pulled out my gun and ran down the hall to where the sound was coming from. That's when I noticed someone jumping out a bedroom window. I would have sworn it was a female.

"It was so dark I couldn't see much. I cautiously put my head out the window, as there was broken glass everywhere. I couldn't see anybody. That's when I realized I'm a sitting duck if she's still close by, she could fucking blow my head off! Also, I knew I couldn't leave my post, brass was coming. I shouldn't have been in there, so how would I explain what I saw anyway? Didn't want to get caught inside, ya know?"

Katz was about to say thanks when Aimes reached down and retrieved something from his car. It was Skyann's camera. "I'm taking a big risk here, friend, but I believe I'm giving this to the right person. Almost tripped on it going out the front door. No one knows about this camera, no one. Okay?"

Katz puts his hand on his friend's shoulder, "Thanks, Aimes."

"Sure. Also, if I hear anything proof positive about an abduction, you'll be the first I call, okay, Katz?" Then with a long stare, he said, "We go way back, that amounts to something."

Katz took his hand off his friend's shoulder and said, "Give me a call when you get some free time. We'll go for a few drinks and some pool."

"Yeah, sure. If I can get some free time. Now with this shit happening, might be busy for weeks; hell, years. And then the missus..."

"I get it, Aimes. Take care. I'll just walk around a little, okay?"

"Go ahead, but don't get in the way of the FBI when they get here. Don't want any screwup on this situation."

Katz waved a hand as he walked away.

Katz was deep in thought. How could he tell Aimes that he just returned from the ER where his employee, Natalie Brown, received twelve stitches? Katz was impressed with this employee's tenacity; she broke the bedroom window, and in the process of climbing through, her arm got caught on a piece of sheared glass, resulting in a deep laceration. This didn't stop her heroic behavior, however.

Despite the arm's profusive bleeding, she managed to find a notepad on Skyann's small end table in the living room. She didn't have time to scour the area any longer; she knew she needed medical attention. She called Katz directly and he met her at the hospital, wherein she told him about the notepad and that it was in her pocketbook. He walked over to her pocketbook, retrieved the notepad, said "Thank you," and left.

When Natalie returned to work the very next day, the least she expected was a raise, so she certainly wasn't prepared for what she got: fired. Katz cited breaking and entering was not how he conducted business. He did say the medical bills would be covered, however.

The true reason, of course, was he knew from her mannerism that she didn't realize the importance of her find. He meant to keep it that way.

And what a find! A list of names and their association with Dawn, identified under two categories; Explainable and Unexplainable. After some research, Katz had a clearer understanding of the people on Dawn's list. But, more to his surprise, was the reference to so much alien association!

So now, Dawn meets this alien, Actok. Dr. Kaplan feels he's been abducted before. Ah, so Henry is really a plant at my paper, and a...Light Warrior? What the hell is that? Skyann doesn't seem to have been abducted. Looks like she's just a good friend of Dawn's.

Let's see, what's this reference to the T-HE-RE? Hmm, there's a good lead to pursue.

Now, about the man in black. Why was he following Dawn and Skyann? Sure, I've heard about these guys...in movies! That nut, Inky, who runs around town, writing gloom and doom on the walls and shouting in the streets, wonder what he's got to say about all this? Who the hell knows where he lives? He only shows himself when he wants to.

This Linda person is of interest. Where is she now? Do the red eyes have any significance? Better look up her profile... damn, so much to research.

Katz thought of the work involved in relation to who was abducted and why. If only he could inform his employees of this find, he'd save hundreds of manhours. He was smart enough to realize they'd be in mortal danger if he did. Even Detective Aimes would be in harm's way with this information. Who could he turn to for help?

Katz was happy about the fact that it was his newspaper that could claim the story as their own. Yet, he felt bad for Dawn. If he hadn't had this notepad, he would have sworn she was at the wrong place at the wrong time. Now, he knew she was abducted! *Wait, I'm thinking along the lines that there really are aliens! Fuck! What???*

Katz's thoughts went back to Dawn. He'd withhold her name for as long as he could. The excuse? The *Gazette* doesn't report fake news. So, the only title they would place on their front page would read, "*WHAT IF IT WERE TRUE?*"

57

∞

I'm going to take a break. I need one. It's April and I've been at this...well, it seems like forever!

Haven't been to the authors group for three meetings. Each time was a good excuse. I dread one thing that they do, but it's for a good reason, they always ask when my story will be ready. I DON'T KNOW!!

∞

58

At ten o'clock on Monday, the *Brooklyn Gazette* was buzzing with activity. The presses were hot, the employees exhausted. No rest for Katz either. With his fourth cup of coffee in tow, he walked into his office and closed the door.

He picked up the remote. The same story was being presented: The Brooklyn Abduction. Every single news channel around the world was airing his front-page title, "*What If It Were True?*" and a photo of the event that happened around 8:00 p.m. in Brooklyn, New York on Sunday, September 30, 2018. The picture actually appeared like it was taken around four o'clock in the afternoon, what with the bright lights beaming down onto Skyann's house.

Clearly noticeable was the size of the craft; it covered the entire area around Bragg Street. What was most intriguing and most disturbing was the ship's opened door; allowing a shadowy view of six people floating into the craft.

The gofer dropped the latest competitive newspapers on Katz's desk. Katz was so deep in thought that he didn't acknowledge he had even entered the room. He turned to find them sitting there. Browsing through the first top two, he thought, *Skeptics. Skeptics. Where are the skeptics? Is everyone on board? Not one paper is calling it the hoax of the* century or asking what's next. *Everyone seems to have resigned themselves to the fact that aliens do exist and they did abduct people on a porch.* Katz took a deep breath and thought *Well, by the time the government admits to it, we won't be in such a panic and people will start asking questions. We're so complacent. What the hell's happening to us?*

If truth be told, he didn't want to believe in any of it either. There had to be a rational explanation. Yet...

59

Carole sat down in her living room in her favorite lounge outfit to enjoy a quiet Sunday night supper. Kate, her partner, went to visit her parents two blocks away on East 33rd.

As was her ritual, Carole placed the tray of food on her lap and started switching channels with the remote. No matter what channel appeared, all were talking about the same thing: did an alien abduction really occur on someone's porch in Brooklyn, New York?

Another switch and Carole recognized it: *That's Skyann's porch!* The scene changed to the newsroom where another picture made Carole's fork fall hard onto her plate. She watched as a video depicted her sister Dawn and...*Is that Dr. Kaplan?* They both looked like they were floating up to a ship of some kind. She didn't recognize the other people who were also shown floating helplessly.

Carole's mind was so intent on flipping channels in an effort to gain more insight that she forgot about the food on the tray. So, when the recliner moved suddenly, followed by something hitting the back of her head, it took her completely by surprise. Carole screamed and jumped up, dropping hot food onto her legs and the floor. She turned around and watched as Bella, the cat, scurried off the recliner and ran into the foyer. Carole screamed, "Bella, look what you made me do!"

Carole was wearing a thin pair of lounge pants that didn't protect her legs from the onslaught of hot sauce and food pieces. She started jumping, "Ouch, ouch."

She shook the remaining loose pieces onto the floor then walked to the kitchen to grab a towel. A feeble attempt to wipe away the mess made matters worse. Surveying the mess, Carole decided she wasn't going to deal with it.

A thought was brewing. *Had mom seen this?* Carole headed over to the cell port near the stove where the phone was charging. Thinking of what she should tell her mother; *Mom is already upset, this news might...*Carole stared at the phone. She dialed her mother's number and was surprised she didn't answer. Again, and no answer.

Carole ran to her car, oblivious to the lemon-wine sauce pasted to her skin. While driving, she tried calling again. No answer. She became frightened when she noticed how many cars were on the road at that time of night. She called Kate and asked if she'd seen what was on the news. She said "No, I've been too busy." Carole filled her in on the news being reported on TV. They both agreed they had, of late, been oblivious to what was happening in the world.

Carole requested Kate meet at her mother's. Kate agreed but started crying, "Oh my gawd, what else can happen, Carole? The news, your motha, geez."

It took Carole fifteen minutes to get to her mothers. She ran up the porch stairs and over to the door. Locked. She punched in the code and ran through the door yelling, "Mom. Mom."

Lilly was rubbing her eyes as she walked from her bedroom. She looked down from the top of the stairs. She took one look at Carole and whispered, "What's wrong? Dawn. Its Dawn, isn't it?"

Carole ran up the stairs and hugged her mother. She

asked, "Why didn't you answer your phone? I've been trying and trying."

Lilly replied, "I took a late nap. Jenna, you know, my new neighbor, told me if I really needed some sleep, I should turn my phone off and lock the doors, then put my earplugs in. So, I did. Sorry, honey." Lilly looked pleadingly into her daughter's eyes and said, "Is it Dawn?"

Carole held her mother by the arm and led her down the steps and onto the living room sofa. She could hear Kate's car pulling up in the driveway. She said, "Mom. You've got to be strong now."

Kate was running into the living room. Lilly looked over at Kate who started crying again. "Please, what happened?" Kate could only stand there, wiping tears with her hands. She had never felt so helpless.

Carole began, "Mom, listen. Dawn has...Dawn has, uhm...gee, how do I say this to you?"

"Oh, why do people do that? Just say it, say it," Lilly yelled.

"Okay. Dawn's been...abducted, mom. It's all over the news. I don't think she's dead, but she's been abducted. Do you know what that means, mom?"

Without any hesitation, Lilly announced, "Oh, is that all? That's okay. When I fell into the full REM sleep, I had a vivid dream of her with 'them.' Carole, you of all people know how many times she's been..." She looked over at Kate then back to her daughter and whispered, "abducted!"

For a moment, no one spoke. "She's coming to get me, you know. The thought of leaving you, Carole...but you DO have Kate. So, don't worry. We'll all be together again."

Carole was speechless! She stared at her mother and then heard Kate laugh incredulously.

Just then the doorbell rang. Kate went to see who it was. Jenna was surprised Lilly didn't open the door. Kate could see that Jenna didn't remember their previous meeting. Jenna said, "Oh. Hello." She peeked past Kate as if looking for Lilly.

"Is Lilly okay? It's all over the news."

Kate invited her in. As they walked down the hall, Kate reminded Jenna she was Carole's friend. Carole was hugging her mother. Kate stated she was going to put on some coffee. Jenna walked toward Lilly, stating, "I tried to call you but you must have listened to my advice, right?"

Lilly laughed, "Yep. Sorry to have caused so much bother."

"Oh, don't worry, sweetie. No bother."

Carole said, "Sit down and get comfortable, Jenna, you're about to hear a story." Jenna chose the small couch near an open window. The breeze felt good on her face. With folded hands on her lap, she looked quizzically at Carole then Lilly. Carole continued, "We can't do anything at this point now, anyway. Going to the police would be futile. We're all gonna be playing the waiting game."

60

Actok ordered the abduction. No pods were necessary with this system of transport. It is very much like well-documented alien abductions. With the ship overhead, light beams were infused with vibrational frequencies to transfer the group onto the spacecraft. The warp speed at which this was accomplished allowed all of the bodies to teleport at once, but each would arrive a few minutes from each other. Their bodies would tremble from head to toe for about thirty seconds after arrival. First time abductees usually found themselves lying on the ground. This changed with experience.

The first to physically arrive on the ship was Dawn. She opened her eyes and found herself standing upright. Shuddering from the cold, her entire body was vibrating. Dawn tried to acclimate by moving to the left but was frightened as she noticed the same alien, Actok, standing there. Dawn lost her balance and started to fall, but Actok quickly spread out his arms creating a warm energy field. Immediately, Dawn felt in full control of her physical senses and regained her composure. Actok bowed, "Greetings, Dawn." Dawn bowed in response.

Henry arrived next. He stood upright and looked around. He was still as elated as when he first recognized the ship, so the cold didn't bother him. He knew now that this was his favorite mode of transport. It was quick and not so messy.

He saw Actok speaking with Dawn and walked toward them. Actok bowed, at which Henry smiled and bowed in return. When Actok noticed Henry give Dawn a hug, he knew he could attend to the others who were coming.

Dawn was still locked in Henry's embrace as she watched Actok turn and walk away. Staring at his back, she noticed his clothes slowly disappearing, then his hair! She stared in disbelief as his whole body appeared like a prism of swirling dynamic colors. He still possessed the shape of a human...well somewhat, but as he kept walking, the frame was turning the color azure, mixed with emerald swirls, while the head seemed more cone shaped. He was still breathtakingly beautiful.

Actok purposely exposed his true identity to Dawn as a preface, hoping to accelerate her Awakening. She was the only person privy to this visionary insight. Henry leaned in close and said, "It's okay, Dawn. You know it's Actok."

Skyann realized she was lying on a floor and immediately sat upright. The bright light was blinding. Confusion occupied the next few seconds. *Where am I? I can't see much. The noise, that whirring noise, it's stopped. Damn, I'm cold. Wait, is that Dawn? Who's that with her? What? Oh, they're waving for me to come over.* Skyann stood up but felt dizzy. *Now what? Should I sit back down or run over to them? What if I get sick? I'm so dizzy. Oh shit, I peed. Well, can't do anything about that now.*

Skyann slowly got up and when she felt somewhat stable, she started running. When she neared them, Henry released his hold on Dawn and allowed them to huddle close, hoping to warm up. Dawn took the opportunity to introduce the two.

Skyann was visibly nervous, started crying, then felt so nauseous she threw up. When she fell to the ground, Dawn knelt down and pulled her close. Henry kept repeating, "It's okay, Skyann." Dawn rocked Skyann back and forth, looking all around.

Dr. Kaplan woke and felt immediately disoriented. Part of his psyche knew he'd been in the same situation before: on a floor and cold. With much effort, he picked himself up to a seating position. He just stayed there, shivering, trying to acclimate.

It took time to adjust to the blinding light. With vision gradually focusing, he noticed Dawn comforting Skyann and saw Henry motioning him over. That calmed him down a little and gave him the will to try to stand up.

With all his might, Dr. Kaplan attempted to position himself upright, but his legs were wobbly. He tried again to compose himself: after all, he was a doctor and knew it to be a good idea. He took a deep breath and stared at the floor. When he felt a little more stable, he looked up and noticed all three were walking towards him. Henry said, "Hey, buddy, ha, it's okay. Take your time. Everything's all right."

David feigned a smiled but didn't speak. He was too busy thinking *Why does this feel so familiar? How could it? I've so much to learn...if this is all real.*

Actok understood Teresa and Angelicia would be in shock. It was not yet time to expose himself to the group, so he telepathically communed with Dawn, "Please go to the pods where Teresa and Angelicia are arriving. I will be right there."

Dawn turned her head, realizing a communication was happening. She mentally transferred her answer, "Yes, Actok." Instinctively, she knew where these pods were, but still asked herself: *How do I know?*

Dawn took Skyann's hand and Skyann grabbed Dr. Kaplan's. Henry noticed the exchange and smiled. They all walked to another side of the room where they heard a whishing sound; Teresa was teleporting. When her body was fully intact, everyone could hear the screaming. She was bent over, holding her hands around her midsection and shaking uncontrollably. Dawn let go of Skyann and started to get closer to Teresa when she heard Skyann whimpering then screaming. She stopped in her tracks, turned around to Skyann again but saw Dr. Kaplan wrapping her in a big hug.

Dawn reached Teresa, who grabbed her arm for support. Just then Teresa screeched an unnervingly high-pitched sound. No one could mistake it for anything but sheer terror. Dawn wrapped her arms around Teresa and said, "It's okay, sweetie. It's okay."

Teresa was trembling, nonstop. Then the second wave of shrieking forced Dawn to take Teresa by the shoulders and stare into her eyes. It took a few seconds for Teresa to focus. Soon, she stopped screaming and wrapped her arms around Dawn and cried.

Dr. Kaplan started to walk toward Teresa but turned back to Skyann. Skyann could see he was conflicted. He motioned for her to take his hand. She shook her head and said weakly, "No, you go. It's okay." When he walked away, Skyann seized the opportunity to silently withdraw from the crowd. She thought, *I'm so sick I want to throw up again, or die or something.* Her mind couldn't grasp what her body was experiencing: fierce trembling. She leaned up against a wall, hugging herself. Henry noticed her condition and went to her. He stared into her eyes. Without speaking, she heard Henry say, "Skyann, it's really okay. Dawn will not leave you, nor will I. It's okay."

Skyann thought: *Did he just talk to me? Or...am I going deaf? How did I hear him?*

Henry knew this was Skyann's first experience with telepathy, so he gently took her into his arms and verbally said, "So much is happening to you. Just realize you're with very good friends and try to just take it all in. Don't be frightened. Okay?" Skyann looked at Henry questioningly. His smile was comforting. When he felt Skyann had calmed down, he released her.

The thought *Now, if I just stay here and be quiet, I can get rid of this nausea* entered her mind. Soon, their attention was turned to the arrival of Angelicia, just a few feet away.

Like Teresa, Angelicia was screaming. Disoriented, she stood up too quickly, turned herself around and ran into the transporter wall. The light was so bright she kept her back to the wall and started feeling it as if to find an escape. Everyone watched helplessly as she started scratching the wall, then as she fell to the floor crying. Immediately, Angelicia went into a fetal position, shuddering and moaning.

All but Skyann rushed to her aid, but Henry reached her first. He picked her up and just held her. He whispered in her ear, "It's okay. It's okay. You're with friends, Angie." Angelicia put Henry at arm's length and looked at him. He took advantage of this move and stared into her eyes. He immediately tried telepathy, repeating his calming words, "It's okay. It's okay," but she didn't respond. He pulled her close to him, and this time she just let his arms surround her. They stayed like that for another minute or two while everyone else gathered around them speaking words of comfort.

The strange part to this whole scenario? No one realized they were naked! Their clothes were destroyed during the transportation process.

61

Actok slowly walked towards the group who were still near the transporter pods. He was holding what looked like a large amount of cloth. Skyann was still shaking but that nauseous feeling had subsided. She was standing with Teresa and Angelicia who both were holding one of Henry's arms.

Dawn and Dr. Kaplan were in a conversation next to Henry. Actok knew the group as a whole would soon acclimate to their surroundings. He felt placing that semi-hypnotic technique on them when they arrived was a good choice; who knew what the reaction would be if they all saw their bodies were naked.

When Actok came closer, Teresa stared at him, quietly moaning. Henry released her hand and placed his arm around her. Teresa thought, *Who is he? Where are we?* She huddled closer to Henry, who didn't seem to mind a bit.

Angelicia was in awe of Actok. She thought he was a beautiful being, but wondered if he were human, as his hair was so platinum and he had captivating eyes. She started to feel a little calmer.

Actok stood next to Dawn. She turned in mid-sentence with Dr. Kaplan. They both looked at Actok. He bowed to them. They bowed back. Everyone saw the exchange but no one understood its meaning.

Actok started speaking while he handed Dawn a robe. Addressing the group, "Please put on these robes, you'll get warmer in a few minutes." Dawn put her robe on, then took a few from Actok. She handed them to Dr. Kaplan, Skyann and Henry. Actok looked into Angelicia's eyes and handed her a robe. They exchanged a smile. Teresa hesitantly reached for hers when Actok smiled. While everyone put on their robes, no one spoke.

Henry went over and greeted Actok. They were able to hug. This gesture allowed Teresa to be less frightened. Skyann got closer to Dawn and Dr. Kaplan, who took advantage and placed his arm around Skyann's waist.

Actok noticed Skyann and verbally said, "Hello, Skyann. My name is Actok. I am aware you must have a million questions for which, unfortunately, I cannot give you the time to explain. So, I have..." A tall figure appeared out of nowhere and began rushing fast towards Skyann and she screamed. Skyann ran behind Dr. Kaplan. He shielded her with his whole body, which Dawn found very interesting.

Angelicia and Teresa screamed. Henry went towards them. Actok, a little surprised himself, said, "Please don't be alarmed, Skyann. Sorry for this abrupt arrival. I was about to introduce you to Melek. He is very friendly, yet not one of us. He is a Telosian, and thousands of his kind have volunteered to assist us.

"I have summoned Melek here to help me in... bringing you up to speed, as you say. He's also a great Light Warrior, therefore a protectorate, should the need arise. The Telosians have been our friends for eons and we have shared a very beneficial relationship. Please, come forward and meet your new friend."

You could pass Melek on the street and not notice he was an alien being. He looked identical to an actor in his younger days, Clint Eastwood. That's because Melek was a shapeshifter, and aligned his looks to that of the actor. He looked to be around forty-ish. His skin tone was a light brown texture, which complemented the rugged looking face. He was six-feet-four and very slender in all the right places. Throw in those green eyes...

To add to his persona, Melek wore blue jeans and a T-shirt. Yet, it was his smile that would make you drop your defenses; absolutely sexy!

That smile is what prompted Skyann to look over at Dawn. She was nodding her head yes. With a little trepidation, Skyann came out from behind Dr. Kaplan, and Melek immediately went toward her. He bowed. She looked over at the group, questioning as to what she should do next. Their smiles relaxed her, so she looked toward Melek, did a curtsy, then bowed.

Melek stood by her side and she could tell he wasn't about to leave. She glanced at him and thought *I've seen him before...no...felt him. Ah, was he the presence watching me? Yes, I feel it!*

At this point Actok addressed the group. "I realize you have all been through a trying time and that feeling of being drugged will soon pass. Let me say this now. I have transported all of you aboard my ship as it was obvious your group thought your lives could go on as they were. I'm sorry to inform you, but they could not. If we had not interfered, all of you would have been dead within a few days."

Teresa started screaming, "Juan, oh Juan." In an instant Actok was in front of Teresa and placed his finger on her forehead. Immediately she went into a trance-like state. Angelicia held her tight. Actok looked at Angelicia, "Be strong now. She will need you." Angelicia just nodded her head yes.

Dr. Kaplan took his eyes away from the sisters. He looked down at his hands and wondered *Gee, can I do that now? Can I just touch someone and calm them down?*

Actok turned back to the group. "I wish I could explain in

one sentence how...what you call time, functions in our world versus yours, but I cannot. Just know, it's quite different. We do not operate with time, per se. Just know time inside the ship will pass slowly, while time outside is speeding up." Teresa was staring down at the floor.

Actok walked over and addressed Dr. Kaplan. Bowing, "Hello Ra...David. It's so good to see you again."

Dr. Kaplan was frightened but for so many reasons he couldn't show it. He reached for Actok's hand. "Oh, no. Sorry. I cannot shake your hand. If I touched you for more than a second, I would physically hurt you." Dr. Kaplan withdrew his hand and again stared at both of his, studying them.

Actok turned back to the group. "Everyone, please try to relax. In a very short time, all will be explained. Like why some of you can touch me and some cannot. And I'm sure, more formidable questions are on your mind. I am going to take you to a more comfortable area of this ship. Please follow me."

The group slowly started following Actok, including Melek, who was walking right next to Skyann. She liked his stride—confidant.

While Teresa was walking, she slowly came out of her daze. With her face looking forward, she felt Henry's arm around her. She felt Angelicia holding her right hand and walking along her side. Walking helped her body warm. She took a deep breath.

During the walk, Dr. Kaplan was thinking how impressed he was with Actok and realized he was glad this experience was happening to him. He did wonder though *Why did Actok start to call me by a different name? Do I remind him of someone?*

The group soon walked into a room that very much represented a normal living room on Earth. They were not aware but the room was used to create holograms: three-dimensional images formed with light beams from a laser. These images created the illusion that one was in their natural environment. They could move around and touch and feel objects as if they were real.

Everyone went for the big couch, but only a few made it. Angelica let go of Teresa's hand and opted for a chair next to the couch. The others took the smaller couches across from the big one. Henry didn't take a seat, but stood near the couch, right next to Teresa.

Actok began, "I will attempt to enlighten you on this situation, but as most of you are coming from a different level of clarity, I cannot answer all your questions with one explanation, so please bear with me. Just remember this...you are all much more than you think you are!

"There are some new faces here, so let me introduce myself. I am Actok, a hybrid from the planet of Pleiades, a seven-star cluster..."—he looked at the group, hesitated, then continued—"never mind.

"Our species, along with thousands of others from their home planets, have come to the aid of yours. There is a true crisis developing, and much has happened that you are not aware of, so you must trust you were in grave danger.

"Our assistance offers you the opportunity of hope. We have been involved with planet Earth for eons. We mean to bring you enlightenment about who you really are and what your future holds."

Actok hesitated, looked at his bewildered group, took a deep breath and continued, "To put it bluntly, if left unprotected, Earth will either—soon—be at war with species whose only goal is to totally annihilate you and inhabit your planet for themselves; or worse, you'll become a cyborg being on your own world, under a dictator's rule. Or, you might be shipped off to a colonized world needing assistance. I'll say no more on this topic, as each of you will be individually briefed. Now let's just focus on what presently is happening to you."

Before anyone could question the bombshell Actok just landed on the group, he looked over at Teresa. "Teresa, Juan is safe." Teresa started to rock herself back and forth, mumbling while tears started forming in her eyes. She was still feeling a little incoherent but wanted to scream out, "Annihilation? Enlightenment? Please let me go to Juan. I want to go home." Instead, she looked down at the ground. Henry, as if on cue, sat on the edge of the couch and again put his arm around her.

Actok continued, "He is with your father and his mate. You have inadvertently been exposed to this reality by your association with Dr. Kaplan. But your courage in finding out the true nature of Linda Chalmers's agenda has deepened our commitment to protect you. For that act of bravery, we are very grateful." Through tears, Teresa looked up at Actok. He bowed.

"Angelicia, you too, through your love for Teresa, are here inadvertently. Soon I will introduce you both to an Eben, one very much like Skyann's Melek, that will assist you in understanding what's happening."

Actok realized he was telling half-truths, but knew this diverse group needed to acclimate before everything was exposed.

Actok looked over at Henry and pointed, "Henry here is a Light Warrior, as are Dawn and David."

Henry looked at Dawn and David and smiled. Nodding his head, David just smiled back. Dawn looked at them both and raised her eyebrows up and down, then smiled. She didn't have a clue as to her status in the spiritual realm of the universe. She was so muddled that she played the compliment as if it were a joke.

"Henry is an Awakened Light Warrior, while Dawn and David are not...yet. A Light Warrior, for those that do not know the term, is a trained spiritual being whose highest contribution is volunteering to guide Starseeds. On Earth, this includes every species of humans and human hybrids. The Light Warriors guide the Starseeds to higher frequencies of consciousness, in an effort to Awaken them, to bring them back into the light, back to their Prime Creator. This is a very generalized description but for now will suffice. Oh, before? Only Awakened spiritual beings whose frequency levels are matched can touch each other without experiencing a shock."

Actok turned toward Dawn. "The woman you know as Dawn," and he acknowledged her at this point by bowing, "is unquestionably the mightiest of all the Light Warriors in all the galaxies." Dawn got embarrassed as the group turned their attention toward her. She just looked at everyone and forced a fake smile.

Addressing the rest of the group, Actok added, "Without going into more detail now, just know you, too, are so much more than you realize."

Dr. Kaplan raised his hand. "Yes, David?" Actok said.

"Excuse me, but what is actually happening now on Earth? What is your role in helping us? I don't think I understand. Do you have any idea why I was abducted?"

"Let's hold off discussing this topic for a few hours. You need time to assess what you have just been told. I promise that question and many more will be answered soon. You all must be hungry and then there's the need to settle in..."

Teresa looked up, brushed Henry's arm away, and with all her might asked, "What?" Then she yelled, "I want to go home, now. Please."

Angelicia reached over and hugged her sister. Actok said, "Teresa, if I send you home now, you will be...murdered within two days. So would your family. Right now, they are safe. We have surrounded them with protection that even if they were to encounter any danger, no one could penetrate their space to hurt them." (Actok didn't mention he knew of the bunker but was glad Poppy had the foresight to install one.)

Teresa let go of Angelicia and buried her head in Henry's

chest. He was surprised but happy as she wept inside his embrace. Angelicia turned away from Teresa and wept silently for her, thinking how grateful she was for her decision to not have kids.

62

Gaff appeared out of nowhere, stood in the middle of the living room and bowed to the group. "Oh, my friend Gaff has just arrived," Actok announced.

His presence was alarming. Teresa opened her mouth, fell back on the couch, and fainted. Angelicia screamed and brought her legs up and under on the chair. Even Dawn gasped for air.

Dr. Kaplan got up from the couch and ran over to this creature in an effort to protect his friends. Henry jumped up and intervened. He grabbed the doctor from behind and at the waist yelling, "Hold on, buddy. It's okay."

Dr. Kaplan didn't hear his words and tried to release Henry's hold. All he cared about was hearing Skyann crying and seeing Dawn's frightened face. He was running on pure adrenaline. There was complete chaos.

Actok took control of the situation by waving his arms out among the crowd and all fell into another light stupor. Soon, Angelicia released her legs and sat upright. Skyann stared at the ground. Dr. Kaplan lost all his energy while Henry walked him back to his seat. Then Henry shook Teresa and with a little effort, she opened her eyes. "It's okay Teresa. You are in no danger here."

With a deep breath, Actok said, "Sorry, but my friend seems to think a dramatic entrance is funny." Looking disparagingly at Gaff, Actok stated, "He could have avoided all this!"

The lethargy was obvious, everyone had settled down. Gaff realized he shouldn't move, as this group apparently needed time to adjust to his features. He forgets, he's really monstrous-looking to humans!

The group turned their attention to this weird being, who at this point, smiled profusely. This seemed to help, or was it the sedated mood they'd been subjected to?

Anyone would have reacted to Gaff's physique. This was a small-framed, three-foot tall, mustard yellowed creature who possessed an elongated skull covered in a mop of black shaggy hair. His eyes, which seemed to be moving mechanically, were extremely slanted, like an Egyptian's. He had three fingers on each hand, which also seem to move mechanically.

Gaff stared at the group but didn't say a word, yet they received his message: "Hello everyone. I am honored to be among you today." Henry and Dawn gave each other a knowing look, as they realize what he was doing. Teresa, Angelicia, Dr. Kaplan, and Skyann just looked at Gaff in bewilderment as they realized he was talking to them but not speaking out loud!

Verbally Gaff explained, "You have just received your first group telepathic or interfaced message from me. I knew Henry and Dawn would understand, but I am glad to announce you all did wonderfully."

Gaff returned to communicating with the group telepathically, "Sorry for my dramatic entrance. I must remember you do not realize you are travelers at this point in your journey, and someone like me would scare you."

Before anyone could speak, Gaff continued with his telepathy, "Let me give you a little history as to what my purpose is for being involved with the inhabitants on your

Earth planet. I am a species called the Arcturians. We are one of the most advanced civilization in all the galaxies. I actually function on the eleventh and twelfth dimension of existence; a spiritual plane of pure consciousness.

"Don't let that last comment fool you. We can appear in form. I do not look like an Arcturian per se. Our original race bred with them thousands of years ago, your time. And, our species is capable of fluctuating our frequency levels."

Gaff looked at the group and realized they were still a little sedated and decided to liven them up. "An interesting fact about Arcturians, we can see from the back of our heads." He quickly turned his back to them in one fast motion, put both hands behind his head then...hesitated. Everyone was watching when Gaff grabbed his hair and separated it in half, exposing...his scalp. No one knew what to expect. They started looking at each other to watch their response. When no one laughed, Gaff quickly turned around to face the group. "That was my futile attempt at humor. Please forgive me. Yes, we developed the art of being aware of what is happening behind our view but it is through our senses, our frequency levels, as it were."

Skyann laughed, "Oh, I...see. I...see." She looked around and nodded her head up and down at the other members in her group. That's when they got it and started laughing. Actok was glad the sedated mood was helping.

When they quieted down, Gaff continued, "You might find this detail of interest. We have the ability to move objects. You call this function poltergeist activity." Gaff turned toward Actok, and with a wave of his hand, lifted him off the ground, where he hovered for few moments. The group reacted in oohs and aahs. There was a more relaxed atmosphere taking place.

"We have evolved from needing food for nourishment. Now we "feed" on positive forms of energy to empower us. Sleep, which is necessary only...to what you refer as once a week, is a sacred ritual we use for soul travel.

"An important difference between our species and yours is a quality lost to your kind that we are trying to reestablish— enlightenment.

"We..."

Actok realized Gaff's desire to teach was turning into a seminar, so he interrupted his friend's discourse. "Well, I hope you are not in the mood for me to explain all about our race, the Pleiadians. Let's save that for another time." Gaff got the point.

Actok continued, "You may, if the need presents itself, touch Gaff. You will not react like as if you tried to touch me. His voluntary mission is to assist you during the transition period and therefore he has modified himself to Earth's frequencies."

Actok noticed Angelicia's blank facial expression. He turned to the rest of the group and some were just staring at him. "I believe I've lost some of you in translation. Don't worry.

"Now that you have met Gaff, please follow him to your...temporary living quarters. I would ask David and Dawn to please stay behind."

All but Dr. Kaplan and Dawn followed Gaff out of the room. Henry walked with Teresa and Angelicia. Skyann and Melek walked a few feet behind the group. She looked over at Melek and he turned and smiled. She smiled back.

63

∞

Driving to my authors group last week I was full of anticipation.

There were about ten people in the library conference room when I arrived. A few had a bulky amount of paper in front of them. I assumed that it was an indication they critiqued someone's work. Was mine amongst them? It was surreal, having to wait to know if your work was critiqued and if so, did they like it?

Finally, someone said, "Is it my turn? I want to talk about Eileen's story." Wow, was I nervous! When she was told yes, she looked at me and said, "I loved it!" Oh, the elation. OMG! Someone, someone who writes, enjoyed my story!! All that work, all that time, and it was accepted!

Then, the fact that the book was being written in a few different writing modes was discussed. It was stated, "I didn't think you could pull it off, but you did! If I didn't want to read your dialog, I just skipped over it and went back to it."

After a few minutes wallowing in nirvana, I came back down to earth when yet another author asked, "Where is the violence?" He gave good input as to when there could have been more drama.

Then a woman asked if I believed in aliens. I said, "Yes, I do." That's when she said, "Well, I don't." There was discussion on this issue, and it was understood that not all will enjoy a sci-fi story, (just as I'm not a fan of romance novels) and that writers should keep an open mind when reading other's work.

I came away with the thought that anyone reading this book will draw conclusions from their belief system. I'm hoping to challenge yours, folks: why DO you believe the way you do? This is a work of fiction, but certainly indicates my belief in the reality of other species.

I am so happy I joined this wonderful group of writers. I need the pros to push me onwards and the cons to produce a better product. I went away with more insight, more confidence. I received two edited sets of my work. I couldn't wait to go home, review them and make corrections.

I must add, one woman said to me, "Eileen, you can consider yourself a writer!" I walked on air to my car.

My life was never filled with compliments. I'm not that smart, not that educated, not that pretty. So, to receive this feedback...well, it was...there is no word.

64

Linda's cell phone indicated Vasile was calling, and it was then she found out about the porch abduction. Her heart felt heavy with the knowledge that failing Vasile would have its consequences. Her body felt mortal fear for the first time as a human being.

There had been little sleep since finding she'd been duped. Vasile wanted answers. She must explain how such a simple assignment got so out of hand.

Linda knew now that her only hope was to provide him the proof on the tape recordings. Her plan was to sneak in, take the dossier, tapes, and any proof that Dawn Coleman was ever a client at Dr. Kaplan's office. Then, get the hell out of there—for good.

She arrived at Dr. Kaplan's office at 5:30 a.m. She covered her tracks, no one saw her enter the building.

Upon entering her own office, she turned on the lights and immediately noticed the room had been ransacked. Drawers were opened and files were strewn on the floor and desk. Her stomach started churning.

She went to the general files listed under "C" and realized Dawn Coleman's files were gone, including the dossier.

She leaned down to unlock her secret compartment inside

her desk. She put the key in but the door was already opened. *No. No. This can't be!* All of Dawn Coleman's recorded sessions were gone. She thought *Don't panic. I handed him all...oh no, not the last one...there is no record of what happened during Skyann's session. I have no proof they were on to us...* Linda was really frightened, as she had hesitated in sending the last recording. She had wanted to find out who was on to her. *Wait, maybe it's a good thing. I can just say...what? That the tape was damaged? That I didn't have time? No, I can say they never met for a session. Yes, that will be my answer.*

Linda stopped moving and stared at the ceiling. *Who could have done this? It can't be that dumbass Dr. Kaplan. Teresa! It's got to be Teresa. Yes. She knew I was soon going to let her go, so she planted that recorder under my desk. Didn't think she had it in her. I'll get her for this. I have to prove to Vasile I can control a situation.*

Linda scanned the office. She thought of all the clients and her mind went to poor Mr. Brown. After two years with no leeway, Dr. Kaplan could not convince him he wasn't an alien. But Linda instinctively knew he wasn't. (In actuality, the Pleiadians planted a hybrid human to get Dr. Kaplan's mind acclimated to the possibility of alien phenomena so when he met Dawn....) It was then that Linda realized the reality of her predicament.

She gathered her belongings and left. No one saw her. All she could think of was killing Teresa and getting back into Vasile's good graces.

65

Dawn stepped into her new living quarters and watched as the doors automatically closed behind her. She was in a square room about twelve feet by twelve feet but it was absent of any furniture, décor, not even a window! *What am I supposed to do in here?* she pondered. *Was I sent to the wrong room?*

She turned around to face the doors and was looking for a way to open them when a visual communication box on the wall started to write words. "This is a hologram room. Please play with all the selections on this box until you find the décor that fits you. It may be changed at any time. Enjoy your stay."

Dawn touched the screen and was directed to numerous decorating themes. She was particularly drawn to a nautical wall scene; large waves pulsating in a sideways pattern, while through the waves appeared three dolphins. When Dawn pressed "accept." the dolphins started swimming playfully under the waves all around the walls of the room.

Next, she selected a queen-sized bed with a headboard made of seashells. The bedcovers and curtains were a perfect match. Dawn, a Virgo in this reincarnation, had to, by her very nature, coordinate everything.

Then a nightstand, shaped like a dolphin and with a glass

top, grabbed her attention. She didn't see a dresser choice, then realized why would she? They only wear robes here.

When Dawn finished selecting all her choices, the once empty room was affixed with her personal design and equipped with all the essentials.

She walked over to the bed, pressed down on it and thought *it's a bed*. She tried the chair in the corner, *it's a chair*. Feeling less apprehensive, she lay down on the bed. She placed both arms under her head and stared at the ceiling. She allowed herself to relax. At that time, in that moment, she felt protected. Closing her eyes, she fell sound asleep.

I'm having a real tough time visualizing Dawn as a docile character; timid and in the dark. Yet, I don't picture her as a queen or a superhero either. When I write of Dawn, she will be an enlightened, spiritual leader, able to reach the highest levels of consciousness!

Her reputation was widely known throughout the galaxies. Her highly respected tactical victories have been implemented on thousands of planets. So, as a new author, keeping her humble...this is going to be hard!

∞

66

Rosalee and Kristian were standing at the podium engaging their crowd when someone yelled, "Get down. Get down." Whizzing bullets and gun shots were heard throughout the arena. Kristian noticed two men falling to the ground. Then he saw a woman fall as a knife went deep in her chest. Kristian grabbed Rosalee's hand and they both landed on the floor. He motioned for her to crawl in front of him to the back of the stage. As they were crawling, more shots rang out. Everyone was running and screaming. A woman was pushing through the crowd with violent force, screaming over and over, "No Light Warriors, No Light Warriors! Die Starseeds! Die now!"

It was only when Rosalee was safe behind the curtains and surrounded by crew members that she noticed Kristian wasn't behind her. He had tricked her! *I should have known!* Rosalee peered from behind the curtain and saw Kristian running to the stage steps and into the crowd. She started screaming, "No. No. Come back. Kristian...," but he didn't hear her.

The shooter had enough artillery wrapped around her to kill hundreds in attendance. The waist belt was filled with guns and ammo. Her shoulder hosted an AR15, while both hands were shooting 45 mm guns. Both legs were strapped with knives. She meant to kill as many as possible before killing herself. This was definitely a suicide mission.

While rushing to the scene, Kristian realized the security guards were engaging in a diversion. The shooter's attention was focused on the last person she shot, a young man, perhaps 18 or 19. She aimed right for his forehead. It was a direct hit.

While her mind was preparing for yet another victim, she didn't see the guard sneak up behind her with a rope. With lightning speed, he secured it around her neck and began a strangling technique. The rope was twisted at an angle; just enough to immediately knock the air out of the lungs but not cause death. She was startled, yet with all her might tried to break free. She dropped the gun as she needed both hands to pull at the rope cutting off her air. The other guards grabbed her arms. They threw her down and removed the weapons on her body one by one. All the while she was frantically sneering, screaming the same words.

Still running, Kristian looked around to see if the shooter had an accomplice nearby. He didn't notice anyone trying to assist her, but it was hard to tell, as people were still scrambling over seats and over themselves. Some guards were running to assist the victims. It was pure chaos.

When Kristian arrived at the scene, the guards were picking her up off the ground. She noticed Kristian and looked straight into his eyes. She communicated a telepathic message: "You think you have time, fool. Too late. Too late. I have destroyed your chance to bring these Starseeds to fruition. Leave this planet. You cannot help Earthlings. He's here."

Kristian and the shooter kept their stare as the guards secured the handcuffs. He communicated, "What could I say that would make a difference?" She communicated her answer—she shrieked a laugh that made a shiver go through his body. "You stupid fool! It's too late! You have no defense. He's already here." Kristian knew she was pure evil. A true tell? Her eyes were fire red.

67

Skyann chose a modern motif for the room; black and white functional, practical furniture with a splash of red as the accessory color. She too, felt the need to experiment with her surroundings prior to accepting it for real. She was surprised the room had no windows, no view. She'd love to know how far away they were from Earth.

Skyann found comfort knowing her apartment was adjacent to Melek's. She thought *Melek will sleep...does he sleep? He'll be right in the next room.*

Walking toward his room, Melek felt her dilemma. He informed her, "Sleep well, you are perfectly safe here." With those encouraging words, she was finding Melek to be very accommodating. Of course, she didn't realize she wasn't really alone. She was being monitored, as were the others. Not with cameras but with sensing devices, which offered more privacy!

After preparing for bed, she thought of her new friend. *Melek doesn't say much but can speak my language, fluently. He's not acting like a human, but not like a robot either. Somewhere in between. I don't understand much yet but I feel safe here and answers will come; yes, answers will come.*

With that thought, she fell into a deep restful sleep.

Melek's expertise was Guardianship and Protection. He mastered weaponry and physical techniques at age six and became an Avatar at twelve. He'd never found a mate, never produced any offspring. He has incarnated one hundred and thirty-four times, each time swearing loyalty to the Prime Creator.

∞

The similarities between what we, as humans, have been told about our creation story and what numerous species from other galaxies are actually communicating...is extra-ordinarily similar!

Millions of alien species believe in a Prime Creator. What I have come to learn is quite revealing, and if I didn't do this research would never have realized.

The Bible speaks of the Rapture (not that word, though) and of a Tribulation. My research shows that these entities are speaking of a time wherein we will experience a scenario called the Ascension. It's not our physical bodies getting abducted off Earth but that our bodies will change, our frequency levels will enhance, we will not be so physical anymore. We will still be on Earth and look slightly human— reminds me of *The Grays*! It's a great read, look it up!

What IF it were true? That Almighty God created us with so much of himself implanted within us, a wonderful experiment...perhaps in a holographic scenario, placed us on Earth with free will, and if we didn't do anything to seek him, and didn't help our fellow man, then we would fail the experiment, fail to wake up to knowing Him?

What IF the answer to the question of why Almighty God allows negative proponents to happen on this planet is because He created the free will policy? Could that in itself be the reason for so much chaos?

Can you live with that?

∞

68

∞

I think I've learned something new writers must experience. I've offered a few people to read my book as I progress. I would have to say two percent said they wouldn't mind. The rest? They'll wait till it's done, or they don't have the time, and all too often, they don't like to read. So, I stopped the offer. It made for a very uncomfortable conversation.

∞

Every day it seemed more and more people were... missing? At first, it wasn't a huge media-grabbing event, but lately, with more people unaccounted, it was becoming an issue that had to be addressed. Vasile took total advantage of everyone's anxiety and was finding it a platform to control the masses.

Everyone was accepting Vasile as their new leader, especially after announcing all the world tune in to his Universal Clarification Speech, promising an explanation of what was happening. He also stated that he has planned the way for humanity's future.

It wouldn't matter, really, where Vasile chose to give his speech. With the technology available, he could be anywhere: at the China Wall, on the White House lawn, but his choice was very symbolic. He was being presented to the world, literally the whole world, for the first time.

The house was painted a light blue, and located on Theresienstrasse Street, in Bavaria, the home of the Weishaupts, the home of the founder of the Illuminati.

The Weishaupts' house and grounds were filled with at least a thousand guests; three presidents, two dictators, bodyguards, two hundred waiters, and at least twelve hundred observers. Yet, the food and alcohol kept coming.

The podium was positioned on a platform to give an advantage to the crowds far from the front line. To the right of the podium was built a metal circular frame, surrounded by a hanging curtain. This naturally gave way with much ado; who would occupy that seat?

Sitting on the left side of podium was the highest-ranking official in the Illuminati, Dieter Franc. Mr. Franc could trace his family's name back to the beginning of this organization, all the way back to Bavaria in 1776. His family assisted the Weishaupts in gaining affluent members to this movement. And it was a good movement, based on sound principals, it possessed an enormous following, but like so many organizations, subtle underlying factors...

Mr. Franc is seventy-three now and knows his time as head of the Illuminati is over. He knows Vasile has had control in all but the formal induction, which will happen today.

Mr. Franc is a widow with four children. He is a good man, a serious man. Even though he loves his children, everyone recognized his true love was the Illuminati. He is not in good health—prostate cancer. This short, stubby bald man was considered a book worm by most. Some thought he was a die-hard conservatist; wanting the organization to get back to its original roots—"Oppose superstition, suppress religious influence over a person in public office, and any form of abuse of state power." His hope is perhaps the organization can return to the true values it upheld for hundreds of years.

The anticipation was rising. The mood was set.

It's at this point I wish I knew more of the Illuminati; I'm limited in watching the Tom Hanks movie, *Angels and Demons*, and what I can find online. The Illuminati is considered a dead society, yet conspiracy theories abound! I am finding that they might be associated with another secretive society, the Freemasons.

The Common Purpose is another elite group rumored to be the force behind the façade of leaders we see daily (and filthy rich controlling them!) A lot more research is needed here.

But there is hope, too. A spiritual group, The Light System (TLS), apparently works for the good of planet Earth and its people. They accomplish this by elevating our spirituality in order to welcome in humanity's "age of love."

I don't want to copy and paste information easily found on the internet, so I suggest you research these societies on your own.

∞

69

There was no introduction. Vasile walked out from the atrium and up to the podium. With his striking looks and mild manner, he just stood for a whole minute in total silence, allowing the world to take in his presence. His façade of being Brian Rivers was washed away, but the ones who would really take notice were not watching his speech.

Vasile waved at the crowd then looked at the hundreds of cameras allowing millions to witness this event from every corner of the world. He took hold of the microphone. This dramatic gesture demanded silence all around the globe. He certainly received attention when he looked out at the crowd and softly announced, "I'm Vasile, and I am here for you. In the next few minutes, I will explain what has been taking place on planet Earth. Listen and learn." Before the crowd could shout questions at him, he said, "Yes, aliens exist."

For the first time on Earth, the world was silent. One would think the crowd would go into a frenzy, but not a word was spoken. Everyone was trying to internalize the words Vasile had just announced. He continued, "You have been exposed to the possibility through your radios, then movies. Millions of you swore you witnessed sightings and abductions. You did! Yet for thousands of your Earth years, few believed or wanted to believe it was possible. It was possible, and now, with everyone owning a camera, it became futile to hide you from the truth.

"You know the old adage—the truth will set you free? Today freedom prevails. Today, the camouflage is being lifted.

"I want to introduce you to my closest advisor and bodyguard. His name is Jaqui. Now, he might at first look frightening, as he is not of your world. Yes, you heard me right."

You could hear if a pin dropped in the audience; everyone was deathly still.

Vasile continued, "Jaqui is a Yahg from the Andromeda galaxy. He is my friend and protectorate."

The curtain was slowly drawn back. Where that seat was at first empty now sat a frightening beast. No one could mistake Jaqui as a human. No, his species looked alien, like the kind that scared the hell out of you!

Where once the crowd was deathly still, now every news reporter pushed and shoved at each other to vie for position near the patio to get a closer look at Jaqui. The cameramen were moving in, slowly pushing their way toward the front of the podium. People started screaming. Others fainted and more scattered from the area.

Wherever one was in the world, the sight of Jaqui stopped them in their tracks. Scenes of pandemonium occurred all over the world.

The most obvious feature was Jaqui's skin; a dark gray-blue color with large growths of hairy pustules protruding all over his body. He had eight eyes scattered throughout his face and neck, and all moving at the same time. His mouth was slightly off to the left and stayed permanently open, with sharp teeth protruding from every side. His arms hung down to the middle of his stubby legs. The hands were thick with sharp, long nails.

Jaqui wore no clothing, his belly bulged over in rolls of fat making it impossible to know if he was male or female. An intriguing feature, and one difficult to ignore were his feet: disproportionate in size, and flat, with only three toes on each foot.

∞

Oh wait, you might ask how can Jaqui protect anyone? He's morbidly obese and doesn't appear like he's capable of moving fast. So, what do you think his hidden ability could be?

∞

Vasile finally raised his hands out to the crowd in an effort to quiet them. Newspaper reporters started screaming over each other to question him. Vasile waved his hands up and down and soon the audience was in attention.

"I am very aware that today marks the first time some of you have even heard of me. I too am an alien. And so are you! No one is truly FROM Earth. We are all just visitors here. Today I tell you this, that fact is going to change."

Globally, people started running out of bars and away from other social gatherings. "See? I told you!" was the cry heard on the lips of millions. Parents closing their children's eyes so as not to see this monster. In areas where large projection screens were available, all were seeing this creature firsthand. Some shrieked in horror. More fainted right where they were standing.

All over planet Earth, cameras and cell phones were flashing pictures of this alien being. In huge auditoriums, amphitheaters, restaurants, even inside office conference rooms. Everyone had access from one device or another to hear Vasile's message, and everyone was listening; that is, those that hadn't fainted—or immediately committed suicide.

"I come from a planet called Nibiru. We are the Anunnaki. We have been monitoring Earth's plight for eons and have come to assist in your time of need. We love your planet. It is the most beautiful of all we have ever visited. Millions of our species will be arriving soon. But have no fear. We are here to help. To guide.

"Your world is experiencing horrific changes, I know. Please realize I understand your confusion, your anger. I too am angry. I also lost loved ones.

"No one likes change, but you must prepare for it. The world you knew, the life you held is...gone." Then, in the true fashion of a dictator, he raised his hands in the air and announced, "I am your savior!"

The inhabitants of Earth stood still once again when they heard this grave statement. "I know, I know," Vasile said with a voice soft as silk. "It's happened so quickly and you have had no time to acclimate. So, I say this, please keep calm. There's nothing that can be done for your lost loved ones. I tried, believe me. We must look forward to the future now, with me at the helm. Obey me and you will be saved."

Vasile left the podium and sat down in a chair on stage. Jaqui continued to sit in his seat. No clapping, no questions, it was as if everyone in the world didn't know what to do next. The silence was deafening. Not even the reporters could speak.

Katz was watching, also speechless, as he recognized his newfound friend for the first time! Unfortunately, he also recognized that his association with Vasile had just begun.

After about twenty seconds, Mr. Franc took center stage. He started to perform his third Induction Ceremony. People in shock everywhere just watched in silence. Without a hitch it was over. Those in the audience that could, applauded their new leader.

Mr. Franc walked in front of Jaqui, hesitated, then kept walking off the stage. This was not his problem. Yet he knew, deep in his heart, the Illuminati organization he loved, and had fought so hard to preserve had been destroyed from within. As he stepped off the stage, Mr. Franc felt an inner peace, as thoughts drifted to the scene played over and over in his mind; to die surrounded by family and friends.

Almost overnight, Vasile had become the most powerful man on planet Earth, and no one would question his right to this new position.

To the mainstream world this man is the awaited savior of humanity. To the spiritually Awakened? Humanity's doom.

There are three ways I can go with this story; all are swimming around in my brain. Guess it's better to have all these different scenarios rather than writer's block.

70

The day after the porch abduction, Little Juan was pulling on his ears while sitting on Poppy's lap. He kept hearing this ringing noise, but how could he tell anyone? He was only three. Thoughts of his mother were foremost. Poppy noticed Juan's tugging and took a look inside his left ear. No swelling or redness was noted. He felt around the throat and neck area, nothing unusual. He asked Juan, "Are you okay, little buddy?"

Juan replied by saying, "Mama," then laid his head on Poppy's chest and whined.

Poppy and his girlfriend Selma didn't get much sleep. He was worried sick about his daughters who hadn't called. Selma's family were calling, begging that she come to them in Philadelphia right away. They told her that the world was going crazy and she should be there with them.

The decision was made. Both realized this was a very serious matter, and public transportation could be shut down at any moment. After breakfast, they walked to the front door. Poppy picked Juan up so Selma could kiss him. Poppy and Selma both shed a tear, hugged, and promised this was only temporary.

Poppy turned, put Juan down, and went over to the front window. He watched as Selma drove away. His eyes glanced over just in time to see his next-door neighbors hurriedly throwing suitcases in their cars. When he looked across the street, most of the neighbors' cars were gone. That's when he started to panic.

Poppy turned the TV volume up. Vasile was giving his speech. After the speech, the screen showed highways filled with traffic jams as people rushed to get to their loved ones. Scenes flashed of banks and other financial institutions trying to close, but the mobs of angry citizens were demanding they remain open and give them their money.

Then, a flashing news alert—a video of the porch abduction will be shown at 3:00.

Poppy could only think of his daughters. *Both my daughters are gone without a word. Could they have been on that porch? How can I find out the names of the ones that were taken?*

He started to think about filing two Missing Persons Reports but realized it hasn't been twenty-four hours yet, the time needed before he could file. He also knew it would probably be a fiasco there, and that he was probably better off sitting it out at home. Yes, he had to be there if they came back.

For the rest of the morning Poppy kept the news on. He heard Vasile's speech three times before twelve o'clock, but his mind was thinking only of the porch abduction video. *What will the video show? People going up in a ship? Perhaps Angelicia and Teresa?*

Poppy placed Juan in his seat and tried to feed him some lunch. He made a bowl of soup, but Juan would have none of it. He peeled a banana and handed it to him, which Juan grabbed. After Juan finished the banana, Poppy changed the child's Pull-Up. Then he put Juan in his little bed, hoping against hope that he would lie down. All was well; Juan was closing his eyes.

Poppy knew he would probably only have an hour or less to do the task at hand. He walked into his bedroom and over to his closet. Using morse code, he tapped on the furthest wall. Immediately, the door slid sideways and he walked inside his bunker. He turned on the light and immediately started taking inventory. All the necessary items were there: food and water for at least a year, all necessary survival equipment, ammunition and batteries, an air ventilator, hand-held games, lots of reading materials and a generator. A first aid kit and an oxygen tank were sitting on a shelf.

The bathroom area was stocked. The only things he needed were Pull Ups and some changes of clothing, which were in plenty right upstairs. Poppy was so grateful now that he had spent the money creating this bunker. No one knew of its existence. He thought of what it would be like if the neighbors ever found out.

Almost an hour had passed when he heard Juan crying on the monitor. He took a last look around and exited the bunker.

Poppy entered Juan's room and found him standing up and banging on his ears again, yelling for his mother. Poppy picked him up and brought him to the rocking chair in the living room. He looked pleadingly at his Poppy while he repeated, "Mama, Mama." He finally rocked Juan to sleep in his arms.

Poppy placed Juan in his bed and he dozed off on the couch. It wasn't until he heard Juan screaming that he woke up. He ran in to Juan, who again was banging on his ears, yelling, "Mama, Mama." Poppy couldn't know that his daughter Teresa was aboard an alien ship, sitting in a hologram room, communicating with her son—telepathically!

71

The group have chosen their personal holographic living quarters. Actok hoped this would help them adapt to their new situation with less stress.

Nocren and Saghi, Actok's best friends, had just arrived on the ship. Actok wished only to spend time with them but knew that wouldn't be possible. Their mission was to aid in the situation the unexpected six occupants had caused.

Actok couldn't quite put his finger on it, but sensed something was wrong with Saghi, and realized Nocren seemed unconcerned about her condition.

Observation of the group noted all were resting quietly, with the exception of Teresa; the sensing device noted her hands on the sides of her head deep in thought. Actok knew she was practicing telepathy.

His mind drifted to Khacee. *Imagine seeing Dawn and not being able to tell her your true identity. Poor Khacee secluded himself in his apartment, fearing seeing her again till after her Awakening.*

Actok's main concern was Dawn. He had hoped being on the ship would have accelerated her mind to remember her true identity. That was not happening.

I marvel at these emissaries volunteering to go through the process of Awakening every time they take on a new mission. The gift, the thrill of being human on planet Earth, even if just for a little while is the most surreal expression of sense. Functioning on such a low frequency level to experience immense challenges, seems...well, I just enjoyed the process more in my youth. Still, converting from one aspect of my being to another is not only challenging but very elating.

I'm glad my essence is more crystalline, more spiritual, and that I can serve Him on a higher level of enlightenment. As Gaff would say, "You're so cerebral."

Living in eternal spirit close to my Prime Creator is my reward, my happiness.

I'm growing in my ability to write. I feel it. My age and inexperience with writing doesn't faze me as much. Just plugging away gives me confidence. Yet, having no one at this point to really sit with me and dissect the body of this work hinders me somewhat; am I on the right track? Does my story have a flow? Would my readers relate to the characters?

I can't and don't expect anyone from my authors club or any family member or friend to devote serious time to read/edit my work. It's my work. So, I'll continue to write and re-write and re-edit until the story "feels right."

I do have one friend...

Perhaps other writers feel this way too: it's kinda lonely.

72

Angelicia was in Teresa's room watching her practicing telepathy. She said, "I'd like to learn that, it can't be hard. We were doing it with Gaff, right?"

"No, not really, Angie. He was in control. You weren't communicating back. I want that control. Here, sit here. Let me try something on you."

"Whoa, wait sista, I love ya and all, but I'm not going to be a guinea pig here. What if you screwed with my brain?"

Teresa laughed. "That's funny. But come on, trust me." Angelicia positioned herself on the couch and Teresa sat on the small lounger facing her. She pressed her hands to her head and thought really hard.

Angelicia wasn't at all comfortable, thinking *Am I supposed to react somehow?* Teresa gave her sister a questioning look. Angelicia just shrugged her shoulders. She tried again. Nothing.

"Angie, think, come on be serious."

"I am serious, serious as shit. I'm feeling nothing."

After a few attempts they heard a light knock on the door. The sisters looked at each other. Angelicia questioned, "Who is it?"

A soft voice answered, "Henry."

"Oh, come on in," said Teresa a little too quickly, a response that didn't go unnoticed.

Henry stepped into the apartment and without any warning started to telecommunicate with both of them. "Hello, girls."

"Whoa, I can hear you, so why can't I hear Teresa?" Angelicia verbally asked.

Teresa verbally exclaimed, "I can hear you plainly, Henry."

Henry said, "Now, think without talking."

Teresa and Angelicia stared at each other, then tried to connect to each other's thoughts. Angelicia heard Teresa's commune, "We can do this." Angelicia tried to reply but couldn't.

Henry walked over to Angelicia and placed both hands on the top of her spiky hairdo, squashing it till he had a good grip of her head. She cringed, then tried to relax. Actually, relaxing was coming...naturally. Total focus on saying a few words to Teresa initiated her first telepathic thought: "I think we can, too."

Henry removed his hands and smiled at the two of them and proceeded to walk out of the room.

Teresa and Angelicia looked at each other in total amazement and began to laugh. They didn't even question how or why Henry showed up when he did. They just spent the rest of the day developing their newfound skill.

Teresa told Angelicia she was trying so hard to communicate with her son. Little did she know her Juan was being comforted now, and stopped banging his ears when he felt his mommy talk with him!

Henry ran into Actok when he left Teresa's room. "It's done."

Actok questioned, "Any problems?"

"No, Angelicia figured my intervention was all she needed."

"What did you do? The hands on the head trick?"

"Yep." They smiled and walked down the corridor together.

73

For four weeks, Earth time, the group have been in daily consultation with Gaff and Melek. The sisters adjusted so quickly that Actok decided they didn't need a personal Ebon guide. Skyann sat with Melek who was impressed with how well she was grasping the situation.

Gaff and Melek took turns explaining Earth's imminent plight and the choice most in the group must ultimately make: to remain as Starseeds or Awaken as Light Warriors. It was through a visual presentation of Vasile and Jaqui in action that the group got a taste of what was really happening to planet Earth! Actok reiterated again that everyone's families were protected.

Then it was time for them to meet Nocren and Saghi.

On Pleiades, Nocren, as Actok's representative, met with the Ministry of Enlightenment, a duty he performed with great honor. One of the major points of discussion was whether Nocren and Saghi were needed to assist Actok in preparing and guiding this group of six. The committee unanimously agreed yes.

All were assembled in a small holographic conference room, equipped with notepads, pens, and donuts. This, (minus the laptops) was Actok's understanding of what constituted a meeting on planet Earth. He found it so unnecessary, but it was accepted by the group as quite a normal setting.

Actok welcomed his visitors. He hadn't had time to greet them when they first arrived. What alarmed him was when he noticed Saghi lagging behind as she entered the room.

Actok stood in front of his entourage. Sitting from left to right were Dawn, Nocren, Saghi, Dr. Kaplan, Henry, Skyann, Teresa, and Angelicia.

He introduced Nocren and Saghi. Angelicia couldn't take her eyes off Saghi. She thought *What beauty she possesses, along with an elegance, a grace. I always thought that if there were aliens, they'd all be ugly and certainly wouldn't possess any human traits. And, her husband's not bad to look at either!*

Nocren and Saghi turned their attention to Henry, whose grin was recognized as one acknowledging old friends. They bowed to each other. Nocren and Saghi then turned toward David, who, not wanting to insult, stood and bowed. They smiled a knowing smile, one David couldn't understand, then they bowed.

Meanwhile, Teresa and Skyann looked at each other. Skyann whispered to her, "So, what do you think we're supposed to do?" Teresa just shrugged her shoulders up and down in a gesture that indicated, "I don't know." Nocren and Saghi did not turn their attention towards the girls, but back at Actok. No one acted as if a protocol had been broken.

Dr. Kaplan started to sit down when he noticed Dawn had her eyes closed. He looked over at Actok, who communicated, "She is all right, David. She is fully conscious; just heavily sedated with a drug Nocren brought to support her physical body during her Awakening." When the group was fully seated, Dr. Kaplan glanced back at Dawn, whose eyes were opened, but now had changed color from aqua green to a sapphire blue. The group all stared at Dawn and were witness to this manifestation.

Actok began, "There is so little time, and the necessity of

Nocren and Saghi to visit on this ship reaffirms the need to speed up our mission. You have been given some insight, but may ask, what is our mission? During our first meeting, when you were introduced to Gaff, I told you I'd hold off giving a formal explanation of who I was. Remember?"

The group all nodded their heads yes. "We," as Actok pointed to Nocren and Saghi, "are Pleiadians, sovereign emissaries for the inhabitants of planet Earth. We are just a part of the...how do I describe this in your terms? The integral force, willing to assist Earthlings who must be made aware of their eminent danger.

"I'm sure most of you think you are somewhere far away in space." Actok looked over as he noticed Teresa start to cry. She was comforted by Angelicia. At this statement, Skyann's ears perked.

"I'm sorry to seem insensitive but time..."

Teresa interrupted Actok, "Where are we? Please, please let me see Juan. Can't you bring him here?"

Nocren and Saghi looked at each other with an understanding heart.

Actok sadly continued, "Teresa, you are much closer to Juan than you know. Yes, you are on our ship, but not out in space. We have purposely created your living quarters without windows.

"We knew beaming you up onto our ship would not go unnoticed by Earth's enemies. A diversionary plan was created using a rogue ship they followed to the Milky Way; but actually, you are underground, in the Antarctic Ocean. Melek's species, the Telosians, live here and have graciously given us shelter and assistance. Melek, Gaff, and Oonsay have devoted their lives to our endeavors, for which we are very grateful."

Skyann silently thought *Oh, I'm so glad. I thought we were so far away!*

Actok continued, "Teresa, you, Dawn, Angelicia, Skyann, and David have been informed of the difference between

Starseeds and Light Warriors. You have an understanding as of what it takes to Awaken. You have had a little time to consider if you would join in this delegation of galactic warriors to assist your planet.

"All of you have shown great promise, and it is the will of the Prime Creator that you be given this honor now, if you desire it. At this time, I will ask Nocren to speak with you."

Nocren slowly turned his head in recognition of the group. He stood up and declared, "Your Earth is in turmoil. Due to the unforeseen catalyst of the actions of your little group, we, along with thousands of other alien races are preparing to Awaken all the Starseeds on your planet...a little earlier than was planned. This is quite the undertaking, as we need to provide a safe environment for the actual Awakening to occur. Usually, Awakenings are a profoundly personal ceremony, but with all that is happening, the timetable dictates we promote mass Awakenings.

"You have come to understand that you did not come from planet Earth originally. So, know this. You chose to experience a life here. In the time spent here, some of your hidden abilities have come to light and have had room to expand. We would be deeply privileged if you decide to Awaken into your full potential.

"We are aware, under these unforeseen circumstances, that you might desire to be transported back to your home planet, wherever it may be. With deep respect, we would honor your decision."

The room was still. No one wanted to answer. They had all known this moment would come, a moment when they would individually decide their fate.

Finally, Skyann asked, "I know Gaff and Melek have explained what is happening on our planet, yet it's sad to know life as I knew it won't be the same. My role as a Starseed is hard enough to figure out, but as a Light Warrior, how much will I change?"

Nocren replied, "Good question, Skyann." Nocren addressed Henry, "Henry, want to explain that to her?"

Henry stood up and replied, "Of course. I'm sure Gaff mentioned that you will still be you. That it's a matter of your brain's capacity to accept higher levels of frequencies, which enables higher levels of consciousness. In other words, to know. To know there is a Prime Creator and that we are all connected.

"You were given to understand that you chose to come to planet Earth, that you were given a mission..." Henry gestures like he's quoting, " should you choose to take it. " The sisters chuckled, Skyann gave a funny smirk and Dawn and David outright laughed, all remembering the *Mission Impossible* slogan. "The mission being that you assist humanity in remembering their existence and bring them into to the light of consciousness. That's it!"

"Well said, Henry," Nocren stated. "Skyann, does that help you in understanding who you will be? It's your personal choice."

Skyann thought for a moment, then answered, "I want to...know. I want to help. I...I want to be Awakened."

Angelicia looked over at Actok and without hesitation said, "I'm ready, Actok. I will serve the Prime Creator." Dawn and Henry looked at Angelicia and smiled.

Dr. Kaplan and Skyann looked at each other in surprise. Teresa turned to her sister and said, "But, what about dad? Kate...Juan? How can you just leave them behind to start this new life, Angie?"

Angelicia looked pleadingly at Teresa, "I'm looking at it this way. There's no use pretending life is like it was, and I'm needed here. I like the training they are willing to offer me; this is my calling. Dad, well, I'd love to see him again. Hug him, hold him so close. Kate, I love her very much, yet I know in my heart she's safer where she is. Knowing she's surrounded by a big family that will protect her helps. I can only hope we'll meet again...."

Teresa interjects, "And? Juan? What about Juan?"

Angelicia turned to Actok. He bowed his head but looked down at the floor. Nocren intervened, "Teresa, Juan can hear you. Did you know that?"

Teresa looked up at Nocren, "Really? Can he really?"

"Yes. He knows it's you. You have an innate ability that, if further developed, will reach far and wide in the universe to help others communicate. Our wish is that you stay with us. We will work hard to get Juan and your father to you. Teresa, we cannot promise anything, but the effort to protect them is working."

Teresa tried to relax. "I guess more thought is needed. This...gift, this ability, it's kinda cool. And if I can help others..."

A silence lulled the group till David started to speak. "I'm aware of my options. I know now that my life on Earth was predestined, I was there to enact a scenario. I accept that. Never seeing my sis...sister and family...and friends...well, in my heart... Anyway, it would be an honor to be Awakened and perform this mission."

74

Saghi knew that to get to Earth from her planet took around 445.5 light years. Their highly sophisticated spaceships, which they boasted were the best in all the galaxies, could transport hundreds of her kind within hours.

It's the transformational effects that Saghi experienced when she is on Earth that she didn't care for. Her major difficulty was adjusting to Earth's very dense atmosphere; it was hard to breathe our compounded oxygen. Her situation was heightened by the fact she was dying. Perhaps her body's deceleration, of which she had become profoundly aware, wouldn't be noticed during the transition.

Saghi could always use the excuse of the photon belt anomaly. Astrologers and scientist knew our solar system transverses this belt of electromagnetic energy and light every ten thousand years or more, and it was due to come into our planetary alignment. It was a fact that this encounter always interferes with Earth's cataclysms. But, to whose advantage is the speeding up of this process? Who really profits? Saghi knows the answer; it would be the perfect cover-up for her physical aging dilemma.

More than anything, Saghi wanted to see her husband Nocren attain the seat his friend now held: Most-High Unifier in the Ministry of Enlightenment. She knew it took every ounce of his precious time and energy to achieve that goal. She'd made the choice...she wouldn't complain.

Nocren found the ship limiting, and wished to be back on Alcyone. He'd been too long in the political realm of the Ministry and knew that was his true calling. He understood the need to be right where he was, on a ship, assisting six people to realize their full potential, and preparing them to use their newfound skills. It's just, well, he'd much rather address a crowd of thousands and be recognized for his decisions.

He wasn't blind to his wife plight. He noticed when she lagged behind. He noticed her lack of interest in the political shift occurring back home. But, for both their sakes, he acted unaware.

Actok was telecommunicating with Gaff in the reception area when they noticed Henry enter. They motioned for him to join them. Gaff said, "Henry, we were discussing the Akashic Fields and their quantum waves in relation to what are called 'visions.' Do you feel a person is more receptive to these visions if they are meditators or dreamers?"

Henry replied, "Studies have proven that the human brain, genetically modified as it is, can reach cosmic consciousness or visions. Dr. Ervin Laslow learned that radiation fields are all around Earth where zero-point energy exists. He felt this energy didn't just carry the physics of the universe, but also the quantum waves the Akashic Fields are made of. This finding showed human brains can activate electrons capable of tapping into the quantum waves.

"Richard Feynman said the human brain is full of electrical activity with radiation that others should respond to. He thinks humans can receive radio signals from our future, as the brain is the receiver.

"My hypothesis demonstrates that a dreamer, a meditator, a shaman, those that can relax their brain, are more receptive to this ability."

Actok put his hand on Henry's shoulder, looked at him, then turned to his friend, "Well, Gaff, you asked for it."

Actok noticed Gaff seriously thinking and knew he wanted to ask Henry another question. Actok took the opportunity to say, "Henry, I would like a few minutes with you."

Gaff looked up and said, "Oh yes, yes of course. You two go ahead now." Gaff walked away in serious thought.

Actok and Henry smiled and walked toward a room where there would be more privacy. After closing the door, Actok said, "Henry, I'm sorry we haven't been able to talk much privately until now."

"Yeah, but I understand. Actok, don't worry about that. We've got a few minutes now."

"I wish we had time to catch up. Unfortunately, having to create such an exposed incident has fast forwarded the timeline to rouse Dawn...and David. Even others will have to be Awakened earlier than their prearranged time.

There was silence. Then Actok said, "Henry, I'm going to require your assistance.

"I know you have been Dawn's protector and you have become attached to her as a good friend. She's here with us now, safe, and we must prepare her."

Henry hesitated, looked up at Actok, and communicated, "Yes, yes of course. I think what you're saying is Dawn's okay now and you need me elsewhere. Am I right? I will be honored to serve in any way I can."

"Thank you, my friend. We're working on a mission for you now."

Henry asked, "First, can I ask...what is happening with the inhabitants now that they realize other species do exist and are on their planet? It must be total chaos."

"Well, as I mentioned, and to put it bluntly, our timeline was drastically changed by the actions of the six of you. Dawn, David, and you, Henry, we couldn't risk having harmed. You are invaluable to this cause.

"But, to answer your question, I'm sure you are aware our ships were canvassing the New York and New Jersey area. The purpose was to seek out an alien rogue known as Jaqui. He, along with a few hundred of his kind, the Yahgs, created a penetrable laser equal to that of our security field around Earth."

"Wait, how can they do that? We've been protecting Earth for thousands of years from just such raiders."

"Well, Henry, I'd like to say our security is impenetrable, but it's not. We have known of some races sneaking in for various reasons lately, and we have not been able to stop them. These aliens are buccaneers, pirates of sort, and they work for the highest bidder. Our intel determined their newest beneficiary is none other than Vasile, who I believe you know works for Satan. Hence, the chaotic state Earth finds itself in right now."

"No. I didn't realize that. I know he is...well, was...posing as Brian Rivers, but I couldn't find anything incriminating with either name," Henry said. "Guess money and power..."

Actok shook his head yes. "Hide in plain sight, as you always say." Actok hesitated, then added "Henry, the reason you couldn't find anything incriminating on Vasile is he's a human hybrid cyborg, created by Satan with the assistance of the Draconians. This group have also created the most secretive AI organization in your world, AIM, which shelters through the T-HE-RE."

"The Draconians! Wow. I would have guessed the Anunnaki."

Henry continued, "So, you know what those acronyms stand for?" When Actok shook his head no, Henry continued, "The abilities possible now with AI. So, these Yahgs wanted to find and abduct Dawn and David before they were Awakened?"

"Henry, perhaps you especially, since you were already Awakened. That's why we placed an impenetrable stealth shield around you during your last abduction. It's the same application we have in place for Teresa's and Dawn's families. Still, when we knew of your plans to keep things as they were, it was time for an intervention."

The choice in making the Draconians my "bad guys" vs the Anunnaki was difficult. The problem lies in understanding the role the Anunnaki played in our advancement. I disrespect what they did—changing what our Almighty God created. Yet, the more I learn of their culture, the more apparent it is that they manipulated, or as some would argue, created us to perform as higher advanced hybrids! I contend, that if left to our own, as Almighty God made us, wouldn't we develop to their advanced stage with time?

The Draconians on the other hand don't have any redeeming qualities...

I was sitting on the "throne" when I noticed a silhouette in my rug. I studied it. A few outlines with my toes and voila! An Anunnaki.

Better hurry up and finish this book!!

75

Dan Katz was worried sick about Dawn, but what could he do? *I can get busy locating an expert on ETs,* he thought. He spent the morning rummaging through online printed stories on the subject. Still, he knew he needed someone, someone who had been saying all along that ETs are for real.

That one picture of the ship, the beam and the door, had gone viral. What luck. The *Brooklyn Gazette* was the hottest in the...well, anywhere on the planet.

Phones were ringing twenty-four seven. Anyone who wanted to hold on to their job knew not to argue about working double shifts.

HR was frantically going through discarded resumes. Allegis, Manpower, and Kelly Services had depleted their list of temporary help; anyone who could type, take notes, and talk on a phone were hired.

Ten minutes later he caught a break. Percy Mills, his gofer and part-time assistant, opened the door and yelled, "Dan, line two. It's Inky Yavonovich, says a friend of a friend gave him your number." Katz thought *Oh great! I don't have time for this. Wait, maybe...maybe this is the break I'm looking for. Guess I'd better take the call.*

Katz looked up from his computer and shouted, "Yeah, I'll

take it. Thanks."

Inky, on the other hand, couldn't wait to talk with Katz. To him, this abduction was confirmation of his stoic announcement; ETs really did exist!

Katz reached for the phone while thinking *Hope he's not going waste my time.*

"Katz here. Whatcha got, Inky?"

"Well, so much for introductions," Inky said.

"Sorry, going nuts here as you can imagine. Deadlines, the pressure, you know?"

Inky said, "I get it. You guys are all scrambling now because you wouldn't prepare for such an event, like I've been saying for years."

"Yeah, well, can you help? What do you know, Inky? I need to understand, and so do our readers, what the hell just happened. I heard some shit's going down at the Pentagon. There's panic the... aliens are going to come down in droves...soon. All airlines are on a need-to only basis. There are rumors Old Faithful is ready to explode! You can't even get near Mt. Rainier! All federal and state parks are closing. The military is calling in all its reserves. It's a "stay home, or you're on your own" situation now. What do you know?"

"Whoa there, Katz. Too many examples. Can't answer them over the phone. I'm not too far from your office. Wanna meet?" Inky suggested.

"Yeah, when?"

"Now, I'll come now. Put the coffee on, this is gonna take a while."

76

Percy opened the door and yelled into the office again, "Katz, line three. Ah...Vice President, James Dorsett."

James Dorsett. That's not his real name of course. His real name is so hard to pronounce: Sheatagi.

What he lacks in looks he excels in physique! He is almost seven feet tall with a muscular torso and arms, and a bald head accenting his deep violet eyes.

James' race, the Alpha Centaurians, were the most technologically advanced species in the Milky Way. They have monitored all Earthling events for centuries and have been responsible for most of the underground sightings in the last twenty years. It was believed thousands were living among us. Although usually not concerned in integrating with humans, some circumstances required it; for example, the plea from the Pleiadians to assist in this mass effort to support planet Earth.

The Alpha Centaurian race could easily destroy Earth and the annoying grays that keep infiltrating and abducting humans. James' assignment was to infiltrate with government officials and position himself close to the president. He'd done an outstanding job in the last four years: liaison for two warring European presidents, two shifts of political change, militarily ending the terrorist group Ghai, and, comforting his president with the loss of his family.

Spies, lobbyists, whistleblowers, they all had something in common; they know something worth telling. James' army is fortified with Light Warriors who associate with these groups. They infiltrate and obtain secret knowledge which has enabled the government to sustain itself. Still, James didn't kid himself, he realized Vasile was in charge now, and that it's just a matter of time before the New World Order is initiated.

James needed an ally, a spy. Someone close to Vasile. His informants have been watching Dan Katz. His spies have noticed Vasile positioned himself alongside Katz, and recently, they have been seen everywhere together. James needs to get Katz on his side. But, how can he convince Katz that's where he needs to be?

Purchased a Google Mini—love it! All I have to do now is ask it a question and it gives me an answer.

77

Inky knew his way around the *Brooklyn Gazette*. He had penetrated this newspaper posing as a delivery boy, a truck driver, even as a temporary employee for a day. He didn't care if he got caught. His message was too important; spread the news, they're here!

When inside the newsroom he caused havoc, circulating notes of doom, printouts of UFO activities, and writing on bathroom walls with indelible ink. He almost got caught—once.

Inky felt so comfortable walking into Katz' office. They exchanged a handshake and Inky walked over to the window. This surprised Katz, but he said nothing. He sized Inky up: he hadn't changed from the picture his paper had posted of him prophesying in the streets a few years ago; five-foot-ten, thin, maybe thirty, a face that got lost in a crowd, cheap clothing. But his demeanor surprised Katz; he was expecting...well, from his reputation, he expected a freaked out, high-strung individual. That just wasn't the case. What Katz couldn't comprehend was the need for a woolen hat; after all, it was only September. And why was it pulled down over his ears? Was it to hide all that carrot-top hair?

For a long minute, neither said a word. Then Katz said,

"Sit down, Inky. I haven't much time."

"No, no you don't," Inky replied.

"Now, what's that mean?"

"The timetable has been pushed up. This abduction was a necessity, not a tactical event. This doesn't fit the profile I've been studying for years. We're in for drastic changes Katz. And now. Not soon, now."

Katz said, "Yeah, well, I'm a believer...now. How about I apologize for the bad press we gave you...what, three years ago?"

"You mean when you guys said I was a nuisance and should be taken off the streets? Yeah, I remember that. Ah...okay, all is forgiven. Actually, we don't have time to get into it anyway. Wait, on second thought, while we're apologizing, might as well tell you, I'm the one who infiltrated the *Gazette* and printed the gloom and doom stuff that got around."

"Kinda figured. Okay, grab some coffee and donuts and let's get into this."

They both prepared their food and got comfortable. Inky said, "Have you ever given thought as to what's gonna happen to the human race?"

"Do we have time for this?"

"I'm trying to draw you a picture of what's happening, but you don't know even a little about the reasons, Katz."

"Okay, okay. Go ahead, Inky. I'll be quiet and still, promise."

"Earth, as we know it, is going through dramatic changes. You know, nothing stays the same. Alien races have been involved with us since our creation. Some humans even believe they created us! Now, don't ask me what I mean, just listen."

"I am, I am," Katz replied.

Inky gave a heavy sigh and looked at Katz, "They're here, Katz. Have been for eons. More are coming on a daily basis now, good and bad species. The security of our planet has been infiltrated, but I believe it's supposed to happen.

"Remember when I was talking about Earth being invaded by a group known as the Anunnaki? I got flak on that one."

Katz gives Inky a look as if to say, "hurry up."

"Listen, this isn't easy, Katz. You're gonna think I'm crazy!"

"I told you I'm a believer now, so go on, Inky."

"So, you're admitting you believe in aliens?"

"I do now. Go, go."

Inky continued, "Well, there's this other group, a good group called the Pleiadians. They're our protectors. They have this huge group, millions of other aliens, willing to help Earthlings from being annihilated, or worse, turned into cyborgs.

"The Pleiadians have been observing Earth's development for thousands of years. They watched as humans learned to expand their minds from doing menial, everyday tasks like learning how to make fire, create the wheel, learning social skills, stuff like that. So, things were going quite well until we advanced to the industrial revolution. They watched our greed and power grow to unprecedented levels."

Inky takes a deep breath. "Still with me?"

"Yeah, yeah" was all Katz could say.

"The Intergalactic Federation..." Inky pointed toward the ceiling, "felt the time had come to contact the occupants of Earth. Up until this point, they have protected us from invasion of rogue alien races as best they could.

"But now, with our rapid advancements in all areas of technology, the Federation predicted the future we were rushing towards. We're talking about moving to Mars for Christ's sake. Also, all the AI advancements have got them nervous—for mankind, mind you, not them.

"The Pleiadians have created a cutting-edge technology so advanced it would take Earth...well, humans probably could never advance to their level.

"Their system of surveillance is leading-edge, way surpassing any other species in all the galaxies. They've invented sensing adaptations and wave length surges, allowing advanced warning of a rogue attack. Through these senses, they can detect a good race from a bad.

"With all this going on, the inhabitants of Earth are involved in a very life-changing experience. Earthlings are questioning themselves now but soon will realize they are only visitors here: everyone is from somewhere else, Katz. They are displaying a desire to contact their inner self. It has to do with the shift of the axis causing higher frequency ranges, but that's for another time.

"Okay. Still with me?" Inky asked.

Katz changed position in his chair from a restful, laid-back one to both hands on his knees, and both eyes staring into Inky's.

"Yeah. It's true. Damn."

Inky said, "So, let me take you to what's now happening. From what I can gather, an incident occurred in Brooklyn involving six people. They were on this porch..."

"Yeah, I know that, Inky. Go on."

"Hey, what about a little tit for tat here, huh? How about filling me in on that incident; you know some inside info?"

"Just that six people were standing on a porch. One had a camera but dropped it, probably during the abduction. One of my...uh employees found it and when we developed it, well, there is the now that infamous picture. That's all I know."

"I sense you're protecting someone, Katz, and you know more, but I'll let it go for now. Perhaps when you have time to affirm all this new info, you'll trust me."

"Are we being invaded, Inky? Where are these...Pleiadians now? Are you...you one?"

Inky hesitated, gave yet another deep sigh and admitted, "Good insight, Katz! Yes, I am. I am a Light Warrior, an Avatar if you will. Maybe now I can discuss this with you on a new level."

Katz sat back in his chair, stunned. The only movement was in his mind, and that was totally focused on Inky. He remembered Dawn referred to Henry as a Light Warrior in her notepad.

His mind started racing; more questions were swirling in his brain. *Is Inky really an alien being? Am I really sitting and talking with a being from somewhere other than here? How many times did I see him on the street and just pass him by? Have Earthlings been that blind?*

Inky let Katz have his moment. Light Warriors are most patient.

Slowly, like awakening from a dream, Katz announced, "Okay, so I guess since aliens exist, they would have different species and organizations. Why not? How important is it that I know about Starseeds and Light Warriors? Will anyone else get abducted? Jesus, I don't even know what to ask you."

Katz stared at Inky, and noticed a change in his demeanor. "I've already mentioned, your kind are involved in the most dynamic change ever to be experienced; one of contact with the inner self. The human species is becoming conscious of more than their materialistic life and greed for power. Your minds are evolving at such a pace that soon there will be two sides to life here: stay in the materialistic physical Earth wherein you will be a cyborg or a slave, or live on Earth as a highly advanced spiritual being. Their decision positions them on the spiritual battleground to come.

"It's all about how Earthlings will adapt to change. The great news is you're not alone. There is a tremendous army of Light Warriors willing to assist, like me. Speaking of battles, this Vasile guy is the one...okay, how do I say this without you throwing me out of your office?"

This is when Katz throws Inky a defensive look. "Wait, what do you know about him?"

"Let's save that discussion for now. I wanna keep the flow of this intel going before we're interrupted. Okay?"

Katz shakes his head in agreement.

"Earth is slowly shifting into a new orbit, which makes our body's frequency levels expand. Have you been getting ringing in your ears? Do you get excited when you see certain numbers, like eleven-eleven...maybe six-six-six? Have you started questioning...?"

When Katz gave him a weird look, he said, "Never mind."

They both got quiet. Then Inky stated, "You should be aware of something. This is the first time in your recorded history that Earth is experiencing such dramatic cycle shifts while spinning around in orbit. We're here on the planet now, so this change will affect our evolution.

"It's a lot to take in, I know."

78

Over a period of a few weeks since the porch abduction, Vasile's influence on the inhabitants of planet Earth superseded all major global leaders. Everyone was waiting for his second upcoming speech, his Understand the New World Order dialog, this time at the United Nations building in New York.

All were waiting to hear the how's and why's their family and friends were swooped off the planet in one great rush. Millions were not satisfied with his stating there isn't anything to be done.

Why were they being subjected to wearing this embedded piece in the hand called the Chip? And why were all subjected to loss of wages and positions, and forced to live and work in a communistic venue, some in inhumane conditions? What had happened to free will, free enterprise? Why couldn't one visit friends or family without documentation? What had happened to their rights of freedom of speech, freedom of religion, freedom to bear arms? Jaqui!

Jaqui was a Yahg from the Andromeda galaxy. His planet, Urchee, had yet to be discovered. That was fine with his race. They didn't want to be discovered.

Jaqui was ugly, no doubt. His presence had erased any

resistance to the fact that alien beings existed. One exposure, one global mass-look at this creature from another world, and Earth's inhabitants were shocked into submission.

With all the abilities in Jaqui's repertoire, the most impressive and deadliest was his power to read the human mind. He'd focus his stare, which initiated an immediate feeling of intense heat. Facing you, he scanned your body frequencies and immediately detected your thoughts, and whether or not you were lying! Once he identified your position in relation to his, either he'd release the energetic hold or generate more heat and fry you right on the spot!

No one on planet Earth would attempt to challenge Jaqui's control, not after two full days of this visual on every major network and viewing screens. Jaqui was making Vasile's new regulatory implementations to bring forth the New World Order just a day at the office.

Visiting Earth created physical problems he must endure daily. His breathing was labored; making it difficult to adapt to Earth's atmosphere. His many eyes had to work in unison more than on his home planet. He found bathing in extremely hot water a temporary relief for his body's constant shivering. The daily application of mind control over hundreds of humans was exhausting.

Everyone assumed Jaqui enjoyed his position alongside Vasile. Truth be known, he really didn't like Vasile or Earth or this mission. Jaqui was forced to assist dark spiritual entities holding his planet hostage. They were commissioned by Satan. So, really, what choice did he have?

79

In one way or another, the inhabitants of Earth had been affected by Jaqui's cruelty. If not physically, one was subject to the New World Order on a daily basis. No freedom existed. Cyborgs were created and placed all over the world as the new police force.

It had taken Vasile only two years of preparation to position himself as the savior of mankind. With the assistance of the Illuminati, he had manipulated all world governments and situated himself in a manner that no one dared challenge. Not now. Not ever.

Vasile was ready to give his speech as the new Secretary-General of the UN. Hundreds of millions were watching their TVs, others were focused on their cell phones or computers. Stadiums and bars across the globe were having to turn people away, their establishments packed solid. All waited for this man and his message.

James Dorsett was waiting also, sitting next to President Fredericks in a secluded room at the White House. Dorsett knew he had to tell him his real purpose and now was a good opportunity.

James felt great relief when President Fredericks told him he already knew, that Actok had informed him when he first went to work there.

He was also glad to report that with just one meeting, Dan Katz of the Brooklyn Gazette would be at their service!

80

Melek and Skyann were sitting in a little kitchenette area Skyann had decorated in a Coca Cola theme: anything was possible with the hologram.

She was finding Melek to be great company, and was making her very comfortable. Skyann got up, swayed back and forth over to the fridge, and asked Melek if he wanted anything to drink. She was singing, "...whip it up right here in the sink." He didn't get the analogy. He just shook his head no.

Melek asked Skyann if she was adjusting well, if there was anything she needed, questions along those lines. She was taken aback, wondering why he would ask those questions yet again. She felt he was purposely resisting what he really had come to say. "Melek, is there anything you want to tell me? Should I be worried? Are you trying to prepare me for something?"

Melek shook his head no but proceeded to say, "I think you know that it was me you felt watching you. I was assigned..."

"I felt it, Melek, when I first saw you. Why were you assigned to watch me? Even then?" Skyann questioned.

"For your safety. You are a very important person who was placed in a dangerous situation. Your association with Dawn deemed it necessary you be protected. I just want to say

I'm sorry if I frightened you."

The room got very quiet as Skyann sorted this new information. Melek was feeling uncomfortable. "Well, perhaps I should leave you now."

"No, no, Melek. I was thinking how I felt when I was in your presence. It happened a lot in my life, that feeling. You know, like before I walked into a room, I'd know who was in there and actually the mood of the place. Way too often I'd be able to tell the outcome of a situation. Things like that."

"You are not aware yet, Skyann, but you have an ability that if you want to explore, I can assist you. Chakras act as an interface between the dense physical world and the non-physical world of pure consciousness. Your chakras' vibrational level is such that you can expand your sixth and seven senses more readily than the others in this group. That's what I hope you want to learn."

Skyann thought a minute, then asked, "I'm already experiencing a higher consciousness, it's like a...knowing. If I do this, will I change yet again? Will I still be me, Melek?"

"You will still be Skyann but with a new cognizance. Look at Henry! He's a Light Warrior, but he's...Henry, right?

"You can tap into your extrasensory perception, or ESP, anytime your mind wants to jump from a five senses reality into a psychic realm reality. It was your forte. Once Awakened, this talent will come naturally but until that time..." Skyann stared at Melek.

Melek continued, "This ability I can assist you with."

Skyann looked seriously into Melek's eyes and requested, "Give me a little time to think this over, okay?"

81

Actok and Dawn were seated next to each other in Dawn's chambers. "But what happens when I wake up? Is it a process? Does it happen immediately? Will I physically be different?"

"I understand, Dawn, you are anxious and have many questions," Actok replied. "We will be applying a regression technique to begin your Awakening, wherein, soon, you will start to remember on an elevated level.

"We are concerned, Dawn, as this is your most important mission ever. We have purposely protected you physically and shielded your mind, as your mission is crucial to Earth's survival."

Actok looked deep into Dawn's eyes and her body immediately slipped into a state of relaxation, but not hypnosis. She felt the sensation of falling back gently onto the couch. She was receiving a subliminal message from Actok. "Let us go back to what you felt when you first saw me in the airplane hangar."

Immediately she replied, "Ah, funny, now I remember knowing you. Yes, I was frightened at first, then curious, but not really afraid."

Actok acknowledged, "That's correct. Your mind was bringing forth suppressed memories."

Actok hesitated. Dawn asked, "What's the matter, Actok?"

"I'm concerned about your physical strength, Dawn. You have shown signs of withdrawal, weakness."

"Have you been observing me since I was born?" she questioned.

"Yes, of course. We have been monitoring you and everyone associated with you. We had placed Dr. Kaplan...David...in your path as your guide...well, as your psychiatrist...to assist you with remembering your childhood. So, when you were prepared to lead your spiritual army, we could fast-track your mind with little stress. There is good news here, as he is showing promise in his ability to influence—well, deceive. He's enjoying the training here in the art of spying and reconnaissance.

"Henry was positioned by your side as a protector. He has been with you through many incarnations. Now, with his development in mind subversion, he will be quite an asset in seeing into the future, enabling you to know where you are most needed. He also possesses a unique quality; he can find hidden materials!

"Skyann has proven herself a loyal friend with abilities she's unfolding. Melek has received permission to start her lessons in ESP and she's a natural. She will be a great benefit to you, should you choose.

"Teresa and Angelicia were unfortunately collateral..."

Actok noticed Dawn's expression and her body squirming as if she were upset, and realized the choice of words he'd used was wrong. "I'm sorry, Dawn. That doesn't mean to imply they will be annihilated! We are working on developing mind techniques with both sisters and they are proving to be very receptive. This too will be an asset in your mission.

"Dawn, perhaps you won't need to do anything when the war ensues. I say war but no one knows how our Creator will end this state of affairs on Earth. We are here to prepare; in case the need arises. All of you, even the sisters, are more than you know, but for now preparation is in order."

Dawn's body immediately started to settle back down.

They both became quiet. Then Dawn inquired, "The symbol on your shirt, Actok. Nocren's too. I've seen it before."

"Yes! Good. Our Pleiadian Light Symbol. This symbol comforted you on many of your abductions, Dawn. This is progress, your memory is expanding."

Dawn inquired, "How much time do we have before Earth is in real danger, Actok? Please don't try to shield me from information, I need to know."

Actok looked over at Dawn and with a sadness that expressed gloom, said, "None, Dawn. To be honest, none. The stage is set. Vasile and his followers have infiltrated governmental agencies, and even have many presidents around the world in his pocket. As your Bible prophesied, Earthlings are going to be tricked in believing he really is their savior. His power has even reached far beyond the influences held by the religious institutions around the world."

Dawn questioned, "How could this have happened so fast? I never once saw him on TV or in a public setting, or in any arena setting. How did he reach so many so quickly, Actok?"

"Their influence over world leaders was swift. In no time, they had them in their pockets. What leader wouldn't want someone else to take the blame for all that was happening? What leader wouldn't want the benefits of siding with such a massive faction? Secret governments and corporate conglomerates had the means to hide Vasile till the timing was right to expose him.

"Remember, the time continuum indicates you have been on this ship for a week now, our time; that's approximately one month and four days, Earth time.

After your abduction to this ship, Vasile introduced himself and his counterpart, Jaqui, a Yahg, who had abilities that frightened Earthlings into submission. Jaqui has no loyalty, usually he's available to the highest bidder, yet...I sense..."

"You should know that thousands of hybrid cyborgs are being created daily...with...humans who would not succumb to wearing a device known as the Chip. It's embedded in your hand and..."

Dawn became very sullen. Actok continued, "If you were to return now, life as you knew it would not exist; you know that. A state of worldwide submission has occurred. In religious terms, the prophetic Rapture and Tribulation have befallen the inhabitants. In reality, we have undertaken measures to Awaken Starseeds before their time. Left unprotected, they would fall.

"All are looking for a redeemer; your Earth has chosen one, the Antichrist, first known as Brian Rivers and now Vasile. You, Dawn, are the other, chosen by our Prime Creator; you, Dawn, are the Bringer of Light."

"I have one more question, Actok. What will happen to Carole and Kate?"

"We have noticed the empathy they have displayed and in commune with the Prime Creator, he has chosen to protect them from all harm. You will see them again."

Dawn closed her eyes. Actok knew what that meant and was grateful she was already demonstrating a subdued ability. He realized there would be no more need for regression; she was already displaying signs. Without having to place his finger on her forehead, with only one lesson, Dawn was deep in meditation. He got up and quietly walked out of her quarters.

I'm loving writing. What an escape, and to know it's being created in my brain! No one sitting beside me offering their ideas, just me, just me!

Have any of my readers had the desire to write a story? It's said everyone has one to tell. I started this one cold turkey at 71! Give it thought, write something down, just start it...

82

Katz wasn't feeling good—his heart. He was sitting yet again on Vasile's private jet. They were headed for Jerusalem. He knew Vasile would want him in his circle; after all, it was his paper that had introduced Vasile to the world.

The strain of his sudden jump to stardom, the influx of worldwide attention, traveling alongside Vasile, has affected him greatly. He didn't have anyone to comfort him. He knew a trip to a doctor would be beneficial, but his life now consisted of appeasing Vasile. He hated not being at the *Brooklyn Gazette,* hated leaving it in the charge of...Inky!

Now, his face was noteworthy and Vasile was taking every advantage. Since the infamous abduction picture hit the internet, the world had gone wild with speculation and abduction stories. No one doubted their existence now; it was "what do they want" that was on everyone's mind. The world, the entire world was in panic mode.

Vasile's notoriety was instantaneous standing alongside Katz. His money and his influence had trapped the elite and powerful leaders before they could do anything but succumb. If they did know, would they care?

Just prior to their trip, Vasile had promised Katz his paper would be exclusively in charge of the set-up for. Katz knew the enormity of the task and immediately hired the best to accomplish it. Vasile had promised Katz their association would reap enormous benefits, and this broadcast had all eyes on his newspaper.

Seems Katz forgot his arrangement with Dorsett!

Vasile was all smiles when his face appeared to the whole world, while behind him, in a corner of the screen, millions of drones scattered throughout the world were filming the mass shooting murders of anyone, including women and children, if they were caught without the small raised mark of the Chip.

No more were the passive lies. Vasile's message was straightforward: the Earth was in turmoil, new species were arriving daily, and if you wanted to survive, worship him.

The religious leaders and pious followers around the globe were cognizant of what was taking place but powerless to intercede. This Chip was foretold. It was called the "Mark" in the Book of Revelation in the Bible. The presence of Jaqui, Earthlings' first look at a bona fide alien being, gave no solace to those who wouldn't think of wearing the Chip.

For almost two thousand years, generations had been awaiting an Antichrist. Now Vasile, with his message, had proven that was exactly who he was. At the end of his speech, no one doubted he had positioned himself as a god. He even referred to himself several times as "Earth's savior."

Two important statements were made during his speech: "There is no heaven or hell." Then, to the great dismay of the masses, he admitted, "An abduction did occur. I prefer to call it a cleansing. I didn't do it, honest, but in hindsight it was necessary. Do not trouble yourself, profess your loyalty to me and you will not suffer."

The inhabitants of Earth came to realize the millions of people taken had one thing in common; they were spiritual in nature! People rushed to their churches hoping for answers and salvation, but the churches were receiving threats should they were to go against the New World Order. They were not allowed to offer sanctuary; it was an offense with the penalty of death.

The way you spent money, banked, shopped, received an education, and obtained medical assistance were all under one totalitarian rule. Everything was changing so fast that millions couldn't stand the strain. Suicides were an everyday occurrence.

Vasile and Jaqui had, in one afternoon, conquered the world; one in a soft, hypnotic manner, the other with the threat of annihilation. There was no defense.

83

The first time Henry had set eyes on Teresa, he had this urge to be with her, in any way that he could for...whatever she needed. It just felt right that he was by her side. She had this vulnerability that was so attractive. She was quiet, but certainly not boring. She was really cute. He felt her best quality was her love for Juan.

So much had changed for Teresa and Angelicia. They were thrown into a reality so unlike what they had experienced on Earth. Here there was constant training. Both Teresa and Angelicia had responded well, Angelicia in the area of defensive maneuvers. It was a benefit that her forte was in martial arts.

Teresa, with Gaff and Melek's assistance, had fine-tuned her telepathic facilities to such a degree that she could "talk" with Juan whenever she pleased and knew he'd be listening. She was a natural for the technique of remote viewing; a method seeking impressions of a distant unseen target using ESP.

Technically their ship was in Antarctica, yet telepathically, Juan was right in her head. This had enabled her to accept her present condition with less stress.

At first glance, Teresa felt Henry was very special. So kind, easy to lean on. Then, during the time at Skyann's house, when he put his arms around her, she knew, she just knew, those were the arms, that was the face, he was the man.

84

∞

At my age, it's good to know one can have a passion. Think I found mine. Just wish I had an editor, an agent, and extra money in my pocket!

∞

Dr. Kaplan loved his new reality. He was fast becoming friends with Henry. His only sadness was not being able to communicate with his family. Actok had informed him they were safe, but how could he get a message to them? He was thinking of asking Teresa for help.

Something else had developed; he thought he was in love with Skyann. Every avenue of psychoanalysis he could perform on himself didn't produce any other answer; it was love. Excuses for not believing in his feelings were simple: it was just because she was new in his life, they had shared an experience, she was available, all the nuances he told his patients are reasons they think they're in love, but probably are not. Still, the feelings persisted.

David was confused about being abducted. He really

wanted to speak with Actok about it. Getting him alone was the problem. So, when he noticed Actok walking towards his apartment, David walked up to him. "Hello, Actok. Got a minute?"

"Yes, David. What's on your mind?"

"Well, it's about my abduction."

Actok smiled and kept walking, with David following behind him. "Which one, David?" It wasn't until then that David realized he actually was abducted twice: once in his room and when he was beamed up to the ship.

"Oh, ha, yeah. Well, the one in my room."

Actok stopped walking, turned, and offered, "David, that abduction was staged."

David was shocked. He looked at Actok but couldn't speak. Actok continued, "Your mind is skeptical, you don't readily believe. Hence, your question.

"We had to create the feeling that you were abducted to more readily accept what Dawn was telling you. What better way than to experience one yourself?"

Both were silent for a moment. "I need to tell you something, David. There's still more to you than you know. In time, all will be revealed and you will Awaken. Please be patient with this process."

"Of course, Actok. Sure."

Actok felt he had something else on his mind. "Go ahead, David, ask."

"Well, it's my family. I know they're safe, but..."

"They are, and to tell you the truth, they're grieving for you. They have resigned themselves to never seeing you again."

Actok questioned, "Do you remember during your first training day the video Gaff showed from Skyann's camera of the six of you entering our ship, David?"

"Yes," David replied.

"One member, your sister Gail, insisted that was you in

the picture entering our ship."

David dropped his head down and tears welled up in his eyes. Actok placed his hand on David's shoulder. "Trust me, my friend. They are your Earth family, true, but love never dies; you will see them again."

85

Every day alien species attempted to enter Earth's atmosphere. Some could make it through, but others, despite their efforts, realized they could not survive on the planet.

Other races were here already and seizing laboratories and implementing their own genetic experiments. Vasile had no problem with this situation, as long as the outcome produced a cybernetic hybrid slave system. The offspring would be both male and female. Needless to say, men, women and children were disappearing daily.

Still other races, already existing on the planet above and below Earth, were fully operating their own agendas. Some would back Actok, others Vasile.

The media didn't have time to create fake news; everyone was now in panic mode. The totality of Vasile was monumental, but still hundreds of millions around the world wouldn't wear what was labeled the Chip.

Vasile did not expect such a negative response to his bogus proposal to save the planet. He knew he had worked formidably against the Light Warriors, yet they continue to be the thorn in his side. The plan now was to starve the population of the unwilling, keep them in chaos, let their family and friends die in front of them, and they would succumb.

Vasile and Jaqui were headed to China, trying to track down the lead that Renu was there, underground, somewhere. He must destroy her and her massive following. Since the abductions had started, millions had poured into China in the hopes that Renu could save them.

Vasile contested that it was the likes of these fake saviors that were causing all the chaos on the planet. He'd convinced Earthlings that Renu was in partnership with Kristian and Rosalee's massive entourage. His best defense against the Light Warriors was his ability to blame them for the abductions, and he'd be right.

There was, and continued to be, an exodus of Starseeds disappearing daily. Despite his efforts, not even Vasile knew who was responsible for this occurrence.

One theory was they were being taken to a "safe place" off planet Earth to prepare for a great spiritual war. Another is they were being placed in safehouses or hostels all over the Earth.

86

Henry had just remembered something important enough to find Actok. After half an hour of searching, he noticed Actok coming out of the Isolytic Chamber. "Actok. I've got to talk with you, got a minute?"

"Yes, of course, Henry. Let's go to your room."

They walked together down the long corridor into Henry's room. Actok walked over to what looked like a small temperature knob, pressed a few keys, and turned off the recorder and camera devices. This didn't bother Henry; he was well aware of them in his room.

Actok turned to Henry, who stated, "I was thinking of the series of events prior to us coming here, and I remembered Dawn had asked me if I could get her extra security on her computer. We never got a chance. I know its safe right now, but is there any way it can be beamed up here? I'm wondering if there's anything on her computer implicating her or anyone here on the ship."

Actok didn't say anything. He was deep in thought.

"Actok?"

"Yes, yes, Henry. I heard you. Do not concern yourself, we shielded everyone's residence immediately upon your arrival. Anyone who gets near an entrance have their memory repressed. All guards patrol the perimeter a distance away from the door. This has worked so far, but intel suggests the military have realized this maneuver and are trying to penetrate our shields. There are armed guards stationed at all of your homes, but to date, they are concentrating on Teresa's father's house.

Actok got quiet and Henry knew he had something else on his mind. "What is it, Actok?"

"It's regarding a cuneiform, Henry..."

Henry interrupted, "Are you talking about the Timeline Cuneiform. The one that looks like a sheet of papyrus?"

"Yes. That's correct. We need the cuneiform to accurately position the time our warriors are to be placed everywhere on Earth. During their last incarnation, Dawn and Emissary Renu...you remember her, yes?"

"Yeah, sure."

Actok added, "Dawn and Renu had devised a plan to hide the cuneiform. When the timing was right, they'd use the code they created to retrieve it. They were acutely aware of the consequences should this cuneiform be placed in the wrong hands.

"Khacee was made aware that the timeline situation was becoming crucial. He contacted Renu to see if she could divulge where she had hidden the cuneiform, but she was sworn to secrecy. After much coaxing, she revealed only that it was in Dawn's apartment.

"The council would not allow Renu to undertake the mission to retrieve the cuneiform. She was needed elsewhere. So, the council permitted Khacee to find it, bring it back, then return it to its hiding place again." Actok took a deep breath. "But there was a problem. The urgency of the situation did not allow a briefing. Khacee was on his home planet when he learned of the dilemma and went straight forth to retrieve it without informing us. His heart was in the right place but, not being briefed, he couldn't have known that Dawn hadn't

Awakened yet! Both were caught off-guard."

Henry asked, "So, Renu hid it, thinking Dawn would be Awakened soon, and Khacee went to retrieve it, thinking she was. That must have been some reunion."

"It was, Henry. It didn't go well. Of course, Dawn didn't recognize him. This is when he realized she was not Awakened. He felt jeopardized, and was afraid to say too much to her. He only mentioned he was there looking for...he called it a book. So, he left her without saying anything more. This naturally left Dawn with more questions than answers."

Henry took a deep breath. "Huh, so Dawn had no idea she had in her possession the oldest written form of writing ever on Earth!"

Actok stared at his friend then continued, "I'm gravely concerned, Henry. Our friendship is very dear to me, so what I am about to request has been given serious thought...I wish you to undertake a mission that would put your very life in danger.

"You remember that, right, Henry? When we last talked and I said I needed your help?"

Without hesitation, he replied, "Anything, Actok. Just ask."

"Know this first, Henry, much consideration for your safety was discussed in counsel. We were going to ask Khacee to make another attempt at obtaining the cuneiform, but he is in the midst of a neighboring dispute that only he has the ability to suppress. We don't need intergalactic interference now. He's also concerned that if Dawn were to see him again on his return, it might trigger their relationship, which wouldn't help our situation.

"I understand, Actok."

"The mission is twofold. One, go to Dawn's apartment and retrieve the computer and cuneiform. Two, retrieve Teresa's son and father..." Actok hesitated, as he noticed Henry's whole face beam. Sorry to break Henry's elation, Actok continued, "If the shields are broken, they will be interrogated and put to death."

Actok looked closely at Henry. Their bond of friendship was strong. He knew if anyone could accomplish this feat, it was him. "I received information that our protective shield is under attack only at Teresa's house. This makes sense, the militia wants Juan. We're sure they realized he would telecommunicate with his mother and they want to tap into his psyche to retrieve info on where our ship is. They are not focusing on any of your group's other family members right now.

"Henry, it will be easy to get the items from Dawn's home, as we can transport you in and out by shutting off the security for three minutes. This will trigger an alarm that certainly would be detected, but by then you'll be far away. The hard part is that we know they're watching Poppy's house. We need to plan your exact entrance and the three of you must be in close proximity when we use our transporter. It's risky, Henry. I would understand if you decided not to undertake such a mission."

Henry couldn't suppress his smile, as he thought of how happy Teresa and Angelicia would be with their immediate family on board the ship. Henry said, "I understand. When do I leave?"

"Tomorrow." Actok was concerned about Henry's smile. "Henry, this is a dangerous mission I'm asking of you. Be aware, do not be complacent; it may be your demise."

"I will be careful. Thank you for this assignment, Actok. I'll go now and prepare."

Henry turned to go just as Actok said, "Henry, it would be prudent not to mention this to anyone...just in case the mission fails."

"Of course, I agree. If all goes according to plan, I shouldn't even be missed."

87

Henry, by his own description, was a geek Light Warrior. Reincarnated hundreds of times, he never gave thought to volunteering for a dangerous mission. True, most were strategic in nature; he could end a problem from a desk, yet never hesitated to be "out in the field." It's never been about the glory; Henry really didn't enjoy the spotlight. So why now question the acceptance of this mission? Now, when he's alone in his room? Teresa!

Henry has had numerous wives, lovers and close relationships during his incarnations, yet he sat thinking *What am I doing? Why am I feeling this way towards her? I just met her yet why this immediate attraction? Do I somehow...know her?*

Always willing to take the risk, Henry was confused to find that personal feelings were entering his psyche. Torn between duty and physical emotion, he was considering delegating the assignment. *What if I'm not successful? I'll never see Teresa again.* Henry was in love!

Henry forced his attention on the problem before him. He knew every ounce of concentrated effort must be utilized to prepare possible scenarios for the challenge ahead. Henry contemplated. *Timing is of the utmost importance. That* security field around Teresa's home must be turned off to allow entrance. *I'm not going to have but three minutes to get the two of them beamed up before the guards realize what happened. I'm going to need a diversion.*

Again, Henry is disrupted by thoughts of Teresa's smile, how it felt when his arms were protectively around her. He listened with his mind and could clearly remember the sound of her voice. *So familiar somehow...what's the matter with me? I have to concentrate. I can do this!*

Henry, with squinted forehead and closed eyes, forced his mind to think. *All I need is to telecommunicate with Actok the exact moment I need the security removed and when to beam us up.*

Allowing total open-mindedness, the first scenario started forming. *I arrive in Poppy's home to find him walking out of the kitchen with little Juan in his arms. In less than a minute, he's convinced I'm here to help, but Juan on the other hand takes to a tantrum, kicking and screaming as I try to gather the three of us for transport. I start telecommunicating to Actok, who immediately turns off the security system.*

Henry's mind was whirling...*Everything happens so fast. With the security system down, the guards hear Juan screaming and go on high alert. They quickly take advantage of the inactive security system and barge into the house fully armed and ready for battle.*

Poppy thrusts Juan on me, breaking my communication with Actok. Trying to concentrate while Juan is punching my face, I notice Poppy reaching into his pocket for a...gun? He moves quickly away from us and takes position to shoot. I run towards them in an effort to huddle us for transport and commune, "Now, Actok," and just seconds before the transporter beam locks, I witness Poppy shooting every guard that came in sight.

Henry had to admit *Well, that won't work, but it's only my first attempt at creating possible scenarios! Let's try another.*

Perhaps a more positive one.

With all his might Henry released any thoughts and soon a scene appeared wherein he arrived safely inside Poppy's living room. *To my surprise, Poppy greets me with a gun to my face. I slowly place my finger up to my lips in a gesture to be quiet. Then, I poke at the printed picture of his two daughters on my shirt. Poppy looks down and reads, "It's okay Poppy, I'm a friend of your daughters, I'm here to rescue you and Juan."*

Poppy looks up into my eyes, hesitates then nods his head okay. This time, Juan is sleeping. Poppy motions me to follow him into the bedroom and carefully he picks the child up so he doesn't awaken him. We're huddle together and are beamed up successfully!

Now that's better, Henry thought. *But, wait, there's no printing shops on board...perhaps a holographic print... somehow?*

Henry kept this up for about three hours. Good scenarios and bad ones. What weapon(s) should he take? Should he go during a changing of the guards? Should he try to drug Poppy and Juan? All that was weighing on his mind, yet he can't shake his most worrisome question. *What if I get caught and...and die? I'll never see Teresa again.*

Henry started to receive a telepathic message. It was from Dawn. "Henry, Actok informed me you are going on a dangerous mission. Thank you.

"Sorry we don't have time to grab a cup of coffee and talk of our brief time we shared. You are a great asset to me, Henry, and know I am anxious to go on yet another mission with you by my side. Know this—you are an invaluable asset to this cause and its with great honor I say the Prime Creator smiles when we discuss our dear Henry!"

Henry was glad he was alone, his face turned beet red with embarrassment and love.

88

∞

Notes: at least forty pages of reference, then twenty more YouTube videos that I took notes on. It's beginning to form a huge pile.

Found I made a mistake in my timing on this story! Mentioned it to my authors club and was surprised how many people have gone through the same thing! It also surprised me how many could offer me ways of fixing the story without too much work! Love this group.

I'm apprehensive lately, wondering if this story will ever mean anything to anyone, or is it actually just for me? You know, a way of expressing my innermost feelings.

I hate the thought of proofreading this whole book, geez, then getting it published! Yikes. Honestly, when I started writing I did not seriously think of this going to print. It was more of an exercise, a determination to finish a story started so many years ago.

Must say, it's the authors club's fault I even thought of getting my book "out there." All their talk of success, it's addictive!

∞

89

Henry always got uneasy right before saying the words, "Energize." He didn't like not being in control, and certainly wasn't when his entire body changed into molecules, was transported, then reassembled somewhere else. The Pleiadians had adopted the word from our *Star Trek* TV series. They consider it very funny.

When his ears stopped ringing and he felt like a whole person again, an assessment ensued. *Damn, Actok's good. I'm right where I'm supposed to be; in Dawn's bedroom.* He listened before moving and heard shuffling noises outside the apartment. He walked over to the window and observed armed guards walking around. There were two military jeeps parked right outside. Henry knew no one could have entered Dawn's apartment, what with the security system Actok had immediately implemented after the abductions.

He stood near the doorway. From this angle it was easy to scan the room perfectly. Spotting the computer on the desk table, he started walking over to the bed, but stopped. He froze, immediately feeling edgy then tense. For a full minute Henry listened...nothing. He rationalized it was just his nerves and continued to walk to the table where he unplugged the computer and put it in his backpack.

Henry stood for a moment and closed his eyes. Concentrating only on the cuneiform, he remotely viewed the entire house and found where Renu had hidden it—under the kitchen sink. Renu had installed a concrete box beneath the plywood where she knew the cuneiform would be safe.

Henry walked into the kitchen and over to the sink, knelt down, and was in the process of lifting the plywood when he sensed a presence. His frequency levels went on high alert. Tilting his head left, he noticed a figure wearing a pair of jeans standing right next to him. His eyes cautiously traveled up to see the face of the intruder. It was Khacee. Henry stood up to where they were eye to eye. They both looked at each other in complete surprise. They laughed and exchanged a hug. "Hey man, what are you doing here?" Khacee whispered.

Henry replied, "First, let me get my bearings. I didn't expect to find you here." Henry took a deep breath. "But to answer your question, I'll bet it's the same reason you are; to obtain the cuneiform. So, what happened? Thought you couldn't make this mission."

"Yeah, well, not to brag or anything, but my message was to the point, it didn't leave much open for debate. So, the issue was solved." Khacee looked around the room. "But hey, listen, seems you were sent in my place, and you found it, so it looks like you got this under control, mind if I just...leave?"

Henry gave his old friend a curious look, "Khacee, I know you. What are you up to?"

Khacee knew he couldn't hide much from Henry, "You might as well know..."

"Wait, let me guess. Am I right in assuming you're on a rogue mission?"

"Ah, can't get much past you, can I?" Khacee replied. "Since I accomplished my mission back home, there was free time. My thought was I'd come down here to find the cuneiform, then find out what I could about this Vasile guy and this Yahg he's got with him. You know, infiltrate his organization, get his confidence, and report back to Actok my findings. Might speed things along, ya know?" Both knew what this statement indicated; that Actok was in need of help.

Henry asked, "So you know the code, too?"

Khacee replied, "Well...no, but I've figured out harder things than that!"

Henry couldn't hide his smirk. He felt he finally had a heads-up on his friend. Khacee let him have his moment. He really did have other, more pressing matters to worry about.

Henry offered, "Khacee, let me help."

Khacee shook his head, "Henry, I know what you're thinking, and thanks, but right now you've got to get this cuneiform back to the ship. Even if you beamed it up and stayed with me, who's gonna protect Dawn like you? I trust her with you more than anyone else. So, for right now, do this for me. Let me do this knowing she's safe, okay?"

Henry was honored that Khacee thought so highly of him. He also knew the cuneiform was only part of his mission. He gave Khacee a pat on the back, "Sure, sure, Khacee." They gave each other a last look, then Khacee disappeared.

Henry then turned his attention to the task at hand. He removed the plywood and noticed a plastic box over the cuneiform. He tried to pick it up but it wouldn't budge. With intense concentration, he initiated a frequency level four times higher than his norm, forcing the box to open. Henry immediately visualized Dawn programming the box with a code. He noticed a very small indentation on the side of the cuneiform with letters. Henry entered T-O-M-E. Retrieving the cuneiform, he placed it along with the backpack and said, "Beam 'em up, Scottie."

At the precise moment Henry beamed into Poppy's house, the guards were preoccupied with the changing of their shifts. They were all talking amongst themselves and didn't notice the faint, static noise generated by the beam. This was all the diversion Henry needed. Actok's timing was perfect. So far, so good.

Henry found himself in the small bathroom area off the kitchen. He heard a TV on but when he slowly entered the living room, it was dark and quiet. He followed the noise to a bedroom but no one was there. That's when Henry realized Poppy and Juan were in the bunker!

"Now...where's that bunker? Henry closed his eyes and scanned the room with his mind. *"Ah, right behind this bedroom closet!"* Henry walked toward the back of the walk-in-closet and just stood there. Closing his eyes once more, he pulsated a frequency wave across the back wall which resulted in the door quietly sliding sideways, allowing him entrance. He found Poppy and Juan sound asleep on a futon bed.

This was not the first time Henry had to awaken a sleepy human. He remembered far too well the chaos with his first encounter. This time he was more prepared. Henry slowly walked over to the bed and immediately stuck a small device near Poppy's nose and squeezed. An aroma, much like that of cloves, was emanated, the fumes directly streamed into Poppy's nose with each breath. Poppy didn't have a shot; he was drugged prior to waking.

Reacting to the stimulant, Poppy's body shuddered. When he opened his eyes and noticed Henry, he was immobile and could only watch as Henry infused Juan with the same aroma.

Then he stood near the edge of the bed, waved hello and pointed to his T-shirt, which read, "Hello Poppy, I'm Henry. I'm here to take you and Juan to your daughters."

90

∞

My research has enlightened me to the fact that all who inhabit the Earth, be they considered humans, humanoids, hybrids, are already a Starseed. Every Starseed knew when coming here that they would not remember who they really are. It was purposely fashioned that way. Almighty God created this Earth as a free-willed planet, giving you a choice to work on your predetermined challenges to seek a higher self. Some get here with good intentions, but succumb to wealth and power, and lose all interest in their soul. Others tune into their psyche and work diligently to overcome their challenges.

Seekers like myself are always feeling the nudge to find out about our true identity and purpose. Is mine to write this story? Or was my challenge my mother? We successfully met that challenge, and to date it was the hardest in my life.

It's actually helped me tremendously to realize that when I'm confronted with a challenge, it's up to me to take responsibility for it and work through it. When I do, I feel freedom from the burden and...enlightenment regarding its purpose on my journey!

Ever wonder why you chose to be born at this particular

time on Earth? Do you really believe you were just a product of your mom and dad having fun? Have you ever said, "I didn't ask to be born?"

Do you feel apprehension for the future of our species? Do you ever think that perhaps you being on this planet at this time is vital? It is!

Let's ponder the future of the human race. How do you perceive your children or grandchildren will live out a lifetime here? Will you agree with me that even now it seems no matter where you go, no matter what time of day or night, almost all of us are texting with our cell phones, reading from some type of computer, playing with virtual reality goggles and own smart speakers?

Even the youngest are being taught on handheld tablets or computers. Perhaps soon the only source of education you will need is the internet. Could this eliminate the need for schools?

Look around you. Conversation between humans is less than ever. There is a symbiosis occurring and we'd better pay attention. Technology and humans are fusing together at a fanatical rate.

There are now companies introducing technology to embed computer chips into our brains, inject our blood with tiny cholesterol-eating nanobots, build synthetic limbs controlled by our minds, and use genetic editing tools like CRISPR to modify our genome, and quite literally engineer an enhanced version of ourselves!

Soon all the technology that lives outside our body—smartphones, hearing aids, reading glasses watches and such—will be incorporated INTO our bodies to such an extent that we will no longer be able to consider ourselves homo sapiens!

You don't believe this, do you? Well, if you tell someone you got your information from the "internet", what do they ask? "How do you know it's accurate?"

What reply can you give? Try asking, "Where do you get

YOUR information?"

What I've found so shocking is that we don't have to wait till the government and private sectors impose on us this technology. We're voluntarily desiring this for ourselves! Watch some YouTube videos of people already utilizing their embedded technology.

So, is there any good news with all this highly advanced technology? Sure. The rise in environmental technologies can allow us cleaner energy. Our drinking water, dairy, meat, and vegetable products will be processed more efficiently, allowing for longer shelf time. They might even find the cure for cancer in our time due to a new scientific treatment, genomic medicine.

Now, of course, the companies in charge of these technological advances can impose on humans a price for these amenities. Those in charge will mandate that you wear a mark, perhaps the same mark being prophesied for ages—666, that of the Antichrist! And if you don't? You huddle in groups that survive in an "underground society."

Without the identifying Chip, not only can't you purchase the basics but you won't get a license, a mortgage, nothing! Even now as I write this, we are being forced with mandates for this and mandates for that. How do YOU feel about being told you need a vaccine card that allows you access to travel, go to sporting events, etc.? What's next? It's a slippery slide, folks...

If you believe this to be true, what a bleak future for mankind. If you don't, what do you see? Reflect for a minute.

What if it were true?

I've never done this before: I'm finding myself outside almost every night, looking up at the sky. The stars, their clusters, never meant much; but now, with all this research, I'm appreciating them. I'm praying to my Almighty God and stretching my arms out to the universe, allowing all my worries and requests to be released. I'm loving that!

∞

91

∞

Since typing my first word of this novel in December 2018 to now, our planet has plunged dramatically into chaos: the COVID-19 scenario (which in my opinion was purposely imposed upon us), and the aftershock of its implications, along with a political unrest never before witnessed to this extent, demonstrate to me that we are in the end of this system of things.

Even suffering with persistent vertigo for over six straight weeks, I have been writing. An urgency has come upon me to keep writing. Now, three days without vertigo, I plan to do just that!

Our world is experiencing a downward, depressive trend. It's not intended that my story be a definition of this, but more that we become mass-mindful of how responsible each and every one of us are to its outcome!

On a lighter note: I have forwarded excerpts of my story to members in my authors club and have been offered tremendous feedback.

I've touched on who/what is Vasile. Much thought was placed on whether I should detail what Vasile would say to the populace regarding the Rapture. I wasn't interested in reiterating the event. So, please research online and in religious books, perhaps your church, and draw your conclusions from your findings.

Hey, I can't do ALL the work for you. I think of the information in this book as "the seed". You're being offered hundreds of hours of my research but you must "bloom" by informing yourself and opening your mind and heart to new possibilities.

92

Vasile had given the order to release Linda from jail, only to take her into his custody. When Linda heard of this, she erased any thought of escape. She knew there were no options when confronted with him and his sidekick, Jaqui.

Linda doesn't know how she awoke in a car, but realized right away she was blindfolded, frightened, and drugged. Her movements were slow and each caused a wave of nausea. No one spoke and she knew better than to engage in conversation.

With every new movement of the vehicle, her nausea prevented her ability to concentrate. *If only I could sense where I am, perhaps...*but she had no idea where she was, and the drug inhibited her detection abilities.

Vasile was no fool; he wasn't taking any chances with this alien from Lacerta. Hence, Linda lost all hope that she would live to see another day.

When the car stopped and her door opened, Linda immediately felt a tugging on her legs. There was something cold wrapped around her ankles—chains! She moved both legs and noticed they weren't locked. Without any warning, someone picked her up and threw her over their shoulder. Their hold was intense; she knew it futile to scream or even cry.

It wasn't long when she felt her body being taken down stairs. Without sight, it was the sense of smell that told her wherever she was going it was damp and enclosed.

Still on the shoulders of her captor, Linda heard a clinking, like that of many keys. After a few seconds, a door creaked. Before sensing anything else, Linda felt a massive jolt to her body when thrown down onto a stone floor. Both her right shoulder and hip bounced twice, while the chains dragged and dug deep into her ankles. She felt something...wait, huge hands grabbed her ankles and dragged her a few feet. The chains tugged somewhat, lacerating her skin, as she realized they were locking. The slamming of the door produced a scream she didn't know she possessed.

Panicked, she immediately took off the blindfold, only to find she was in complete darkness. Dazed from the drugs, weak from hunger, Linda just lay there on the cold ground. Was her body going into shock? She was about to cry, but then a strange thought made her chuckle—*Why would anyone want to be human? They're so helpless in a crisis!*

Another thought, this one more aligned with her predicament, popped into her head. *I'm in a room...a cell, a...a dungeon. It's dank, musty. Knowing Vasile, this is his compound, but I have no idea where I am.*

Further thought on why Vasile hadn't murdered her already made her realize something horrible; there was going to be torture first!

With blood oozing onto the chains, Linda carefully stood up. Not an easy task, what with the chains digging into her skin with every move. *No broken bones, just dizziness, great,* she sarcastically thought. The deafening silence was broken only by the sound of the shackles rattling as she moved.

Blinded by darkness, the only way to realize her environment was to slide one foot in front of the other while both hands were stretched out in front as a bumper shield. Steadying herself, it didn't take long to knock into a softness on the floor. After a few gentle kicks, she bent down and was glad to realize it was a mattress. She felt around for a blanket, a pillow, a sheet. Nothing.

Now on both knees, Linda felt all around the mattress to satisfy the curiosity of its size. When her hand reached an edge, something moved, yet it didn't make any noise. Fearful of an animal or insect, she slowly moved to the opposite side of the mattress, and with one great swoop, attempted to lift the mattress off the floor. The mattress was much heavier than she imagined but she did hear something roll onto the floor, then silence. She didn't dare move. Her ears were on high alert. Silence. In an instant, Linda felt a weight grab around the back of her leg, just below the knee, followed by an intense pain of a bite. Before she passed out, she could have sworn something was sucking on her leg.

Upon awakening, Linda found herself still in the darkened room. She screamed in terror. Shaking violently, she threw up. Her leg was swollen to the touch and extremely hot. She was sweating profusely. She passed out again.

Linda awoke when she heard someone unlocking the cell door. A mountain of a man came barging in. Linda could barely see the light in the doorway for his size. She tried to sit up but couldn't; she felt extremely weak.

This massive beast of a man stomped over to the mattress, grabbed his prisoner around the waist and lifted her up to a seating position. Without giving her a moment to react, he leaned in and whispered, "Guess you met Brutus." With that one statement, Linda felt yet another sting, but this time it was an injection. "This will help you sleep."

After he pulled the needle out, he said, "Here's some food. I'll check on you in a few hours." Starving, Linda could faintly see the plate and grabbed the food. The beast watched as she ate without questioning.

The beast continued, "Once Brutus strikes, he doesn't care to bother you again."

Linda hardly heard him, with some food oozing out of her mouth, she was lulled into a deep calmness and started to feel the sensation of her body falling sideways, then...nothing.

Twelve hours later Linda woke to the sound of the beast unlocking the cell door. Some light came through as he hesitated near the door. He reminded Linda of a cyclops; a monster of a man with a huge face and only one eye in the middle of his forehead.

A quick movement near her feet turned her attention, and for the first time Linda saw Brutus, just a few feet away, peering into her eyes. Traveling from galaxy to galaxy, she had been exposed to thousands of creatures, but this...form...this almost human form, she had never seen before. He was maybe three feet tall, no arms, huge eyes, no hair, but a mouth surrounded by fatty gums that constantly but silently opened and closed. His legs bent inward at the knees, while his feet bent outward. No smell emanated from him. He was truly repulsive.

When Brutus saw the beast walk over to the prisoner he bent down and scurried to a dark area of the cell and made no further attempt at movement or sound.

Linda, tried to sit up but immediately peed, then defecated. Her leg felt numb. Finally, she sat up and submissively waited.

Her captor came closer, noticed her condition and announced, "Pig, you're being presented today. Get up. Here, wash yourself." The beast threw a wet rag in Linda's lap. She hurriedly rubbed the cold cloth all over her face and neck, then started to use it on her body.

The beast bent down and unlocked the ankle chains. He didn't react to the smell of the body fluids. She realized then he wasn't human. He stood up and grabbed Linda's right arm and lifted her off the mattress. This humongous creature towered over her, and when he again threw her over his shoulders, she knew he was the one who had carried her to the dungeon.

While upside down on the back of this creature, Linda fought in vain to gain a bearing; but the nausea was overpowering her thought process. She dared not vomit. A few deep breaths kept the queasiness at bay.

Vasile was standing in a jury chamber; a hologram room, created to play out his scenario. You could tell he was anxious, angry.

Upon entering the jury room, Linda could barely focus when forced to stand up alone. Feeling like throwing up, she did, but it was only bile. She almost passed out from the open-handed slap she received from her captor.

Forced to her knees, she swayed and hung her head down, waiting.

Walking in a slow circle around Linda, Vasile leaned in and picked up her chin. "Look around. There is no escape. Today is your judgement day; your day of reckoning has arrived!

"You know why I have released you from jail? Because I will be your judge and jury. You have failed me...twice." He released her head with such force she fell to the ground and started wailing. Oblivious, he continued, "Your father would be very disappointed even if I were to consider sending you back to Lacerta! A trial would ensue, the judgement would be delivered..." Leaning on one knee, he picked Linda's head up by her hair, and placed his face alongside hers, exclaiming, "...then...to the devastating humiliation of your family and friends, you'd be annihilated."

Linda's head was slammed to the ground just hard enough that she didn't pass out. Vasile stood up and started to walk around her. His face was contorted. There was more of this abuse to come.

Looking up into Vasile's eyes, Linda started to show submission to her plight. Silent tears spilled down her cheeks as she licked the salt on her lips. Slowly the drug was wearing off. She rolled herself up into a sitting position. Her head was bleeding. The pain was excruciating.

Vasile turned to face Linda and leaned in once again, grabbed her hair and...was interrupted by a cough coming from the right side of the room. He looked over angrily and saw Jaqui coming toward him. This time, the force to shove Linda was so great, her head crashed to the ground, causing her to black out.

Vasile was surprised when Jaqui quickly stated, "Whoa, hold on there. I don't think you're seeing the benefits in keeping this one alive."

"Explain."

"She's a devotee, you don't get many of them nowadays. She's like a dog, Vasile. She'll take the abuse, the little bones you throw at her, and go back to do your bidding, over and over. To kill her now is a waste of talent."

Vasile reflected, considering his options. "She's sloppy, downright stupid!" Jaqui let him have his moment.

Vasile had to admit, Jaqui made a good point. "Okay, but someone has to take her and train her properly, I don't have the time."

"I'll take that responsibility, Vasile. I'll teach her in my ways. I'll supervise her directly. You're going to need someone with superior abilities, like mine, if you're to defeat this enemy we know is coming. Who better to assist me than a Terran from Lacerta? She...Dawn won't fight a physical war, you know this, but her tactics will induce one. Anyway, I can use a sidekick. Don't most great heroes have one?"

93

It's been almost three months Earth time since the mass exodus of humans disappeared. Christmas was a time of deep sorrow, the likes of which the world had never experienced. Businesses were folding, families were starving, depression was the norm.

The Rapture concept circulated throughout the globe. Believing that Almighty God removed his chosen off the planet pacified the masses. Needless to say, those left behind considered themselves unworthy but still hoped for answers. Even Vasile didn't challenge the biblical account. He used it to his advantage, twisting the event to align with his lies.

Earth's inhabitants quickly acclimated to his claim of being their savior. He embraced this title, using it constantly when seen on hologram projection screens all over the world.

Vasile successfully manipulated Earth's inhabitants with his well-rehearsed fabrications spoken in his soothing voice. His powerful presence and words were so believable that they calmed many a poor soul. If that didn't persuade one to join him, Jaqui would. Rumors were ramped that Jaqui was a satanic alien.

No one on planet Earth now questioned the existence of aliens living among them. You couldn't, they were arriving daily in huge ships or were presenting themselves to Earthlings in their true form. The aliens living underwater were now establishing terrain bases everywhere. Why not come out of hiding? As expected, some were benevolent, some not.

President Fredericks had resigned himself to the fact that his wife, two children, his father, and sister were taken in the Rapture. His mother was beside herself with grief, and he felt hopeless to comfort her. Despite all his loss, he continued to face the populace with stamina and courage every day.

Regrettably, every minute that went by, he was made to look foolish with his cry, "Everything is under control." The people didn't believe everything was under control; they were way beyond being mollified. They wanted an understanding of why it happened. A "what's next" approach to help them acclimate to this epic pandemonium that had been forced upon them.

Obtaining intel from the military, his staff, and the millions of calls being screened down in the basement's War Room took time.

There was so much destruction during the Rapture, what with airplanes crashing into homes and buildings, trains colliding, auto accidents, and suicides, that millions were kept busy cleaning up the mess with very little compensation.

Funeral parlors had resorted to applying dry ice procedures until they could properly give a burial. All too many reports were noted of people bringing their deceased loved ones to a parlor and walking away, never to return.

Couple that with the virus threats like Ebola, HIV, norovirus, and monkeypox plaguing the Earth, which had left many wishing they were dead and endangering the limited supply of vaccines.

The worst menace preying on Americans was Jaqui. Secret military plans to seek out and destroy Vasile and Jaqui were thwarted; no one could locate them.

In the eyes of the populace, the once loved and well-respected President Fredericks had lost control to the new rising star and his ever-present subordinate. Other countries followed suit. The emissaries for all major countries succumbed to him. The people were demanding answers, Vasile was supplying them.

The most influential figures in the world of government, technology, medicine, and religion all clamored to meet this man. If given private audience, it was understood that he owned you.

Even with a heavily funded, secretive effort by the CIA to find Vasile's residence, the search led to a dead end.

President Fredericks had one ace in the hole, one ally his military didn't know anything about yet and he had not been given the go-ahead to inform them. He had agreed to play this charade until the timing was right. No one could know about the clandestine meeting with the Pleiadians in the War Room just a few hours ago. No one was to know the stage was being set.

94

I'm changing. I can feel it. It's a good change, I'm becoming more aware of how I present an argument, and the criticizing of others (a Virgo trait) has diminished immensely. I attribute this to my research.

Everything happens for a reason has become my mantra and everyone is on their own journey, my acquiesce.

∞

95

Tina Woods had just received her long-awaited promotion at the *Brooklyn Gazette*. In a hurried fanfare, Dan Katz announced she was now their lead investigative reporter. With that promotion and this worldwide event, Tina was given carte blanche with two assistants at her beck and call. Katz knew no one at the paper would work harder, seeing that all her family had been lost in the Rapture. Katz also felt he could keep Tina at bay, unlike Natalie Brown.

For Tina, this promotion came at a price; all thoughts of a personal life were lost to her now. Getting the "true story" was her driving goal. Katz didn't know Tina was attempting to document it all; she was writing a book!

Tina was savvy enough to know her looks had factored in this promotion. She was a size six, tall, with beautiful olive skin, long black hair and deep brown eyes.

Tina wasn't stupid; she knew Natalie was fired after performing that great piece of investigative work. She knew protecting her findings was paramount. So, she devised a plan: keep Katz hanging with tidbits of information, just enough to satisfy him and his readers, but delve deep enough to find the truth. She knew there was a story out there, and she wasn't afraid of the work.

96

Teresa was asleep in her room when she heard a slight knocking. She listened again and thought she heard, "Mommy?" She sat up and listened once more. "Mommy?"

Teresa ran to the door and quickly opened it. Overwhelmed with the vision standing there, she immediately fell to her knees. Oh, the joy! "Juan!" she screamed. "Juan!" In an instant, she had him in her arms. Tears were flowing down their faces. Juan hugged her so tight she could barely breath.

When she looked around, she noticed Henry and her father standing nearby. She released Juan and ran into her father's embrace. Teresa was besides herself with happiness.

Angelicia heard Teresa's screaming Juan's name and started running toward her sister's room. When she saw the gathering, she too started screaming with joy. She grabbed Juan in her arms and hugged him so tight. What a reunion, what elation.

Angelicia then handed Juan to Teresa as she ran over to her father. Tears flowing down their cheeks, they just held onto each other. Teresa looked over at Henry, and when their eyes locked, she communicated, "How? How is this possible? Oh, Henry, I just know this is your doing. Somehow, you're responsible for this...for my happiness. Thank you, thank you with all my heart."

Henry took total advantage of Teresa's embrace.

Prior to writing, I like to listen to Enigma or Enya. The music gets my juices flowing and allows me to create scenes. Yet, lately, my family gets upset with me when I try to play games. I cringe while the loud music is playing and I'm trying to decipher whose turn it is. That's because...they start talking on top of the music and the game. Geez. Okay, I'm getting older, everything's bothering me!

∞

97

Oonsay, an Eben, arrived battered and bruised from his collision with an asteroid headed straight for Earth. He was commissioned to intercept Coppevi's trajectory, forcing it to shift away between Jupiter and Mars. His craft suffered damage, but still landed safely in Antarctica, where he was picked up and taken to Actok's ship. The inhabitants of Earth were shocked to learn the asteroid was only 3,852 miles away. How much more would they have been shocked if they had known how close to death they had been?

Oonsay had traveled from Zeta Reticuli to Earth, a 39.5 light-year journey for humans—for him, three Earth days. His ancient race existed outside Earth's space-time continuum; meaning, in part, that it was very difficult to even detect them, and although considered skilled warriors, they avoided confrontation.

This particular species were not the beings considered the little grays. They were tall, at least eight feet, with large, black, almond-shaped eyes, a pear-shaped head, and four fingers. Their skin color varied; some were brown, pale green, or the most common color, a dull ashen gray. What separated Oonsay from the grays was the foulest of descriptions—he looked like a praying mantis!

The Ebens were telepathic in nature and masters of psychic phenomena. The Ebens and the Pleiadians had aligned themselves to the preservation of Earth and all that reside upon it eons ago. They were the best-known environmentalists out there.

What made Oonsay so valuable was his ability to move not only small but massive objects. It didn't hurt that he could shapeshift at will.

Oonsay was a very friendly Eben known throughout hundreds of galaxies. He was your go-to alien.

Actok was anxious for Oonsay to meet his guests and other members of his crew. Yet he was aware that just the sight of his friend would frighten everyone on board. He suggested to Oonsay to use his telepathic ability to have them "see" him prior to their meeting. This tactic worked and when they were introduced, no one demonstrated any hesitation in shaking his claw-shaped hand. Nor were they concerned about his apparent bruises.

When Actok was alone with Oonsay, he took notice of his fragile condition and was torn about assigning him to another tour of duty: transporting Renu, Rosalee, and Kristian back to the ship. He thought of Henry but felt it prudent to allow him time with Teresa and her family.

Actok's fears were soon dissipated, as after only two days of rest, Earth time, Oonsay was ready for the task.

Even though Light Warriors were aware they were not from Earth originally, some alien forms would still appear visually repulsive. And, without the presence of Actok to introduce him, Oonsay realized he'd better apply his highly advanced telepathic ability to prepare Renu, Kristian, and Rosalee for his encounter. Through mental visual presentations they became used to his appearance and all went well with the transport.

Getting ready to Awaken Dawn now. This is the hardest part of my story...well, so far. She's truly not aware of her magnificent spiritual legacy. How do I incorporate the qualities you know about her into the makings of the Bringer of Light, yet keep her...approachable? I believe I mentioned this before...but see? It's a...predicament!

I am entrenched in this novel now. I find daily the question arises...did I write today? If I'm busy and an idea comes into my head, I hurriedly stop and grab a sticky note to jot down the thought.

Have to admit, I've been thinking of little else...

∞

98

One thing was clear: Vasile had relied on Katz to propagate his message and Katz took full advantage of the notoriety and financial gain. In his attempt to justify the relationship, Katz willfully overlooked the daily backstabbing practices and under the table deals that caused millions to go bankrupt, get kicked out of their homes, or die from lack of food and medical attention. Up to this point, Katz had kept this inside knowledge to himself but now, he was feeling ashamed.

Katz was also fully aware of the rumors that underground safehouses were popping up all over the world. Tina Woods even supplied him the location of one such place. From what Katz could ascertain, Vasile's spies were unable to locate these sanctuaries...yet, and he wasn't about to tell him either.

It all climaxed for Katz the day he inadvertently heard Jaqui discuss Linda's ordeal and threaten a senator with the same treatment. He also came to realize his suspicions were true; that Dawn Coleman was their target. He wasn't privy to where she was taken, but now knew that she was definitely among the abductees snatched off the porch that night.

He listened long enough to learn of the league of evil entities preparing to invade the world. They were arriving in droves, all to have an audience with Jaqui and if approved, with Vasile.

Katz called for a clandestine meeting with the only people he knew to trust, Detective Aimes, Inky, and Tina Woods. The meeting took place in a secured conference room at the *Brooklyn Gazette*.

Tina was introduced to Inky and Detective Aimes. When Katz started to introduce Inky to the detective, he was surprised to hear Inky say, "We've met."

After a few cordial conversations Katz said, "Okay, now that we're acquainted, lets delve into it. I'll start. Vasile is evil incarnate and his sidekick Jaqui is a personified killing machine. I've seen them both in action."

The three were speechless. For Katz to admit he'd been wrong... "I know I've been in with them thick as thieves and yes, I've benefited from my association." Katz hesitated and held his head down. "I can't do it anymore. I...honestly, I didn't understand the scope of this man's plan. I was tricked just like the masses into thinking he was our liberator. It wasn't until recently..."

Katz looked up at his little group, "Vasile is Satan's voice, his protégé, yes the Antichrist. He's directing Satan's plan to annihilate all unnecessary inhabitants and make cyborg and hybrid slaves of the rest.

"Only recently was I able to see Jaqui in action behind the scenes. You've only been privy to his being able to expose a person lying, you've seen his torturous approaches, but I've seen his strategic military mind at work. He's gaining an army of millions right now, alien species of all types with different...ah, abilities."

Aimes shouted, "I knew it! I just knew it! Not that I was a believer in ancient prophecy but this was foretold, right? We're actually living on this Earth during this predicted time! These characters...these creatures do exist. Look at the ones we're starting to see taking over our way of life! It's unbelievable how we're adapting, just accepting this as our norm. Jesus."

Tina leaned in and added, "I can only believe it was by divine intervention that I stumbled onto the underground city in Italy. How else? Why hasn't Vasile's people been able to?

I heard there were what's being referred to as Light Warriors Awakening Starseeds. I'm using all my resources to seek out other such sites. I've got another lead in China, also by accident. Some woman named Reenu or Raynu, is supposedly heading up millions to do this Awakening thing."

Inky knew but he didn't say anything as he looked pleadingly at Katz. Katz could tell Inky wasn't ready to reveal himself as a Light Warrior, so he kept his mouth shut.

Katz continued, "It's obvious now that Vasile has chosen America for his control center, knowing most of the world follows our lead. The political unrest and divide in our own country are the likes of which we've never seen. As we try to inform our readers, the disrespect for law and order has developed into anarchy, infuriating an already suppressed population. But what I have come to know is Vasile was allowing this upheaval, he controlled the damn narrative, the perception, and realized how, with that control, he singlehandedly could rule the world. And that's exactly what he's done."

Detective Aimes said, "Seems to me the time to get Vasile is now before his army is fortified any further! You know, I could advise President Fredericks on what we have figured out. Katz, you know I've worked with the man on many occasions. He can be trusted."

"Yes, I believe that's true. Does anyone have anything to say to the contrary?"

No reply. "Good. You follow up on that and let us know what he's planning and if we can help."

Katz got quiet. His head looking down at the table, he mumbled, "There's something else."

Aimes questioned, "What? What is it, Katz?"

"Not sure how, but I feel I'm being watched. Vasile has

been slowly but surely pulling away from me; as you know I was there by his side daily for quite a while. It's as if he doesn't trust me anymore. I suppose that's a good thing but of course I wonder, am I in danger now?"

The room was devoid of any sound as everyone was in deep thought. Then Tina said, "We can find out. I'll send my best trackers…"

"No Tina. I'll not lose another employee."

With that, the group looked at him. The cat was out of the bag. With all eyes on him, Katz admitted, "Dawn, Dawn Coleman. I believe she was abducted on the porch along with the others."

"That's where…" Tina stopped talking and scribbled frantically on her pad. Her mind drifted to all the facts she now could categorize.

Katz continued, "Anyway, we've got to be careful now. I think Vasile is too busy to really worry about me right at this moment, being fully focused on implementing his New World Order system. And I want nothing but to get back to my world, my paper, and view life from an easier platform: the written word."

The group agreed to meet every third day at a local upscale pub called Nicky's to keep abreast of any new developments. They all felt it was too dangerous to meet again at the paper.

99

∞

I've mentioned that planet Earth is experiencing a virus, COVID-19.

It's not the lack of toilet paper, the six-foot distance rule or even the anxiety of wearing a mask that concerns me, it's the consequence of this manifestation upon us as a society.

What I'm experiencing as an elderly female, now writing a book about man's future, is the clarity in which I witness this event—knowing...well, okay, this is MY belief: alien entities have completely infiltrated every aspect of our lives. THEY have created the chaos we are living through now. It's THEM that feed, and gain strength from stealing our frequency/ energy.

All over the internet people are expressing their opinions on why Earthlings contracted this horrific virus. There is this theory that China didn't start this virus, it just happened to manifest there. This theory suggests that an asteroid that just missed Earth in January of 2020 was the culprit. While passing us, it released smaller asteroids that landed on Earth with devastating virus-producing material.

Another theory is China deliberately did this in retaliation for President Trump embarrassing them: stating to the world that they cheated, lied and stole from us for years, and he was going to stop it.

The conspiracy theories go so far as to propose that our Almighty God, our Jehovah, or however you wish to call Him, ordered this to happen!

I delved further into other theories to extrapolate that position. Seems we, as Earth-bound citizens, needed a "wake-up call," a reprimand that had to be unilaterally applied. We were on a collision course; the negative band of our collective frequencies was so loud and chaotic that it was interfering with the balance of the universe! Our Almighty God needed to put a halt to our way of life. Literally, our way of life! A mass-consciousness attempt to stop the madness.

What if it were true?

Did you know that the last time Pluto transitioned the degree of Capricorn the American Revolution occurred? That the last time Uranus transited Taurus was the end of our Great Depression? That the last time Neptune transited Pisces the major movement to end American slavery started taking place?

Do you see what I see? Do you believe the Earth's shifting polarities are at work here? We're shifting now! Some reports indicate more than ever before! So, what does it mean that we're transitioning from Pisces to Aquarius? What will history record as this time for us?

100

In the weeks since they met, Katz and Inky had become good friends. Katz was very impressed with Inky's running of the paper in his absence!

The end of the day was fast approaching at the *Brooklyn Gazette* and Katz was a little surprised to realize Vasile hadn't asked for an audience in a few days.

Inky said, "Let's go get something to eat, I'm hungry. You run a tight ship, Katz, but let's get out of here."

"Yeah, all right," Katz replied. "Let's stay close to here though. How about checking out Nicky's before our first meeting with the group?"

"Anywhere, sure."

Walking the two blocks from the paper, the two of them got into an intense discussion of man's future. Entering Nicky's, Katz asked, "But what's its true meaning, Inky? More governmental control? A socialist takeover? I heard talk of wearing the Mark, so could this chip be...the Mark? It's rumored now that without this device one won't have access to food, education, money, nothing. It's also supposed to contain one's personal information, right down to the mole on your ass."

The waiter recognized Katz immediately and for the first

time offered their best table, away from the crowd and private. Walking over to their table, Katz lowered his voice and leaned into his friend, "It's true, isn't it? There's gonna be an embedded piece of equipment in our body in our near future?"

Inky didn't reply, and when he sat down, Katz noticed his demeanor had changed. A sad look was on his face. Almost inaudibly, he replied, "You'd better sit down before I answer, friend. In the near future, you won't believe what's coming your way."

Katz looked intently at Inky as he sat in his chair. His glare was interrupted as the waiter stood over them ready to take their drink and food orders. Katz took a moment to look around and was glad to see they were enjoying an atmosphere of anonymity. One could not detect who was sitting in those seats, what with the wooden room divider shielding the area. It was known that this section was for the who's who—that didn't want to be noticed!

Inky started the conversation up again as he took the first sip of his rum and coke. Katz was lifting his scotch and water up to his mouth when Inky stated, "You have been listening to me for a while now and I'm honored, Katz, really. You know a lot more about me, too. Guess you've noticed I've been staying out of your spotlight. I must. Too much is at stake and a run-in with Vasile..."

Katz put down his drink and stared at his friend. "Go on, Inky. I think you know you can trust me. You don't see anything quoted in my paper from you, I don't speak to Vasile of you. So, what? What's going to happen to us, you know, us...and...and this planet?"

Inky stated emphatically, "The Chip will become the norm by 2024, Katz. All the bullshit talks about it linking us to Vasile are true. He'll know everything, manage everyone. He'll use it as his weapon of choice. No need for armies or even bloodshed, not with beings like Jaqui at his command. This will be a war of wars, true, but unlike any man's history has encountered. It's not like man hasn't been warned this time would come. For thousands of years, we've had prophets, shamans, books predicting the gloom and doom that we're witnessing right now. Well, it's here, Katz. You're actually living in the last days of Earth as you know it."

101

The waiter coughed, which prompted Katz and Inky to stop their conversation and place their order.

When the waiter walked away, Inky continued, "Prior to the introduction of Vasile, only the elite or geek radicals were exploring how an embedded computer chip would eliminate the need for numerous electronical devices. Now? This device, and other replications are being manufactured in the private sector!

"Underground markets and the very rich are already selling devices for an astronomical fee: the more technology built into it, the more it would cost. Naturally, adults would vie for such a device, it would make their lives easier.

"Imagine a woman cooking dinner: with a wave of her hand, the programmed chip enables her to read the time, preheat the stove, answer an incoming call, and turn on the TV all while standing in one spot. Then, when done with dinner, turn on the dishwasher, and turn off the light.

"A man could wake up to his alarm playing a prearranged music station, review his phone messages, turn on the bathroom light, start the shower water, then turn the light off when done. That's all before he goes to his office (be it in-house or not)! Who WOULDN'T want the Chip?

"Now, the children. Can you picture this? In the near future, your kids are begging for Chips as presents. Even if you tried to reason with your kids, warning that people have died using them, all they'd see are the really popular kids in school showing off their Chips' attributes all day long. Try saying 'No, they're not good for you. You'll understand when you get a little older.' Sure, that'll work!"

Katz leaned back in his seat and ran his hands through his hair. "Damn. Everything's happening so fast. I'm too old for this shit. I'll admit it, I'm tired. So, what do you know about Vasile, Inky? Don't hesitate, you can tell me. I think we're on the outs anyway."

"He's Satan personified! A foretold creature of evil here to do the work of destroying this planet from within. Some say he's a rogue warrior while others think Satan created him! His plan is to create a league of cyborgs, hybrid robotic humans, with what's left of humanity."

Too bad, but both were oblivious to the true meaning of being given the best table Nicky's had to offer. Katz's ego was inflated, so he accepted this gesture as a perk of the business. He didn't have a clue that their every word was being recorded and the info would be forwarded to Vasile!

Good time to mention I just received a really cool gift: high tech ear plugs! Now, talk about not desiring new gadgets...

102

Oonsay was preparing for his arrival on Actok's ship. As with Kristian, Rosalee, and Renu, he telecommunicated to all he was coming aboard, eliminating any dramatic scenes when they first set eyes on him. Actok had simulated the same process on the group prior to their arrival when no one realized their nakedness.

The mission went smoothly. Oonsay was pleased he was actually ahead of schedule.

Kristian, Rosalee, and Renu had little time to get acquainted while on their flight to Antarctica, but the couple did inform Renu of their close call with Linda. Renu, in an effort to relax them, informed them of their growing popularity in the Starseed and Light Warrior underground communities.

Skyann watched as they stepped onto the ship and thought, *Gosh I hope they can help Dawn. She's so withdrawn. I haven't had much private time with her this week at all, Actok's been by her side. Wow, that's gotta be Renu; the other two are holding hands. Gee, Renu is different than what I expected. So small, so unassuming. You'd never guess she is at the forefront of the Light Warrior movement. She's shaking everyone's hands, better get over there.*

Dawn didn't meet the entourage; she hadn't left her quarters. For most of three days, Dawn had been sitting in her favorite position on a large pillow. If the group could see Dawn, they'd realize she wasn't withdrawn but very much in her element. Dawn was meditating day and night, getting ample sleep, and...chanting. Actok found his presence was not needed as much as just a few days ago! Dawn sat quietly today, waiting...waiting...

Actok requested everyone to meet for dinner after they had a chance to settle in. This would include Oonsay, Melek, Nocren, Saghi, and Gaff. Teresa and Juan sat next to Angelicia and Poppy. Henry sat alongside Teresa. Dr. Kaplan and Skyann sat across from one another, both realizing their feelings towards each other were getting stronger.

Missing was Dawn, and all just knew not to ask.

Within hours of their arrival, the group found themselves in a holographic dining room designed to make even the most defensive feel completely comfortable. The room was decorated as if it were hosting a Thanksgiving dinner, complete with a blazing fireplace. There was an ample display of foods intended to satisfy anyone's palate.

During dinner, one could not help but see Saghi was breathing rather heavily and didn't touch her food. She asked to be excused, stating she was tired. It also didn't go unnoticed that Nocren paid little heed to his wife's condition.

During dessert, Teresa sensed something exciting was about to happen. Her frequency levels rose even higher when a woman Juan had come to know as Nana approached and asked if he and Poppy would like to play with her. Juan readily agreed, and Poppy knew he wasn't going to be privy to what was coming. He stood up and looked at his two daughters. Passing Angelicia, she stood, and with all the love she had, put her arms around his neck and hugged him. Teresa reached for Juan and gave him a hug. Then she stood up and kissed her father on the cheek. Poppy continued his exit, nodding his head to Actok, who bowed in kind, and the three walked out of the room.

Teresa's senses heightened yet again. Henry, fully aware, took her hand, and held it tight. He wouldn't let go until he felt her grip relax.

Angelicia noticed this display, as very little passed her acute sense of awareness. Tonight, she had also witnessed Dr. Kaplan writing on a napkin and handing it to Skyann, and she in turn, wrote back to him. She couldn't miss the calmness of Kristian and Rosalee, who had fully acclimated to their new surroundings.

It was at this point Angelicia and Teresa received a telepathic transmission from Gaff, "All is well, all is as it should be." Teresa softened her hold on Henry.

After coffee, Actok stood up and slowly looked at each one of his guests. Then, almost in a whispered voice, announced, "It is an honor for me to be a part of this most exciting time in the history of Earth's evolution. Serving the Prime Creator with His plan to bring back to Earth His vision of unity and wonderous love has been my greatest privilege.

"Thank you Gaff and Melek for your steadfast patience and training, assisting this group of six, who are prepared now for what is their destiny. Oonsay, for eons, your willingness to perform a mission at a moment's notice has been one of my greatest assets."

Actok stopped talking and gazed over at the people he had come to know and love. After a few long stares, he stated, "I speak to my newest of friends now. You have not arrived at this point in life's journey by mistake; everything happens for a reason. Yes, from Dawn's early life, some of you started to enter her realm. Especially you, dear Skyann. You truly were her protector and we thank you."

Skyann blushed and looked at Dr. Kaplan. He was smiling.

"Dawn's mission on planet Earth, unbeknownst to her, was to raise awareness and gather you together. Regrettably, her ability to acquire Starseeds was cut short due to the untimely situation that occurred. But know this, our Prime Creator had ordained it so. Now, you are more aware of what her role really is—the Bringer of Light!"

Actok turned to address the sisters: "You two were no accident! Even I didn't realize what the Prime Creator had in store when I was forced to abduct you off the porch along with the others. But look what talents you are bringing to assist Dawn in her mightiest of endeavors. You might need them in your physical role. Still...there is more you will soon come to know.

"Kristian and Rosalee...look at them. A perfect match! Their hearts and souls are bound, both ready and willing to bring forth Starseeds into their true purpose! We honor you." With this, Actok bowed. Kristian and Rosalee stood up and bowed back.

Actok smiled and continued, "In the little time we have shared together, all of you have made life-altering choices. You learned you are Starseeds. Then, with realizing the plight of your planet, you made choices. First choice? Accepting this new reality, second, choosing to allow our guides to enhance your abilities.

"But, most of all, it's your third choice: the six of you expressing readiness to stand alongside Dawn in this period of Awakening. That choice, knowing the danger, is a tribute to your human spirit. The human spirit the Prime Creator values above all; as it decides with free will!"

Actok took time to again look at all present at the table. "All of you will empower planet Earth with the knowledge that the time has come, the inhabitants must choose: live life in the divine light of knowing, or accept surviving in spiritual darkness."

Stretching out his hands to all his guests, Actok announced, "Tonight, I ask my new friends to join with us in the most sacred of chambers. One that will open your eyes to see beyond time and space, life and death. I invite you to join us in the Isolytic Chamber, where you will get a...sense of the Prime Creator and all He is!

"But before we continue..." Actok slowly turned his head to his great friend. "Nocren..."

Nocren wasn't paying attention. His whole body was experiencing a pain he couldn't understand. It was mostly centered around his heart, but he could feel his pulse beating and his legs felt tingly, like they had gone to sleep. "Ah, Nocren..."

Nocren looked over to Actok and exclaimed, "Oh, yes, yes, Actok?"

"After deliberation with our Prime Creator, and with the full acceptance of my being, tonight I am stepping down as head of the Ministry of Enlightenment..."

"What? No, wait. Not now, Actok. Wait." Nocren couldn't take this news, news he's waited to hear, had even longed for. He stood up. Forgetting he was in the presence of a group who probably shouldn't hear any of his conversation, he cried, "Actok, please." Nocren looked beseechingly at his friend.

At first Actok was taken aback but quickly realized where Nocren's mind was—with Saghi. He too started feeling pain in his heart. Actok now recognized it was just an act between them not to acknowledge how sick she was. It was their way of handling the grief they knew was coming. Actok just bowed his head and said, "Of course, Nocren, of course."

103

∞

A blank page. I'm staring at a blank page. The question foremost on my mind is why the hesitation to keep going? Still looking up to the universe with arms stretched up high, I ask for help all the time.

So, I asked myself, does the need for help mean I feel this is going to be a hell of a story, a big hit and it better be with "spiritual" assistance? Or, am I thinking more of a *Game of Thrones* kinda thing...I'm inwardly hoping for a movie deal or in the least, a great book? I'm sure there are those who would think the story line isn't even close to making a movie, but weirder things have happened, ya know!

∞

104

Actok addressed the group. "Skyann, Angelicia, Teresa, David, it is now time for your Awakening to begin." Nocren stood up, slightly bowed, and with no excuse, left the room.

All stood and followed Actok toward the Isolytic Chamber area. Teresa was holding Henry's hand so tight it hurt, but he wouldn't complain. Angelicia was excited yet felt trepidation. Skyann and David walked side by side but when they reached the chamber, she hesitated, then stopped walking. Actok sensed this and turned around. He noticed Skyann leaning against the wall with her arms folded in front of her. The group all stopped when they saw Actok make his way toward her.

Skyann felt as if she would faint. "May I?" Actok asked as he placed his finger near her forehead. Skyann looked at him as if seeing this being for the first time. His body became brighter and she could almost see...

Actok didn't wait for an answer as he took advantage of her trance-like state. Skyann immediately calmed after his touch to her forehead. David drew near and Actok smiled as David put his arm around her shoulder.

The chamber itself was breathtaking: white walls as large as three stories, and the floor shaped like a triangle. Soft lights were flickering behind the walls at eye level, completely surrounding them. Actok allowed his entourage to explore the scenery before them.

Immediately David noticed the walls seemed to be moving. He noticed strange hieroglyphics appearing and walked over, hoping to decipher them. Skyann followed behind him, also enjoying the strange writings.

"Look here, Sky." Skyann was surprised at hearing David call her Sky but she liked the way it sounded, so she made no comment.

David was bending down near a wall full of symbols and pictures. He hesitated then decided to touch them. Without sound, the whole wall lit up immediately. David, stunned, stood, and backed up. The others walked toward him.

A vision of Earth's solar system filled the entire wall, depicting in real time its sun, moon, and surrounding planets. The group huddled closer as the scene changed yet again. All stood in wonder as planet Earth came into view.

Slowly the hologram revealed the beauty of the planet, hovering above her as if not to interfere. Green were the rainforests of Africa, South America, Indonesia, Southeast Asia, and Australia, each more beautiful than the last.

Yellow-gold were its deserts of the Sahara, Namib, Gobi, Atacama, and Thar. All were enthralled when displayed were the Seven Wonders of the World.

A sense of sadness enveloped the group as the scene changed, showing large cities and buildings all over planet Earth. One watched as thousands of people went to and fro. With no explanation, they felt Earth's pain in supporting and withstanding the significant changes man kept inflicting upon it.

The hologram went deeper in its vision to show humanity in its essence. Scenes of sickness, disease, starvation were vividly displayed. Man killing man, prison cells filled to their limits.

Blood stains upon her ground and mountains revealed the sacrifice of the wars upon it.

Then, the group were witness to a future event: Earth's inhabitants, all coexisting in peace and harmony. Everyone playing their part in Earth's rehabilitation. They watched as the Earth healed, and love for each other and of the planet returned.

No one spoke; there was no need. Angelicia turned to her sister and hugged her tight. David took Skyann in his arms and kissed her. Henry and Actok watched and smiled.

Actok finally broke the silence. "If only the inhabitants would realize their true reason that they visit Earth…"

Henry interjected, "To express love. Just that, to express love."

105

Dawn's withdrawal was expected, as she had been spiritually weakened by this incarnation. In this lifetime she wasn't practicing a religion and didn't have a background of faith to apply to her everyday life. This weakened her spiritual connection with the Creator. It was a very difficult challenge in that she allowed herself to separate to that degree.

The formula of the drugs to boost her immune system, and the time given to strengthen her chakras, enabled Dawn to prepare for her destiny. She was given techniques to assist her in recharging her body and her soul. All she needed now was a kick-start, and she had just arrived!

Awakening Dawn.

I'm going to do it today. I'm not leaving this desk, not getting coffee, not…anything, till I get my most important character to realize who she is!

Why is this so hard? I've done the research, I know pretty much how it will happen for Dawn, so why this hesitancy? Perhaps criticism. I'm fearful of feedback from spiritual people who might not agree that's how an Awakened person finds their true self? Wait. Since this is a sci-fi fantasy, I'm going to elaborate my own thoughts on how I feel she should Awaken. It's my story, it's my story, I've got to own it!

Okay, it's April 15, 2020, 12:17 pm...

∞

Dawn felt different; a lighthearted wonderful feeling of awareness swelled inside her being. She was sitting in the middle of the room on her pillow, in the same yoga position she had applied for a week, the Om. Holding completely still, she allowed her body to yield to what she felt was a tingling sensation. Soon, in a complete state of awareness, all of her body was gently consumed with pure energy. She felt so happy she silently cried.

It was during this intense sitting that Dawn heard a knocking. Her heart started beating faster. She was acutely aware all she had been waiting for, all she needed to know, was on the other side of the door. "Come in."

Renu quietly entered. Without speaking, she walked over and sat on the floor in front of Dawn. Although Dawn had never met Renu, not in this lifetime, they looked into each other's eyes and smiled. Dawn felt only elation and peace; this was who she had been waiting for. Dawn closed her eyes as Renu took her hands.

Both immediately felt a powerful rush of energy opening their heart centers, throat centers, their third eyes, and crowns. Being "grounded," their reality was magnified. Uniting as one entity triggered yet another powerful surge of vigor, transporting them to a higher realm of consciousness. On this level, both sensed a loss of their physicalness, replaced with the essence of crystalline energy. The very next sensation was one of an awareness of spirit, a...knowing!

Dawn's body felt lighter, yet she sensed the blood flowing through the veins. Her mind and body were absorbing the energy source surrounding her at an intense level.

Renu and Dawn remained in their seated position, holding hands, eyes closed. Both allowed the influx of energy to engulf them while it lasted.

A true Awakening was occurring; they had entered the highest dimensional state of being; they had connected to the Divine, the Prime Creator of all that is!

When the energy flow slowly diminished, Renu released Dawn's hands. They both stood up, they both smiled, and then Renu bowed.

It was as that moment, watching Renu bow, when Dawn Awoke as her true self; fully aware of her association with the Prime Creator and fully aware of her persona as the humanoid Dawn.

This Awakening had not changed her outward physical appearance nor her mental acuity. What did occur was a force to create a sense of perceptiveness within her.

Even with her elevated position, even with realizing she was in league with the Prime Creator, Dawn still bowed back to Renu. No words were exchanged.

Both stood up and smiled. Walking Renu to the door, Dawn pressed the panel to open it. Immediately, she felt a jolt of energy rush through her and she quickly removed her hand. Renu noticed the action and remarked, "You're going to have to get used to that again." They both smiled, remembering similar incidents from other incarnations.

Oh wow! It's 1:28 pm, on the same day! All that worry, all that stress and it took me just over an hour to write Dawn's Awakening. I just asked my Dave what he thought of it. He liked it! Being a spiritual person himself, he said it made sense!

What a feeling of accomplishment!

∞

106

Actok watched quietly as his little group walked around in awe at their findings in the chamber. He was pleasantly surprised when Angelicia separated from them to check out a huge picture of Seraphin angels on one of the walls. Massive were these beings, tall, with enormous wings, a vision so inspiring it was difficult for her to look away and return to the group.

Actok knew it was time. "Excuse me. The time has come. Please follow me."

Everyone gathered together and walked behind Actok, who led them over to the section of the room where a triangle appeared on the floor.

All were given directions as to where to stand. They were surprised when the room became void of any scenes or symbols on the walls. Standing still, waiting, all were subjected to an immediate changing of their clothes: soft white robes appeared on their bodies with no effort from them at all! For a few seconds, they were startled, but then looked at each other and smiled.

Actok was standing at the tip of the triangle with his eyes closed. He waved his hand across the room, which placed his friends in a very relaxed frame of mind.

No one spoke or moved. Actok opened his eyes, turned to Henry and said, "Henry, I am grateful you have offered to assist with your friends' Awakening process. You have served me well, and the Ministry is grateful. You, Kristian, and Rosalee have been invited to commune with your friends if desired. Of course, you will receive His love on a much higher frequency level, as this is not your first time."

Henry was honored. "Thank you, Actok. With all my heart I say there is no better compensation than your generous offer."

"As do we, dear Actok. Thank you for the offering," Kristian said.

Actok looked over at Kristian, "It is He who has offered." Actok then turned his attention to the group.

"Friends, you have decided to Awaken in this manner, at this time. The Prime Creator is very pleased."

As was the communal ceremony with Actok and his emissaries, the Awakening ceremony happened to this group of four humans, so humbled, so honored.

All were immersed for a short period of time with the total pure essence of their Creator, and Skyann, David, Teresa, and Angelicia were Awakened.

107

There was no doubt: Nocren would be the choice to replace Actok. He had proven himself on the battlefield, surpassing his father's reputation as a skilled warrior. He had a powerful presence with both his peers and the general masses. Notwithstanding all these acclimates, Actok sensed it was Nocren's unselfish generosity that would always be his most endearing quality.

Actok reflected on the Ministry of Enlightenment and its benefit with his comrade's leadership. He knew the will of the Prime Creator would always be at the forefront of Nocren's every decision.

Yet now, after this revelation about Saghi...how could he entrust this heavy burden on Nocren while he was losing his love? Actok sensed from his last meeting that Saghi was dying. It wasn't his place to recognize the fact. The truth would soon expose itself; there is nothing to do but wait. Soon though, he must inform the Ministry about stepping down. Soon...

108

∞

The next section of this story has me all in a tizzy! For days, my thoughts are like scattered bolts of energy running through my brain. Dawn is Awakened. Now on to setting up the war of wars! Or do I? Maybe offering scenarios and not an actual ending to humanity is the way to go...

It's October 1, 2020, and the COVID-19 virus is still plaguing us. The kids are mostly being homeschooled here in our neck of the woods.

I've had to stop and take inventory on...well me. My weight was out of control, my face was drying up like a prune, my hair looked plain ugly and yikes, I needed to pay attention. So...for the past month I've...lost thirteen pounds, utilized the new treadmill, got a dental cleaning, started walking our new dog Rusty, treated myself to a facial, and actually paid to have someone shape my eyebrows and dye and highlight my hair! Great, I feel better!!

When I write, I hear every noise. Like now, a hummingbird is whizzing through my flowers, right outside my door. Must admit, this could be my high frequency levels coursing through my body. I've experienced ringing in the ears for most of my life. My audiologist recently was impressed with my hearing test, stating he hasn't tested many my age with the ability to hear such high-pitched sounds! It's truly annoying, though, when I place my head on the pillow—any movement sounds like I'm in a cave, or worse, I hear the crunch, crunch, crunch of the stuffing!

109

Standing alone, Dawn surveyed the living quarters as if noticing them for the first time. Her mind raced as thoughts of numerous manifestations roused her being. Her visual senses noted each object, though still, as if they were alive with pulsing energy. Her hearing sharpened, capturing the murmur of the ship's integral humming. As if blended in harmony with all around her, she allowed time to absorb familiar yet distant memories of past incarnations.

110

∞

I was stuck, plain and simple. Stuck. Putting off my writing until a thought would enter my head. I allowed myself time to contrive a believable scenario. Think as I might, nothing was coming. I know my author's club would be disappointed that I stopped writing yet my whole being felt I couldn't. Where am I going with this entourage of six? Does anyone relate to my characters?

I know most writers go through these times.

The COVID-19 virus is still with us, our economy has taken a huge hit, and being separated from some of my family is emotionally killing me.

Days have gone by. Then...

Funny how the universe attends to you...when the timing is right!

111

It was with great surprise that the whole group found themselves entering the cafeteria at the same time. All were sensing something was about to happen, but no one expressed an opinion. They all were aware that Dawn was to give individual audience later that day, but this was different.

So, when they noticed Renu enter the cafeteria...

She didn't look over at them nor did she speak. The group all looked quizzically at each other but said nothing. Renu poured herself a cup of coffee and sat down at the end of their bench. No one wanted to speak first, but with egging from the group, Kristian took the initiative. "Renu, excuse...us, but we're really concerned for Dawn. We were wondering if she is okay, you know, what should we expect?"

Smiling, Renu replied, "You will see Dawn, the friend you know and love. She will be communing with all of you separately soon."

David interjected, "Yes, but will she remember us? Will she be...different towards us, you know, a more distant Dawn?"

Renu was a little surprised at that remark. With a questioning look, Renu asked, "Distant? In what way, David?" She was purposely making him uncomfortable.

David rationalized his inquiry was too personal and that Renu picked up on it. He became quiet, looking for the right words. He stood up and slowly walked towards Renu. "Well, it's just that I...we...care so much about her and now that she's Awakened...I guess I'm hoping she remembers us the way we were...on Earth."

Renu wanted to laugh loudly but she suppressed the urge. "You have nothing to be concerned about. Dawn is still Dawn. Just now she is aware of her purpose. I'll say no more, as during your private session all will be explained."

Angelicia walked over to Renu, who clearly felt her anxiety. "Excuse me, but am I to understand that with our...Awakening process...Dawn will be the same person I know, yet she is now in her element? You know, a more spiritual human?"

Renu looked into Angelicia's eyes. She wasn't bothered by the question, she knew this person, knew of her tenacious fortitude. "To answer simply, yes. Do you feel different now, Angel...can I call you Angel? Are you not exactly who you were prior to your Awakening? Yet now, you can know or sense on a higher level of your consciousness, a higher spiritual plain, but not everything has been revealed to you yet."

At that moment, Angelicia felt this woman could see right through her. She certainly wasn't going to admit that, it wasn't her style. She simply replied, "Yeah, you're right. And sure, call me Angel, I kinda like it."

They both exchanged a smile when Angelicia stated, "I am sensing something."

Then Renu tilted her head, almost like she was listening. In an instant, she moved so quickly there was no time for Angelicia to react. She stood up, and with both hands, grabbed Angelicia's shoulders from behind and stood perfectly still. Immediately a shockwave swept through Angelicia's whole body. The intense burning sensation ended as quickly as it had started.

To the onlookers, it seemed that Angelicia just froze in her spot, but that's not what Angelicia was experiencing. In reality, she felt extremely weak. She noticed a vision appear; a human-like figure with massive white wings descending from above. She couldn't determine if it were male or female, even though there were no clothes on its body. When the being softly landed, it walked quickly towards her. They locked eyes yet the being kept walking. Angelicia couldn't move as each attempt to remove Renu's hands offered her another jolt to her body.

Angelicia sensed that she had seen this manifestation before, but where? No time to think, as this being wasn't stopping. With eyes focused on Angelicia, and the pace towards her picking up speed, she watched helplessly. The wings folded behind its body with a whishing sound and tremendous force. That sound, that force, she had heard before...

The figure neared Angelicia, intently looking into her eyes. At that moment, Renu removed her grip and stepped aside, just as the figure entered Angelicia, who immediately stepped back, bracing the impact.

All the onlookers just gasped at her movement. They couldn't comprehend what had just happened as they were not privy to her true experience. They only sensed a presence.

"Oh no!" screamed Teresa as she started toward her sister. Henry instinctively turned to Teresa and wrapped his arms around her, holding her back.

Henry whispered, "It's okay, Teresa. It's okay."

Skyann started moving toward Angelicia, but David held out his hand in a gesture to stop. David moved closer and was about to touch Angelicia when Renu extended her arm in an effort to halt the excitement. She exclaimed, "Be calm. She's all right." With just the sound of her voice, the group unanimously responded to her command.

Renu looked at Angelicia who was still reeling from the

impact. It was shocking for the onlookers to watch as Angelicia suddenly began a transformation from her physical form into one of a giant spiritual angelic being.

Angelicia looked deeply into Renu's eyes. No one could talk, everyone was focused on the interaction between Renu and Angelicia.

Renu questioned, "Michael?"

A voice within Angelicia spoke as if an echo, "Hello Renu! It's an honor to see you again." The group looked at each other in awe, fully engrossed in the scene before them.

Renu responded, realizing that those in the room would not know who this figure was unless properly addressed, "As it is to see you, Archangel Michael."

112

Teresa watched helplessly as her sister was embedded with a spiritual being, a huge Seraphin angel that towered over her by at least four feet. His body was that of a human and one couldn't help but notice how masculine he was. His wavy brown hair accented his blue-green eyes. His three sets of golden wings were softly flapping, but they were not completely exposed.

Henry noticed his shining blue-purple sword; proof he was Archangel Michael.

But, Renu and Michael didn't notice any of them! They were deep in telepathic communication.

Henry gently whispered to Teresa, "Come with me. Renu and your sister, well...Archangel Michael, need a little time. Henry placed his arm on Teresa's shoulder wherein he felt her body trembling. They walked without speaking to her apartment, where Juan and Poppy were playing a game.

Melek watched behind the doorway as Skyann folded her arms in an effort to withdraw. He hesitated, then watched David hug her. He slowly withdrew.

What Melek didn't witness was the fact that Skyann wasn't comforted. She looked at David and faked a smile. She'd been feeling edgy, anxious the last few hours and figured this event was probably why. She was wrong.

An hour passed, finding Michael in Angelicia's room, acclimating. He gave thought to what to say when he met with Teresa, Juan, and his Earth-father. He understood too well the emotional state humans could immerse themselves in.

Renu, too, had gone back to her apartment.

Dawn cerebrally summoned Actok to her apartment and was pleased she could finally communicate with her mentor and best friend in the format they had shared for eons, one of mind and spirit.

Actok stood near her and slightly bowed, then looked into her eyes. "There you are!" He again bowed, this time with a slow, deep bending of his body. "Dawn, Bringer of Light."

Dawn smiled. For a moment, they stood still and locked together their minds.

"Renu indicated all went well with your Awakening. I must say there was much worry with your Earth-body this time around."

"Yes, my friend, all went well. I am grateful for your assessment that my physical form was weak and needed attention.

"I also know now it was you who saved me during the bus accident. I can see it all." With a slight chuckle, "I remember, too, our meeting in the hanger."

Actok laughed. "Yes, that was quite an encounter. You surprised me that the urge to scream was upended by your curiosity. Very little was needed to suppress you."

"Yes. Humans are very curious creatures and I have always enjoyed acting the role."

Dawn said, "It feels wonderful to once again be with you. Please, sit, Actok. I must inform you of my commune with the Prime Creator."

113

Angelicia and David walked with Skyann and Oonsay to a table in the empty recreation area.

David questioned, "Skyann, are you okay? You seem...well, like you're in shock. I'm...so concerned about you."

He was interrupted in his commune with the entrance of Melek, who said, "Excuse me, David, but we're going to sit over there. You've got this." Melek and Oonsay shared a quiet smile with David, who was grateful for their display of confidence.

David turned his attention to Skyann. "Listen, let's try a calming technique." Skyann's blank look said it all. She was frightened, shocked to her core. David took her hands and whispered, "Try to look at me, Skyann. Skyann?"

Slowly she turned her head towards the voice. She recognized David sitting across from her. Looking down, she noticed he was attempting to hold her hands. The warmth of his touch reacted to her energy flow, her senses heightened, as did his. A spectrum of green and amber colors burst forth from their beings, swirling around them. For a moment, their minds were connected. Then, with a bolt of powerful emotion, their minds separated, and the colors subsided back within their bodies. At that moment, Skyann and David knew.

Still holding her hands, David looked deeply into Skyann's eyes. He was tilting his head in recognition. He leaned in, then telecommunicated, "Uriel!"

Renu was sitting in her room when she sensed a presence. She instinctively started running towards the recreation area. As she was running through the hall, she felt yet another presence. *Run, Renu, run.*

Renu saw Skyann and David holding hands. She arrived at their table just at the moment Skyann telepathically communicated to David, "Raphael!"

In a daze, David released Skyann's hands and held his in front of his face. He felt he wasn't himself, wasn't David the psychiatrist, but knew touching Skyann had brought into his psyche his real persona; he was the Archangel Raphael!

"Uriel!" was all he muttered.

Uriel started laughing. "Well, I must admit, this is the most fascinating Awakening moment I have ever experienced! So easy! And, look at me, I have always relished being in form, but this time I'm a woman! Can't remember the last time that happened. Ha."

Renu said, "This is all happening so fast. Uriel...welcome."

Uriel recognized Renu. "Forgive me, Renu, I was in the moment. It is wonderful to see you again. There is only high praise on your mission here. We know millions of souls will be saved due to your untiring efforts." Uriel bowed to Renu from her seat as Renu responded with a full body bow.

Then Renu turned to Raphael. They exchanged a look that only soul mates could comprehend. It was that of a deep affection, born of trust and loyalty that had supported them throughout many incarnations. Renu said, "Raphael, it is so wonderful to see you. How I have waited for this moment!"

Raphael replied, "Renu. Beautiful Renu. I too have waited to work on yet another mission together."

They were just smiling at each other when Uriel turned to Raphael. "And to think I was falling for you! Wait, should I blush?"

Renu laughed then sat down at their table. Raphael, being the more somber angel, replied, "The human heart goes where it will, Uriel. It's going to be fun to continue this charade knowing the feelings we had."

"Well," Uriel announced, "We could start..."

Renu coughed and the two angels looked at her, then at each other and laughed.

Oonsay and Melek walked over to pay their respects and were offered a seat at the table.

Although it might seem strange to humans, angels are often believed to dwell within a human body to perform a mission. It's very easy to switch back and forth when necessary. The level of intensity they felt when their hands touched was all the catalyst Skyann and David needed.

Renu wished Rosalee and Kristian could have participated in the Awakening of Skyann, David, Teresa, and Angelicia. But it was not to be. *Where were they? Sleeping?* she wondered. She'd been busy training them in the art of precognition. This event would have given them insight into the many methods used to Awaken.

Renu was proud of the work they had performed gathering large masses of Starseed spirits and assisting them evolving into Light Warriors. She also realized the urgency to get them back to their followers to prepare for the upcoming Battle for Enlightenment.

Little was Renu aware that Kristian and Rosalee were cognizant of all that was taking place in the recreation area of the ship! Dawn, who instinctively knew what was happening outside her door, informed them during their private sessions.

It was Uriel who asked, "Where is Actok?"

Renu answered, "Uhm, your arrival, like everything else with this mission, happened unexpectedly. And..." Renu stopped talking as she watched Uriel smirk.

"What? What are you smiling about?"

"That you commented everything happened unexpectedly.

You of all people should realize if something is not moving in its direction, the Prime Creator made it so! In this case, I'd venture to say it was a tactical diversion."

Renu realized she had spoken out of frustration, as she was perfectly aware everything happens for a reason. She replied, "Yes, of course. I would agree. But to answer your question, Actok's meeting with Dawn as we speak."

Uriel turned just in time to notice Raphael was silently smiling. Uriel questioned, "Okay, give. Why are you smiling now?"

"Oh, only that every incarnation makes me feel more of an affinity towards humans. Their ability to love. I can laugh now thinking that I had actually had emotional thoughts towards Dawn when I first met her. Until I met you, of course, Skyann, uh Uriel."

Uriel, always the jokester, was not going to let that statement go unanswered. Coyly she replied, "So, now I suppose you're just going to let it all go?" Turning towards Renu, "And I worked so hard."

"Uriel...I warn you!" Raphael remarked.

"Oh, how I enjoy toying with you, Raphael! And why do humans have all the fun?"

David added "And, now Awakened, I've come to realize we're like a brother and sister!"

"Well, I'm glad you figured that out!" laughed Uriel.

This camaraderie was interrupted with the presence of Michael, who appeared out of thin air.

"Oh, Michael!" Renu stood and bowed.

"Michael!" Raphael exclaimed, stood, then bowed.

Uriel stood, bowed and respectively uttered, "Michael. It is good to see you, my friend." Walking closer to Michael, Uriel stared approvingly at his body. "You certainly would have fooled me with the feminine choice you made!"

Michael smiled then opened his wings and flashed them at his friends. "Don't forget who's in charge here."

"Oh, we won't. You wouldn't let us anyway!" Uriel announced. They all shared a knowing smile.

Renu addressed Michael, "Will Arial be joining us on this mission?"

Michael, folding back his wings, said, "No, there is a great need for her conservation services on Venus but she does send her love."

It was Raphael who halted the chatter. "We'd better get acclimated quickly."

The group agreed and all sat at the table to discuss their assignments.

114

∞

Hurdles. I'm learning writing a story comes in hurdles. Awakening Dawn being the most challenging.

Moving forward the goal is to set the stage for the upcoming spiritual battle...or not!

∞

115

Planet Earth changed drastically under Vasile's rulership. While he focused all his efforts to implementing his New World Order system, the populace was forced to adjust to new alien entities arriving daily. Adapt, hide, or die.

There was also drama happening on the ship. Saghi was dying. Nocren hadn't left their room, even though he sensed the presence of new arrivals of a very high nature. He thought he'd be torn between the position in the Ministry of Enlightenment and his wife's condition. To Nocren, there was no choice to make: he wouldn't leave Saghi's side.

Nocren had been sitting near her for four days, watching as his wife was losing her battle to hang on. On day five: "Nocren, please dear, come closer."

Nocren stood at the bed and leaned in close to hear his wife's words. "Now listen to me. You and I have had a wonderful life together. I regret nothing. I could not be prouder of you or our children.

"My time is coming soon, Nocren. You have been with me day and night. I am very appreciative but we both know this arrangement is not the best for anyone. You must consider letting me go home to the children and grandchildren. Now."

"No, no, I cannot, Saghi. Saghi, how can you ask this of

me? Actok can handle everything here. Let me be with you through...through..."

"You must see the whole picture now, Nocren. You are needed here. Actok will be moving on."

"What? Is he sick, too? I didn't sense..."

"No, of course not. Don't you see, Nocren? He will be aligned with the Prime Creator. His work on Earth will be completed. He can...go home."

"But how...do you know this?"

Saghi smiled at her husband. "Nocren, all is in place. Soon it will be incumbent on you to fulfill his position for all that is to transpire. Please, please Nocren give this thought...now." Saghi turned her head and fell into a deep sleep.

Nocren continued to stand over his wife. *How beautiful she is! Even facing death, my Saghi looks like the young girl I promised my life to. I could not have partnered with any other. Her commitment to me and the children was exemplary. How fortunate we have all been to have shared our lives in her presence.*

She wants to go home. Of course, how selfish I have been. How did she know I needed her insight to see what had to be done? How did she know about Actok? I really shouldn't be surprised. There has always been a side to Saghi that was strange to me. A knowing of how future events would play out!

Nocren knew she didn't have long to live. With a heavy heart, knowing he was putting into play the hardest decision he'd ever had to make, Nocren made arrangements to send Saghi home to Alcyone.

116

∞

A realization has occurred during all this research. I believe my home planet is Arcturia. What a statement to make! You can easily research this on your own, for free. There are sites on the internet to help. Yes, okay, internet help. What can I say?

I've often wondered why I haven't been successful in finding any UFO groups or spiritual groups around here while I'm writing this book. Could it be because Almighty God wanted my inner feelings and nothing "outside" those feelings interfering with this work? Hmmm...

∞

117

Lately, as Katz had mentioned, Vasile had been too busy to bother with him, what with establishing his New World Order and accommodating his massive alien race to planet Earth.

Everyone attended the first meeting at Nicky's: Katz, Inky, Detective Aimes, and Tina Woods.

Katz cleared his throat, "So, Aimes, the reason..."

Aimes cut him off. "Listen, I know now. I believe now. I've seen too much. How can I help?"

"Tell us all you know."

Little did Katz and Inky realize how insightful and forthcoming Aimes was going to be! "Okay. I'll bring you up to speed from our perspective. This Vasile guy, he's no good! It's rumored he's the Antichrist! He's got all the character-istics..."

"Yeah, I agree. I've seen firsthand what he's capable of." Katz said.

Aimes sarcastically said, "Well, you'd know. You were hanging out with him pretty heavily the last few weeks."

Both men looked at Inky when he loudly placed his hands on the table. "He IS the Antichrist!"

Aimes said, "I knew it! Everything points to it. His ability to charm the populace into believing everything's all right.

That this New World Order is what the planet needs right now. Yeah, sure it is!

You know, soon you can't get anything without having that chip, the...the Chip it's called, embedded in your hand. We're getting reports of underground hubs being created now so people can get organized and not have to get the damn thing.

"Some swear Vasile's the answer to prayer. Others, like me, see right through that prick! Okay, so it appears he's stopped a lot of the chaos, but he's responsible FOR it!

"You know who's behind this movement to welcome his...his kind, right? Jaqui, that's who! He's one mean son of a bitch! Did you know he can read you? Something about sensing if you're lying. It's been reported thousands are missing now, and not just those taken in this...Rapture thing, but those Jaqui saw fit to annihilate! Now, these...these aliens are coming down in droves and we're supposed to WELCOME them?"

Inky mentioned, "They've been coming for eons. Not just this species, numerous ones."

Aimes said, "You know, Inky, I wouldn't have given that statement any credence until now. The understanding that it's true, Jesus.

Aimes continued, "Now it's rumored Jaqui has a sidekick. A woman who does his every bidding. She's one sick bitch. Jesus, what are we to do? Who's here to help us?"

Katz replied, "Let's just concentrate on what else you might know. Anything, Aimes. I know you've got great contacts. What's really going on at the White House, the Pentagon? How about getting help from other countries?"

"From reports, it looks like the Pentagon has fallen. Supposedly, all our secrets are now in the hands of this Vasile guy. The White House isn't releasing any information. President Fredericks is in lockdown, apparently of his own volition. Nobody really knows what he's up to. Some say he's lost it, you know, from losing his wife and kids.

"My friends in Germany, you know, Katz, the ones that worked with us on reigning in that terrorist group, have informed me that countries are falling every day. China just fell yesterday, they said. It was that or starve. Dictatorships are dropping quicker than democratic countries, but it's just a matter of time. It sucks. And, none of this will hit the news...unless," Aimes looked at Katz, "...unless, Katz, you..."

"What? Print this shit? Seriously?"

The room got still. It felt like all the air was taken up in their last breath. Everyone waited for a reply. It didn't come.

118

Dawn smiled when Teresa, Poppy, and little Juan entered her apartment. "Please, sit, make yourselves comfortable. I won't keep you long."

As Teresa passed Dawn, Dawn bowed. Teresa didn't know how to respond, so she bowed quickly and kept walking toward her seat. When they all found themselves seated, Teresa started looking quizzically at Dawn. With a smile, Dawn commented, "Were you expecting me to look different now, Teresa?"

"Well, I'm not sure what I expected, really. Actually, all this is so new."

Juan was being fidgety, arching his back and trying to climb over to his mother. Dawn asked, "Can I?"

Teresa, educated now in the art of healing with frequencies (thanks to Gaff and Melek), understood what Dawn meant. She hadn't mastered the technique herself yet, but allowed Dawn to touch Juan's forehead. No major bolt occurred, just a slight tap that made him immediately sit down in his seat. He would remain relatively quiet for the rest of their meeting.

Poppy was amazed. But then again, everything amazed him since his arrival. His personality was such that he adapted well and even relished the new abilities he was learning from Gaff. So, Poppy was taken aback when Dawn suddenly and without warning placed her finger on his forehead. He, like Juan, went into a slight stupor, listless but comprehensible. Teresa watched in amazement, but understood Dawn must require they be still during this meeting.

Dawn addressed Teresa, "Everything happens for a reason. There are no chance encounters, no sudden catastrophes; everything happens for a reason." Teresa nodded in agreement.

"Yes, you are Awakened, and are displaying an ability to telecommunicate far and wide. Your remote viewing skills are no accident. This is...innate in you, and soon you will understand what I mean. You, like Angelicia are much more than an Awakened Avatar."

Dawn allowed this information to take hold of Teresa's psyche. A few seconds of silence ensued. Then Teresa looked into Dawn's eyes and surprisingly announced, "I know what you are about to do. Guess I've been waiting for this moment to happen. I'm...I'm someone else, aren't I? I am, right?"

Dawn gave the biggest sigh and said, "Oh Teresa, yes, yes you are!"

"Well then, let's get on with it. I know I'll still be Teresa too, so let's do this."

Dawn laughed. "I love your resolve but I'm hesitating, as what I am about to expose to your son and your father might frighten them at first, hence the suppression technique. They must see, to...to understand...Are you ready?"

Teresa was resolved. She stood up and walked over to Dawn. She started to say something but Dawn immediately stood up and grabbed Teresa around the shoulders and held on tight. As with Skyann, Teresa received a severe shock to her body that dissipated as quickly as it happened.

Poppy and Juan watched as Teresa slowly transformed

into a figure of bright light. Poppy tried to stand up in an effort to help his daughter, but Dawn communicated, "Sit back, she is not being harmed." As if in slow motion, he did just that. Juan, still pacified, sat motionless.

This figure began to glow, first white, then yellow. Dawn released her hold and took a step back. Immediately, Teresa's physical body disappeared, replaced by an ethereal angel. Her feet left the ground and she floated a few inches in the air. Then a thunderous noise filled the room as this angel opened her wings. Glorious was the sight in front of them. Teresa was now Angel Sariel, the Communicator. Dawn bowed before this graceful creature and Teresa acknowledged the gesture. Sariel turned slowly and glided closer to Poppy and Juan. She smiled and communicated, "You are loved."

As quickly as Teresa had transformed herself, she was able to appear in her former body once again. Now with the added powers of Sariel, Teresa was in full control of her senses. Her first act was to wave her hand over Poppy and Juan, bringing them out of their stupor. They both looked at her and smiled.

She then nodded her head to the side to show she wanted them to follow her. She turned to Dawn, who bowed. Sariel smiled, and proceeded to walk to her room with Poppy and Juan in tow.

Dawn was used to witnessing Sariel's quick demonstration of transference. She also knew from numerous missions working alongside her that even though she was known for her communicative abilities, very little was spoken.

119

∞

Creating my main six characters, Dawn, Dr. Kaplan, Skyann, Henry, Teresa, and Angelicia was fun. Transforming them into Light Warriors and Archangels, challenging!

Countless box office hits introduce superhuman beings with special powers. I didn't want to follow that scenario. I worried and worried...then...the universe answered...create their personalities to transform into who they really are! It fit!

Thank you, Universe! Okay, it took three weeks of stress and worry but I have received and acted upon the answer.

∞

120

Those left on Earth who weren't of a religious nature began hearing of the Tribulation and what it meant for mankind. Of course, the die-hard amongst them wouldn't acquiesce to words of wisdom or accept any reassurances.

Some agreed they had nothing to lose. You'd find this group turning to religious leaders holding secretive underground meetings. At least there they could be forgiven of their sins, and commune with others of the same frame of mind.

Every single survivor were now living in a morbid state of suppression. Almost overnight, in every country on Earth, the New World Order was established. The process happened so smoothly there was no time allotted for a rebellious movement and no heroes came forth. Earth's inhabitants would now answer to Vasile, Jaqui, and their army of aliens.

No longer could one practice religion at a place of worship. No longer could one walk about freely in their environment. A personalized, monitored device, smaller than a grain of rice, embedded in one's hand, informed the new government, the T-HE-RE, of every move from waking to sleeping. If survival was the goal, the populace had to conform.

It was easy enough to get the Chip; ask for it and it shall

be given! You need only to show up at any designated building and get one for free. It didn't hurt, just a quick jab on the side below the left thumb.

This little gadget allowed one anything that required a monetary transaction.

Yet, the privilege of choosing your own doctor was taken away and replaced by an assigned government physician!

Schools and municipalities were now governed by the T-HE-RE who created their own guidelines.

No one knew what the T-HE-RE acronym actually meant, but there was a universal acceptance when it was described as "They're Here!" Especially when it was noted that on a daily basis, alien ships were landing, unloading hundreds of their own kind all over the planet.

Lodging for some of these newcomers was easy; they seized what they liked, and if you thought of defending your home...you were annihilated.

Onlookers watched in panic. These aliens demonstrated they had no interest in Earthlings, and did nothing to assist them in their plight.

An intolerable, impossible toll was being placed on mankind.

121

Raphael appeared in Dawn's chambers unannounced. When she pretended to ignore his presence, he coughed. She ignored. He coughed. Silence.

"Raphael, you have to knock, just like everyone else. When will you learn?"

Laughing, he responded, "Since when do I enter through a door?"

Dawn walked over to him. "It's wonderful seeing you again, Raphael. I must say I missed you! Not sure if you've had enough time in your Awakening process to...well, process... what we meant to each other on Earth?"

"Humans exploit their emotions without much insight! I'll admit I had thoughts...but I kept getting this feeling we knew each other...somehow. Then I met Skyann, and who couldn't fall for that one?"

Dawn nodded her head and laughed, "Yes, I understand. I was experiencing everyday life at hyper speed and didn't have time to process any further feelings. Perhaps that was a good thing.

"I wanted to have this moment with you to say thank you, Raphael. I am always honored when we can share a mission together."

"It's my honor, Dawn." And he bowed.

122

Dawn surprised Uriel with her hurried entrance to her apartment. Upon opening the door, Dawn grabbed her and they huddled together for about a minute without talking. They released their embrace and both bowed.

"This is the best part of Awakening, isn't it, Uriel? When we get to realize our true selves and our mission is clear. It never gets old."

"The best!"

"Oh, how I'd love to sit with you, my friend and discuss all we've just been through together and..."

Uriel interjected, "I know, Dawn. I am aware. Even on this ship, time is a factor and we haven't much of that to enjoy."

"Thank you for understanding, but of course you would. The Prime Creator has announced all is being prepared. Now, we must.

"I believe first and foremost in sending Rosalee and Kristian back to Earth to gather the mass of Starseeds ready to assist us.

"I must send Renu back to Asia where she has emissaries she can post throughout the world, places Kristian and Rosalee cannot penetrate. It's time for all Earth's Starseeds to Awaken into Light Warriors. Oh, what a powerful message we will be sending to Vasile and Jaqui. And the Draconians have arrived."

Dawn looks sadly up at Uriel, "The war of wars is upon us. All the inhabitants of Earth…"

"Dawn, I feel there is something…let me guess. You wish of me to go with them, to protect them. Yes?"

With a heavy heart, Dawn said, "Ah, what insight. Yes. That is my request, yes."

"It is good to know what my role was going to be and it's my honor to do so. When do I leave?"

123

As Lilly passed the living room window, she noticed something. "Carole, come here. What are those little bubbly lights outside? I've never seen anything like it before."

Carole got up from the couch and pulled back the curtain. She noticed the same strange lights as her mother. "Kate, quick, come here."

Kate ran to the window. "What are you guys seeing out there?"

"Not sure. Looks like white balls...big and little ones. What the hell?" Carole commented.

Lilly looked at the two women and smiled. "Oh, perhaps it's our Dawn!"

Carole was used to comments like this from Lilly, yet she stared at her mother. The past few months have been so devastatingly heartbreaking. It was affecting Lilly the most. Every day she'd ask Carole and Kate to pray with her for Dawn's return. Up to this point, Carole had shielded her mother from what was happening to Earth and its inhabitants, and Kate did her part. Kate and Carole explained that there was a dangerous virus killing hundreds of people daily and they must stay put. Kate coded the TV and radio so only certain channels were available. They were both a little surprised at how easily Lilly had accepted these answers...

Both women kept Lilly in the dark regarding the New World Order, the wearing of the Chip and the danger both faced every time they'd go to an underground community for food and needed supplies. When Lilly questioned where her friend Jenna was, the girls remarked that she was no longer next door and had moved in with some relatives because of the virus. Even this was accepted without hesitation. Truth be known, Jenna was taken off the planet along with millions of others.

Carole quickly noticed the balls of lights were descending in a condensed manner the closer to Earth they came. Soon, they were hovering right outside her door!

Lilly feigned tiredness and announced she was going to take a nap. The girls were relieved, as they could discuss what was happening without scaring her.

Carole whispered, "Orbs, that's what they are! Quick, unlock the TV. Let's see what everyone is saying about this."

Kate first walked quietly to the stairs and listened. When she didn't hear any noise coming from Lily's room, she ran to the TV and unlocked the TV with her code. "Okay. It's ready. I'll keep the volume down low, though."

That's when Carole realized, "Oh, don't bother. It won't be reported. We should know that by now. Anything newsworthy is edited out." Sure enough, no matter what channel Kate selected, not one was reporting this phenomenon. Carole whispered frantically, "Damn it, knew it. Something is happening right in front of us. You see this, right? Wonder if it's happening all over the planet or just here?"

Kate rationalized, "Well...these...orbs are not spewing anything out at us...yet. Maybe that's a positive thing; we sure as hell could use some of that! But we're running low on food and money, and we can't take a chance driving anywhere, so what the hell are our options here?"

Both women felt panic setting in. A minute passed, then

Kate suggested, "Perhaps it's time we have a heart-to-heart talk with that group we purchase food from. Who knows how much longer we'll be able to stay here, Carole? Maybe they'd be able to help us."

Carole looked at her partner with a frightened look. "How do we know we can trust them? Who are they? Okay, so they provide food for the ones who won't take the Chip. They are known to..."

Kate hushed Carole with a wave of her hand. She was bending down, focused on the window again. Both met at the window at the same time and watched as the orbs turned bright yellow. Neither noticed as Lilly snuck down the steps and slipped her way past them. Then she started running full blast out the front door.

Carole and Kate watched in horror as they noticed Lilly running into the orbs, screaming, "Dawn, Dawn! It's mommy! Come and get me!"

The orbs were moving slowly at first, their color changing constantly now: yellow to green, green to blue, blue to purple.

Kate and Carole stared at each other then started to run toward the front door. When Carole tried to open it, nothing happened. Kate pushed her out of the way and pressed her whole body on the door. Nothing. They ran back to the window just in time to see Lilly standing still with her hands in the air. "Dawn, it's me. I know this is you. Please, honey, come and get me."

Carole started screaming and banging on the window "Mom. Mom. Stop. Please."

Right in front of their eyes they watched as the orbs surrounded Lilly, and through pulsating lights the girls watched in horror as Lilly ascended. She looked so happy, so content. With a brilliant flash of light, all the orbs vanished in an instant and she was gone.

Carole again ran to the door and this time it opened without delay. Tears streaming down her face, Carole started to run but Kate grabbed her, wrapped her arms around her waist and stopped her from moving. The comments Lilly had made about Dawn coming to get her came vividly back into Carole's mind. Carole, notably weakened, looked into Kate's eyes and succumbed to her hold.

124

Nocren was busy demonstrating viewing tactics to Henry and Teresa. It had been noted they displayed a similar talent: the speed at which their thoughts would reach a target. No one else in the group was even close to their perceptional abilities.

Out of nowhere, Nocren pressed both hands on his stomach and bent over. So fast was this gut-wrenching attack that it caused him to lose his balance and fall. Teresa and Henry immediately went to his aid, but Nocren just stared at the floor and announced, "Saghi, she's dead."

Teresa said, "Oh my goodness, Nocren..."

Henry interjected with, "I'm so sorry, Nocren. Is there anything..."

Nocren stood up slowly. "No, thank you. I...I just need some time..."

"Of course," Teresa and Henry stated in unison.

Nocren excused himself and walked slowly away.

Actok felt the loss. He instantly knew Saghi's light was gone. He went looking for his friend. He wasn't hard to find. Nocren had ordered a holographic session wherein memorable events spent with Saghi were recorded. When Actok realized this, he knew it best to leave Nocren alone.

While in her spiritual form, Dawn sensed Saghi's demise;

it was as if her heart just stopped beating. She knew Saghi felt no pain, just a "knowing" it was her time.

Trying hard to figure out whether the book should end because I've been at it so long, over a year and a half, or keep it going until I'm damn well ready to end it! Think what's really stopping me is how much I'm learning!

Still out on this one...

125

Henry was the last to assist Rosalee, Kristian, and Skyann aboard the shuttle. Once inside, they were surprised to realize there was no seating, no windows, actually nothing at all resembling an airplane. A familiar voice came over the intercom, "Welcome aboard, friends," Actok announced. "Don't worry. You won't feel a thing."

They were getting used to Actok's simplistic display at humor, and this last attempt, a holistic shuttle, was just too much!

Henry looked at his friends. Kristian placed his hand on Henry's shoulder and stated, "Glad we had this time. You've made such an impression on me...on us. Don't know where our duties will bring us, but just know, it was an honor!"

Henry's heart welled up. Kristian noticed and patted his shoulder. "It's true. Only our Prime Creator knows if we'll meet again. Be watchful my friend. Be diligent. Godspeed."

Henry's heart was pounding so loud he could hear each beat. After a fervent hug, Henry was able to blurt, "Goodbye, Kristian."

Rosalee put down her last piece of luggage and walked over to Henry. "I'm more optimistic, I won't say goodbye. I want to believe we'll see you again, Henry. Kristian and I have less to worry about now, knowing you are a great avatar, ready to protect our mother Earth and its people. We pray for your safety and that of all of the wonderful species willing to assist us. It was right we met during this incarnation. Dawn was the catalyst to bring us all together."

Henry could only nod his head yes. Rosalee continued, "Henry, I...I want to mention something before you go. Your aura. It's amazing. Please realize if I can read it so clearly, others will too."

Henry replied, "Yes. Dawn and I had quite the conversation about it. I will Rosalee."

At this point Skyann interjected, "Hey, I'm standing here Henry. What about me? Hugs, hugs."

Henry didn't hug her, he picked her up, swirled her around and kissed her on the cheek. That's what she wanted!!

The door closed behind Henry. Rosalee turned to face Kristian and Skyann. No sooner had they looked at each other than they materialized in Kristian and Rosalee's living room.

Henry stood still, and watched the shuttle doors close. His head hung low. He was deep in thought. When he looked up, he was surprised to see Actok standing there. "Oh, you surprised me, Actok. Is everything okay?"

"I need to speak with you, Henry."

"Sure, sure. Where?"

"My apartment will be adequate."

"Lead the way," Henry said.

Henry was surprised to see Teresa, Melek, Khacee, Gaff, and Oonsay joining them in the hallway. After pleasantries, all walked into Actok's apartment.

They didn't get a chance to sit, as Actok wasted no time delving into his purpose for the meeting. "The time has come. Dawn is Awakened. Rosalee, Kristian, and Renu are going to Awaken all of the Starseeds in the very near future. Soon Earth will have its warriors. These warriors will be able to save millions of other lost souls."

"The deliverance of the orbs went as planned. We successfully abducted Dawn's Earth-mother, Lilly, to our ship using them.

"Vasile has had little success gathering data on us, but we must still be very diligent in that respect."

Orbs? What orbs? Henry was thinking. He also wondered why he was called to a meeting with Melek and Gaff. He didn't have to wait long for his answer.

Actok turned his face, "Henry, my friend. We realize that even as an Awakened Light Warrior, you have always preferred anonymity with each incarnation. Your highly advanced technical skills and your willingness to well...put yourself out there, has often been praised by our Creator."

Actok was having a terrible time trying to find the right words. He stumbled, "As you know, time...We...well Henry, we..."

Gaff interrupted, "Excuse me, Actok. Let me, may I?"

Actok took a deep breath and sighed relief, nodded and stepped back.

Gaff said, "Henry, Actok's heart is too full. What he was trying to say...what we are gathered here to do is...honor you."

Henry was speechless. He looked around at the friends he has known throughout many incarnations, and at the new faces he's come to love, especially Teresa!

Gaff continued, "Simply put, we all admire your knack for daredevil maneuvers, risk-taking, seeing hidden objects, placing yourself in harm's way and...well, your compassion, Henry, above it all, your compassion is what our Prime Creator loves most."

Henry looked directly at Actok. "I am honored, of course." Truth be known, his chest was swelled and he could barely talk, his throat was all choked up.

Actok seemed to get a hold of his emotions and requested, "Then, please, Henry, accept this title of Honorary Avatar within the Ministry of Enlightenment!" He turned, picked up a brilliant white buttonless shirt, walked closer to Henry, and placed it over his head. The insignia in the middle was the same as on every member of the Ministry.

The group inducted Henry by bowing four times, signaling Henry's acceptance by all. Henry's chest swelled with love.

Actok coughed then continued, "Let us sit." The group waited for Henry to sit first. He felt so honored.

"Now, Henry, you might have seen some of us in action, but as a collective, we'd like to tell you of our abilities. Melek?"

Melek stated, "My strengths lie in my protective abilities. I can be in many places at the same time, through mind control. That's not to say telepathy, it's more within the frame of frequency interference. I can stop movement of time...for a time."

Actok nodded toward Gaff. "Gaff?"

"I can create positive or negative energy. I have the ability to walk through solid objects as easily as flowing through a wormhole. I can see from the back of my head." Henry's eyes widened and he started to smile. "Yes, I really can, Henry. I just didn't want to scare the group any more than they were already. I can also move faster than the speed of light."

Oonsay interjected, "Oh please, not to brag...much, but I'm not your go-to favorite avatar for nothing! You have seen me demonstrate my abilities, heard I can move asteroids from their trajectories, that I can walk through solid objects, and yes, I too can stop time...well, somewhat, but I can do something else...want to know, Henry?"

"Sure," Henry replied.

Oonsay smirked and announced, "My frequency levels are such that, for a short period of time, I can make myself invisible!"

Henry's mouth opened in awe, but he just smiled.

Actok stated, "Melek, Oonsay, and I will be joining forces with Nocren. Soon after, Uriel, Michael, Raphael, Sariel, Dawn and I will meet up with Jesus and his..."

Henry looked surprised and questioned, "Sariel? Who's Sariel?"

Teresa stood up quietly and confessed, "I am, Henry."

Actok tried to interject, tried to prepare Henry to realize she was both an angelic being yet still Teresa as he knew her.

Teresa walked toward Henry then stopped. She smiled, leaned over and kissed him sweetly on his lips. He was taken aback, but before he had time to react further, Teresa raised her body off the ground and presented herself as Sariel.

Henry stared at her, his love, now an angelic being. She smiled down to him and immediately folded her wings and transformed back into her earthly body.

He couldn't speak, couldn't move. Teresa stared into his eyes and it was then Henry knew she was still his Teresa. He started to cry. She sat down and this time she was hugging him. She whispered, "I'm sorry, I couldn't find the right time to tell you—until now." Henry turned, faced his love and they embraced, then kissed, oblivious to those in attendance!

Actok faked a cough, which brought the couple out of their revelry. "Do you understand now, Henry? Are you okay to continue?" Actok asked.

Henry looked over to Actok then to everyone else in the room. He was so full of love. "I...yes, please let's continue."

Henry wanted the attention off of him while he accessed this new reality. That wasn't going to happen, as he immediately realized Actok had mentioned Jesus also. Actok started to speak but was interrupted with, "Wait, Jesus? You said Jesus. You mean...you mean...Jesus himself?"

Actok took the time to laugh. "Oh yes, Henry. Jesus himself! What did you think? He'd like to be left out of the most-worthy of causes? To protect the most precious creation? His people?"

Henry thought, "Well, no, of course not. I guess I was thinking we're sort of alone down here, I didn't expect...well, so much assistance."

Actok continued, "I truly enjoy your human terms, so let me inject one here. 'We got this covered, man.'"

Gaff laughed so hard, he bent over, grasping his knobby knees. Melek just grinned; he couldn't think of a response anyway.

While Gaff was still laughing, Actok said, "This is the spiritual war of wars, Henry. Time is up for Satan and his puppets—Vasile and all his dark forces and species like the Draconians and Anunnaki. Satan will lose the temporary control over Earth he has been given.

"Dawn will be the catalyst to bring the planet's Starseeds into their new reality, into their truest of manifestations, into their own light.

"Jesus must return, in all his glory, to unify Earth and its people back to their true home—in the heart of their Almighty God! His presence will bring comfort and trust to the inhabitants that have been waiting for his second coming. They must feel worthy again, loved. Dawn will expose the darkness to all the inhabitants. Some will feel they recognize her..."

126

Renu was using another form of travel to return to China—the Projectile Beam. She had no need to worry, as she'd utilized the beam hundreds of times in her reincarnations.

While packing, Renu was reviewing all she had been told. Her meeting with Dawn, Actok, Skyann, Rosalee and Kristian was insightful. She was content with all the plans being set forth. What was upsetting was the heartfelt pain of seeing Dawn and the Archangels again. Seeing old friends and meeting new ones, then having to leave, knowing the great war was upon them.

No time was wasted when she arrived at her apartment in a remote area near Beijing. A quick scan indicated her environment was safe.

She spent time unpacking and took a shower. She dressed, then went into the kitchen to put on some coffee. A quick glance at the clock indicated it was 5:00 p.m. *Good,* she thought.

Coffee in hand, Renu stood in her living room and telepathically requested her best friend Victor come over. He arrived in less than ten minutes. With him was Renu's personal body guard, Big John. Both had a thousand questions but knew Renu well enough not to ask them.

Victor has been with Renu throughout all her incarnations. They have been siblings, lovers, friends. Once they agreed to challenge their friendship: on Orion they were bitter enemies, and through a series of trials, they came to realize their true enduring bond.

With this incarnation, more was required of Victor: he had sworn to be Renu's Avatar Warrior! He lived only to serve her and their Prime Creator's agenda.

While on the ship, Renu and Henry devised a plan: create a network of Starseed geeks to encode Starseeds' cell phones to respond to a special ring. This was implemented, and Vasile hadn't a clue of its existence. So far, so good!

I see this story now as if it's playing out in a movie. Renu is preparing for her biggest night wherein millions of souls will be saved, enabling them to save others.

Every time I write a scene, I see my characters acting out their part. Their personalities determine how they will react to a situation. Cool.

127

Vasile's feigned attention to Katz dropped immediately after his projection screens were situated all over the world. He didn't require a mere newspaper to reach his audience now, he had the whole world watching him.

Katz wasn't sure at first if he should feel happiness or anger that he was being brushed aside so quickly. After all, the notoriety and financial gain was exhilarating. That phase soon passed. It took one incident of Jaqui interrogating someone for Katz to realize his good fortune...he got a free pass.

Another benefit was now that he was working with Inky, he didn't have to worry so much about watching his back. Inky was a sensitive, an empath. Katz felt safe when in his presence.

Katz and Inky had been meeting for a few weeks now at Nicky's but also at a secluded area in Owl's Head Park, near the Belt Parkway. When he could get away, Aimes would meet up with them.

The recordings didn't tell Vasile any pertinent information he wasn't expecting. He knew Katz wasn't an ally but he also didn't consider him a threat. Even if he wrote negative information now, even if his paper went rogue, the damage was done. He owned the world. He just didn't care what Katz thought.

Inky, on the other hand, might prove beneficial. His recorded answers were reserved at best. He didn't even admit to knowing Dawn, but did he? Did he know anything about his archenemy, the Draconians, and their plan of action? He'd heard rumors they were on their way. Vasile thinks, *He's too evasive...perhaps a little aggressive questioning? Nah, not at this point.*

Vasile felt invulnerable. What with Jaqui and everyone who was a who's-who adhering to his every demand, control was his.

Ah...but what Vasile didn't know could hurt him. Khacee was slowly but surely infiltrating Vasile's immediate circle. But not militarily, not as a consultant, but as...enter Kylie Styles.

What? You didn't think Khacee could shapeshift? Why not? Our human bodies were created to manipulate the world we are living in. This hinders us from understanding/ accepting that other species are not limited in their abilities to adapt.

Did you ever hear that if we learned how to manipulate our frequency levels, we could walk through walls? So many abduction stories include this scenario—they actually see their captors coming right through the walls or down from the ceiling!

Did you know...it's rumored that our own military work alongside humans who possess super-human abilities? Look up the story of Uri Geller on YouTube. As a child he was able to bend spoons. His abilities soon grew and undercover intelligent agencies as well as private corporations paid him well for his services, to include finding oil. Excellent read!

∞

128

Vasile sat deep in thought in his favorite lounge chair on his veranda. Reaching to get a sip of his first cup of coffee, he turned to the sound of someone coughing. It was Jaqui standing in the entranceway. "Excuse me, Vasile, but I have confirmed information you must hear."

Vasile doesn't offer Jaqui a seat. "Yes?"

"We just received intel, just now, Vasile! It's what you predicted. A few minutes ago, the Draconians introduced themselves to the world. Undetected, they set up holographic projectors in every major city, hacking into networks we couldn't penetrate. We assume billions were watching and with the Chip...well, everyone on the planet will know of this communication today.

"Chikah has taken the role of leader, and at his command, positioned scenes of their uncloaking, much to the dismay of humans. Seeing them in their true form is causing immediate worldwide havoc."

"Go on, Jaqui."

"Scenes of his sizeable army positioned all over the world displayed millions of 'em, Vasile. Of course, it's just a hologram right now. But he's preparing to attack.

"This morning Earthlings were informed of his hatred for

you, Vasile...that..."

"That what? Speak!"

Jaqui inhaled a deep breath, while slime dripped onto the floor. He continued, "Yes, my friend. He's telling Earthlings you have been lying to them all along, promising hope and salvation. He's calling you Satan's Puppet while addressing himself as their True God. In the broadcast, he said he's coming for you!"

One would expect Vasile to jump from his chair, sound the alarm, and prepare for war. Vasile didn't do any of those things. He placed his elbow on the edge of the sofa, lifted his arm, and with two fingers, supported his head and...smiled.

129

At 8:00 a.m. President Fredericks walked into the Oval Office, where a cup of his favorite peppermint herbal tea was brewing on his desk.

He watched the announcement with a saddened heart. If only he could warn his people, warn all the people, that this was inevitable, and that even more alien species would attempt to control Earth, seeing it in its weakened condition.

He was sworn to secrecy. Only those Actok approved were in the know. But to see the people he was sworn to protect...he never touched his tea.

During the day he kept blowing his worsening runny nose. He started to feel feverish. When his temperature of 102.1 was realized around 2:30 p.m., it prompted a visit with the House Physician.

Along with the usual medical exam, he was tested for the second onslaught of what was now titled the Alpha and Delta Variants, affecting millions worldwide. Not ten minutes later his throat felt sore and he had a headache.

For both his health and safety reasons, he was flown to his home in nearby Maryland. The house was in Chattahoochee Hills in Fulton County, not too far from the College Park Airport.

Accompanying him in the helicopter was the Physician to the President, Dr. Abby Garced, with two nurses and two Navy Seal officers.

When President Fredericks and Dr. Garced were settled, the Navy Seal officers positioned themselves around the perimeter. They were in constant contact with James Dorsett, now the Acting President, since it was obvious President Fredericks was in no position to make decisions of any kind.

President Fredericks was confident James would abide by the covert actions designated by Actok and Nocren. All he need worry about was getting better.

It was evident that after two hours, the newest trial of intravenous medication, Remdesivir, wasn't doing its job. He was still sneezing profusely, his lungs were still manufacturing fluid, and it was difficult to keep him awake.

It was around 9:00 p.m. when Dr. Garced, exhausted from working diligently with her patient, announced to the two nurses she would try to get some sleep. They were in total agreement and had decided their turns at watch.

The three-story house was surrounded by woods on all sides. There was only a small driveway on which to maneuver a car, which would arrive dead smack in front of the sprawling porch. Of course, there are cameras strategically positioned in the woods and constant helicopter surveillance day and night. With the Navy Seal officers and all this protection, how could what occurred have happened?

130

Dawn was to meet personally with all who were on the ship. She was to commission them, using the cuneiform for positional guidance.

Since Awakening, Dawn preferred her natural state, that of a beam of brilliant light energy. There was no sense of weight, no breathing issues, no physical maintenance, and no need for sleep. Her sense of self was as if she were swirling within an energy field, the force of a bolt of lightning.

This outward change in appearance didn't occur with Light Warriors, as she resided on a higher plane of consciousness, more spiritual than physical. More crystalline in nature, like Actok. This was due to her body and mind resonating to a higher frequency, that of the fourteenth dimension. With a little practice, Dawn was able to shapeshift back and forth with little effort.

The first few sessions were with the Prime Creator, then Actok, Nocren, Gaff, Melek, and Oonsay. They were used to spiritual entities and enjoyed communing with Dawn in her element.

Not so when meeting her little entourage of 6! What fun she had reveling in their confusion whether to converse as their true self or not!

Dawn especially enjoyed her time with Skyann, who naturally reminisced of their friendship and close calls they shared.

It was during her greetings with Teresa, Henry and Poppy that she knew to approach them in a gentler manner. The first thing they noticed was a glow around her body, a softening of her anatomy, almost as if visualizing her through a light fog. The blonde hair, usually seen pulled back in a ponytail, was more platinum in color and settled over her shoulders.

Yet, it was the eyes one noticed immediately. One almost felt rude watching them swirling slowly, displaying prism shades of amber and aqua blue. All felt the same sadness when they first saw her, that the Dawn they knew was gone. Yet, by the end of their session, her welcoming gestures assured them she was still their friend, their Dawn.

One more person was on Dawn's mind, and she couldn't help but smile knowing her Earth-mother had just arrived. This was the first time Dawn had chosen this entity, who played the role of her sweet, unassuming Earth-mother to perfection!

131

Actok beamed into President Frederick's bedroom. Not one guard or any household personnel knew he was there. How effortless a maneuver to destabilize all the top-of-the-line security equipment in and around the President's home. He stood beside his friend's bed and telepathically announced, "Hello, Bill."

President Fredericks opened his eyes, smiled and tried to raise his arm.

Actok took his hand, "We haven't much time. You are physically dying. I have been granted permission from our Prime Creator to heal you so you may continue your wondrous work."

President Fredericks smiled but could do no more. With one slow wave of his right arm, Actok projected a beam of blue light that burst forth onto his friend's chest. President Fredericks felt a hot searing sensation so intense his whole body arched up. The heat quickly subsided, and his back landed with a thump. He immediately fell into a deep sleep.

Three hours later, Dr. Garced was back on duty and walked into the president's room. The other nurses were whispering in a corner—something about a miracle. Dr. Garced walked over and was handed the patient's chart. After reviewing the findings, Dr. Garced looked at the nurses then turned her attention on President Fredericks. She immediately took his temperature and questioned *How can his temperature be normal? How come he doesn't look flushed? Should I wake him to give him his meds? Wait, something had to have happened. Did the medication take hold so quickly? How can this be?*

132

∞

I'm frustrated. It's October 2020 and I have been at this story since December 2018. I'm so fixated on how it should end. Not even reviewing my extensive notes is helping me get to the war of wars.
DEEP BREATH! STOP FORCING IT. REST IN THE POWERS THAT BE!

∞

Linda didn't have time to heal from her injuries inflicted by Vasile, as Jaqui immediately started the training program he designed specifically for her. Reeling from a swollen head, she had difficulty hearing his commands. She was presented still in her filthy clothes. His words were inaudible, yet out of sheer terror for this creature's capabilities, Linda tried to apply the technique she thought he was saying.

Frustrated, Jaqui demanded she stand in front of him as he slowly applied his burning method of punishment. The intense heat felt like a warm enclosure around her body. Swaying and on the verge of fainting, Linda absorbed the heat, actually taking comfort from it. Her mind was lost to the reality of her situation. She didn't even realize his abuse wasn't having any effect nor that her body didn't burn when more hot pressure was applied.

Jaqui, shocked at watching his subject's reaction, stopped applying heat. Never had anyone been immune to his torturous actions, but never before had Jaqui ever dealt with the Lacerta race.

Watching Linda swaying back and forth, covered in filth, Jaqui got disgusted. He yelled to a servant, "Get this piece of shit out of here and clean her up. I want her back here tomorrow same time."

Linda was forced to walk. She was so dizzy she threw up and on the second attempt, fainted.

Linda awoke to a dark, damp room. Bred on Terran, a reptilian planet, her body instantly reacted to the cold floor. She started shivering uncontrollably. The only light emanated from a small open window high above and to the left.

Immediately she realized there was someone else in the room, as the sound of persistent yet faint scratching noises was gnawing at her psyche.

She tried to get up but her head was pounding. Touching her right temple, she felt a depression and realized blood was still oozing. The smell from her feces and previous vomit was almost overwhelming.

Not knowing who was making the scratching noises, she immediately realized she could be considered bait.

With all the strength she could muster, Linda pulled up to a seated position. Screening out the scratching noise, she listened intently for any indication of movement, so she became agitated when all she heard was a very human sound— her stomach growling.

Just as she was cautiously attempting to stand up, Linda heard a key unlocking the door. A bright light lit up the room and her attention immediately turned to where the scratching noise was. At first, she was surprised, as no one was there.

As the cyclops lifted her up on his shoulders, Linda noticed who was sharing her cell—a small bird, frantically trying to find its way out, but it never would; Brutus bit its wing and was done with it.

Something happened to Linda at that very moment. Something...

133

While traveling to her underground meeting, Renu had time to reflect on the human race. Elation at having seen her favorite trio yet again—Michael, Uriel and Raphael—reestablished the conviction deep in her heart that all was as it should be. Almost there, her thoughts turned to President Fredericks. *Everyone thinks him the fool. Not even Vasile is concerned with him. A mistake, a big mistake. I'm excited to see him tonight and to meet his little entourage: Daniel Katz, Detective Aimes, and Inky.*

The cavern was destroyed over sixty years ago, totally crushed by an earthquake. It was deemed safe for the congregation of thousands, yet precautions had to be met. Positioned alongside the Bezeklik Thousand Buddha Caves near the Taklamakan Desert, there would be no way anyone would realize people were there. The debris of man-made buildings and foliage had completely covered the entire area for over a mile.

There was no need for a holographic cloaking screen. It was easy to bring in the multitude of attendees as one could simply walk through the forest hidden under the trees. This, of course, took several days of preparation. Still, everyone was to be as quiet as possible so as not to draw any unwanted attention.

Renu stood on the podium, and looked lovingly at the massive amount assembled. She spoke into the microphone, "There is love here tonight. Wondrous love. Our Prime Creator is present and all of you are feeling His essence. Isn't it wonderful?"

The assemblage all responded by whispering, "Yes," hugging each other, crying joyfully. There was no holding back, love filled every corner of their being.

"Thank you all Light Warriors for your ceaseless efforts to bring forth those that would enhance the course of the human race on Earth. Your untiring patience and steadfastness are true attributes our Prime Creator loves to witness within you."

With that, every Starseed turned to a Light Warrior and hugged them.

"My precious Starseeds, be not afraid in your hearts, as all is as it was ordained.

"Most of you have been told, perhaps been brainwashed, to believe you are suffering through a tribulation which you caused. Your loved ones were taken because you didn't love them enough, you didn't love your Prime Creator enough.

"Tonight— enough! Yes, you are the "left behind" but there were reasons so. Tonight, my beautiful Starseeds, you will elevate to an understanding that our Creator loves everyone, unconditionally. Tonight, you will Awaken, tonight you'll be given the insight to understand why you were left behind."

134

∞

    Wow. I'm seeing the numbers 319 every single day lately! Every single day. So, I did what I do best...research. I found that 319 is an angelic message meaning the universe is with me, go for it! It's getting so obvious that I'm embarrassed when I see 319 and don't write my story!!!

    Due to COVID-19, our authors club meetings are on Zoom. Have to admit, I miss the camaraderie! I really enjoyed going out to lunch after our meetings to discuss our personal writing journeys.

135

The crowd drew quiet when Renu stopped speaking. She took her time gazing out at the thousands of people in attendance. Then she said "Please, all take a moment to look at the people near you. Take hold of someone's hand, preferably a stranger. How else can you get to know them? There. That's wonderful."

Renu became silent yet again. She lowered her head and the crowd mimicked her. No one spoke, no one moved. No one broke the contact chain.

Three full minutes went by, then Renu whispered into the mike, "Close your eyes now. Be in peace."

Not one eye remained opened as all responded to her command. Some people started squeezing hands, some started swaying slightly, but all eyes remained closed and all voices were still.

A miracle started to unfold. When Renu closed her eyes and raised her hands over her head, small, dimly lit orbs began to appear and individually hover above each and every Starseed.

Soon, a brilliant light burst forth from each orb, entering their bodies and surrounding them with warmth and a sense of overwhelming love. Some started humming, some swayed, but not one wanted the experience to end.

The brilliant flash of light that entered through the Starseeds enabled them to "see" into their souls. Immediately, all knew why they were on planet Earth. All understood their mission: to express themselves to others, thus performing the Prime Creator's mantra: *Love each other as I have loved you!*

The Awakening, the powerful message, the feeling of complete love for each other, created the need for some to quietly hum, while others grabbed the nearest person and started dancing. Lots of hugging ensued; some were even weeping with joy.

The Light Warriors mingled with their newest members, but no commands were issued—they weren't necessary. All understood their mission: go out to the world spreading the word that the time had come to choose.

136

Dawn prepared her body to acclimate to her Earth-mother's frequency levels. She didn't want to give Lilly a shock when she hugged her. Then she quietly walked to Lilly's apartment on the ship. She knocked and Lilly immediately opened the door and grabbed her daughter with the tightest hug Dawn had ever received.

They both laughed, then Lilly said, "Come sit, Dawn. We have so much to discuss. My first question, of course, is do you know if Carole's all right?"

Dawn smile and stared at her Earth-mother's face: full of questions, so innocent, like a young child's. "Yes, mom, she's fine. So are Kate and Jenna."

"Oh, that's great. I must admit I was worried." Lilly looked around and stated, "What a beautiful ship. And the people, every one of them, so nice." Dawn was surprised that Lilly could change topics so quickly, and that her first question wasn't about her.

"We haven't much time, mom, so let me explain..."

"You don't have to, dear. Gaff explained it all. Guess I've always known you were destined for...something...something more."

"Mom, I couldn't have asked for a better Earth-mother.

You understood me. I am honored."

Lilly started crying. "You're honored? Oh Dawn. And...look at you now. Look who you really are. I don't know if I should hug you again or keep crying."

"Let's just start discussing what your future holds. The choice is yours: go back to Earth after this event is over and live out your life with Carole, or go back to Orion, your true home." Lilly just stared at her daughter. She realized either way, she might never see Dawn again.

When Dawn started to lift her hand to Lilly's face, she thought it was to wipe away her tears, but Dawn pressed her finger on Lilly's forehead where immediately visions of her home, family, and friends on Orion appeared. It only took a few seconds when Lilly took her daughter's hands and said, "It was an honor to have you as my child, Dawn. And, I can always go home. So, I want to go back to Carole. She needs me."

Dawn held her Earth-mother once more. "Soon, mom, soon."

137

Nocren and Actok were walking into the recreation area where they noticed Lilly and Henry sitting close together in deep conversation.

Lilly questioned, "Really? So, what you're saying is there wasn't a Rapture? The planet isn't going through a Tribulation right now?"

Actok and Nocren looked at each other and their expression showed they couldn't wait to hear this dialog.

They made their way to the table. "Hello there. Can we sit down?" asked Nocren.

Lilly said, "Sure. We've just started talking about whether Earth has truly experienced a Rapture and Tribulation."

Henry said, "Have a seat. I was addressing the idea that perhaps the people on Earth didn't get taken off the planet the way the biblical account describes, but that something else occurred."

"And I was about to tell Henry some would consider that blasphemous. And that's when you came over."

The two sat down and said nothing. Henry and Lilly looked at each other. Henry said, "Oh, I get this. You guys wanna see where we're going with this. We're supposed to talk and look dumb and then you'll fill us with your wisdom. I get it! C'mon guys, give."

Nocren smiled incredulously at them. "What? We didn't mean to interrupt your conversation. So, go on, we want to hear your views on this."

Lilly laughed. "Okay, well, I was always taught to believe..."

Henry interjected, "There, let me interrupt you right there. Taught. That's the word, not felt or experienced but taught. I want to know what you feel, Lilly."

Lilly contemplated, "I've always felt the truth was hidden and it was up to the individual to find it. And...what's true for one isn't necessarily for the other. So, who's to say what I've been...taught...isn't the truth?"

Henry smiled. "You're evading an answer. But that's okay."

"No, I'm not," Lilly laughed. "I'm really trying to buy time so I can answer intellectually, if that's even possible around you guys."

Actok turned his head to face Lilly directly. "You do know already. You have powerful intuition. Use it. What do you think? Have some of Earth's inhabitants been taken up by the Prime Creator? If so, why? If not, where did they go?"

"Okay, applying biblically prophetic events to this present...ah, Rapture, I notice a pattern: that prior to releasing His wrath upon the people, all were warned. There are examples, like Ezekiel, Noah, Moses, and...lets forward to Jesus. All inhabitants at those times had their chance to change but many didn't repent.

"I'm not experiencing nor do I have access to what the inhabitants of Earth believe is happening to them now. So..."

Nocren interjected, "Yes, you do, Lilly. Think."

Lilly's mouth opened as she looked at Nocren. Her mind was racing. She answered, "Ah...okay, I'm...sensing they believe they're going through the Rapture and Tribulation foretold in the Book of Revelation. They are anxiously awaiting what was promised...Jesus will return and claim them.

"So...to answer your question, I believe the inhabitants feel God the Almighty has taken his chosen as was prophesied."

Lilly was looking up at the ceiling at this point and didn't notice the excited expression on her friend's faces. Her mind was deep in thought and no one interrupted her. "The taken must be...well, I don't think they're in spirit yet, I'm not getting that. Wait...no, they are still in their physical bodies. They're...being prepared..."

Lilly continued, "But, not sure as to the why—yet." Actok and Nocren turned to each other and smiled.

Henry said, "There's a story in Numbers about Moses warning the people about Almighty God's wrath, and the ground opened up and swallowed only the immoral, wicked ones. Do we consider that a Rapture? There really wasn't any account that they went through a time of tribulation.

"How about Sodom and Gomorrah? Ezekiel forewarned the people. The whole city was burned and only Lot and his children survived. Was Lot in a way...Raptured?"

Lilly, still deep in thought, added, "Uhm, now think of this! It's always been that the bad were taken off the planet, for example, Noah's story, and the servants of the Lord were left behind. In our modern-day Rapture, we're told all the good were taken!! Why's that?"

Actok said, "You should consider that in your human form, you created ideologies, formed religions, secretive cults, all to try and understand yourselves. So, ask yourself now, was any of this what our Prime Creator envisioned for His people?"

With everyone deep in thought, Actok continued, "Many would argue that man had divine intervention to bring forth the books of knowledge...like your Bible or the Koran. Was our Creator's hand really in on this?"

When no one answered Nocren asked, "Can you find the word Rapture in your Bible or the Koran?"

Henry said, "No, actually I tried myself to locate even one word and it's not there. The word Rapture was popularized by a man named James Nelson Darby in the 1830s. He belonged to a group called...ah...the Plymouth..."

Nocren interjected, "Brethren."

"Yes, that's right. Brethren," Henry replied. "They were of the belief the Bible held all the truths of church and its doctrines."

Henry continued, "There are those of course that will argue just because the word Rapture isn't in the Bible, the references of such an event are. Many argue the words Judgment Day is a synonym for the word Rapture."

"Yes," Lilly agreed. "That's the problem. That's where one's faith has to take a part. Do you believe or not?"

Actok smiled. "Lilly, you were chosen as Dawn's Earth-mother because of your devotion to the Prime Creator. I know He would allow me to speak now. You are from Orion, you know this. Recently, you have been given a quick peek at your family and friends there. What you don't know is your position on the Counsel of Enlightenment, Loving Mother. Not only did Dawn choose you for this incarnation, but you chose her! You purposely forgot prior to arriving here."

So much information started to filter into her mind. "Of course, of course," she mumbled. Lilly was surprised when at that point Nocren, Actok and Henry stood and bowed.

Actok and Nocren turned to leave. "Is that it?" questioned Henry.

"Actok, should we interfere at this point on his journey?" Nocren jokingly asked.

Actok, looking down at Henry, smiled and replied, "No, contemplation on his part will do the trick."

Henry then added, "Wait. I do have one question. It has been my honor to work with you on other missions, Actok. You know that. But what is your real purpose, the Pleiadians, for this mission?"

Actok replied, "Conspiracy theories abound, but know this. We are one with the Prime Creator. We administer His will, which on this particular mission means we assist His precious planet to rejuvenate and all who reside upon it to prepare for the greatest Awakening of their consciousness. Life as you have known it on Earth is about to get a face-lift. He wants love to flourish, as was His plan from the beginning. Exuberant, joyous love, the highest frequency one can experience. The catalyst for all..."

Nocren quickly chimed in, "Actok..."

Actok caught himself. "Oh, I apologize. I get so filled..."

"Yes, you do, Actok, and that's His greatest compliment."

Henry and Lilly watch as they walked away, deep in their dialog on love. That's when Teresa walked over and sat down next to Henry. "Hope you don't mind. I eavesdropped a little."

Lilly and Henry both chimed, "Oh, that's okay."

Lilly felt they should have some private time so she excused herself. Immediately, Teresa looked into Henry's eyes and said, "I've never felt this powerful a presence of love in my incarnations, my missions, not really. Henry, have you?"

Henry looked into Teresa's eyes. "I haven't either...until now. I'm beginning to appreciate my existence, my purpose and...and you, Teresa."

Much to Henry's delight, Teresa grabbed his shirt and pulled him into her. She planted a kiss on him. Neither cared if anyone was watching.

138

∞

For my readers who have difficulty expressing their feelings: all your life, in one situation or another, you've had to face the emotion love. You have experienced the pain and joy of putting yourself out there.

I firmly believe that love is the ultimate lesson, and that our Almighty God has given us Earth to EXPERIENCE it!!

And, by now, do you understand that my writing alludes to your reason for being here?

I'll offer you this:

"We are not here to live for ourselves but to live for each other."

– Nancy Stewart, a 107-year-old Irish resident

"Our purpose is simple, to love. To love each other, to love all life, and to love our Earth."

– Anthony Douglas Williams, *Inside the Divine Pattern*

"The purpose of your time here on Earth is not primarily about acquiring possessions, attaining status, achieving success, or experiencing happiness...those are secondary issues. Life is all about love—with God and with other people. You may succeed in many areas, but if you fail to learn how to love God and love others, you have missed the reason why He created you!"

— *Cannot find an author*

139

Signs posted throughout the assembly area requested silence. But, when Renu introduced President Fredericks, the assembled were caught off guard. Even Light Warriors can feel offended.

An apprehensive president said, "Thank you. I ask for your attention while I explain to you what is really happening on planet Earth now.

"You have been lied to. Yes, by your own government. I understand and accept the false narrative that had to be created around me. The façade had to be fashioned that our allies and their governments looked weak and easy for the taking. One crucial reason can be understood with the cliché *Keep your friends close and your enemies closer.*

"We had to obtain intel from within their worldwide organization, the T-HE-RE, whose leader is none other than Vasile himself. Vasile, the false prophet, the deceiver that so many have placed their trust in, is the Antichrist!" The crowd softly booed. "He has now received the highest position of power, Secretary-General of the United Nations!

"Let me explain some things Vasile will never tell you. The Antichrist is a genetically created cyborg. He is the weapon of choice for his maker, Satan."

The crowd quietly hissed their hatred of Satan.

"You know now that other species—ah, aliens—are real. Some are new here and some have been living among us for eons. And...you have figured out that for whatever reason, if their goal was to annihilate us, we'd all be gone. So far, you've noticed they're not interacting with us...yet. Know this. That's about to change!"

While the president was talking, Katz, Inky, and Aimes arrived. They had all received a private invitation to the event of which all were sworn to secrecy. They could not even discuss it amongst themselves. Every detail was meticulously executed.

Victor and James brought them over to Renu and introductions were made. They all turned their attention to the podium where the president was still speaking.

"I can tell you now, as the President of the United States, that we are preparing for the war of wars. This will be a spiritual war, one that entails not only Vasile versus Earth but Vasile versus an alien force he trusted, the dreaded Draconians. Fear not, for the weapon at our disposal will surely destroy the Draconians, Vasile and his armies, along with his creator, Satan!

"Vasile would love nothing better than to fight this war with military tactics. He knows he would win hands down. Satan has instilled in Vasile that our Prime Creator's strategy will bring forth a power stronger than any physical weapon ever invented. Oh, Vasile knows our Creator's weapon, he just doesn't know how to combat it!"

140

Dawn enjoyed the one-on-one conversations she had with her friends. Everyone was aware of their mission and now Dawn's mission could begin.

Throughout all her incarnations, Dawn's favorite place to visit was planet Earth. During those visits, she witnessed thousands of situations wherein there was war, conflict, and love.

She was in her room for two days deciphering the cuneiform, and was thrilled to realize the tablet not only directed her positions, but Dawn could now decipher the whole mission—if the timeline embedded on the tome matched exactly with what the Prime Creator had indicated during their last consultation, the time had come! It did!

Dawn knew that no "so far, so good" attitude would win this war of wars, only precision. This would not be a war of man versus man, but of good versus evil!

There would be no need for strategically assigned military zones. No naval stations or ships. No arial maneuvers. No satellite assistance. The Prime Creator needed none of these man-made armaments to bring forth the most devastating thrust of power ever imposed upon planet Earth.

Dawn understood that war, in and of itself, identified with

conflict, hatred, fear, loss of precious life. Love? If there were love between two opposites, a compromise would emerge! However, this time there would be no compromise.

This war would be the prophetic outcome of humanity's rejection of all their Creator offered!

141

Linda was very conscious of Jaqui's wariness when teaching her a technique, but instinctively knew he wouldn't apply his infamous burning procedure again. Why would he? She was immune.

Jaqui knew she had hidden abilities, especially that she was a shapeshifter, but he instilled upon Linda another form of torture, a psychological one: if she opposed him, she'd never see her home planet and family ever again.

With six days of incessant training and pumping vitamins and energy foods, Linda was back. Her mental acuity was intact, despite the head injuries imposed by Vasile.

Yet, to Jaqui's great dismay, Linda wasn't exhibiting the loyal dog submissiveness he had told Vasile she would. Yes, she performed his assignments. Yes, she killed if it were needed. But there were no signs of gratitude, no humbleness. He would keep a close eye on her.

Whenever Linda was granted a few moments, she found herself constantly assessing her situation. She had come to hate her captors and felt no loyalty towards them.

As was her Terran nature, she started questioning *Who deserves my loyalty now? What side would benefit me? Will Jaqui really allow me to see my family again? Wait, am I softening? These humans, that bird...*

It only took a short while to re-evaluate her circumstances, and a lesser amount of time to act on it.

Jaqui awakened to a thunderous sound. At first, he thought it was lightning, but soon realized it was his two trusted soldiers banging on his bedroom door. "Sir Jaqui, come quick, come quick, Linda has escaped us."

As Jaqui made his way to the door, huge globs of saliva escaped from the side of his crooked mouth. This always happened during times of great anxiety. The saliva made the floor slippery so to avoid falling, he had to move slower than he preferred.

He reached the door, unlocked it, and allowed his soldiers entrance. They noticed the saliva and tried to avoid walking through it. Being that the saliva was thin in its composition, it spread quickly and one of the soldiers fell to the floor, at which time Jaqui grew angry and hissed heat at him. While attempting to stand, he again fell backward and landed in the middle of the worst accumulation of the slimy substance. This embarrassed Jaqui so he burnt him alive.

The other soldier backed up in total horror. All he could think of is he was next.

"How?" he asked him.

Obviously scared for his life, the soldier announced, "We...heard her weeping incessantly, but when the noise abruptly stopped, we went to investigate immediately. When we entered her room, it was dark. Jori..." The soldier looked down at the burnt body. "Ah...we immediately turned on the light and found Linda was gone. The light prompted a lizard and two spiders to jump out from a corner and slither out the door under our feet."

"Sir Jaqui, it happened so fast we didn't associate these creatures with Linda. We immediately searched everywhere. When we regrouped, we realized she must have...have changed her...her form into the...the lizard. We of course did a search of the grounds but..."

Jaqui looked at his loyal soldier. He wanted to incinerate him, but now, with the loss of Linda and the burning of Jori, he needed all the help he could get.

142

Linda made it safely to a hotel room in Beijing, China. She reached out to her counterpart, a Lacerta alien named Rhen, who possessed the ability of remote viewing. It took him two intense hours of silence to gain the intel Linda required: finding Renu.

Rhen informed Linda that Vasile and Jaqui had all intention of ruling Earth with the inhabitants who would obey them. He also mentioned that the general consensus was the Draconians were telling Earthlings the truth —Vasile had been lying to them and now he's lost a majority of support. He needed to win this war to stay in power.

Rhen could foresee the Draconians were about to strike at Vasile, annihilate him and his entire regime, and reside on Earth as dominant rulers. They would, in turn, wipe out any inhabitants who would not conform, including the Anunnaki. The remaining humans would go through a process of DNA manipulation, resulting in the creation of a half human, half cyborg creature. There was no escape for humanity if either side won.

Even Linda abhorred this futuristic prospect; truth be known, living among humans DID soften her up. She was beginning to see the light...

Linda had a plan of action: with the coordinates Rhen supplied, infiltrate Renu's assembly and get an audience with her.

Linda arrived late and was startled at the desolated area she was in. The directions required she travel on a road walking in a downward motion. Soon she noticed many underground caves, once used for nuclear shelter. Considering the enormous amount of people, it was eerily silent.

Linda felt she was undetected amongst the crowd. President Fredericks was winding up his speech.

Linda knew who Renu was from photos her spies had supplied. As Renu walked away from the podium area, Linda cautiously followed her. She neared the front and began hiding herself within the curtains. When she peered out, Renu was not in sight.

All of a sudden, the curtains seemed to be swaying on their own. Linda attempted to move away from them but became tangled among the tassels. The more she stirred, the tighter the tassels seemed to wrap themselves around her.

Linda felt protected by the curtains yet frightened by the tightening of the tassels. In an effort to free herself, she bent down to loosen the ropes. She was jerking the tassel on her left leg when she suddenly felt a presence. She stood up and found herself face to face with Renu.

No one could see the pair hiding among the curtains. Strangely, Linda felt as if she was receiving a telepathic message. "You've arrived. I knew you were coming, Linda. What is your real name?"

Linda's mouth opened in awe and could only mumble, "Phetah." She stopped struggling with the tassels and stared at Renu.

Renu looked deeply into Linda's eyes and inquired, "What brings you here, Phetah?"

Linda replied, "Please, call me Linda. I...I do not deserve the name given to me by my birth parents. I..."

"I sense a betrayal in you...yet you're saddened...I feel that. Quick, tell me."

"Only now do I see what the plan for Earth is. I...I didn't care prior to arriving here. I have been a rogue, a pirate, willing to work for the highest bidder.

"Vasile bid far more than his adversaries. He assigned me a position immediately. I was to infiltrate a Dr. Kaplan's psychiatric office and produce recorded information on a Dawn Coleman. Easy assignment, I thought. Although the transformation process was..."

"Move on, Linda. We don't have much time. I need proof of your mission now, quick."

"Of course. Short end of it? He's the Antichrist, Satan's right-hand man. That didn't bother me so much, but Jaqui. Well, let me just say I wished Vasile would have murdered me when he had the chance. His fire burning torture did not work on me, but he used another form, a mental..."

"Yes, we have also seen him on the projector screens performing his techniques. Go ahead."

"Renu, they plan to take over this planet, soon. Their cohorts have been arriving daily. They're even coming up from under the sea!

"Well, I had time to reflect and realized I was on the wrong side! I want to help. I really do. I'm...sorry.

"There was this girl...Teresa...well, her example...let's just say she kept popping up in my head while in my cell. I almost killed her, Renu. And her little boy, too. I was almost there.

"I want to be part of this event, then I want to go home to Lacerta."

Renu's senses were on high alert. The flow of energy between them allowed Renu to "read" her. She was telling the truth.

Renu asked, "You must have had a game plan coming here. What did you expect after meeting me?"

Linda leaned in close to Renu's face. "With or without your

help, I am going to kill them. Annihilate them, as they would us. Then I would inform the people to stand up to the other alien races and merge with the Pleiadians. Fight. Fight."

"So, you know of the Pleiadians? Where do you get your information?"

"Sorry, Renu. My sources are my only means of defense, I cannot expose them."

"I see," Renu answered. "But, before you meet the president, know, I led you here. I allowed your spies our coordinates. We had to test you."

Linda looked at Renu with a deeper respect, as she knew it were true.

At that moment, Linda felt the tassels around her loosening.

"President Fredericks has just finished. Come, follow me."

143

Actok called a meeting. Present were Gaff, Nocren, Oonsay, Melek, David, Teresa, Skyann, Angelicia, and Henry.

"Our Dawn is ready. Soon you will be escorted to your assigned positions on Earth.

"Our Prime Creator is honored that His little band of six have come to recognize their full potential. The transitions are complete.

"Getting word from Renu, Rosalee, and Kristian that millions of Light Warriors are busy seeking out Starseeds in the darkest corners of the planet and assisting them into the Awakening state of their true existence, hence creating billions of warriors throughout the planet.

"Renu and President Fredericks have worked tirelessly convincing top leaders of each country to outwardly comply with Vasile's New World Order. The element of surprise would reap millions of followers. The only countries having difficulty are the dictatorships. Their countries are infiltrated with Light Warriors reaching millions, but the warriors are fully aware danger is right around the corner if caught.

"Dawn's presence will promote the onset of what is to be. She will bring light into this world, allowing all willing souls an affinity with our Prime Creator."

Sitting there, David's mind wandered off. *Will I, as a human, get the opportunity to demonstrate my newly acquired abilities as an espionage spy master?* He wondered how Uriel and Michael were feeling with their learned human capabilities. As an angelic being, there would be no need for deceitful tactics or the use of earthly weapons. But, he's David too.

As Dr. Kaplan, he was well suited for implementing the art of psychoanalysis. As Raphael, he already knew it wasn't necessary! The play never gets old: angelic beings relish any opportunity to act out scenarios in a physical body.

"David?" Actok asked.

David looked over to Actok, whose face had a questioning look. Immediately he announced, "Oh, I'm sorry Actok, I didn't realize...I was in deep thought."

Actok just smiled and continued, "The advent of Dawn is upon us. Her protection is utmost. She will, in only a few hours, be presenting herself to the world.

"Before we send you out on your mission know this: the Ministry of Enlightenment is proud of your training, your use of free will, and your steadfastness to this cause. Whether your training will even be necessary in this particular event is yet to be seen, but your particular abilities are a part of you now, and ready to utilize on other missions, should you desire."

With the deepest of bows, Actok continued, "Our Pleiadian race and other brethren races are honored to assist you to return Earth to its glory in the name of our Prime Creator."

David bowed. Yet he was torn: as Raphael the Healer, he hadn't had the desire to assist with wars on other planets prior to this request from Michael to get involved. But as David, he couldn't wait and was up for the challenge!

144

Yes, to the entire world, it was truth—one world leader running the show with his grotesque side-kick, Jaqui. They ruled utilizing the media, which was everywhere one looked: projector screens, TVs, cell phones.

Everyone was waiting for the announcement of a technological breakthrough: a little chip embedded in one's hand that would eliminate the need for watches, cell phones, car keys, and so many other handheld devices. Besides that, it was a personalized, flawless ID method every human would eventually need for obtaining...anything!

Yet, there was a growing populace seeking answers to where their loved ones were. They were sick of Vasile's unwillingness and disregard to address this situation with more than the same rhetoric that he really doesn't know. The subject was gaining momentum, with Vasile quickly losing the support of influential allies everywhere.

∞

Oh geez, I have to stop a minute. What am I trying to project here? What I've been told about the Mark? What was

prophesied about a false messiah? I don't want my story to delve any further down this path! Anyone who remotely cares about their future has already figured out that prophecies are relative, subject to interpretation!

I will admit this: my research has convinced me that the Mark is the embedded chip we will be mandated to wear.

145

The stage was set.

In Beijing, Renu and Linda walked over to where President Fredericks was speaking to a small crowd. He felt a presence; it was so strong he stopped mid-sentence and turned to see Renu standing with Linda. He immediately excused himself from his present company and greeted Linda with a smile. He held out his hand, which she hesitantly shook.

"Don't be surprised Phetah, I can read you. I knew you were coming. I just knew."

Renu looked surprised, while Linda was having a tough time keeping her mouth closed. When she finally realized how she must have looked, she released his hand and smiled.

Renu said, "Let's go over here and get acquainted." The three were seen walking away but no one felt they should intervene.

Renu started to speak, but Linda interjected, "President Fredericks, I…"

"Please, call me Bill or if you'd like, Berah, my native name. I am from Aldebaran, in the Pleiades. We are proud of our involvement with the Prime Creator and have volunteered our entire energy force to assist in this conflict.

"I've been Awakened since I took office and have come to

know Earth has many allies. As you are probably aware, the Draconians have arrived and are preparing to war with Vasile."

After a moment of silence, Linda said, "Yes, I have been informed. All right then. I swear my allegiance to you and your cause. We are not a race of warriors, although being reptilian, many species see us as such. I will do my part to engage my planet's support."

Linda wanted to mention the horrific episode she had just experienced at the hands of Vasile and Jaqui, but thought better of it.

Renu took Linda's hand, at which point Berah took the other. In unison they both telepathically acknowledged, "We are aware of your ordeal and we are sorry."

Linda was awestruck and started crying.

Renu was pleased to hear Linda promised support, but it was to be seen if her planet would bother interfering.

146

On a hidden island, Vasile allowed himself a well-deserved vacation. He was enveloped in the arms of the most beautiful human he had ever seen, Kylie. She had overnight charmed her way into his heart and mind. It helped, of course, that her persona was fortified with the power of pure love.

His reputation gained some credence when the media exposed the affair. They were seen as the most beautiful couple; people even commented they hoped they would marry.

A well-documented dossier was created for Kylie. It had to be; she had always kept out of the limelight considering her professional trade, call girl. Since Vasile owned most of the media, he made it known: no negative press or death.

Feeling energized yet saddened that my story is winding down. Lots and lots of editing. At least fifty hours this week alone and it's the day after Christmas! Already drumming up scenarios for my third book. Writing has become an obsession.

∞

147

Nocren and Actok, dressed incognito, arrived at Nicky's at 7:30 p.m. Sitting in a cordoned-off area were Katz, Inky, and Aimes.

Inky sensed a presence, a frequency that felt higher than his own. He didn't want to bring attention to this situation. Therefore, he slowly scanned the room so his companions would not notice.

Soon Nocren and Inky were locked in eye contact from across the room. Nocren immediately sent a telepathic message for Inky to nonchalantly bring his friends over to their table. He answered in the affirmative.

It was then Inky recognized Actok. He couldn't help but smile at Actok's attempt at dress. He was too handsome to ignore, even with a pair of casual slacks and a collegiate sweater; the Scandinavian appearance was just too much. Everyone stared at him; well, he looked like an Adonis.

Aimes and Katz were in a deep conversation when Inky coughed. They looked over at their friend. Inky then relayed a telepathic message that they were being called over to another table and to follow him without question. Katz was a natural at telepathy, while Aimes was practicing every day. How proud when given and understanding his first real command!

"Katz, Detective Aimes, I'd like you to meet some friends of mine," Inky announced when they reached the table, "Nocren and Actok." It was then that Nocren and Actok just bowed with their heads at Inky, as not to bring attention.

Nocren was dressed in a brown suit minus the tie. He too was strikingly beautiful, and his facial scar no doubt attracted unwanted glances, but his demeanor affected a don't-get-friendly attitude, so no one tried.

A round of drinks was ordered. While waiting, Nocren jumped right in. "I am speaking low so as not to attract any attention..." Nocren stated as he noticed at least three women eying Actok. "Which is quite difficult with everyone staring at you, Actok."

Actok just brushed off the compliment. "Well, we can't sit at their table now, can we?"

Katz asked, "Who are you guys, really? And why can't we sit at my table?"

Nocren whispered, "I'll tell you now. Your every word sitting at that table has been recorded." Katz's mouth dropped. He never felt his blood rush to his feet, and so pressured was the feeling around his heart, he was speechless.

Inky said, "And that means, ah...oh shit, Vasile. I should have known!"

Aimes stated, "I should have known. Oh fuck, what did we say?"

Actok said, "We believe not much damage has been done. Vasile has lost interest in you, Katz. We monitor his every move, best we can."

Katz finally addressed Nocren, "So, you're an alien. Okay, getting used to that fact. Hell, there's a few of 'em harassing me every day now. Yet, you're here to tell us we've been blabbing our mouths into a recorder for a few weeks now. And you...Ac..."

"Actok."

"Yeah, Actok. Have I got questions for you! I've seen your

name before. A friend of mine's missing and, well...she wrote your name..."

Actok interjected, "Yes. Dawn. You're speaking of Dawn Coleman."

"That's right, Dawn Coleman."

"Mr. Katz, Dawn is fine."

"So, I suppose you're not going to tell me anything else about her?"

When Actok failed to respond, Nocren said, "Not here, not now. You must listen. We have come to ask for your help. Vasile and the Draconians are going to engage in war any time now. I'm sure Inky has told you both what's going on in your world right now.

"We are hoping to create a diversion, using a false narrative, one you could propagate from..." Nocren points to Katz's table, "that table over there."

It took Aimes under a minute to acclimate to this situation—he was in the presence of aliens. And, being the gumshoe detective he was, immediately offered his assistance. "I'm in. What can I do? I know Bill...ah, President Fredericks... he's..."

Nocren placed a hand over Aimes' shoulder. "Thank you. Yes, he has told us about you. He has informed us of your courageous behavior and we are pleased."

Katz said, "And I'm in. Tell me what you want said and it will be done. I am also offering my paper at this time. Can't hide my head in the sand any longer. Since I'm on the outs with Vasile anyway, and he hasn't tried to kill me, but maybe that's just a matter of time..."

Inky, silent up to this point, knew what their clandestine meeting really meant. Knew what was really in store for them. Looking over at his two friends, "You know, you two are still Starseeds, you're not even Awakened yet and..."

"That hadn't gone unnoticed," Nocren admitted. "All the

more reason we are dedicated to protecting you at all costs. You have chosen to help of your own free will. You're a race of many dimensions."

148

It was getting dark quickly in Egypt, as Rosalee and Kristian walked away from the makeshift podium and stage. Everyone became quiet, wondering what was next. Why would the two speakers leave without going through an Awakening process with their audience? No one mentioned a break. People started to question each other. Some became frightened that their hideaway was jeopardized.

A small group started to move towards the stage, hoping to get answers, when a little blonde woman walked slowly toward the podium waving her hand across the crowd. The crowd hushed in unison. They knew something spectacular was about to occur. Those watching at every corner of the world on their coded cell phones were rushing to find a quiet area to witness what was coming.

Dawn looked lovingly into the masses and announced, "Fear not, for I am with you. I am Dawn, your Bringer of Light. I speak to you tonight the words of your Prime Creator. He who loves."

Dawn raised her hands yet again over the crowd. All felt the presence of someone profound speaking to them—no, vibrationally through them. The feeling of love was overpowering. Those few words, just hearing her voice brought tears to everyone's eyes. All were smiling, hugging. Rosalee was standing behind the stage curtain and was caught off guard when Kristian turned to her and kissed her passionately, lovingly.

Soon, everyone participated in "the wave" with their hands in the air swaying back and forth, humming quietly.

After a few minutes, Dawn again addressed the crowd: "Tonight my precious Starseeds, tonight you will be Awakened, as you have chosen. You have been in darkness long enough. Tonight, you will know who I am."

Dawn continued, "Warriors, I honor you for your loyalty and assistance but most for your expression of love toward all my Starseeds. You have worked tirelessly on my behalf and you hold a special place in my Kingdom, should you choose."

While Dawn was speaking the words of her Creator, every Starseed in the world felt something happen to their bodies: all felt grounded where they were standing. The pleasant vibration felt with Dawn's words was starting to intensify. Toes tingled. A warmth in the vibration slowly worked its way up through their legs, hips, chests, arms and heads. No one moved or spoke. They were completely absorbed in a euphoric stupor, and love was their only sense of being.

It didn't matter if you were there at that moment or on your cell phone thousands of miles away, all Starseeds were Awakened, who now knew who they were and what their purpose was on planet Earth.

The process took only a few minutes but the aftermath of overflowing love for each other took longer. No one wanted to stop expressing themselves to each other. So much hugging, laughter, dancing. The warning of being quiet was overlooked, but Dawn didn't seem to mind. She knew this was to be the last necessary Starseed assemblage.

"My loving children," Dawn began. The crowd quieted down and turned their attention to Dawn. "I am honored to have you amongst my Light Warriors. Tonight, as you stand newly Awakened, you now know why you chose to come at this time in Earth's history: to spread His words, 'Love conquers all.'"

"The war is upon us. Tonight, we tell the world we are ready. I ask you now, hush for a moment and stay steadfast."

The crowd was soon to understand those words. Cameramen and their equipment came out of hiding and were flashing pictures of Dawn as she spoke, "I speak for the One, your Almighty God. I say unto you my children of Earth, fear not. This time in your evolution was preordained. All will come to pass and Earth will once again be free."

Dawn looked directly into the cameras and smiled. "Hold fast and trust. All is prepared."

149

∞

Christmas has come and gone. I've promised myself I'd have this story done by December 31, 2020. I am diligently working hard to reach that goal.

Wondering what you are thinking at this point in the story. What would be some of your questions?

I can tell you this now. I have grown in my spiritual development and yes, my frequency levels are higher than ever before. I pay attention to "signs" placed before me. I am more emotional in my dealings with everyone.

Another change—my eyes are becoming greener in color! Is this just to be attributed to age? Research shows that's a no! Most eyes remain the same color throughout one's life. I'll take that fact and run with it—I'm Awakening!

Hasn't it been an awful year, this 2020? Why? Really, why? Do you believe it's for us as a species to look inward, to stop the hatred and express our love for one another? So, perhaps this was a test? From whom? Another alien race or...Almighty God?

Or, do you feel this is our new norm? An everybody-out-for-themselves future? Do you think we're going to have a New World Order soon?

Do you believe in the actions of these political and social movements—Black Lives Matter, Critical Race Theory, #Metoo, the LGBTQ? Do you agree with the taking down of statues and plaques reminding us of our history? Are you aware what the teachers are imposing on our children? Are you at all politically aware of what is happening in your government?

What are your thoughts on Elon Musk's and Jeff Bezos' futuristic plans for humankind? What would you do if you were in a position of immense financial power like they are?

Think about walking around next to cyborgs. How does that make you feel?

It's said history always repeats itself. What if it were true?

150

Chikah and his Royal Draco army were a force to be reckoned with; they have positioned a death-star planet over the northern hemisphere of Earth. They are prepared to nuke Earth with a neutron prana bomb, a thousand times more powerful than the Anunnaki's bomb used over 4,000 years ago.

There would be no empathy, no consideration for the inhabitants of Earth; theirs would be a total annihilation of all life forms.

For millions of eons the Draconians and Satan were allies. That was, until Satan became obsessed with their new creation, a Neo-Cehahr race of Draconian-Human hybrid machines, which, once functional, he would command.

Chikah refused to pay this homage to Satan, citing even though the creation idea was conceived on Earth, the machines were manufactured on their home planet, Cekahrra. Satan knew not the coordinates to Cekahrra, a blunder he regretted. He could only sever his association and swear vengeance.

Satan held steadfast to that call. He had his spies obtain the design by torturing rogue Draconians operating on Earth. After many futile attempts, a replicated human-cyborg creation bore fruit, Vasile.

This blatant copying of their technology enraged Chikah. He sought now total annihilation of the human race including Satan.

Tina Woods, along with two reporters, sought out a tip and were able to hide themselves nearby where a meeting of disheartened Draconians leaked Chikah's plans. All was captured on tape.

This event was the catalyst for Katz to authorize the printing of the truth: a war was inevitable and the participants were in position. Daily, the *Brooklyn Gazette*, now the most-read newspaper in the land, was considered the "Combat Zone," where the truth was told, regardless of retaliation.

That leap, Katz understood, meant he could have just signed his death warrant.

151

Khacee was not enjoying his role as Kylie, to say the least. Acting as a female prostitute who must bed Vasile, well, aversion and degradation consumed his being. Hiding that, while Vasile wined and dined him, while he stared lovingly into his eyes, was decidedly the hardest undertaking ever.

Informing Actok and Nocren of his rogue mission wasn't easy either. After the reprimand, they understood Khacee's desire to be in the midst of the enemy camp, but in such a disguise?

Vasile was obsessed, his human traits were in overdrive. He would do anything Kylie wished and Jaqui was getting sick of it. For a week he was shunned as Vasile was in front of cameras flaunting his new love.

That's when Jaqui realized there must be a spell on Vasile and he was going to get to the bottom of it. With the loss of Linda, his favor had diminished greatly in Vasile's eyes.

Jaqui wondered why his spies couldn't find Linda. *Was she this Kylie woman? I know she can shapeshift but would she be so brazen?*

It was wise of Satan and Jaqui to question Kylie's intentions—her position made her privy to Vasile's world. She found out the meaning of the evil intent with his organization, the T-HE-RE: Tenet—Human Eradication— Reclaim Earth. The subdivision AIM was Artificial Intelligence Mars. Now it was true, any humans who wouldn't willingly comply would be eradicated and they were going to colonize Mars with human hybrid cyborgs as well. Perfect acronyms.

Satan suggested to Jaqui to kill Kylie immediately, and that he would have a talk with Vasile! Secretly, Satan wondered if there was a flaw in his creation, and having him submit to a "tune-up" was on the agenda.

Jaqui quickly called Kylie to join him in his private chambers under the pretense of getting to know her better. (Up to this point, he hadn't been able to get a definitive read on Kylie, as she was always with Vasile.) He was glad she quickly accepted his offer. *She's probably thinking we'll be making wedding plans for her! The minute she walks in, I'm going to burn her alive. That is, IF she's not Linda!*

Jaqui opened his door and welcomed Kylie in. She walked over a pool of slime and heard him lock the door. She turned to see Jaqui smiling a vindictive smile, his body becoming a crimson red.

He immediately wanted to determine if Kylie were Linda. He still couldn't get a read, couldn't tell what she was thinking. He started to emanate intense heat on her legs, knowing if it were her, she would be impervious to this treatment. To his surprise, he wasn't given time to find out, as with the first burning attempt, Kylie shapeshifted into his true self. Fast as lightening, Khacee's wings flew open in one blasting whishing noise. The shock of this transformation, this little nothing human now hovering over him with enormously loud, flapping, giant wings, took Jaqui off guard. He backed up and slipped on his own slime. His body lost its ability to generate heat. His color turned back to normal. He was panicked, shocked, so each attempt at rising off the ground failed. "Who are you?" Jaqui questioned.

Khacee stated in an echoed voice, "I am an emissary of

your worst enemy, the Prime Creator of all things." Hovering, Khacee enjoyed watching Jaqui squeal, slipping and sliding in his own slime. The angel's wings started flapping harder as Khacee lifted himself higher above Jaqui. He announced, "And I have a message—you reap what you sow—burn eternally." With that, Khacee blew a blast of golden liquid heat over Jaqui that enveloped his body and the entire floor around him. He didn't die, but was permanently embedded within a shield of perpetual molten fire, unable to move for eternity.

It was the sight of Jaqui unable to speak to Vasile through the impenetrable plasmic shield that broke the spell Khacee had on him.

The Prime Creator made it so!

152

There were no more safety nets. It was rumored the Draconians were ready to strike. They were close by, no doubt, but where?

Vasile and Satan had organized the largest army of human cyborgs ever created: dark evil entities with no souls. They were intermingling with humanity, as if already the victors.

Daily, thousands of hungry souls desperate for food were captured, tortured, and murdered by these cyborgs. Only those that wore the Chip were ignored. The underground system was overwhelmed in their efforts to help everyone.

Every day the inhabitants of Earth were exposed to Light Warriors and maleficent alien beings. They were being forced to choose. Some swore the Tribulation was upon them.

Satan realized Vasile had been unable to seek out Dawn, unable to find Linda, and unable to protect Jaqui. Without the aid of Jaqui, Satan recognized Vasile's ability to rule was greatly diminished. He knew Vasile was losing his edge, and dictators were the first to notice and comment. Soon after, other nations were becoming disinterested in his leadership. Conspiracy theories abounded, all with Vasile going down.

Satan was stunned, his first blow in the war. How could Vasile, his prize creation, have failed him so? Who killed Jaqui?

Where was Kylie? How could his league of spies and his intelligence networks fail to find Dawn? Satan thought *Why aren't the Anunnaki assisting in this war? Do they know something I don't? Are they waiting to sweep down after the carnage? Are they working with the Draconians? Or worse...have they sided with the Prime Creator?*

Actok had at his disposal hundreds of thousands of alien warrior ships from all corners of the universe cloaked behind holographic clouds, just waiting for word...

Satan's army was closely watching for the Draconian ships. Their weapons were armed and ready. So, he was shocked when he received yet another blow—intel that Dawn was not in Brooklyn, but in Jerusalem at the Wailing Wall with hundreds of cameras taking in her every move. *How prophetic*, Satan thought, *of course, the Wailing Wall.*

One of Satan's drones hovered over the area where he noticed Renu, Kristian, Rosalee, Henry, James Dorset, President Fredericks, Victor and Rhen, standing all together near the wall.

He didn't recognize one man standing alongside them...Khacee! He wondered *Where is Dawn?* He couldn't have known that Raphael, Sariel, Michael and Uriel were also not present!

He also understood Katz and Inky would stay at the Gazette, alert and ready for any news. Satan knew he had problems on two fronts: there were no Draconians and what was his mortal enemy up to?

Although the Pleiadians laugh at the old cliché— history repeats itself —they realized some situations do cause previous scenarios to come into play over and over. Thus, the Pleiadians' trick—to plant false information provided by Aimes and Katz while at Nicky's, worked.

The Draconians thought they had the upper hand, but they were given the same incorrect information Vasile received: that Dawn was addressing the inhabitants of Earth in the

Brooklyn Stadium! They also realized where Dawn was Satan would be! Thanks to the work of David, Skyann, Henry, Teresa and Angelicia, powered up from their training, all Light Warrior internet information was controlled telepathically and false information was forwarded to the enemy.

Both Satan and the Draconian armies scurried to bring their fleets to Israel. But was it too late?

The underground system, working in alliance with the best technical geeks on Earth, prevented Satan's attempts at blocking the air waves. The message was sent to all Light Warriors that Dawn, the Bringer of Light, was going to appear once again. This news was broadcasted and it created an upheaval of anticipation and excitement.

There was no need to hide this assemblage; there would be over 3,450,000 people in Jerusalem alone, with billions all over the world watching while in a secured area, on a secured network, using a code embedded in the phones of only the Light Warriors.

No enemies were in sight, they were still in transit.

No one knew where Dawn had been when she suddenly appeared before them. Dressed in a white robe and wearing no shoes, she walked up onto a large mound of dirt placed directly in the middle of the newly created male and female divide. Not one person interfered with this arrangement. It was as if it just felt right when it was being prepared. There was no podium, no microphone.

Dawn stood still and closed her eyes. You could have heard a pin drop. She placed herself in a deep state of meditation. Then, Dawn cried out loud, "I am Dawn, the Bringer of Light. I speak for the one, your Almighty God, your Father!"

Silence. Then Dawn's voice resonated, "I am your Almighty God. I created your essence, your spirit in the likeness of Me. You are my precious ones."

In that very moment, her appearance transformed. A brilliant light beamed down on her from above the clouds. Her physical body slowly faded, as an azure, crystalline body with swirling glittering lights flickered before them. She started to float above the mound. To the astonishment of all, Dawn exposed her true self—The Bringer of Light!

So bright were her colors, so awesome her expression that people screamed her name while others fell to the ground in worship.

A deep voice resounded from within her. "My children, how proud I am. You were free to travel anywhere in the universe, but you chose to assist Me in an experiment of the human condition. All understood that while upon this planet free will ruled. Not even I would interfere for a certain period in your time."

Everyone's eyes and ears were attuned to the precious words. "You have heard that a Rapture has occurred and all the spiritually good people were taken from you. Yes, the spiritually Awakened among you were removed off Earth but only for a brief moment of time. They were trained to assist in your Ascension. All will be reunited in due course."

No one moved. Everyone was on high alert, inwardly feeling excitement but they knew not why. The people watching on their cell phones were glued to their screens.

Dawn's spectral body started moving downward, landing softly on the mound. Slowly, she turned back into her physical body.

Standing, looking out at the audience, she tilted her head as if listening. Everyone watched as a man dressed in a white robe and wearing no shoes appeared onto the platform and stood next to Dawn. He raised his hands above his head and said, "As foretold, I am here." And with that, a powerful gush of warmth and love was felt by every enlightened being standing there or on their cell phones.

The crowd roared with excitement. Cries of, "Jesus has returned! Our Savior, Jesus! The prophecy is fulfilled!" All over the planet, the Enlightened were crying with joy, dancing, hugging or praying.

Dawn smiled at Jesus and they waved their hands in front of the crowd then placed them on their chests, a gesture expressing pure love for all.

Then, as Jesus walked off the mound with Dawn, someone yelled "Mary? Are you...Mother Mary?"

The crowd went wild with adoration. "Mary? No, Mother Teresa!" Others screamed, "Ruth, Ruth." A man yelled, "Who are you? Please, who are you?"

Jesus smiled and said to Dawn, "Here it comes!"

As they walked into the background, chants were heard that could not be ignored. "Jesus? Or, are you the reincarnated Ezekiel? Moses? Noah?"

As if on cue, all the spiritually Awakened realized their cell phones were vibrating. The time had come...

153

∞

There are a few scenarios swirling around in my brain as to how to finish this story. Oh, wait, were you expecting me to come up with just one ending? I did give that a lot of thought, but really...how could I? What's the name of this book?

I'm sure you've noticed my stance is one of a spiritual nature, of which I have alluded to often. So, let's start with my scenario.

ONE:

The underground system created a worldwide spiritual network with all Light Warriors informed that the Prime Creator's most powerful weapon was about to be unleashed upon the planet. They were given their instructions.

Actok's mothership and its crew hovered over Jerusalem, cloaked in a hologram of clouds. Aboard were Actok, Khacee, Melek, Gaff and Oonsay.

Renu, Henry, Rosalee, Kristian, Lilly, Linda, James Dorsett, President Fredericks and Dr. Abby, along with Rhen, Victor & Big James, were beamed aboard when the ship arrived. Immediately it was obvious there was an attraction between President Fredericks and Linda.

Despite drastic failures, Satan and Vasile had tirelessly attempted to find what weapon of love they were up against. It had to be a physical weapon, didn't it? They expected it to be, as how could love in and of itself be a weapon?

Some of the alien species left Earth in fear of the outcome. Others figured they'd take their chances. There were many alien races who offered the Pleiadians military assistance at the last minute, but were informed it would not be necessary.

The hologram was lifted and the skies above Jerusalem quickly turned black as the massive army of Pleiadians ships, along with their hundreds of ally ships, exposed their mighty fleet.

Within minutes, the rest of the world noticed the gigantic ships hovering above them. Everywhere the world turned dark with the presence of them.

Who else were in each and every spaceship? The faction who were taken, the most spiritual humans on Earth. Their mission was to be trained to assist in this moment; trained to display the most powerful force—ever!

All the military might on Earth was ready to engage.

The Draconians arrived but quickly assessed that they were outnumbered.

Satan's ground army stood ready for battle. They believed their neutron assault weapons would wipe their enemies out of the skies. Fools—the Prime Creator didn't need destructive technology or military tactics to win His war. Remember the parting of the sea, the great flood, Jericho?

Before the enemy ships could drop a bomb or spray deadly gaseous chemicals, before they could even realize what sort of strategy was being applied all over the world, every Light Warrior felt the vibration. No matter where they were, all stood still and closed their eyes.

Dawn and Jesus, standing once again on the mound in front of the Wailing Wall, closed their eyes too, allowing their spiritual force within them start to hum. The humming became louder and louder. They raised their hands and looked up to the sky. Dawn again morphed into the crystalline being, humming in a pulsating rhythm, while Jesus transformed into a brilliant white light, emanating the same pulsating rhythm as Dawn. People had to look away, the energy and light were too powerful a force to look upon.

While the enemies were scrambling to understand what was coming next, every single Light Warrior on the planet started humming in unison.

At that moment, the faction on the ships beamed down into every corner of the world. There, they took the positions Dawn had given them using her cuneiform.

Immediately, billions of white orbs dropped from the Pleiadian ships and all their ally ships. The faction unilaterally belted out a high-pitched shrill so forceful that the orbs landed right above the head of every Light Warrior on Earth, and released an oscillated beam into the minds of Awakened humans, resulting in all being of one consciousness.

Yet, the un-awakened souls heard nothing, felt nothing. Absolutely nothing.

Satan and Vasile rushed to destroy the floating orbs but found their weapons could not penetrate the force field of love's consciousness. Still, Satan demanded his armies to fire their weapons on everyone, but the frequency waves of love knocked them out of their hands, rendering them useless. It was as if every Light Warrior were the weapons, weapons of love!

Then, from their ships, in a futile effort, the Draconians attempted to release their deadly gaseous chemical onto the masses, only to find a gathering of angelic beings had surrounded their ships, inhaling the gas and exhaling it back inside their ships.

Alone in the Command Station, Chikah realized his dilemma. He didn't assume he needed to fight anyone other than Satan. Kill Satan and all would fall to his knees. He was caught completely off guard.

Chikah watched, as one by one, his fleet dropped from the

skies. He stood firm, acknowledged his defeat, then deeply inhaled his last breath.

Michael, Khacee, Uriel, Sariel and Raphael, along with Oonsay and Gaff guided the falling ships, via the cuneiform position, to an abandoned compound outside Jerusalem.

Satan too realized defeat. Even with his force of unprecedented evil, and with his creation Vasile, he was unable to deduce the weapon that rendered him helpless— UNIFIED LOVE!

At that moment, hundreds of millions of lost souls fell to the ground and died. They had made their choice.

All of this was broadcast throughout the world on big projector screens or on home televisions. Great joy and contentment abounded as Earthlings watched Khacee, Uriel, Raphael, Sariel and Michael round up Vasile and Satan and present them to Dawn and Jesus.

For the spiritually inclined, beautiful, isn't it?

TWO:

Everyone on the planet assumed they were preparing for a spiritual war of wars, as did Actok and every alien species on Earth or in the skies.

All was set. All knew their positions. All thought the war would take place—tomorrow!

Therefore, it took every single being by surprise when one Draconian ship came into view, showing their ships with a white mist. Actok watched from his mothership, but was defenseless. The gaseous chemical seeped through their vents and with one breath, all were dead.

Everyone in the crowd, Jesus and all of Dawn's entourage watched in horror—disbelief—then they too fell to the ground, dead.

Vasile and Satan's armies had no time to create a defense. They weren't prepared, and all intel suggested that the Draconians were coming tomorrow. Within seconds all were annihilated.

Chikah knew he didn't require thousands of ships to position themselves all around the world, as within minutes, the chemical spread so quickly into every single human being, along with every alien species, hybrid, and cyborg on the planet.

After a cleansing was performed on Earth from their aerial ships, they arrived on Earth and started a new colony of purebred Draconians.

There is no prophetic outcome here. It's a law of war in this battle: appear weak, then show your strength.

Does this scenario perpetuate in you the belief that there is no Almighty God? Can you accept that every single spiritual person on this planet were worshiping a false entity?

Is it ALL a façade? There really isn't any spiritual and religious truth? Jesus, Dawn, the Archangels, all of it, was it just another form of mind control? You WERE just a product of your mom and dad having sex?

Can you picture a total annihilation like this occurring on Earth?

In this scenario it's, "We didn't act quick enough, we wouldn't work with each other, we kept believing world governments would protect us." Blame, blame, blame. No love here!

If we, as a species ARE an experiment, and you did AGREE to come to Earth, how do you feel that we were here, had the opportunity but...failed?

For eternity, the Draconians will tell this story to their children, offering proof they are the true deities of the universe.

THREE:

Almighty God needed no military armies, no angelic beings, no Light Warriors. That whole scenario was to divert attention away to His real plan: to put an end to the experiment he placed on the inhabitants of Earth.

Almighty God watched as his creations prepared to die for

Him. That was the only catalyst He needed.

With nothing more at His disposal than the thought to do so, He removed the shield of darkness from within the minds of every inhabitant and manifested a New Earth, filled with his blessings, where the promise was made never to impose the free will statute again. With love as the ruling agent, there was no need.

Humanity was saved.

Jesus and Dawn immediately went to seek out Satan and Vasile. But what they found was Almighty God's form of punishment.

Satan thought of hiding himself inside his creation, Vasile. While thinking of ways, he played out a scene in his mind. *Why not enter him, upgrade his abilities from within? I could create the most powerful hybrid cyborg ever.*

This was Satan's worst course of action! Little did he know Khacee had weakened Vasile's defense system daily, with doses of a lingering euphoric perfume used when alone with Kylie.

Satan had no problem entering Vasile, as he was too weak in his ability to resist. Immediately Satan went mad with thousands of frequencies shocking his body upon impact. The potion seeped through his spectral form leaving him defenseless against the power of love. It was...actually...that effortless.

All Jesus and Dawn had to do was bind what was left of him and present him before Almighty God for judgement.

Any beings, to include humans, hybrids, cyborgs or visiting species were welcomed to inhabit Earth.

FOUR:

I'd lead you to a confrontation but offer no ending. Oh, if I could only be with you when you create a scenario of your own.

Here's my question: would you still create the same scenario as before you read this story?

Now let's see if you agree with the outcome of my characters. I'm hoping you were involved with them enough to understand and approve of my choices.

154

New Earth. Almighty God gifted all their choice—to finish out the lifetime or go to their real homes.

On Earth, the words Light Warriors and Starseeds would be titles mentioned in stories that would be told for eons.

Much work was needed to bring Mars into fruition for those who wished to establish a colony there. Who better to train the inhabitants than cyborgs who were created for just such an undertaking?

Other alien races returned to Earth and more arrived daily, some to visit, some to stay.

The Anunnaki were not in Jerusalem and had not accepted Satan's offer to assist. After their eons of watching, manipulating, and interfering with Almighty God's human experiment, He gave them an ultimatum—"Side with me and continue to do good to my creation, or die." They sided, and with their advanced technologies, offered Earth's population their knowledge and...love.

The Prime Creator formerly announced Actok's promotion during a ceremony on the Pleiades. He received the highest position alongside His Creator: Prime Minister of Enlightenment.

Nocren, too, was honored at this event and humbly (but

gratefully) accepted the position his good friend had held, the Most-High Unifier of the Ministry of Enlightenment.

The first order of business for Nocren was to offer Oonsay the recompence position of Chief Sentinel with an army of thousands at his command. Being they were in the Pleiades little need was warranted of an army. Oonsay accepted the position knowing it would not hinder his ability to travel on other missions throughout the galaxy when needed.

Khacee and Dawn wanted to explore New Earth in their physical form. They decided to embark on a long, overdue vacation. There was no reward offered them; this mission was their calling.

Even as a Light Warrior and the Bringer of Light, they represented the real meaning of...soulmates. Eventually, Khacee would return to Schedar and Dawn to where she held a prominent position, next to Jesus—wherever He was needed.

Dr. Kaplan knew he could assume his true identity, Raphael, at any time, yet decided to live out his life on New Earth. There were those who required emotional adjustments to their new lifestyle so his psychiatric business was thriving.

He was happy to find his sister, mother and brother-in-law were saved. He listened tirelessly to their story of redemption.

And yes, Dr. Kaplan finally does meet a woman at his sister's house, an enlightened being in training, Leigh. Their goal is to volunteer on off-world missions together!

Ah...Skyann. Deep in thought she pondered, *Despite the fact that, as a human, I'm easily frightened and now realize David and I were never meant to be in a long-term relationship, I like my existence this time round. There's so much opportunity to express oneself. I'll stay in Brooklyn and write my next book. It will be a documentary of all that's happened. I'll ask Tina Woods to work with me. She has expressed the need for some assistance at the Gazette...*

Skyann and Dawn said their goodbyes quietly, and not

without the shedding of tears. They looked forward to the undoubtedly numerous missions they would still be called upon to perform together. They both agreed, though, this one was fabulous!

Angelicia preferred her true role, that of Archangel Michael, and would assist Actok in his new position. There were tears and promises of a reunion when she said her goodbyes to her father, Juan, and Teresa.

Renu, Kristian, Rosalee, and yes, Rhen (Linda's counterpart turned Light Warrior—with the assistance of Khacee) created and managed the New Earth Enlightenment Center, the hub of the cosmic library right inside the White House.

The cuneiform, now considered a piece of history, could be found on display at the National Archives building in Washington, DC.

Linda and President Fredericks are considered the "cutest couple" when seen walking around the White House together.

She requested and was given the opportunity to privately apologize to Teresa and Dr. Kaplan.

She also ventures to Lacerta with Rhen to visit family and friends. Her race had offered their full assistance but it was not needed. They swore their allegiance to the Pleiadians.

Gaff and Melek accepted the commission from the New Earth Enlightenment Center to train willing souls in the arts of self-defense, telepathy, and remote viewing.

Henry was offered a permanent position in Oonsay's army, but he rejected the offer...with good reason. Teresa accepted his proposal of marriage. They both wanted to live out their human lives on New Earth, but have volunteered to assist on other missions.

Poppy and Juan would remain with Teresa and Henry in Brooklyn. Poppy is still looking for Selma. Seems she tried to get back to him...

Juan had been noticed frustrated with his friends of late. They just don't get why he's banging on his ears like that in front of them. But others realize he's already displaying his desire to teach his awesome new found abilities in telecommunication.

Lilly desired to return to Carole and Kate, as she knew Dawn's true purpose now. To her great pleasure, Dawn granted them access to visit other worlds alongside her when it was feasible to do so.

Life on New Earth hadn't stopped its usual day-to-day routines. There was still a paper to run in Brooklyn, so Inky and Katz shared in the duties of publishing the news together.

Natalie Brown was rehired and promoted to Managing Editor/Investigator, along with receiving the most-sincere apology Katz had ever made. With Katz's blessing, Natalie promoted Tina Woods to the position of News Editor.

It seemed all four have not yet adjusted to the warp-speed articles their recently hired alien beings produce before lunch!

Almighty God protected Katz, Natalie Brown, Tina Woods, Victor, Big John, Carole and Kate throughout their ordeal. He knew their hearts.

Poppy, Nurse Abby, James Dorsett, Detective Aimes and his wife, had pronounced their love for the Almighty God and were Awakened prior to the war, in their churches, despite the fear of exposure and death!

Katz and Inky would remain best friends for the rest of their lives.

Detective Aimes retired and only assisted the force on a consulting basis. Yes, situations arose but were quickly investigated with justice served. He enjoyed spending more time with his wife, a few yearly dinner engagements with his friend Bill Fredericks, and more games of golf with Katz.

New Earth's government did not require a man sitting full-time on a king's throne or at a desk in the White House. Actok and Nocren introduced a foolproof system of checks and balances, eliminating the need for much decision-making. No communistic regime here; the people were given back the power, and with President Fredericks leading his people with love...

James Dorsett was given a new title: Administrator of New Earth, answering to or obtaining advice from Nocren. He could perform any duties required of him right from his home.

James was pleasantly surprised when informed Dr. Abby Garced was of great assistance to the cause. She proved her loyalty when asked to perform a dangerous rogue mission: deliver the elixir Khacee needed to seduce Vasile. It was made in the basement of the White House, and had to be brought over to Vasile's apartment undetected. This required numerous road trips, which she performed with tenacity and courage...and never spoke of it to anyone.

Lately she's been very busy in her new position of Chief of Surgery in an office in downtown Washington, DC...removing everyone's Chips! This made James quite happy, as he thought Dr. Abby to be quite nice...

Throughout the world love was the deciding factor with the inhabitants on Earth. The spreading of the desire for unified love prevented future famines, wars, and unnecessary havoc.

All was well on Almighty God's precious planet—Earth!

There is so much I have not been able to cover in this book. Like quantum theory conspiracies, alien abduction phenomena, parallel worlds, conscious AI technology, life on Mars, and seek the true agendas of hidden organizations.

What if I were to tell you that there are those who know every single alien being in the universe shares our DNA? Would you feel more of an affinity towards beings from other worlds?

The intention of writing this story was to devote the time

to research the what-ifs, in an effort to find my way and share the findings with you.

I truly believe the soul of our humanity is at stake at this time in our evolution! I also believe the heightened violence is going to wake up millions of Starseeds. Everyone is becoming aware of something happening. Isn't that why you chose to read this book?

Here's what I found—we're all searching for...love. Love in all its' wondrous forms of expression!

I believe you have a purpose and that you're on a journey here. Are you living a life that constantly moves you in a forward direction, or, are you feeling lost—just existing day to day?

Wars aren't bringing us the promise of peace, the political divide isn't benefiting our lives. Could it be that? Just...love?

What if it were true?

Due to all this research, I feel in a slight way that perhaps I can offer some advice to those spiritually inclined? Don't stress if your beliefs change, you're growing! Don't stress if family or friends get angry or upset with your new way of thinking, and start to weave in and out of your life.

If questioned on a topic, realize you're being questioned because they are seeking answers! IF they knew all the answers, they wouldn't be looking for yours! Just have faith that your words will resonate some sense of "ah-hah" within them! You know, drop the seed...

Try to join spiritual or UFO groups in your area. I too will keep trying... Remember—Everything happens for a reason!

I've grown, much has been answered for me, and I must say, this was the best bucket list item I've ever scratched off!

It's Thursday, September 2, 2021. OMG! I started this story on a Thursday! How apropos!

To my readers, my sincere hope is that I challenged you to question your belief system. Perhaps this work has affirmed your confidence that you are on the right path. Perhaps the work has offered you a new means to see your world and why you're in it—now.

Thank you so much for your interest in my book!

ALIEN CHARACTERS

ACTOK
From Pleiades .... Most-High Unifier within the Ministry
of Enlightenment

KHACEE
From Schedar...............Chief Counsellor, Ministry of
Enlightenment

VASILE
From Nibiru .... Anti-Christ/Anunnaki warrior

LINDA CHALMERS
From Terran .... Rogue agent and spy for Vasile

JAQUI
From Andromeda .... Assists Vasile in annihilating Earthlings

MELEK
From Telosian .... Light Warrior/Assists Pleiadians

GAFF
From Arcturia .... Light Warrior/Assists Pleiadians

NOCREN
From Pleiades .... Celebrated Light Warrior

SAGHI
Nocren's devoted wife

OONSAY
From Zeta Reticuli...... Go-to alien/Assists Pleiadians

RHEN
Linda's counterpart

OOTAJ
Saghi's dad................. Peacekeeper—deceased

BULI-NASA
Nocren's father........... Renowned Light Warrior—deceased

CHIKAH
Draconian leader

BRUTUS
Creature in Linda's cell

CYCLOPS
Creature working for Jaqui

HUMAN/OID CHARACTERS

DAWN COLEMAN
Bringer of Light/Foremost Light Warrior

DR. DAVID KAPLAN
Dawn's psychiatrist

SKYANN PETERS
Dawn Coleman's best friend

HENRY JACKSON
Light Warrior/Geek

KRISTIAN BROWN
Charismatic Light Warrior

ROSALEE BROWN
Charismatic Light Warrior

TERESA DEL
Mom to Juan—sister to Angelicia

ANGELICIA ROJAS
Teresa's sister

RENU
Programs universal secret events for Starseeds/Warriors

DAN KATZ
Owns *Brooklyn Gazette* Newspaper

INKY YAVONOVICH
UFO expert/Light Warrior

DETECTIVE AIMES
Assigned to recent abduction case

CAROLE COLEMAN
Dawn's older sister

POPPY
Teresa and Angelicia's father—Grandpa to Juan

SELMA
Poppy's girlfriend

KATE DUPREE
Carole's love interest

LILLY COLEMAN
Dawn and Carole's mom

NATALIE BROWN
Private investigator at the *Brooklyn Gazette*

TINA WOODS
Reporter/journalist at the *Brooklyn Gazette*

WILLIAM FREDERICKS
President of the United States

DIETER FRANC
Stepping down as leader of Illuminati

DR. ABBY GARCED
Physician to the President

JAMES DORSETT
Vice President of the United States

VICTOR
Renu's soulmate

BIG JOHN
Renu's bodyguard

JIM and GAIL
Dr. Kaplan's brother-in-law and sister

JENNA
Lilly's next-door neighbor

MARTIN WELSH
Witness to abduction

MEGAN
Detective Aimes's secretary

LT. MASON
Detective Aimes's boss

PERCY MILLS
Katz's gofer at *Brooklyn Gazette*

DR. RICHARD A. STONE
Referred Dawn to Dr. Kaplan

DR. JESSUP
Psychiatrist who offered Linda to assist Dr. Kaplan

DR. STEIN
Covers for Dr. Kaplan

MRS. TAYLOR
Dawn's principal

LEIGH
Dr. Kaplans new love interest

JOAN FRISK
Congresswoman

MAYOR BORSKI
Mayor of Brooklyn

HILLY SCHULTZ
Skyann's friend/ex-boss

JORI
Jaqui's soldier

ART & NORMA
Friends of the author

ACKNOWLEDGEMENTS

Carolina Forest Authors Club—there would be no book!

*Katherine Dostie—your steadfastness in
commenting on the entire book*

*Linda Rac & Dawn Williams—I truly felt your pride...
it was a great catalyst*

*Rosalee Brown—as busy as you are...
you were there for me*

David Wesel—thanks for the privacy and all the waters

Kristian Brown—the technical support I needed

*Carole Bertekap—for the self-help book
and your optimism*

Terri Sackett—knowing you believed in me

Albert Wilson & Mary Coll—for info on Brooklyn

*To others who helped with suggestions and
encouragement, I thank you!*

ABOUT ATMOSPHERE PRESS

Atmosphere Press is an independent, full-service publisher for excellent books in all genres and for all audiences. Learn more about what we do at atmospherepress.com.

We encourage you to check out some of Atmosphere's latest releases, which are available at Amazon.com and via order from your local bookstore:

Twisted Silver Spoons, a novel by Karen M. Wicks

Queen of Crows, a novel by S.L. Wilton

The Summer Festival is Murder, a novel by Jill M. Lyon

The Past We Step Into, stories by Richard Scharine

The Museum of an Extinct Race, a novel by Jonathan Hale Rosen

Swimming with the Angels, a novel by Colin Kersey

Island of Dead Gods, a novel by Verena Mahlow

Cloakers, a novel by Alexandra Lapointe

Twins Daze, a novel by Jerry Petersen

Embargo on Hope, a novel by Justin Doyle

Abaddon Illusion, a novel by Lindsey Bakken

Blackland: A Utopian Novel, by Richard A. Jones

The Jesus Nut, a novel by John Prather

The Embers of Tradition, a novel by Chukwudum Okeke

Saints and Martyrs: A Novel, by Aaron Roe

When I Am Ashes, a novel by Amber Rose

Melancholy Vision: A Revolution Series Novel, by L.C. Hamilton

ABOUT THE AUTHOR

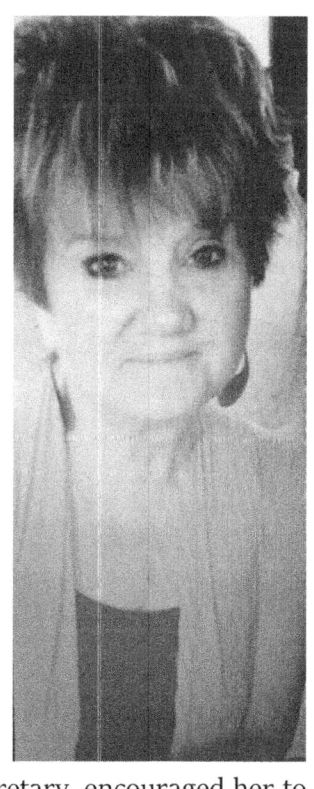

It's fair to say Eileen made her most critical decisions before she was 21. This is not to imply they were all smart ones!

In 1980, she found herself divorced, raising three children alone, and desperately holding onto her full-time job. There was no avenue available to pursue any dreams.

Therefore, her one smart move had to wait—a bucket list item: *Write a book!*

Fast forward to 2018. Married and enjoying an easier lifestyle, Eileen wanted to check off that item. She never envisioned that one little project would create within her an obsessive passion to write!

The Carolina Forest Authors Club, of which she is Recording Secretary, encouraged her to delve into writing, thus producing her first self-published book, *Help Me, Help Me!* in 2020.

Her novel, *What If It Were True?* is an in-depth, three-year research epic sci-fi of mankind's future plight, wherein the reader is challenged throughout to question their beliefs.

She is currently working on her third book, *The Nap*.

Eileen enjoys traveling, listening to Enigma and Enya, playing Texas Hold 'em and sharing time with her family.

ALSO BY EILEEN WESEL

Help Me! Help Me!

Made in the USA
Las Vegas, NV
24 December 2021

39323101R00288